FREE PUBLIC LIBRARY
DALTON, MASSACHUSETTS

First opened, May 1861   Accepted by Town, March 1885

LIBRARY RULES

1. A fine of 5¢ a day will be charged for each adult book kept overtime, beyond the due date; for Juvenile and Young Adult books, the fine will be 2¢ a day for each book. All overdue records are 5¢ a day.

2. Full value must be paid if a book is LOST; a reasonable fine if it is damaged.

3. No books or other library materials may be borrowed by persons with a record of unreturned materials or unpaid fines or losses. However, use of the reading rooms and references and advisory service are always available to everybody.

   Please note that all materials may have the due date extended, either by phone or in person, unless a reserve for same is on file.

THE BOOK OF LOST TALES
Part II

THE HISTORY OF MIDDLE-EARTH

I
THE BOOK OF LOST TALES, PART ONE

II
THE BOOK OF LOST TALES, PART TWO

III
THE LAYS OF BELERIAND
(in preparation)

IV
THE SHAPING OF MIDDLE-EARTH
THE QUENTA, THE AMBARKANTA AND THE ANNALS
(in preparation)

J. R. R. TOLKIEN

THE
BOOK OF LOST TALES

PART II

Edited by Christopher Tolkien

BOSTON
HOUGHTON MIFFLIN COMPANY
1984

Library of Congress Cataloging in Publication Data
(Revised for Part II)

Tolkien, J. R. R. (John Ronald Reuel), 1892-1973.
The book of lost tales.

(The History of Middle-earth ; 1)
Includes indexes.
1. Fantastic literature, English. I. Tolkien,
Christopher. II. Title. III. Series: Tolkien, J. R. R.
(John Ronald Reuel), 1892-1973. History of Middle-earth ; 1.
PR6039.032B6   1984   823'.912   83-12782
ISBN   0-395-35439-0 (v. 1)
ISBN   0-395-36614-3 (v. 2)

CONTENTS

PREFACE

This second part of *The Book of Lost Tales* is arranged on the same lines and with the same intentions as the first part, as described in the Foreword to it, pages 10–11. References to the first part are given in the form 'I. 240', to the second as 'p. 240', except where a reference is made to both, e.g. 'I. 222, II. 292'.

As before, I have adopted a consistent (if not necessarily 'correct') system of accentuation for names; and in the cases of *Mim* and *Niniel*, written thus throughout, I give *Mîm* and *Níniel*.

The two pages from the original manuscripts are reproduced with the permission of the Bodleian Library, Oxford, and I wish to express my thanks to the staff of the Department of Western Manuscripts at the Bodleian for their assistance. The correspondence of the original pages to the printed text in this book is as follows:

(1) The page from the manuscript of *The Tale of Tinúviel*. Upper part: printed text page 24 (7 lines up, *the sorest dread*) to page 25 (line 3, *so swiftly.*"). Lower part: printed text page 25 (11 lines up, *the harsh voice*) to page 26 (line 7, *but Tevildo*).

(2) The page from the manuscript of *The Fall of Gondolin*. Upper part: printed text page 189 (line 12, "*Now,*" *therefore said Galdor* to line 20 *if no further.*"). Lower part: printed text page 189 (line 27, *But the others, led by one Legolas Greenleaf*) to page 190 (line 11, *leaving the main company to follow he*).

For differences in the printed text of *The Fall of Gondolin* from the page reproduced see page 201, notes 34–36, and page 203, *Bad Uthwen*; some other small differences not referred to in the notes are also due to later changes made to the text B of the Tale (see pages 146–7).

These pages illustrate the complicated 'jigsaw' of the manuscripts of the *Lost Tales* described in the Foreword to Part I, page 10.

I take this opportunity to notice that it has been pointed out to me by Mr Douglas A. Anderson that the version of the poem *Why the Man in the Moon came down too soon* printed in *The Book of Lost Tales I* is not, as I supposed, that published in *A Northern Venture* in 1923, but contains several subsequent changes.

The third volume in this 'History' will contain the alliterative *Lay of the Children of Húrin* (*c.* 1918–1925) and the *Lay of Leithian* (1925–1931), together with the commentary on a part of the latter by C. S. Lewis, and the rewriting of the poem that my father embarked on after the completion of *The Lord of the Rings*.

I

THE TALE OF TINÚVIEL

The *Tale of Tinúviel* was written in 1917, but the earliest extant text is
later, being a manuscript in ink over an erased original in pencil; and in
fact my father's rewriting of this tale seems to have been one of the last
completed elements in the *Lost Tales* (see I. 203–4).

There is also a typescript version of the *Tale of Tinúviel*, later than the
manuscript but belonging to the same 'phase' of the mythology: my
father had the manuscript before him and changed the text as he went
along. Significant differences between the two versions of the tale are
given on pp. 41 ff.

In the manuscript the tale is headed: 'Link to the Tale of Tinúviel, also
the Tale of Tinúviel.' The *Link* begins with the following passage:

> 'Great was the power of Melko for ill,' said Eriol, 'if he could indeed
> destroy with his cunning the happiness and glory of the Gods and
> Elves, darkening the light of their dwelling and bringing all their love
> to naught. This must surely be the worst deed that ever he has done.'
> 'Of a truth never has such evil again been done in Valinor,' said
> Lindo, 'but Melko's hand has laboured at worse things in the world,
> and the seeds of his evil have waxen since to a great and terrible
> growth.'
> 'Nay,' said Eriol, 'yet can my heart not think of other griefs, for
> sorrow at the destruction of those most fair Trees and the darkness of
> the world.'

This passage was struck out, and is not found in the typescript text,
but it reappears in almost identical form at the end of *The Flight of the
Noldoli* (I. 169). The reason for this was that my father decided that the
Tale of the Sun and Moon, rather than *Tinúviel*, should follow *The
Darkening of Valinor* and *The Flight of the Noldoli* (see I. 203–4,
where the complex question of the re-ordering of the *Tales* at this point is
discussed). The opening words of the next part of the *Link*, 'Now in the
days soon after the telling of this tale', referred, when they were written,
to the tale of *The Darkening of Valinor* and *The Flight of the Noldoli*;
but it is never made plain to what tale they were to refer when *Tinúviel*
had been removed from its earlier position.

The two versions of the *Link* are at first very close, but when Eriol
speaks of his own past history they diverge. For the earlier part I give
the typescript text alone, and when they diverge I give them both in

succession. All discussion of this story of Eriol's life is postponed to Chapter VI.

Now in the days soon after the telling of this tale, behold, winter approached the land of Tol Eressëa, for now had Eriol forgetful of his wandering mood abode some time in old Kortirion. Never in those months did he fare beyond the good tilth that lay without the grey walls of that town, but many a hall of the kindreds of the Inwir and the Teleri received him as their glad guest, and ever more skilled in the tongues of the Elves did he become, and more deep in knowledge of their customs, of their tales and songs.

Then was winter come sudden upon the Lonely Isle, and the lawns and gardens drew on a sparkling mantle of white snows; their fountains were still, and all their bare trees silent, and the far sun glinted pale amid the mist or splintered upon facets of long hanging ice. Still fared Eriol not away, but watched the cold moon from the frosty skies look down upon Mar Vanwa Tyaliéva, and when above the roofs the stars gleamed blue he would listen, yet no sound of the flutes of Timpinen heard he now; for the breath of summer is that sprite, and or ever autumn's secret presence fills the air he takes his grey magic boat, and the swallows draw him far away.

Even so Eriol knew laughter and merriment and musics too, and song, in the dwellings of Kortirion – even Eriol the wanderer whose heart before had known no rest. Came now a grey day, and a wan afternoon, but within was firelight and good warmth and dancing and merry children's noise, for Eriol was making a great play with the maids and boys in the Hall of Play Regained. There at length tired with their mirth they cast themselves down upon the rugs before the hearth, and a child among them, a little maid, said: 'Tell me, O Eriol, a tale!'

'What then shall I tell, O Vëannë?' said he, and she, clambering upon his knee, said: 'A tale of Men and of children in the Great Lands, or of thy home – and didst thou have a garden there such as we, where poppies grew and pansies like those that grow in my corner by the Arbour of the Thrushes?'

I give now the manuscript version of the remainder of the *Link* passage:

Then Eriol told her of his home that was in an old town of Men girt with a wall now crumbled and broken, and a river ran thereby over which a castle with a great tower hung. 'A very high tower indeed,' said he, 'and the moon climbed high or ever he thrust his face above it.' 'Was it then as high as Ingil's Tirin?' said Vëannë, but Eriol said that that he could not guess, for 'twas very many years agone since he had seen that castle or its tower, for 'O Vëannë,' said he, 'I lived there but a while, and not after I was grown to be a boy. My father came of a coastward folk, and the love of the sea that I had never seen was in my bones, and my father whetted my desire, for he told me tales that his father had told him before. Now my mother died in a cruel and hungry siege of that old town, and my father was slain in bitter fight about the walls, and in the end I Eriol escaped to the shoreland of the Western Sea, and mostly have lived upon the bosom of the waves or by its side since those far days.'

Now the children about were filled with sadness at the sorrows that fell on those dwellers in the Great Lands, and at the wars and death, and Vëannë clung to Eriol, saying: 'O Melinon, go never to a war – or hast thou ever yet?'

'Aye, often enough,' said Eriol, 'but not to the great wars of the earthly kings and mighty nations which are cruel and bitter, and many fair lands and lovely things and even women and sweet maids such as thou Vëannë Melinir are whelmed by them in ruin; yet gallant affrays have I seen wherein small bands of brave men do sometimes meet and swift blows are dealt. But behold, why speak we of these things, little one; wouldst not hear rather of my first ventures on the sea?'

Then was there much eagerness alight, and Eriol told them of his wanderings about the western havens, of the comrades he made and the ports he knew, of how he was wrecked upon far western islands until at last upon one lonely one he came on an ancient sailor who gave him shelter, and over a fire within his lonely cabin told him strange tales of things beyond the Western Seas, of the Magic Isles and that most lonely one that lay beyond. Long ago had he once sighted it shining afar off, and after had he sought it many a day in vain.

'Ever after,' said Eriol, 'did I sail more curiously about the western isles seeking more stories of the kind, and thus it is indeed that after many great voyages I came myself by the blessing of the Gods to Tol Eressëa in the end – wherefore I now sit here talking to thee, Vëannë, till my words have run dry.'

Then nonetheless did a boy, Ausir, beg him to tell more of ships and the sea, but Eriol said: 'Nay – still is there time ere Ilfiniol ring the gong for evening meat: come, one of you children, tell me a tale that you have heard!' Then Vëannë sat up and clapped her hands, saying: 'I will tell you the Tale of Tinúviel.'

The typescript version of this passage reads as follows:

Then Eriol told of his home of long ago, that was in an ancient town of Men girt with a wall now crumbled and broken, for the folk that dwelt there had long known days of rich and easy peace. A river ran thereby, o'er which a castle with a great tower hung. 'There dwelt a mighty duke,' said he, 'and did he gaze from the topmost battlements never might he see the bounds of his wide domain, save where far to east the blue shapes of the great mountains lay – yet was that tower held the most lofty that stood in the lands of Men.' 'Was it as high as great Ingil's Tirin?' said Vëannë, but said Eriol: 'A very high tower indeed was it, and the moon climbed far or ever he thrust his face above it, yet may I not now guess how high, O Vëannë, for 'tis many years agone since last I saw that castle or its steep tower. War fell suddenly on that town amid its slumbrous peace, nor were its crumbled walls able to withstand the onslaught of the wild men from the Mountains of the East. There perished my mother in that cruel and hungry siege, and my father was slain fighting bitterly about the walls in the last sack. In those far days was I not yet war-high, and a bondslave was I made.

'Know then that my father was come of a coastward folk ere he wandered to that place, and the longing for the sea that I had never seen was in my bones; which often had my father whetted, telling me tales of the wide waters and recalling lore that he had learned of his father aforetime. Small need to tell of my travail thereafter in thraldom, for in the end I brake my bonds and got me to the shoreland of the Western Sea – and mostly have I lived upon the bosom of its waves or by its side since those old days.'

Now hearing of the sorrows that fell upon the dwellers in the Great Lands, the wars and death, the children were filled with sadness, and Vëannë clung to Eriol, saying: 'O Melinon, go thou never to a war – or hast thou ever yet?'

'Aye, often enough,' said Eriol, 'yet not to the great wars of the earthly kings and mighty nations, which are cruel and bitter, whelming in their ruin all the beauty both of the earth and of those fair things that men fashion with their hands in times of peace – nay, they spare not sweet women and tender maids, such as thou, Vëannë Melinir, for then are men drunk with wrath and the lust of blood, and Melko fares abroad. But gallant affrays have I seen wherein brave men did sometimes meet, and swift blows were dealt, and strength of body and of heart was proven – but, behold, why speak we of these things, little one? Wouldst not hear rather of my ventures on the sea?'

Then was there much eagerness alight, and Eriol told them of his first wanderings about the western havens, of the comrades he made, and the ports he knew; of how he was one time wrecked upon far western islands and there upon a lonely eyot found an ancient mariner who dwelt for ever solitary in a cabin on the shore, that he had fashioned of the timbers of his boat. 'More wise was he,' said Eriol, 'in all matters of the sea than any other I have met, and much of wizardry was there in his lore. Strange things he told me of regions far beyond the Western Sea, of the Magic Isles and that most lonely one that lies behind. Once long ago, he said, he had sighted it glimmering afar off, and after had he sought it many a day in vain. Much lore he taught me of the hidden seas, and the dark and trackless waters, and without this never had I found this sweetest land, or this dear town or the Cottage of Lost Play – yet it was not without long and grievous search thereafter, and many a weary voyage, that I came myself by the blessing of the Gods to Tol Eressëa at the last – wherefore I now sit here talking to thee, Vëannë, till my words have run dry.'

Then nevertheless did a boy, Ausir, beg him to tell more of ships and the sea, saying: 'For knowest thou not, O Eriol, that that ancient mariner beside the lonely sea was none other than Ulmo's self, who appeareth not seldom thus to those voyagers whom he loves – yet he who has spoken with Ulmo must have many a tale to tell that will not be stale in the ears even of those that dwell here in Kortirion.' But Eriol at that time believed not that saying of Ausir's, and said: 'Nay, pay me your debt ere Ilfrin ring the gong for evening meat – come, one of you shall tell me a tale that you have heard.'

Then did Vëannë sit up and clap her hands, crying: 'I will tell thee the Tale of Tinúviel.'

★

The Tale of Tinúviel

I give now the text of the *Tale of Tinúviel* as it appears in the manuscript. The *Link* is not in fact distinguished or separated in any way from the tale proper, and Vëannë makes no formal opening to it.

'Who was then Tinúviel?' said Eriol. 'Know you not?' said
Ausir; 'Tinúviel was the daughter of Tinwë Linto.' 'Tinwelint',
said Vëannë, but said the other: ''Tis all one, but the Elves of this
house who love the tale do say Tinwë Linto, though Vairë hath
said that Tinwë alone is his right name ere he wandered in the
woods.'

'Hush thee, Ausir,' said Vëannë, 'for it is my tale and I will tell it
to Eriol. Did I not see Gwendeling and Tinúviel once with my
own eyes when journeying by the Way of Dreams in long past
days?'[1]

'What was Queen Wendelin like (for so do the Elves call her),[2] O
Vëannë, if thou sawest her?' said Ausir.

'Slender and very dark of hair,' said Vëannë, 'and her skin was
white and pale, but her eyes shone and seemed deep, and she
was clad in filmy garments most lovely yet of black, jet-spangled
and girt with silver. If ever she sang, or if she danced, dreams and
slumbers passed over your head and made it heavy. Indeed she
was a sprite that escaped from Lórien's gardens before even Kôr
was built, and she wandered in the wooded places of the world,
and nightingales went with her and often sang about her. It
was the song of these birds that smote the ears of Tinwelint,
leader of that tribe of the Eldar that after were the Solosimpi
the pipers of the shore, as he fared with his companions behind the
horse of Oromë from Palisor. Ilúvatar had set a seed of music in
the hearts of all that kindred, or so Vairë saith, and she is of them,
and it blossomed after very wondrously, but now the song of
Gwendeling's nightingales was the most beautiful music that
Tinwelint had ever heard, and he strayed aside for a moment, as
he thought, from the host, seeking in the dark trees whence it
might come.

And it is said that it was not a moment he hearkened, but many
years, and vainly his people sought him, until at length they
followed Oromë and were borne upon Tol Eressëa far away, and
he saw them never again. Yet after a while as it seemed to
him he came upon Gwendeling lying in a bed of leaves gazing
at the stars above her and hearkening also to her birds. Now
Tinwelint stepping softly stooped and looked upon her, thinking
"Lo, here is a fairer being even than the most beautiful of my own
folk" – for indeed Gwendeling was not elf or woman but of the
children of the Gods; and bending further to touch a tress of her
hair he snapped a twig with his foot. Then Gwendeling was up
and away laughing softly, sometimes singing distantly or dancing

ever just before him, till a swoon of fragrant slumbers fell upon him and he fell face downward neath the trees and slept a very great while.

Now when he awoke he thought no more of his people (and indeed it had been vain, for long now had those reached Valinor) but desired only to see the twilight-lady; but she was not far, for she had remained nigh at hand and watched over him. More of their story I know not, O Eriol, save that in the end she became his wife, for Tinwelint and Gwendeling very long indeed were king and queen of the Lost Elves of Artanor or the Land Beyond, or so it is said here.

Long, long after, as thou knowest, Melko brake again into the world from Valinor, and all the Eldar both those who remained in the dark or had been lost upon the march from Palisor and those Noldoli too who fared back into the world after him seeking their stolen treasury fell beneath his power as thralls. Yet it is told that many there were who escaped and wandered in the woods and empty places, and of these many a wild and woodland clan rallied beneath King Tinwelint. Of those the most were Ilkorindi – which is to say Eldar that never had beheld Valinor or the Two Trees or dwelt in Kôr – and eerie they were and strange beings, knowing little of light or loveliness or of musics save it be dark songs and chantings of a rugged wonder that faded in the wooded places or echoed in deep caves. Different indeed did they become when the Sun arose, and indeed before that already were their numbers mingled with a many wandering Gnomes, and wayward sprites too there were of Lórien's host that dwelt in the courts of Tinwelint, being followers of Gwendeling, and these were not of the kindreds of the Eldalië.

Now in the days of Sunlight and Moonsheen still dwelt Tinwelint in Artanor, and nor he nor the most of his folk went to the Battle of Unnumbered Tears, though that story toucheth not this tale. Yet was his lordship greatly increased after that unhappy field by fugitives that fled to his protection. Hidden was his dwelling from the vision and knowledge of Melko by the magics of Gwendeling the fay, and she wove spells about the paths thereto that none but the Eldar might tread them easily, and so was the king secured from all dangers save it be treachery alone. Now his halls were builded in a deep cavern of great size, and they were nonetheless a kingly and a fair abode. This cavern was in the heart of the mighty forest of Artanor that is the mightiest of forests, and a stream ran before its doors, but none could enter that portal save across the

stream, and a bridge spanned it narrow and well-guarded. Those
places were not ill albeit the Iron Mountains were not utterly
distant beyond whom lay Hisilómë where dwelt Men, and thrall-
Noldoli laboured, and few free-Eldar went.

Lo, now I will tell you of things that happened in the halls of
Tinwelint after the arising of the Sun indeed but long ere the
unforgotten Battle of Unnumbered Tears. And Melko had not
completed his designs nor had he unveiled his full might and
cruelty.

Two children had Tinwelint then, Dairon and Tinúviel, and
Tinúviel was a maiden, and the most beautiful of all the maidens
of the hidden Elves, and indeed few have been so fair, for her
mother was a fay, a daughter of the Gods; but Dairon was then a
boy strong and merry, and above all things he delighted to play
upon a pipe of reeds or other woodland instruments, and he is
named now among the three most magic players of the Elves, and
the others are Tinfang Warble and Ivárë who plays beside the sea.
But Tinúviel's joy was rather in the dance, and no names are set
with hers for the beauty and subtlety of her twinkling feet.

Now it was the delight of Dairon and Tinúviel to fare away from
the cavernous palace of Tinwelint their father and together spend
long times amid the trees. There often would Dairon sit upon a
tussock or a tree-root and make music while Tinúviel danced
thereto, and when she danced to the playing of Dairon more
lissom was she than Gwendeling, more magical than Tinfang
Warble neath the moon, nor may any see such lilting save be it
only in the rose gardens of Valinor where Nessa dances on the
lawns of never-fading green.

Even at night when the moon shone pale still would they play
and dance, and they were not afraid as I should be, for the rule of
Tinwelint and of Gwendeling held evil from the woods and Melko
troubled them not as yet, and Men were hemmed beyond the hills.

Now the place that they loved the most was a shady spot, and
elms grew there, and beech too, but these were not very tall, and
some chestnut trees there were with white flowers, but the ground
was moist and a great misty growth of hemlocks rose beneath the
trees. On a time of June they were playing there, and the white
umbels of the hemlocks were like a cloud about the boles of the
trees, and there Tinúviel danced until the evening faded late, and
there were many white moths abroad. Tinúviel being a fairy
minded them not as many of the children of Men do, although she

loved not beetles, and spiders will none of the Eldar touch because of Ungwelianté – but now the white moths flittered about her head and Dairon trilled an eerie tune, when suddenly that strange thing befell.

Never have I heard how Beren came thither over the hills; yet was he braver than most, as thou shalt hear, and 'twas the love of wandering maybe alone that had sped him through the terrors of the Iron Mountains until he reached the Lands Beyond.

Now Beren was a Gnome, son of Egnor the forester who hunted in the darker places[3] in the north of Hisilómë. Dread and suspicion was between the Eldar and those of their kindred that had tasted the slavery of Melko, and in this did the evil deeds of the Gnomes at the Haven of the Swans revenge itself. Now the lies of Melko ran among Beren's folk so that they believed evil things of the secret Elves, yet now did he see Tinúviel dancing in the twilight, and Tinúviel was in a silver-pearly dress, and her bare white feet were twinkling among the hemlock-stems. Then Beren cared not whether she were Vala or Elf or child of Men and crept near to see; and he leant against a young elm that grew upon a mound so that he might look down into the little glade where she was dancing, for the enchantment made him faint. So slender was she and so fair that at length he stood heedlessly in the open the better to gaze upon her, and at that moment the full moon came brightly through the boughs and Dairon caught sight of Beren's fáce. Straightway did he perceive that he was none of their folk, and all the Elves of the woodland thought of the Gnomes of Dor Lómin as treacherous creatures, cruel and faithless, wherefore Dairon dropped his instrument and crying "Flee, flee, O Tinúviel, an enemy walks this wood" he was gone swiftly through the trees. Then Tinúviel in her amaze followed not straightway, for she understood not his words at once, and knowing she could not run or leap so hardily as her brother she slipped suddenly down among the white hemlocks and hid herself beneath a very tall flower with many spreading leaves; and here she looked in her white raiment like a spatter of moonlight shimmering through the leaves upon the floor.

Then Beren was sad, for he was lonely and was grieved at their fright, and he looked for Tinúviel everywhere about, thinking her not fled. Thus suddenly did he lay his hand upon her slender arm beneath the leaves, and with a cry she started away from him and flitted as fast as she could in the wan light, in and about the tree-trunks and the hemlock-stalks. The tender touch of her arm made Beren yet more eager than before to find her, and he followed swiftly and yet not swiftly enough, for in the end she escaped him, and reached the dwellings of her father in fear; nor did she dance alone in the woods for many a day after.

This was a great sorrow to Beren, who would not leave those places, hoping to see that fair elfin maiden dance yet again, and he wandered in the wood growing wild and lonely for many a day and searching for Tinúviel. By dawn and dusk he sought her, but ever more hopefully when the moon shone bright. At last one night he caught a sparkle afar off, and lo, there she was dancing alone on a little treeless knoll and Dairon was not there. Often and often she came there after and danced and sang to herself, and sometimes Dairon would be nigh, and then Beren watched from the wood's edge afar, and sometimes he was away and Beren crept then closer. Indeed for long Tinúviel knew of his coming and feigned otherwise, and for long her fear had departed by reason of the wistful hunger of his face lit by the moonlight; and she saw that he was kind and in love with her beautiful dancing.

Then Beren took to following Tinúviel secretly through the woods even to the entrance of the cave and the bridge's head, and when she was gone in he would cry across the stream, softly saying "Tinúviel", for he had caught the name from Dairon's lips; and although he knew it not Tinúviel often hearkened from within the shadows of the cavernous doors and laughed softly or smiled. At length one day as she danced alone he stepped out more boldly and said to her: "Tinúviel, teach me to dance." "Who art thou?" said she. "Beren. I am from across the Bitter Hills." "Then if thou wouldst dance, follow me," said the maiden, and she danced before Beren away, and away into the woods, nimbly and yet not so fast that he could not follow, and ever and anon she would look back and laugh at him stumbling after, saying "Dance, Beren, dance! as they dance beyond the Bitter Hills!" In this way they came by winding paths to the abode of Tinwelint, and Tinúviel beckoned Beren beyond the stream, and he followed her wondering down into the cave and the deep halls of her home.

When however Beren found himself before the king he was abashed, and of the stateliness of Queen Gwendeling he was in great awe, and behold when the king said: "Who art thou that stumbleth into my halls unbidden?" he had nought to say. Tinúviel answered therefore for him, saying: "This, my father, is Beren, a wanderer from beyond the hills, and he would learn to dance as the Elves of Artanor can dance," and she laughed, but the king frowned when he heard whence Beren came, and he said: "Put away thy light words, my child, and say has this wild Elf of the shadows sought to do thee any harm?"

"Nay, father," said she, "and I think there is not evil in his heart at all, and be thou not harsh with him, unless thou desirest to see thy daughter Tinúviel weep, for more wonder has he at my dancing than any that I have known." Therefore said Tinwelint now: "O Beren son of the Noldoli, what dost thou desire of the Elves of the wood ere thou returnest whence thou camest?"

So great was the amazed joy of Beren's heart when Tinúviel spake thus for him to her father that his courage rose within him, and his adventurous spirit that had brought him out of Hisilómë and over the Mountains of Iron awoke again, and looking boldly upon Tinwelint he said: "Why, O king, I desire thy daughter Tinúviel, for she is the fairest and most sweet of all maidens I have seen or dreamed of."

Then was there a silence in the hall, save that Dairon laughed, and all who heard were astounded, but Tinúviel cast down her eyes, and the king glancing at the wild and rugged aspect of Beren burst also into laughter, whereat Beren flushed for shame, and Tinúviel's heart was sore for him. "Why! wed my Tinúviel fairest of the maidens of the world, and become a prince of the woodland Elves – 'tis but a little boon for a stranger to ask," quoth Tinwelint. "Haply I may with right ask somewhat in return. Nothing great shall it be, a token only of thy esteem. Bring me a Silmaril from the Crown of Melko, and that day Tinúviel weds thee, an she will."

Then all in that place knew that the king treated the matter as an uncouth jest, having pity on the Gnome, and they smiled, for the fame of the Silmarils of Fëanor was now great throughout the world, and the Noldoli had told tales of them, and many that had escaped from Angamandi had seen them now blazing lustrous in the iron crown of Melko. Never did this crown leave his head, and he treasured those jewels as his eyes, and no one in the world, or fay or elf or man, could hope ever to set finger even on them and live. This indeed did Beren know, and he guessed the meaning of their mocking smiles, and aflame with anger he cried: "Nay, but 'tis too small a gift to the father of so sweet a bride. Strange nonetheless seem to me the customs of the woodland Elves, like to the rude laws of the folk of Men, that thou shouldst name the gift unoffered, yet lo! I Beren, a huntsman of the Noldoli,[4] will fulfil thy small desire," and with that he burst from the hall while all stood astonished; but Tinúviel wept suddenly. "'Twas ill done, O my father," she cried, "to send one to his death with thy sorry jesting – for now methinks he will attempt the deed, being maddened by thy scorn, and Melko will slay him, and none will look ever again with such love upon my dancing."

Then said the king: "'Twill not be the first of Gnomes that Melko has slain and for less reason. It is well for him that he lies not bound here in grievous spells for his trespass in my halls and for his insolent speech"; yet Gwendeling said nought, neither did she chide Tinúviel or question her sudden weeping for this unknown wanderer.

Beren however going from before the face of Tinwelint was carried by his wrath far through the woods, until he drew nigh to the lower hills and treeless lands that warned of the approach of the bleak Iron Mountains. Only then did he feel his weariness and stay his march, and thereafter did his greater travails begin. Nights of deep despondency were his and he saw no hope whatever in his quest, and indeed there was little, and soon, as he followed the Iron Mountains till he drew nigh to the terrible regions of Melko's abode, the greatest fears assailed him. Many poisonous snakes were in those places and wolves roamed about, and more fearsome still were the wandering bands of the goblins and the Orcs – foul broodlings of Melko who fared abroad doing his evil work, snaring and capturing beasts, and Men, and Elves, and dragging them to their lord.

Many times was Beren near to capture by the Orcs, and once he escaped the jaws of a great wolf only after a combat wherein he was armed but with an ashen club, and other perils and adventures did he know each day of his wandering to Angamandi. Hunger and thirst too tortured him often, and often he would have turned back had not that been well nigh as perilous as going on; but the voice of Tinúviel pleading with Tinwelint echoed in his heart, and at night time it seemed to him that his heart heard her sometimes weeping softly for him far away in the woodlands of her home: – and this was indeed true.

One day he was driven by great hunger to search amid a deserted camping of some Orcs for scraps of food, but some of these returned unawares and took him prisoner, and they tormented him but did not slay him, for their captain seeing his strength, worn though he was with hardships, thought that Melko might perchance be pleasured if he was brought before him and might set him to some heavy thrall-work in his mines or in his smithies. So came it that Beren was dragged before Melko, and he bore a stout heart within him nonetheless, for it was a belief among his father's kindred that the power of Melko would not abide for ever, but the Valar would hearken at last to the tears of the Noldoli, and would arise and bind Melko and open Valinor once more to the weary Elves, and great joy should come back upon Earth.

Melko however looking upon him was wroth, asking how a Gnome, a thrall by birth of his, had dared to fare away into the woods unbidden, but Beren answered that he was no runagate but came of a kindred of Gnomes that dwelt in Aryador and mingled much there among the folk of Men. Then was Melko yet more angry, for he sought ever to destroy the friendship and intercourse of Elves and Men, and said that evidently here was a plotter of deep treacheries against Melko's lordship, and one worthy of the tortures of the Balrogs; but Beren seeing his peril answered: "Think not, O most mighty Ainu Melko, Lord of the World, that this can be true, for an it were then should I not be here unaided and alone. No friendship has Beren son of Egnor for the kindred of Men; nay indeed, wearying utterly of the lands infested by that folk he has wandered out of Aryador. Many a great tale has my father made to me aforetime of thy splendour and glory, wherefore, albeit I am no renegade thrall, I do desire nothing so much as to serve thee in what small manner I may," and Beren said therewith that he was a great trapper of small animals and a snarer of birds, and had become lost in the hills in these pursuits until after much wandering he had come into strange lands, and even had not the Orcs seized him he would indeed have had no other rede of safety but to approach the majesty of Ainu Melko and beg him to grant him some humble office – as a winner of meats for his table perchance.

Now the Valar must have inspired that speech, or perchance it was a spell of cunning words cast on him in compassion by Gwendeling, for indeed it saved his life, and Melko marking his hardy frame believed him, and was willing to accept him as a thrall of his kitchens. Flattery savoured ever sweet in the nostrils of that Ainu, and for all his unfathomed wisdom many a lie of those whom he despised deceived him, were they clothed sweetly in words of praise; therefore now he gave orders for Beren to be made a thrall of Tevildo Prince of Cats*. Now Tevildo was a

---

* Footnote in the manuscript: *Tifil (Bridhon) Miaugion or Tevildo (Vardo) Meoita.*

mighty cat – the mightiest of all – and possessed of an evil sprite, as some say, and he was in Melko's constant following; and that cat had all cats subject to him, and he and his subjects were the chasers and getters of meat for Melko's table and for his frequent feasts. Wherefore is it that there is hatred still between the Elves and all cats even now when Melko rules no more, and his beasts are become of little account.

When therefore Beren was led away to the halls of Tevildo, and these were not utterly distant from the place of Melko's throne, he was much afraid, for he had not looked for such a turn in things, and those halls were ill-lighted and were full of growling and of monstrous purrings in the dark. All about shone cats' eyes glowing like green lamps or red or yellow where Tevildo's thanes sat waving and lashing their beautiful tails, but Tevildo himself sat at their head and he was a mighty cat and coal-black and evil to look upon. His eyes were long and very narrow and slanted, and gleamed both red and green, but his great grey whiskers were as stout and as sharp as needles. His purr was like the roll of drums and his growl like thunder, but when he yelled in wrath it turned the blood cold, and indeed small beasts and birds were frozen as to stone, or dropped lifeless often at the very sound. Now Tevildo seeing Beren narrowed his eyes until they seemed to shut, and said: "I smell dog", and he took dislike to Beren from that moment. Now Beren had been a lover of hounds in his own wild home.

"Why," said Tevildo, "do ye dare to bring such a creature before me, unless perchance it is to make meat of him?" But those who led Beren said: "Nay, 'twas the word of Melko that this unhappy Elf wear out his life as a catcher of beasts and birds in Tevildo's employ." Then indeed did Tevildo screech in scorn and said: "Then in sooth was my lord asleep or his thoughts were settled elsewhere, for what use think ye is a child of the Eldar to aid the Prince of Cats and his thanes in the catching of birds or of beasts – as well had ye brought some clumsy-footed Man, for none are there either of Elves or Men that can vie with us in our pursuit." Nonetheless he set Beren to a test, and he bade him go catch three mice, "for my hall is infested with them," said he. This indeed was not true, as might be imagined, yet a certain few there were – a very wild, evil, and magic kind that dared to dwell there in dark holes, but they were larger than rats and very fierce, and Tevildo harboured them for his own private sport and suffered not their numbers to dwindle.

Three days did Beren hunt them, but having nothing wherewith to devise a trap (and indeed he did not lie to Melko saying that he had cunning in such contrivances) he hunted in vain getting nothing better than a bitten finger for all his labour. Then was Tevildo scornful and in great anger, but Beren got no harm of him or his thanes at that time because of Melko's bidding other than a few scratches. Evil however were his days thereafter in the dwellings of Tevildo. They made him a scullion, and his days passed miserably in the washing of floors and vessels, in the scrubbing of tables and the hewing of wood and the drawing of water. Often too would he be set to the turning of spits whereon birds and fat mice were daintily roasted for the cats, yet seldom did he get food or sleep himself, and he became haggard and unkempt, and wished often that never straying out of Hisilómë he had not even caught sight of the vision of Tinúviel.

Now that fair maiden wept for a very great while after Beren's departure and danced no more about the woods, and Dairon grew angry and could not understand her, but she had grown to love the face of Beren peeping through the branches and the crackle of his feet as they followed her through the wood; and his voice that called wistfully "Tinúviel, Tinúviel" across the stream before her father's doors she longed to hear again, and she would not now dance when Beren was fled to the evil halls of Melko and maybe had already perished. So bitter did this thought become at last that that most tender maiden went to her mother, for to her father she dared not go nor even suffer him to see her weep.

"O Gwendeling, my mother," said she, "tell me of thy magic, if thou canst, how doth Beren fare. Is all yet well with him?" "Nay," said Gwendeling. "He lives indeed, but in an evil captivity, and hope is dead in his heart, for behold, he is a slave in the power of Tevildo Prince of Cats."

"Then," said Tinúviel, "I must go and succour him, for none else do I know that will."

Now Gwendeling laughed not, for in many matters she was wise, and forewise, yet it was a thing unthought in a mad dream that any Elf, still less a maiden, the daughter of the king, should fare untended to the halls of Melko, even in those earlier days before the Battle of Tears when Melko's power had not grown great and he veiled his designs and spread his net of lies. Wherefore did Gwendeling softly bid her not to speak such folly; but Tinúviel said: "Then must thou plead with my father for aid, that he send

warriors to Angamandi and demand the freedom of Beren from
Ainu Melko."

This indeed did Gwendeling do, of love for her daughter, and
so wroth was Tinwelint that Tinúviel wished that never had her
desire been made known; and Tinwelint bade her nor speak nor
think of Beren more, and swore he would slay him an he trod those
halls again. Now then Tinúviel pondered much what she might
do, and going to Dairon she begged him to aid her, or indeed
to fare away with her to Angamandi an he would; but Dairon
thought with little love of Beren, and he said: "Wherefore should
I go into the direst peril that there is in the world for the sake
of a wandering Gnome of the woods? Indeed I have no love for
him, for he has destroyed our play together, our music and our
dancing." But Dairon moreover told the king of what Tinúviel
had desired of him – and this he did not of ill intent but fearing lest
Tinúviel fare away to her death in the madness of her heart.

Now[5] when Tinwelint heard this he called Tinúviel and said:
"Wherefore, O maiden of mine, does thou not put this folly away
from thee, and seek to do my bidding?" But Tinúviel would not
answer, and the king bade her promise him that neither would she
think more on Beren, nor would she seek in her folly to follow after
him to the evil lands whether alone or tempting any of his folk with
her. But Tinúviel said that the first she would not promise and the
second only in part, for she would not tempt any of the folk of
the woodlands to go with her.

Then was her father mightily angry, and beneath his anger not a
little amazed and afraid, for he loved Tinúviel; but this was the
plan he devised, for he might not shut his daughter for ever in the
caverns where only a dim and flickering light ever came. Now
above the portals of his cavernous hall was a steep slope falling to
the river, and there grew mighty beeches; and one there was that
was named Hirilorn, the Queen of Trees, for she was very mighty,
and so deeply cloven was her bole that it seemed as if three shafts
sprang from the ground together and they were of like size, round
and straight, and their grey rind was smooth as silk, unbroken by
branch or twig for a very great height above men's heads.

Now Tinwelint let build high up in that strange tree, as high as
men could fashion their longest ladders to reach, a little house of
wood, and it was above the first branches and was sweetly veiled in
leaves. Now that house had three corners and three windows in
each wall, and at each corner was one of the shafts of Hirilorn.
There then did Tinwelint bid Tinúviel dwell until she would

consent to be wise, and when she fared up the ladders of tall pine these were taken from beneath and no way had she to get down again. All that she required was brought to her, and folk would scale the ladders and give her food or whatever else she wished for, and then descending again take away the ladders, and the king promised death to any who left one leaning against the tree or who should try by stealth to place one there at night. A guard therefore was set nigh the tree's foot, and yet came Dairon often thither in sorrow at what he had brought to pass, for he was lonely without Tinúviel; but Tinúviel had at first much pleasure in her house among the leaves, and would gaze out of her little window while Dairon made his sweetest melodies beneath.

But one night a dream of the Valar came to Tinúviel and she dreamt of Beren, and her heart said: "Let me be gone to seek him whom all others have forgot"; and waking, the moon was shining through the trees, and she pondered very deeply how she might escape. Now Tinúviel daughter of Gwendeling was not ignorant of magics or of spells, as may well be believed, and after much thought she devised a plan. The next day she asked those who came to her to bring, if they would, some of the clearest water of the stream below, "but this," she said, "must be drawn at midnight in a silver bowl, and brought to my hand with no word spoken," and after that she desired wine to be brought, "but this," she said, "must be borne hither in a flagon of gold at noon, and he who brings it must sing as he comes," and they did as they were bid, but Tinwelint was not told.

Then said Tinúviel, "Go now to my mother and say to her that her daughter desires a spinning wheel to pass her weary hours," but Dairon secretly she begged fashion her a tiny loom, and he did this even in the little house of Tinúviel in the tree. "But wherewith will you spin and wherewith weave?" said he; and Tinúviel answered: "With spells and magics," but Dairon knew not her design, nor said more to the king or to Gwendeling.

Now Tinúviel took the wine and water when she was alone, and singing a very magical song the while, she mingled them together, and as they lay in the bowl of gold she sang a song of growth, and as they lay in the bowl of silver she sang another song, and the names of all the tallest and longest things upon Earth were set in that song; the beards of the Indravangs, the tail of Karkaras, the body of Glorund, the bole of Hirilorn, and the sword of Nan she named, nor did she forget the chain Angainu that Aulë and Tulkas made or the neck of Gilim the giant, and last and longest of all she spake of the hair of Uinen the lady of the sea that is spread through all the waters. Then did she lave her head with the mingled water and wine, and as she did so she sang a third song, a song of uttermost sleep, and the hair of Tinúviel which was dark and finer than the most delicate threads of twilight began suddenly to grow very fast indeed, and after twelve hours had passed it nigh filled the little room, and then Tinúviel was very pleased and she lay down to rest; and when she awoke the room was full as with a black mist and she was deep hidden under it, and lo! her hair was trailing out of the windows and blowing about the tree boles in the morning. Then with difficulty she found her little shears and cut the threads of that growth nigh to her head, and after that her hair grew only as it was wont before.

Then was the labour of Tinúviel begun, and though she laboured with the deftness of an Elf long was she spinning and longer weaving still, and did any come and hail her from below she bid them be gone, saying: "I am abed, and desire only to sleep," and Dairon was much amazed, and called often up to her, but she did not answer.

Now of that cloudy hair Tinúviel wove a robe of misty black soaked with drowsiness more magical far than even that one that her mother had worn and danced in long long ago before the Sun arose, and therewith she covered her garments of shimmering white, and magic slumbers filled the airs about her; but of what remained she twisted a mighty strand, and this she fastened to the bole of the tree within her house, and then was her labour ended, and she looked out of her window westward to the river. Already the sunlight was fading in the trees, and as dusk filled the woods she began a song very soft and low, and as she sung she cast out her long hair from the window so that its slumbrous mist touched the heads and faces of the guards below, and they listening to her voice fell suddenly into a fathomless sleep. Then did Tinúviel clad in her garments of darkness slip down that rope of hair light as a squirrel, and away she danced to the bridge, and before the bridgewards could cry out she was among them dancing; and as the hem of her black robe touched them they fell asleep, and Tinúviel fled very far away as fast as her dancing feet would flit.

Now when the escape of Tinúviel reached the ears of Tinwelint great was his mingled grief and wrath, and all his court was in uproar, and all the woods ringing with the search, but Tinúviel was already far away drawing nigh to the gloomy foothills where the Mountains of Night begin; and 'tis said that Dairon following after her became utterly lost, and came never back to Elfinesse, but turned towards Palisor, and there plays⁶ subtle magic musics still, wistful and lonely in the woods and forests of the south.

Yet ere long as Tinúviel went forward a sudden dread overtook her at the thought of what she had dared to do and what lay before; then did she turn back for a while, and she wept, wishing Dairon was with her, and it is said that he indeed was not far off, but was wandering lost in the great pines, the Forest of Night, where afterward Túrin slew Beleg by mishap.⁷ Nigh was Tinúviel now to those places, but she entered not that dark region, and regaining heart pressed on, and by reason of the greater magic of her being and because of the spell of wonder and of sleep that fared about her no such dangers assailed her as did Beren before; yet was it a long and evil and weary journey for a maiden to tread.

Now is it to be told to thee, Eriol, that in those days Tevildo had but one trouble in the world, and that was the kindred of the Dogs. Many indeed of these were neither friends nor foes of the Cats, for they had become subject to Melko and were as savage and cruel as any of his animals; indeed from the most cruel and most savage he bred the race of wolves, and they were very dear indeed to him. Was it not the great grey wolf Karkaras Knife-fang, father of wolves, who guarded the gates of Angamandi in those days and long had done so? Many were there however who would neither bow to Melko nor live wholly in fear of him, but dwelt either in the dwellings of Men and guarded them from much evil that had otherwise befallen them or roamed the woods of Hisilómë or passing the mountainous places fared even at times into the region of Artanor and the lands beyond and to the south.

Did ever any of these view Tevildo or any of his thanes or subjects, then there was a great baying and a mighty chase, and albeit seldom was any cat slain by reason of their skill in climbing and in hiding and because of the protecting might of Melko, yet was great enmity between them, and some of those hounds were held in dread among the cats. None however did Tevildo fear, for he was as strong as any among them, and more agile and more swift save only than Huan Captain of Dogs. So swift was Huan that on a time he had tasted the fur of Tevildo, and though Tevildo had paid him for that with a gash from his great claws, yet was the pride of the Prince of Cats unappeased and he lusted to do a great harm to Huan of the Dogs.

Great therefore was the good fortune that befell Tinúviel in meeting with Huan in the woods, although at first she was mortally afraid and fled. But Huan overtook her in two leaps, and speaking soft and deep the tongue of the Lost Elves he bid her be not afraid, and "Wherefore," said he, "do I see an Elfin maiden, and one most fair, wandering alone so nigh to the abodes of the Ainu of Evil? Knowst thou not these are very evil places to be in, little one, even with a companion, and they are death to the lonely?"

"That know I," said she, "and I am not here for the love of wayfaring, but I seek only Beren."

"What knowest thou then," said Huan, "of Beren — or indeed meanest thou Beren son of the huntsman of the Elves, Egnor bo-Rimion, a friend of mine since very ancient days?"

"Nay, I know not even whether my Beren be thy friend, for I seek only Beren from beyond the Bitter Hills, whom I knew in the woods near to my father's home. Now is he gone, and my mother Gwendeling says of her wisdom that he is a thrall in the cruel house of Tevildo Prince of Cats; and whether this be true or yet worse be now befallen him I do not know, and I go to discover him — though plan I have none."

"Then will I make thee one," said Huan, "but do thou trust in me, for I am Huan of the Dogs, chief foe of Tevildo. Rest thee now with me a while within the shadows of the wood, and I will think deeply."

Then Tinúviel did as he said, and indeed she slept long while Huan watched, for she was very weary. But after a while awakening she said: "Lo, I have tarried over long. Come, what is thy thought, O Huan?"

And Huan said: "A dark and difficult matter is this, and no other rede can I devise but this. Creep now if thou hast the heart to the abiding place of that Prince while the sun is high, and Tevildo and the most of his household drowze upon the terraces before his gates. There discover in what manner thou mayst whether Beren be indeed within, as thy mother said to thee. Now I will lie not far hence in the woods, and thou wilt do me a pleasure and aid thy own desires an going before Tevildo, be Beren there or be he not, thou tellest him how thou hast stumbled upon Huan of the Dogs lying sick in the woods at this place. Do not indeed direct him hither, for thou must guide him, if it may be, thyself. Then wilt thou see what I contrive for thee and for Tevildo. Methinks that bearing such tidings Tevildo will not entreat thee ill within his halls nor seek to hold thee there."

In this way did Huan design both to do Tevildo a hurt, or perchance if it might so be to slay him, and to aid Beren whom he guessed in truth to be that Beren son of Egnor whom the hounds of Hisilómë loved. Indeed hearing the name of Gwendeling and knowing thereby that this maiden was a princess of the woodland fairies he was eager to aid her, and his heart warmed to her sweetness.

Now Tinúviel taking heart stole near to the halls of Tevildo, and Huan wondered much at her courage, following unknown to her, as far as he might for the success of his design. At length however she passed beyond his sight, and leaving the shelter of the trees came to a region of long grass dotted with bushes that sloped ever upward toward a shoulder of the hills. Now upon that rocky spur the sun shone, but over all the hills and mountains at its back a black cloud brooded, for there was Angamandi; and Tinúviel fared on not daring to look up at that gloom, for fear oppressed her, and as she went the ground rose and the grass grew more scant and rock-strewn until it came even to a cliff, sheer of one side, and there upon a stony shelf was the castle of Tevildo. No pathway led thereto, and the place where it stood fell towards the woods in terrace after terrace so that none might reach its gates save by many great leaps, and those became ever steeper as the castle drew more nigh. Few were the windows of the house and upon the ground there were none – indeed the very gate was in the air where in the dwellings of Men are wont to be the windows of the upper floor; but the roof had many wide and flat spaces open to the sun.

Now does Tinúviel wander disconsolate upon the lowest terrace and look in dread at the dark house upon the hill, when behold, she came at a bend in the rock upon a lone cat lying in the sun and seemingly asleep. As she approached he opened a yellow eye and blinked at her, and thereupon rising and stretching he stepped up to her and said: "Whither away, little maid – dost not know that you trespass on the sunning ground of his highness Tevildo and his thanes?"

Now Tinúviel was very much afraid, but she made as bold an answer as she was able, saying: "That know I, my lord" – and this pleased the old cat greatly, for he was in truth only Tevildo's doorkeeper – "but I would indeed of your goodness be brought to Tevildo's presence now – nay, even if he sleeps," said she, for the doorkeeper lashed his tail in astonished refusal. "I have words of immediate import for his private ear. Lead me to him, my lord," she pleaded, and thereat the cat purred so loudly that she dared to stroke his ugly head, and this was much larger than her own, being greater than that of any dog that is now on Earth. Thus entreated,

Umuiyan, for such was his name, said: "Come then with me," and
seizing Tinúviel suddenly by her garments at the shoulder to her
great terror he tossed her upon his back and leaped upon the
second terrace. There he stopped, and as Tinúviel scrambled
from his back he said: "Well is it for thee that this afternoon my
lord Tevildo lieth upon this lowly terrace far from his house, for a
great weariness and a desire for sleep has come upon me, so that I
fear me I should not be willing to carry thee much farther"; now
Tinúviel was robed in her robe of sable mist.

So saying Umuiyan* yawned mightily and stretched himself
before he led her along that terrace to an open space, where upon a
wide couch of baking stones lay the horrible form of Tevildo
himself, and both his evil eyes were shut. Going up to him the
doorcat Umuiyan spoke in his ear softly, saying: "A maiden awaits
thy pleasure, my lord, who hath news of importance to deliver to
thee, nor would she take my refusal." Then did Tevildo angrily
lash his tail, half opening an eye — "What is it — be swift," said he,
"for this is no hour to come desiring audience of Tevildo Prince of
Cats."

"Nay, lord," said Tinúviel trembling, "be not angry; nor do I
think that thou wilt when thou hearest, yet is the matter such that
it were better not even whispered here where the breezes blow,"
and Tinúviel cast a glance as it were of apprehension toward the
woods.

"Nay, get thee gone," said Tevildo, "thou smellest of dog, and
what news of good came ever to a cat from a fairy that had had
dealings with the dogs?"

"Why, sir, that I smell of dogs is no matter of wonder, for I have
just escaped from one — and it is indeed of a certain very mighty
dog whose name thou knowest that I would speak." Then up sat
Tevildo and opened his eyes, and he looked all about him, and
stretched three times, and at last bade the doorcat lead Tinúviel
within; and Umuiyan caught her upon his back as before. Now
was Tinúviel in the sorest dread, for having gained what she
desired, a chance of entering Tevildo's stronghold and maybe of
discovering whether Beren were there, she had no plan more, and
knew not what would become of her — indeed had she been able
she would have fled; yet now do those cats begin to ascend the
terraces towards the castle, and one leap does Umuiyan make
bearing Tinúviel upwards and then another, and at the third he

---

* Written above *Umuiyan* here is the name *Gumniow*, enclosed within brackets.

stumbled so that Tinúviel cried out in fear, and Tevildo said: "What ails thee, Umuiyan, thou clumsy-foot? It is time that thou left my employ if age creeps on thee so swiftly." But Umuiyan said: "Nay, lord, I know not what it is, but a mist is before mine eyes and my head is heavy," and he staggered as one drunk, so that Tinúviel slid from his back, and thereupon he laid him down as if in a dead sleep; but Tevildo was wroth and seized Tinúviel and ·none too gently, and himself bore her to the gates. Then with a mighty leap he sprang within, and bidding that maiden alight he set up a yell that echoed fearsomely in the dark ways and passages. Forthwith they hastened to him from within, and some he bid descend to Umuiyan and bind him and cast him from the rocks "on the northern side where they fall most sheer, for he is of no use more to me," he said, "for age has robbed him of his sureness of foot"; and Tinúviel quaked to hear the ruthlessness of this beast. But even as he spake he himself yawned and stumbled as with a sudden drowziness, and he bid others to lead Tinúviel away to a certain chamber within, and that was the one where Tevildo was accustomed to sit at meat with his greatest thanes. It was full of bones and smelt evilly; no windows were there and but one door; but a hatchway gave from it upon the great kitchens, and a red light crept thence and dimly lit the place.

Now so adread was Tinúviel when those catfolk left her there that she stood a moment unable to stir, but soon becoming used to the darkness she looked about and espying the hatchway that had a wide sill she sprang thereto, for it was not over high and she was a nimble Elf. Now gazing therethrough, for it was ajar, she saw the wide vaulted kitchens and the great fires that burnt there, and those that toiled always within, and the most were cats – but behold, there by a great fire stooped Beren, and he was grimed with labour, and Tinúviel sat and wept, but as yet dared nothing. Indeed even as she sat the harsh voice of Tevildo sounded suddenly within that chamber: "Nay, where then in Melko's name has that mad Elf fled," and Tinúviel hearing shrank against the wall, but Tevildo caught sight of her where she was perched and cried: "Then the little bird sings not any more; come down or I must fetch thee, for behold, I will not encourage the Elves to seek audience of me in mockery."

Then partly in fear, and part in hope that her clear voice might carry even to Beren, Tinúviel began suddenly to speak very loud and to tell her tale so that the chambers rang; but "Hush, dear maiden," said Tevildo, "if the matter were secret without it is not

one for bawling within." Then said Tinúviel: "Speak not thus to
me, O cat, mighty Lord of Cats though thou be, for am I not
Tinúviel Princess of Fairies that have stepped out of my way to do
thee a pleasure?" Now at those words, and she had shouted them
even louder than before, a great crash was heard in the kitchens as
of a number of vessels of metal and earthenware let suddenly fall,
but Tevildo snarled: "There trippeth that fool Beren the Elf.
Melko rid me of such folk" – yet Tinúviel, guessing that Beren had
heard and been smitten with astonishment, put aside her fears and
repented her daring no longer. Tevildo nonetheless was very
wroth at her haughty words, and had he not been minded first to
discover what good he might get from her tale, it had fared ill with
Tinúviel straightway. Indeed from that moment was she in great
peril, for Melko and all his vassals held Tinwelint and his folk as
outlaws, and great was their joy to ensnare them and cruelly
entreat them, so that much favour would Tevildo have gained had
he taken Tinúviel before his lord. Indeed, so soon as she named
herself, this did he purpose to do when his own business had
been done, but of a truth his wits were drowzed that day, and he
forgot to marvel more why Tinúviel sat perched upon the sill of
the hatchway; nor did he think more of Beren, for his mind was
bent only to the tale Tinúviel bore to him. Wherefore said he,
dissembling his evil mood, "Nay, Lady, be not angry, but come,
delay whetteth my desire – what is it that thou hast for my ears, for
they twitch already."

But Tinúviel said: "There is a great beast, rude and violent, and
his name is Huan" – and at that name Tevildo's back curved, and
his hair bristled and crackled, and the light of his eyes was red –
"and," she went on, "it seems to me a shame that such a brute be
suffered to infest the woods so nigh even to the abode of the
powerful Prince of Cats, my lord Tevildo"; but Tevildo said:
"Nor is he suffered, and cometh never there save it be by stealth."

"Howso that may be," said Tinúviel, "there he is now, yet
methinks that at last may his [life] be brought utterly to an end, for
lo, as I was going through the woods I saw where a great animal lay
upon the ground moaning as in sickness – and behold, it was
Huan, and some evil spell or malady has him in its grip, and still he
lies helpless in a dale not a mile westward in the woods from this
hall. Now with this perhaps I would not have troubled your ears,
had not the brute when I approached to succour him snarled upon
me and essayed to bite me, and meseems that such a creature
deserves whatever come to him."

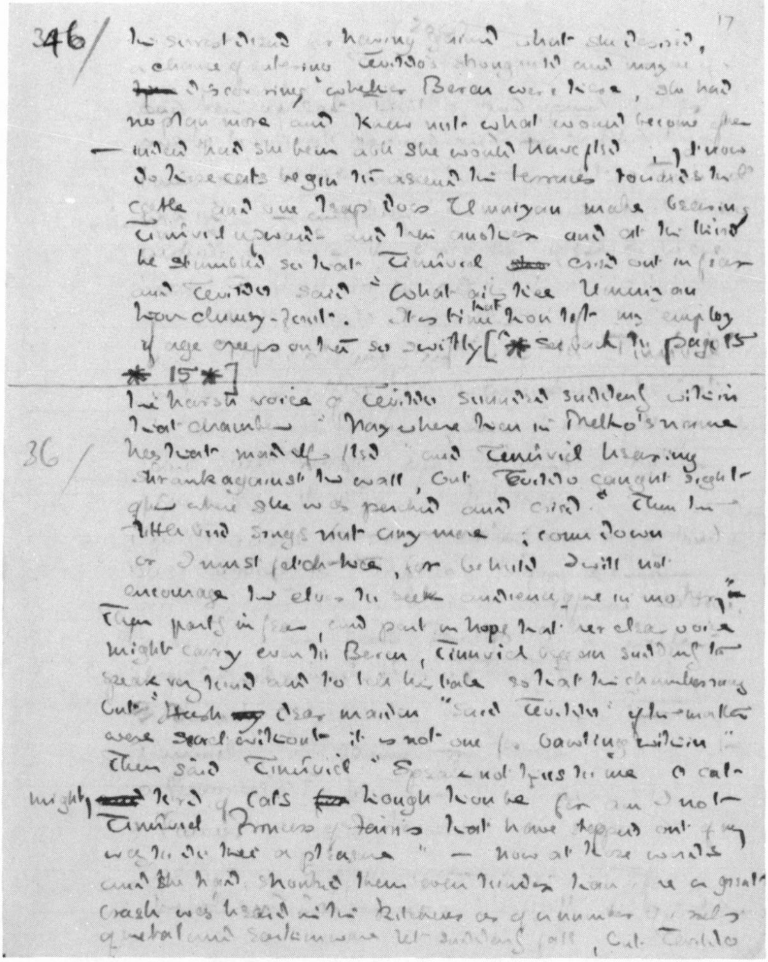

A page from the *Tale of Tinúviel*

"Now therefore" said Galdor "we must get as far hence
toward the Encircling Mountains as may be ere dawn come upon us,
and that giveth us no great space of time albeit it is winter."
Thereat rose a dissension for a number said that it were folly
to make for Cristhorn or Tuor purposed. "The Sun" say
they "will be up long ere we win the foothills and we shall
be overwhelmed in the plain by Orc-drakes and these demons;
~~nay many a host we meet as we fare in front the~~..."

~~And spake around these yet were here for making for~~
~~But Uswen the way of Escape now far less~~.

Let us fare to Bad Uswen the Way of Escape for that is
but half the journeying, and our weary and our wounded
may hope to win so far no further.

But these, led Gove Legolas Greenleaf of the house of the
Tree who knew all that plain by day or by dark, and was
night-sighted made ~~~~ for all their weariness over
the vale, and halted only after a great march. Then was
all the Earth spread with the grey light of that said dawn that
ranked unmore on the beauty of Gondolin. On the plain was full of mists
— and that was a marvel for no mist so fog came there ever before, and
this perchance had to do with the ruin of the fountain of the king.
Again they rose and covered by the vapours fared long past dawn in
safety, till they were already far for any to descry them in those
misty airs from the hill or from the ruined walls.
Now the Mountains were on that side Seven leagues save a
mile from Gondolin and Cristhorn the Cleft of Eagles, another
league of upward going from the beginning of the mountains wherefore
they were now yet two leagues and part of a third from the pass, and
very weary to it.
By now the Sun being
~~Then rose the Sun~~ well above a saddle in the Eastward hills,
and she was very red and great; and the mists nigh them were
lifted, but the ruins of Gondolin were utterly hidden as in a cloud.
Behold at the clearing of the airs they saw, but half a league
away, a knot of men that fled on foot — and these were pursued
by a strange cavalry, for on great wolves rode Orcs, as they
thought, brandishing spears. Then said Tuor! Lo! here
is Earendel my son and my men of the wing, and they are in
sore strait." Forthwith he chose fifty of the men that were
least weary, and leaving the main company to follow, he

Now all this that Tinúviel spake was a great lie in whose devising Huan had guided her, and maidens of the Eldar are not wont to fashion lies; yet have I never heard that any of the Eldar blamed her therein nor Beren afterward, and neither do I, for Tevildo was an evil cat and Melko the wickedest of all beings, and Tinúviel was in dire peril at their hands. Tevildo however, himself a great and skilled liar, was so deeply versed in the lies and subtleties of all the beasts and creatures that he seldom knew whether to believe what was said to him or not, and was wont to disbelieve all things save those he wished to believe true, and so was he often deceived by the more honest. Now the story of Huan and his helplessness so pleased him that he was fain to believe it true, and determined at least to test it; yet at first he feigned indifference, saying this was a small matter for such secrecy and might have been spoken outside without further ado. But Tinúviel said she had not thought that Tevildo Prince of Cats needed to learn that the ears of Huan heard the slightest sounds a league away, and the voice of a cat further than any sound else.

Now therefore Tevildo sought to discover from Tinúviel under pretence of mistrusting her tale where exactly Huan might be found, but she made only vague answers, seeing in this her only hope of escaping from the castle, and at length Tevildo, overcome by curiosity and threatening evil things if she should prove false, summoned two of his thanes to him, and one was Oikeroi, a fierce and warlike cat. Then did the three set out with Tinúviel from that place, but Tinúviel took off her magical garment of black and folded it, so that for all its size and density it appeared no more than the smallest kerchief (for so was she able), and thus was she borne down the terraces upon the back of Oikeroi without mishap, and no drowziness assailed her bearer. Now crept they through the woods in the direction she had named, and soon does Tevildo smell dog and bristles and lashes his great tail, but after he climbs a lofty tree and looks down from thence into that dale that Tinúviel had shown to them. There he does indeed see the great form of Huan lying prostrate groaning and moaning, and he comes down in much glee and haste, and indeed in his eagerness he forgets Tinúviel, who now in great fear for Huan lies hidden in a bank of fern. The design of Tevildo and his two companions was to enter that dale silently from different quarters and so come all suddenly upon Huan unawares and slay him, or if he were too stricken to make fight to make sport of him and torment him. This did they now, but even as they leapt out upon him Huan sprang up into the air with a mighty baying, and his jaws closed in the back close to the neck of that cat Oikeroi, and Oikeroi died; but the other thane fled howling up a great tree, and so was Tevildo left alone face to face with Huan, and such an encounter was not much to his mind, yet was Huan upon him too swiftly for flight, and they fought fiercely in that glade, and the noise that Tevildo made was very hideous; but at length Huan had him by the throat, and that cat might well have perished had not his claws as he struck out blindly pierced Huan's eye. Then did Huan give tongue, and Tevildo screeching fearsomely got himself loose with a great wrench and leapt up a tall and smooth tree that stood by, even as his companion had done. Despite his grievous hurt Huan now leaps beneath that tree baying mightily, and Telvido curses him and casts evil words upon him from above.

Then said Huan: "Lo, Tevildo, these are the words of Huan whom thou thoughtest to catch and slay helpless as the miserable mice it is thy wont to hunt – stay for ever up thy lonely tree and bleed to death of thy wounds, or come down and feel again my teeth. But if neither are to thy liking, then tell me where is Tinúviel Princess of Fairies and Beren son of Egnor, for these are my friends. Now these shall be set as ransom against thee – though it be valuing thee far over thy worth."

"As for that cursed Elf, she lies whimpering in the ferns yonder, an my ears mistake not," said Tevildo, "and Beren methinks is being soundly scratched by Miaulë my cook in the kitchens of my castle for his clumsiness there an hour ago."

"Then let them be given to me in safety," said Huan, "and thou mayest return thyself to thy halls and lick thyself unharmed."

"Of a surety my thane who is here with me shall fetch them for thee," said Tevildo, but growled Huan: "Ay, and fetch also all thy tribe and the hosts of the Orcs and the plagues of Melko. Nay, I am no fool; rather shalt thou give Tinúviel a token and she shall fetch Beren, or thou shalt stay here if thou likest not the other way." Then was Tevildo forced to cast down his golden collar – a token no cat dare dishonour, but Huan said: "Nay, more yet is needed, for this will arouse all thy folk to seek thee," and this Tevildo knew and had hoped. So was it that in the end weariness and hunger and fear prevailed upon that proud cat, a prince of the service of Melko, to reveal the secret of the cats and the spell that Melko had entrusted to him; and those were words of magic whereby the stones of his evil house were held together, and whereby he held all beasts of the catfolk under his sway, filling them with an evil power beyond their nature; for long has it been said that Tevildo was an evil fay in beastlike shape. When therefore he had told it Huan laughed till the woods rang, for he knew that the days of the power of the cats were over.

Now sped Tinúviel with the golden collar of Tevildo back to the lowest terrace before the gates, and standing she spake the spell in her clear voice. Then behold, the air was filled with the voices of cats and the house of Tevildo shook; and there came therefrom a host of indwellers and they were shrunk to puny size and were afeared of Tinúviel, who waving the collar of Tevildo spake before them certain of the words that Tevildo had said in her hearing to Huan, and they cowered before her. But she said: "Lo, let all those of the folk of the Elves or of the children of Men that are bound within these halls be brought forth," and behold, Beren was brought forth, but of other thralls there were none, save only Gimli, an aged Gnome, bent in thraldom and grown blind, but whose hearing was the keenest that has been in the world, as all songs say. Gimli came leaning upon a stick and Beren aided him, but Beren was clad in rags and haggard, and he had in his hand a great knife he had caught up in the kitchen, fearing some new ill when the house shook and all the voices of the cats were heard; but when he beheld Tinúviel standing amid the host of cats that shrank from her and saw the great collar of Tevildo, then was he[8] amazed utterly, and knew not what to think. But Tinúviel was very glad, and spoke saying: "O Beren from beyond the Bitter Hills, wilt thou now dance with me – but let it not be here." And she led Beren far away, and all those cats set up a howling and wailing, so that Huan and Tevildo heard it in the woods, but none followed or molested them, for they were afraid, and the magic of Melko was fallen from them.

This indeed they rued afterward when Tevildo returned home followed by his trembling comrade, for Tevildo's wrath was terrible, and he lashed his tail and dealt blows at all who stood nigh. Now Huan of the dogs, though it might seem a folly, when Beren and Tinúviel came to that glade had suffered that evil Prince to return without further war, but the great collar of gold he had set about his own neck, and at this was Tevildo more angry than all else, for a great magic of strength and power lay therein. Little to Huan's liking was it that Tevildo lived still, but now no longer did he fear the cats, and that tribe has fled before the dogs ever since, and the dogs hold them still in scorn since the humbling of Tevildo in the woods nigh Angamandi; and Huan has not done any greater deed. Indeed afterward Melko heard all and he cursed Tevildo and his folk and banished them, nor have they since that day had lord or master or any friend, and their voices wail and screech for their hearts are very lonely and bitter and full of loss, yet there is only darkness therein and no kindliness.

At the time however whereof the tale tells it was Tevildo's chief desire to recapture Beren and Tinúviel and to slay Huan, that he might regain the spell and magic he had lost, for he was in great fear of Melko, and he dared not seek his master's aid and reveal his defeat and the betrayal of his spell. Unwitting of this Huan feared those places, and was in great dread lest those doings come swiftly to Melko's ear, as did most things that came to pass in the world; wherefore now Tinúviel and Beren wandered far away with Huan, and they became great in friendship with him, and in that life Beren grew strong again and his thraldom fell from him, and Tinúviel loved him.

Yet wild and rugged and very lonely were those days, for never a face of Elf or of Man did they see, and Tinúviel grew at last to long sorely for Gwendeling her mother and the songs of sweet magic she was used to sing to her children as twilight fell in the woodlands by their ancient halls. Often she half fancied she heard the flute of Dairon her brother, in pleasant glades' wherein they sojourned, and her heart grew heavy. At length she said to Beren and to Huan: "I must return home," and now is it Beren's heart that is overcast with sorrow, for he loved that life in the woods with the dogs (for by now many others had become joined to Huan), yet not if Tinúviel were not there.

Nonetheless said he: "Never may I go back with thee to the land of Artanor—nor come there ever after to seek thee, sweet Tinúviel, save only bearing a Silmaril; nor may that ever now be achieved, for am I not a fugitive from the very halls of Melko, and in danger of the most evil pains do any of his servants spy me." Now this he said in the grief of his heart at parting with Tinúviel, and she was torn in mind, abiding not the thought of leaving Beren nor yet of living ever thus in exile. So sat she a great while in sad thought and she spoke not, but Beren sat nigh and at length said: "Tinúviel, one thing only can we do – go get a Silmaril"; and she sought thereupon Huan, asking his aid and advice, but he was very grave and saw nothing but folly in the matter. Yet in the end Tinúviel begged of him the fell of Oikeroi that he slew in the affray of the glade; now Oikeroi was a very mighty cat and Huan carried that fell with him as a trophy.

Now doth Tinúviel put forth her skill and fairy-magic, and she sews Beren into this fell and makes him to the likeness of a great cat, and she teaches him how to sit and sprawl, to step and bound and trot in the semblance of a cat, till Huan's very whiskers bristled at the sight, and thereat Beren and Tinúviel laughed. Never however could Beren learn to screech or wail or to purr like any cat that ever walked, nor could Tinúviel awaken a glow in the dead eyes of the catskin – "but we must put up with that," said she, "and thou hast the air of a very noble cat if thou but hold thy tongue."

Then did they bid farewell to Huan and set out for the halls of Melko by easy journeys, for Beren was in great discomfort and heat within the fur of Oikeroi, and Tinúviel's heart became lighter awhile than it had been for long, and she stroked Beren or pulled his tail, and Beren was angry because he could not lash it in answer as fiercely as he wished. At length however they drew near to Angamandi, as indeed the rumblings and deep noises, and the sound of mighty hammerings of ten thousand smiths labouring unceasingly, declared to them. Nigh were the sad chambers where the thrall-Noldoli laboured bitterly under the Orcs and goblins of the hills, and here the gloom and darkness was great so that their hearts fell, but Tinúviel arrayed her once more in her dark garment of deep sleep. Now the gates of Angamandi were of iron wrought hideously and set with knives and spikes, and before them lay the greatest wolf the world has ever seen, even Karkaras Knife-fang who had never slept; and Karkaras growled when he saw Tinúviel approach, but of the cat he took not much heed, for he thought little of cats and they were ever passing in and out.

"Growl not, O Karkaras," said she, "for I go to seek my lord Melko, and this thane of Tevildo goeth with me as escort." Now the dark robe veiled all her shimmering beauty, and Karkaras was not much troubled in mind, yet nonetheless he approached as was his wont to snuff the air of her, and the sweet fragrance of the Eldar that garment might not hide. Therefore straightway did Tinúviel begin a magic dance, and the black strands of her dark veil she cast in his eyes so that his legs shook with a drowziness and he rolled over and was asleep. But not until he was fast in dreams of great chases in the woods of Hisilómë when he was yet a whelp did Tinúviel cease, and then did those twain enter that black portal, and winding down many shadowy ways they stumbled at length into the very presence of Melko.

In that gloom Beren passed well enough as a very thane of

Tevildo, and indeed Oikeroi had aforetime been much about the
halls of Melko, so that none heeded him and he slunk under the
very chair of the Ainu unseen, but the adders and evil things there
lying set him in great fear so that he durst not move.

Now all this fell out most fortunately, for had Tevildo been with
Melko their deceit would have been discovered – and indeed of
that danger they had thought, not knowing that Tevildo sat now in
his halls and knew not what to do should his discomfiture become
noised in Angamandi; but behold, Melko espieth Tinúviel and
saith: "Who art thou that flittest about my halls like a bat? How
camest thou in, for of a surety thou dost not belong here?"

"Nay, that I do not yet," saith Tinúviel, "though I may perchance hereafter, of thy goodness, my lord Melko. Knowest thou
not that I am Tinúviel daughter of Tinwelint the outlaw, and he
hath driven me from his halls, for he is an overbearing Elf and I
give not my love at his command."

Now in truth was Melko amazed that the daughter of Tinwelint
came thus of her free will to his dwelling, Angamandi the terrible,
and suspecting something untoward he asked what was her desire:
"for knowest thou not," saith he, "that there is no love here for thy
father or his folk, nor needst thou hope for soft words and good
cheer from me."

"So hath my father said," saith she, "but wherefore need I
believe him? Behold, I have a skill of subtle dances, and I would
dance now before you, my lord, for then methinks I might readily
be granted some humble corner of your halls wherein to dwell
until such times as you should call for the little dancer Tinúviel to
lighten your cares."

"Nay," saith Melko, "such things are little to my mind; but as
thou hast come thus far to dance, dance, and after we will see,"
and with that he leered horribly, for his dark mind pondered some
evil.

Then did Tinúviel begin such a dance as neither she nor any
other sprite or fay or elf danced ever before or has done since, and
after a while even Melko's gaze was held in wonder. Round the hall
she fared, swift as a swallow, noiseless as a bat, magically beautiful
as only Tinúviel ever was, and now she was at Melko's side, now
before him, now behind, and her misty draperies touched his face
and waved before his eyes, and the folk that sat about the walls or
stood in that place were whelmed one by one in sleep, falling down
into deep dreams of all that their ill hearts desired.

Beneath his chair the adders lay like stones, and the wolves before his feet yawned and slumbered, and Melko gazed on enchanted, but he did not sleep. Then began Tinúviel to dance a yet swifter dance before his eyes, and even as she danced she sang in a voice very low and wonderful a song which Gwendeling had taught her long ago, a song that the youths and maidens sang beneath the cypresses of the gardens of Lórien when the Tree of Gold had waned and Silpion was gleaming. The voices of nightingales were in it, and many subtle odours seemed to fill the air of that noisome place as she trod the floor lightly as a feather in the wind; nor has any voice or sight of such beauty ever again been seen there, and Ainu Melko for all his power and majesty succumbed to the magic of that Elf-maid, and indeed even the eyelids of Lórien had grown heavy had he been there to see. Then did Melko fall forward drowzed, and sank at last in utter sleep down from his chair upon the floor, and his iron crown rolled away.

Suddenly Tinúviel ceased. In the hall no sound was heard save of slumbrous breath; even Beren slept beneath the very seat of Melko, but Tinúviel shook him so that he awoke at last. Then in fear and trembling he tore asunder his disguise and freeing himself from it leapt to his feet. Now does he draw that knife that he had from Tevildo's kitchens and he seizes the mighty iron crown, but Tinúviel could not move it and scarcely might the thews of Beren avail to turn it. Great is the frenzy of their fear as in that dark hall of sleeping evil Beren labours as noiselessly as may be to prise out a Silmaril with his knife. Now does he loosen the great central jewel and the sweat pours from his brow, but even as he forces it from the crown lo! his knife snaps with a loud crack.

Tinúviel smothers a cry thereat and Beren springs away with the one Silmaril in his hand, and the sleepers stir and Melko groans as though ill thoughts disturbed his dreams, and a black look comes upon his sleeping face. Content now with that one flashing gem those twain fled desperately from the hall, stumbling wildly down many dark passages till from the glimmering of grey light they knew they neared the gates – and behold! Karkaras lies across the threshold, awake once more and watchful.

Straightway Beren thrust himself before Tinúviel although she said him nay, and this proved in the end ill, for Tinúviel had not time to cast her spell of slumber over the beast again, ere seeing Beren he bared his teeth and growled angrily. "Wherefore this surliness, Karkaras?" said Tinúviel. "Wherefore this Gnome[10] who entered not and yet now issueth in haste?" quoth Knife-fang, and with that he leapt upon Beren, who struck straight between the wolf's eyes with his fist, catching for his throat with the other hand.

Then Karkaras seized that hand in his dreadful jaws, and it was the hand wherein Beren clasped the blazing Silmaril, and both hand and jewel Karkaras bit off and took into his red maw. Great was the agony of Beren and the fear and anguish of Tinúviel, yet even as they expect to feel the teeth of the wolf a new thing strange and terrible comes to pass. Behold now that Silmaril blazeth with a white and hidden fire of its own nature and is possessed of a fierce and holy magic – for did it not come from Valinor and the blessed realms, being fashioned with spells of the Gods and Gnomes before evil came there; and it doth not tolerate the touch of evil flesh or of unholy hand. Now cometh it into the foul body of Karkaras, and suddenly that beast is burnt with a terrible anguish and the howling of his pain is ghastly to hear as it echoeth in those rocky ways, so that all that sleeping court within awakes. Then did Tinúviel and Beren flee like the wind from the gates, yet was Karkaras far before them raging and in madness as a beast pursued by Balrogs; and after when they might draw breath Tinúviel wept over the maimed arm of Beren kissing it often, so that behold it bled not, and pain left it, and was healed by the tender healing of her love; yet was Beren ever after surnamed among all folk Ermabwed the One-handed, which in the language of the Lonely Isle is Elmavoitë.

Now however must they bethink them of escape – if such may be their fortune, and Tinúviel wrapped part of her dark mantle about Beren, and so for a while flitting by dusk and dark amid the hills they were seen by none, albeit Melko had raised all his Orcs of terror against them; and his fury at the rape of that jewel was greater than the Elves had ever seen it yet.

Even so it seems soon to them that the net of the hunters drew ever more tightly upon them, and though they had reached the edge of the more familiar woods and passed the glooms of the forest of Taurfuin, still were there many leagues of peril yet to pass between them and the caverns of the king, and even did they reach ever there it seemed like they would but draw the chase behind them thither and Melko's hate upon all that woodland folk. So great indeed was the hue and cry that Huan learnt of it far away, and he marvelled much at the daring of those twain, and still more that ever they had escaped from Angamandi.

Now goes he with many dogs through the woods hunting Orcs

and thanes of Tevildo, and many hurts he got thus, and many of them he slew or put to fear and flight, until one even at dusk the Valar brought him to a glade in that northward region of Artanor that was called afterward Nan Dumgorthin, the land of the dark idols, but that is a matter that concerns not this tale. Howbeit it was even then a dark land and gloomy and foreboding, and dread wandered beneath its lowering trees no less even than in Taurfuin; and those two Elves Tinúviel and Beren were lying therein weary and without hope, and Tinúviel wept but Beren was fingering his knife.

Now when Huan saw them he would not suffer them to speak or to tell any of their tale, but straightway took Tinúviel upon his mighty back and bade Beren run as best he could beside him, "for," said he, "a great company of the Orcs are drawing swiftly hither, and wolves are their trackers and their scouts." Now doth Huan's pack run about them, and they go very swiftly along quick and secret paths towards the homes of the folk of Tinwelint far away. Thus was it that they eluded the host of their enemies, but had nonetheless many an encounter afterward with wandering things of evil, and Beren slew an Orc that came nigh to dragging off Tinúviel, and that was a good deed. Seeing then that the hunt still pressed them close, once more did Huan lead them by winding ways, and dared not yet straightly to bring them to the land of the woodland fairies. So cunning however was his leading that at last after many days the chase fell far away, and no longer did they see or hear anything of the bands of Orcs; no goblins waylaid them nor did the howling of any evil wolves come upon the airs at night, and belike that was because already they had stepped within the circle of Gwendeling's magic that hid the paths from evil things and kept harm from the regions of the woodelves.

Then did Tinúviel breathe freely once more as she had not done since she fled from her father's halls, and Beren rested in the sun far from the glooms of Angband until the last bitterness of thraldom left him. Because of the light falling through green leaves and the whisper of clean winds and the song of birds once more are they wholly unafraid.

At last came there nevertheless a day whereon waking out of a deep slumber Beren started up as one who leaves a dream of happy things coming suddenly to his mind, and he said: "Farewell, O Huan, most trusty comrade, and thou, little Tinúviel, whom I love, fare thee well. This only I beg of thee, get thee now straight to the safety of thy home, and may good Huan lead thee. But I – lo,

I must away into the solitude of the woods, for I have lost that Silmaril which I had, and never dare I draw near to Angamandi more, wherefore neither will I enter the halls of Tinwelint." Then he wept to himself, but Tinúviel who was nigh and had hearkened to his musing came beside him and said: "Nay, now is my heart changed," and if thou dwellest in the woods, O Beren Ermabwed, then so will I, and if thou wilt wander in the wild places there will I wander also, or with thee or after thee: – yet never shall my father see me again save only if thou takest me to him." Then indeed was Beren glad at her sweet words, and fain would he have dwelt with her as a huntsman of the wild, but his heart smote him for all that she had suffered for him, and for her he put away his pride. Indeed she reasoned with him, saying it would be folly to be stubborn, and that her father would greet them with nought but joy, being glad to see his daughter yet alive – and "maybe," said she, "he will have shame that his jesting has given thy fair hand to the jaws of Karkaras." But Huan also she implored to return with them a space, for "my father owes thee a very great reward, O Huan," saith she, "an he loves his daughter at all."

So came it that those three set forward once again together, and came at last back to the woodlands that Tinúviel knew and loved nigh to the dwellings of her folk and to the deep halls of her home. Yet even as they approach they find fear and tumult among that people such as had not been for a long age, and asking some that wept before their doors they learned that ever since the day of Tinúviel's secret flight ill-fortune had befallen them. Lo, the king had been distraught with grief and had relaxed his ancient wariness and cunning; indeed his warriors had been sent hither and thither deep into the unwholesome woods searching for that maiden, and many had been slain or lost for ever, and war there was with Melko's servants about all their northern and eastern borders, so that the folk feared mightily lest that Ainu upraise his strength and come utterly to crush them and Gwendeling's magic have not the strength to withhold the numbers of the Orcs. "Behold," said they, "now is the worst of all befallen, for long has Queen Gwendeling sat aloof and smiled not nor spoken, looking as it were to a great distance with haggard eyes, and the web of her magic has blown thin about the woods, and the woods are dreary, for Dairon comes not back, neither is his music heard ever in the glades. Behold now the crown of all our evil tidings, for know that there has broken upon us raging from the halls of Evil a great grey wolf filled with an evil spirit, and he fares as though lashed by some

hidden madness, and none are safe. Already has he slain many
as he runs wildly snapping and yelling through the woods, so
that the very banks of the stream that flows before the king's
halls has become a lurking-place of danger. There comes the
awful wolf oftentimes to drink, looking as the evil Prince
himself with bloodshot eyes and tongue lolling out, and never can
he slake his desire for water as though some inward fire devours
him."

Then was Tinúviel sad at the thought of the unhappiness that
had come upon her folk, and most of all was her heart bitter at the
story of Dairon, for of this she had not heard any murmur before.
Yet could she not wish Beren had come never to the lands of
Artanor, and together they made haste to Tinwelint; and already
to the Elves of the wood it seemed that the evil was at an end now
that Tinúviel was come back among them unharmed. Indeed they
scarce had hoped for that.

In great gloom do they find King Tinwelint, yet suddenly is his
sorrow melted to tears of gladness, and Gwendeling sings again
for joy when Tinúviel enters there and casting away her raiment of
dark mist she stands before them in her pearly radiance of old. For
a while all is mirth and wonder in that hall, and yet at length the
king turns his eyes to Beren and says: "So thou hast returned too –
bringing a Silmaril, beyond doubt, in recompense for all the ill
thou hast wrought my land; or an thou hast not, I know not
wherefore thou art here."

Then Tinúviel stamped her foot and cried so that the king and
all about him wondered at her new and fearless mood: "For
shame, my father – behold, here is Beren the brave whom thy
jesting drove into dark places and foul captivity and the Valar
alone saved from a bitter death. Methinks 'twould rather befit a
king of the Eldar to reward him than revile him."

"Nay," said Beren, "the king thy father hath the right. Lord,"
said he, "I have a Silmaril in my hand even now."

"Show me then," said the king in amaze.

"That I cannot," said Beren, "for my hand is not here"; and he
held forth his maimed arm.

Then was the king's heart turned to him by reason of his stout
and courteous demeanour, and he bade Beren and Tinúviel relate
to him all that had befallen either of them, and he was eager to
hearken, for he did not fully comprehend the meaning of Beren's
words. When however he had heard all yet more was his heart
turned to Beren, and he marvelled at the love that had awakened in

the heart of Tinúviel so that she had done greater deeds and more daring than any of the warriors of his folk.

"Never again," said he, "O Beren I beg of thee, leave this court nor the side of Tinúviel, for thou art a great Elf and thy name will ever be great among the kindreds." Yet Beren answered him proudly, and said: "Nay, O King, I hold to my word and thine, and I will get thee that Silmaril or ever I dwell in peace in thy halls." And the king entreated him to journey no more into the dark and unknown realms, but Beren said: "No need is there thereof, for behold that jewel is even now nigh to thy caverns," and he made clear to Tinwelint that that beast that ravaged his land was none other than Karkaras, the wolfward of Melko's gates – and this was not known to all, but Beren knew it taught by Huan, whose cunning in the reading of track and slot was greatest among all the hounds, and therein are none of them unskilled. Huan indeed was with Beren now in the halls, and when those twain spoke of a chase and a great hunt he begged to be in that deed; and it was granted gladly. Now do those three prepare themselves to harry that beast, that all the folk be rid of the terror of the wolf, and Beren kept his word, bringing a Silmaril to shine once more in Elfinesse. King Tinwelint himself led that chase, and Beren was beside him, and Mablung the heavy-handed, chief of the king's thanes, leaped up and grasped a spear[12] – a mighty weapon captured in battle with the distant Orcs – and with those three stalked Huan mightiest of dogs, but others they would not take according to the desire of the king, who said: "Four is enough for the slaying even of the Hell-wolf" – but only those who had seen knew how fearsome was that beast, nigh as large as a horse among Men, and so great was the ardour of his breath that it scorched whatsoever it touched. About the hour of sunrise they set forth, and soon after Huan espied a new slot beside the stream, not far from the king's doors, "and," quoth he, "this is the print of Karkaras." Thereafter they followed that stream all day, and at many places its banks were new-trampled and torn and the water of the pools that lay about it was fouled as though some beasts possessed of madness had rolled and fought there not long before.

Now sinks the sun and fades beyond the western trees and darkness is creeping down from Hisilómë so that the light of the forest dies. Even so come they to a place where the spoor swerves from the stream or perchance is lost in its waters and Huan may no longer follow it; and here therefore they encamp, sleeping in turns beside the stream, and the early night wears away.

Suddenly in Beren's watch a sound of great terror leaped up from far away – a howling as of seventy maddened wolves – then lo! the brushwood cracks and saplings snap as the terror draweth near, and Beren knows that Karkaras is upon them. Scarce had he time to rouse the others, and they were but just sprung up and half-awake, when a great form loomed in the wavering moonlight filtering there, and it was fleeing like one mad, and its course was bent towards the water. Thereat Huan gave tongue, and straightway the beast swerved aside towards them, and foam was dripping from his jaws and a red light shining from his eyes, and his face was marred with mingled terror and with wrath. No sooner did he leave the trees than Huan rushed upon him fearless of heart, but he with a mighty leap sprang right over that great dog, for all his fury was kindled suddenly against Beren whom he recognized as he stood behind, and to his dark mind it seemed that there was the cause of all his agony. Then Beren thrust swiftly upward with a spear into his throat, and Huan leapt again and had him by a hind leg, and Karkaras fell as a stone, for at that same moment the king's spear found his heart, and his evil spirit gushed forth and sped howling faintly as it fared over the dark hills to Mandos; but Beren lay under him crushed beneath his weight. Now they roll back that carcase and fall to cutting it open, but Huan licks Beren's face whence blood is flowing. Soon is the truth of Beren's words made clear, for the vitals of the wolf are half-consumed as though an inner fire had long been smouldering there, and suddenly the night is filled with a wondrous lustre, shot with pale and secret colours, as Mablung[13] draws forth the Silmaril. Then holding it out he said: "Behold O King,"[14] but Tinwelint said: "Nay, never will I handle it save only if Beren give it to me." But Huan said: "And that seems like never to be, unless ye tend him swiftly, for methinks he is hurt sorely"; and Mablung and the king were ashamed.

Therefore now they raised Beren gently up and tended him and washed him, and he breathed, but he spoke not nor opened his eyes, and when the sun arose and they had rested a little they bore him as softly as might be upon a bier of boughs back through the woodlands; and nigh midday they drew near the homes of the folk again, and then were they deadly weary, and Beren had not moved nor spoken, but groaned thrice.

There did all the people flock to meet them when their approach was noised among them, and some bore them meat and cool drinks and salves and healing things for their hurts, and but for the harm that Beren had met great indeed had been their joy. Now then they covered the leafy boughs whereon he lay with soft raiment, and they bore him away to the halls of the king, and there was Tinúviel awaiting them in great distress; and she fell upon Beren's breast and wept and kissed him, and he awoke and knew her, and after Mablung gave him that Silmaril, and he lifted it above him gazing at its beauty, ere he said slowly and with pain: "Behold, O King, I give thee the wondrous jewel thou didst desire, and it is but a little thing found by the wayside, for once methinks thou hadst one beyond thought more beautiful, and she is now mine." Yet even as he spake the shadows of Mandos lay upon his face, and his spirit fled in that hour to the margin of the world, and Tinúviel's tender kisses called him not back.'

Then did Vëannë suddenly cease speaking, and Eriol sadly said: 'A tale of ruth for so sweet a maid to tell'; but behold, Vëannë wept, and not for a while did she say: 'Nay, that is not all the tale; but here endeth all that I rightly know,' and other children there spake, and one said: 'Lo, I have heard that the magic of Tinúviel's tender kisses healed Beren, and recalled his spirit from the gates of Mandos, and long time he dwelt among the Lost Elves wandering the glades in love with sweet Tinúviel.' But another said: 'Nay, that was not so, O Ausir, and if thou wilt listen I will tell the true and wondrous tale; for Beren died there in Tinúviel's arms even as Vëannë has said, and Tinúviel crushed with sorrow and finding no comfort or light in all the world followed him swiftly down those dark ways that all must tread alone. Now her beauty and tender loveliness touched even the cold heart of Mandos, so that he suffered her to lead Beren forth once more into the world, nor has this ever been done since to Man or Elf, and many songs and stories are there of the prayer of Tinúviel before the throne of Mandos that I remember not right well. Yet said Mandos to those twain: "Lo, O Elves, it is not to any life of perfect joy that I dismiss you, for such may no longer be found in all the world where sits Melko of the evil heart – and know ye that ye will become mortal even as Men, and when ye fare hither again it will be for ever, unless the Gods summon you indeed to Valinor." Nonetheless those twain departed hand in hand, and they fared together through the northern woods, and oftentimes were they seen dancing magic dances down the hills, and their name became heard far and wide.'

And thereat that boy ceased, and Vëannë said: 'Aye, and they did more than dance, for their deeds afterward were very great, and many tales are there thereof that thou must hear, O Eriol Melinon, upon another time of tale-telling. For those twain it is that stories name i·Cuilwarthon, which is to say the dead that live again, and they became mighty fairies in the lands about the north of Sirion. Behold now all is ended – and doth it like thee?' But Eriol said: 'Indeed 'tis a wondrous tale, such as I looked not to hear from the lips of the little maids of Mar Vanwa Tyaliéva,' but Vëannë answered him: 'Nay, but I fashioned it not with words of myself; but it is dear to me – and indeed all the children know of the deeds that it relates – and I have learned it by heart, reading it in the great books, and I do not comprehend all that is set therein.'

'Neither do I,' said Eriol – but suddenly cried Ausir: 'Behold, Eriol, Vëannë has never told thee what befell Huan; nor how he would take no rewards from Tinwelint nor dwell nigh him, but wandered forth again grieving for Tinúviel and Beren. On a time he fell in with Mablung[15] who aided in the chase, and was now fallen much to hunting in lonely parts; and the twain hunted together as friends until the days of Glorund the Drake and of Túrin Turambar, when once more Huan found Beren and played his part in the great deeds of the Nauglafring, the Necklace of the Dwarves.'

'Nay, how could I tell all this,' said Vëannë, 'for behold it is time for the evening meat already'; and soon after the great gong rang.

★

The second version of the Tale of Tinúviel

As already mentioned (p. 3), there exists a revised version of part of the tale in a typescript (made by my father). This follows the manuscript version closely or very closely on the whole, and in no way alters the style or air of the former; it is therefore unnecessary to give this second version *in extenso*. But the typescript does in places introduce interesting changes, and these are given below (the pages of the corresponding passages in the manuscript version are given in the margin).

The title in the typescript (which begins with the *Link* passage already given, pp. 4–7) was originally 'The Tale of Tynwfiel, Princess of Dor Athro', which was changed to 'The Tale of Tinúviel, the Dancer of Doriath'.

(8)   'Who then was Tinúviel?' said Eriol. 'Knowst thou not,' said Ausir, 'she was the daughter of Singoldo, king of Artanor?' 'Hush

thee, Ausir,' said Vëannë, 'this is my tale, and 'tis a tale of the
Gnomes, wherefore I beg that thou fill not Eriol's ear with thy
Elfin names. Lo! I will tell this tale only, for did I not see Melian
and Tinúviel once long ago with my own eyes when journeying by
the Way of Dreams?'

'What then was Queen Melian like,' quoth Eriol, 'if thou hast
seen her, O Vëannë?'

'Slender and very dark of hair,' said she, 'and her skin was white
and pale, but her eyes shone seeming to hold great depths. Clad
she was in filmy garments most lovely yet of the hue of night,
jet-spangled and girt with silver. If ever she sang or if ever
she danced, dreams and slumbers passed over the heads of those
that were nigh, making them heavy as it were with a strong wine
of sleep. Indeed she was a sprite that, escaping from Lórien's
gardens before even Kôr was built, wandered in the wild places of
the world and in every lonely wood. Nightingales fared with her
singing about her as she went – and 'twas the song of these birds
that smote the ears of Thingol as he marched at the head of that
second[16] tribe of the Eldalië which afterward became the Shoreland Pipers, the Solosimpi of the Isle. Now had they come a great
way from dim Palisor, and wearily the companies laboured behind
the swift-footed horse of Oromë, wherefore the music of the magic
birds of Melian seemed to him full of all solace, more beautiful
than other melodies of Earth, and he strayed aside for a moment,
as he thought, from the host, seeking in the dark trees whence it
might come.

And it is said that it was not a moment that he hearkened, but
many years, and vainly his people sought him, until at length they
must perforce follow Oromë upon Tol Eressëa, and be borne
thereon far away leaving him listening to the birds enchanted in
the woods of Aryador. That was the first sorrow of the Solosimpi,
that after were many; but Ilúvatar in memory of Thingol set a seed
of music in the hearts of that folk above all kindreds of the Earth
save only the Gods, and after, as all story tells, it blossomed
wondrously upon the isle and in glorious Valinor.

Little sorrow, however, had Thingol; for after a little, as him
seemed, he came upon Melian lying on a bed of leaves . . .

*

(9)   Long thereafter, as now thou knowest, Melko brake once more
into the world from Valinor, and wellnigh all beings therein came
under his foul thraldom; nor were the Lost Elves free, nor the
errant Gnomes that wandered the mountainous places seeking
their stolen treasury. Yet some few there were that led by mighty
kings still defied that evil one in fast and hidden places, and if

Turgon King of Gondolin was the most glorious of these, for a while the most mighty and the longest free was Thingol of the Woods.

Now in the after-days of Sunshine and Moonsheen still dwelt Thingol in Artanor and ruled a numerous and hardy folk drawn from all the tribes of ancient Elfinesse – for neither he nor his people went to the dread Battle of Unnumbered Tears – a matter which toucheth not this tale. Yet was his lordship greatly increased after that most bitter field by fugitives seeking a leader and a home. Hidden was his dwelling thereafter from the vision and knowledge of Melko by the cunning magics of Melian the fay, and she wove spells about all the paths that led thereto, so that none but the children of the Eldalië might tread them without straying. Thus was the king guarded against all evils save treachery alone; his halls were built in a deep cavern, vaulted immeasurable, that knew no other entrance than a rocky door, mighty, pillared with stone, and shadowed by the loftiest and most ancient trees in all the shaggy forests of Artanor. A great stream was there that fared a dark and silent course in the deep woods, and this flowed wide and swift before that doorway, so that all who would enter that portal must first cross a bridge hung by the Noldoli of Thingol's service across that water – and narrow it was and strongly guarded. In no wise ill were those forest lands, although not utterly distant were the Iron Mountains and black Hisilómë beyond them where dwelt the strange race of Men, and thrall-Noldoli laboured, and few free-Eldar went.

Two children had Thingol then, Dairon and Tinúviel . . .

*

(10)   'her mother was a fay, a child of Lórien' for manuscript 'her mother was a fay, a daughter of the Gods'.

*

(11)   'Now Beren was a Gnome, son of Egnor the forester' as in manuscript; but *Egnor* changed to *Barahir*. This however was a much later and as it were casual change; Beren's father was still Egnor in 1925.

*

(11)   Manuscript version 'and all the Elves of the woodland thought of the Gnomes of Dor Lómin as treacherous creatures, cruel and faithless' is omitted in the typescript.

*

(13)   *Angband* for manuscript *Angamandi*, and throughout.

*

(14)   Many a combat and an escape had he in those days, and he slew
therein more than once both wolf and the Orc that rode thereon
with nought but an ashen club that he bore; and other perils and
adventures . . .

*

(15)   But Melko looking wroth upon him asked: "How hast thou, O
thrall, dared to fare thus out of the land where thy folk dwells at
my behest, and to wander in the great woods unbidden, leaving
the labours to which thou hast been set?" Then answered Beren
that he was no runagate thrall, but came of a kindred of the
Gnomes that dwelt in Aryador where were many of the folk of
Men. Then was Melko yet more wroth, saying: "Here have we a
plotter of deep treacheries against Melko's lordship, and one
worthy of the tortures of the Balrogs" – for he sought ever to
destroy the friendship and intercourse of Elves and Men, lest they
forget the Battle of Unnumbered Tears and once more arise in
wrath against him. But Beren seeing his peril answered: "Think
not, O most mighty Belcha Morgoth (for such be his names
among the Gnomes), that could be so; for, an it were, then should
I not be here unaided and alone. No friendship has Beren son of
Egnor for the kindred of Men; nay indeed, wearying utterly of the
lands infested by that folk he has wandered out of Aryador.
Whither then should he go but to Angband? For many a great tale
has his father made to him aforetime of thy splendour and thy
glory. Lo, lord, albeit I am no renegade thrall, still do I desire
nothing so much as to serve thee in what small manner I may."
Little of truth was therein, and indeed his father Egnor was the
chiefest foe of Melko in all the kin of the Gnomes that still were
free, save only Turgon king of Gondolin and the sons of Fëanor,
and long days of friendship had he known with the folk of Men,
what time he was brother in arms to Úrin the steadfast; but in
those days he bore another name and Egnor was nought for
Melko. The truth, however, did Beren then tell, saying that he
was a great huntsman, swift and cunning to shoot or snare or to
outrun all birds and beasts. "I was lost unawares in a part of the
hills that were not known to me, O lord," he said, "the while I was
hunting; and wandering far I came to strange lands and knew no
other rede of safety save to fare to Angband, that all can find who
see the black hills of the north from afar. I would myself have fared
to thee and begged of thee some humble office (as a winner of
meats for thy table, perchance) had not these Orcs seized me and
tormented me unjustly."

Now the Valar must have inspired that speech, or maybe it was
a spell of cunning words cast upon him in compassion by Melian as
he fled from the hall; for indeed it saved his life . . .

Subsequently a part of this passage was emended on the type-script, to read:

. . . and long days of friendship had he known with the folk of Men (as had Beren himself thereafter as brother in arms to Úrin the Steadfast); but in those days the Orcs named him Rog the Fleet, and the name of Egnor was nought to Melko.

At the same time the words 'Now the Valar must have inspired that speech' were changed to 'Now the Valar inspired that speech'.

*

(15)   Thus was Beren set by Melko as a thrall to The Prince of Cats, whom the Gnomes have called Tiberth Bridhon Miaugion, but the Elves Tevildo.

Subsequently *Tiberth* appears for MS *Tevildo* throughout, and in one place the full name *Tiberth Bridhon Miaugion* appears again. In the MS the Gnomish name is *Tifil*.

*

(17)   . . . getting nought but a bitten finger for his toil. Then was Tiberth wroth, and said: "Thou hast lied to my lord, O Gnome, and art fitter to be a scullion than a huntsman, who canst not catch even the mice about my halls." Evil thereafter were his days in the power of Tiberth; for a scullion they made him, and unending labour he had in the hewing of wood and drawing of water, and in the menial services of that noisome abode. Often too was he tormented by the cats and other evil beasts of their company, and when, as happened at whiles, there was an Orc-feast in those halls, he would ofttimes be set to the roasting of birds and other meats upon spits before the mighty fires in Melko's dungeons, until he swooned for the overwhelming heat; yet he knew himself fortunate beyond all hope in being yet alive among those cruel foes of Gods and Elves. Seldom got he food or sleep himself, and he became haggard and half-blind, so that he wished often that never straying out of the wild free places of Hisilómë he had not even caught sight afar off of the vision of Tinúviel.

*

(17)   But Melian laughed not, nor said aught thereto; for in many things was she wise and forewise – yet nonetheless it was a thing unthought in a mad dream that any Elf, still less a maiden, the daughter of that king who had longest defied Melko, should fare alone even to the borders of that sorrowful country amid which lies Angband and the Hells of Iron. Little love was there between the woodland Elves and the folk of Angband even in those days before the Battle of Unnumbered Tears when Melko's power was not grown to its full, and he veiled his designs, and spread his net

of lies. "No help wilt thou get therein of me, little one," said she; "for even if magic and destiny should bring thee safe out of that foolhardiness, yet should many and great things come thereof, and on some many sorrows, and my rede is that thou tell never thy father of thy desire."

But this last word of Melian's did Thingol coming unaware overhear, and they must perforce tell him all, and he was so wroth when he heard it that Tinúviel wished that never had her thoughts been revealed even to her mother.

*

(18)   Indeed I have no love for him, for he has destroyed our play together, our music and our dancing." But Tinúviel said: "I ask it not for him, but for myself, and for that very play of ours together aforetime." And Dairon said: "And for thy sake I say thee nay"; and they spake no more thereof together, but Dairon told the king of what Tinúviel had desired of him, fearing lest that dauntless maiden fare away to her death in the madness of her heart.

*

(18)   . . . he might not shut his daughter for ever in the caves, where the light was only that of torches dim and flickering.

*

(19)   The names of all the tallest and longest things upon Earth were set in that song: the beards of the Indrafangs, the tail of Carcaras, the body of Glorund the drake, the bole of Hirilorn, and the sword of Nan she named, nor did she forget the chain Angainu that Aulë and Tulkas made, or the neck of Gilim the giant that is taller than many elm trees; . . .

Carcaras is spelt thus subsequently in the typescript.

*

(20)   . . . as fast as her dancing feet would flit.

Now when the guards awoke it was late in the morning, and they fled away nor dared to bear the tidings to their lord; and Dairon it was bore word of the escape of Tinúviel to Thingol, for he had met the folk that ran in amazement from the ladders which each morning were lifted to her door. Great was the mingled grief and wrath of the king, and all the deep places of his court were in uproar, and all the woods were ringing with the search; but Tinúviel was already far away dancing madly through the dark woods towards the gloomy foothills and the Mountains of Night. 'Tis said that Dairon sped swiftest and furthest in pursuit, but was wrapped in the deceit of those far places, and became utterly lost, and came never back to Elfinesse, but turned towards Palisor; and there he plays subtle magic musics still, wistful and lonely in the woods and forests of the south.

Now fared Tinúviel forward, and a sudden dread overtook her at the thought of what she had dared to do, and of what lay before her. Then did she turn back for a while, and wept, wishing that Dairon were with her. It is said that he was not indeed at that time far off, and wandered lost in Taurfuin, the Forest of Night, where after Túrin slew Beleg by mishap. Nigh was Tinúviel to those evil places; but she entered not that dark region, and the Valar set a new hope in her heart, so that she pressed on once more.

*

(21)   Seldom was any of the cats slain indeed; for in those days they were mightier far in valour and in strength than they have been since those things befell that thou art soon to learn, mightier even than the tawny cats of the southern lands where the sun burns hot. No less too was their skill in climbing and in hiding, and their fleetness was that of an arrow, yet were the free dogs of the northern woods marvellously valiant and knew no fear, and great enmity was between them, and some of those hounds were held in dread even by the greatest of the cats. None, however, did Tiberth fear save only Huan the lord of the Hounds of Hisilómë. So swift was Huan that on a time he had fallen upon Tiberth as he hunted alone in the woods, and pursuing him had overtaken him and nigh rent the fur of his neck from him ere he was rescued by a host of Orcs that heard his cries. Huan got him many hurts in that battle ere he won away, but the wounded pride of Tiberth lusted ever for his death.

Great therefore was the good fortune that befell Tinúviel in meeting with Huan in the woods; and this she did in a little glade nigh to the forest's borders, where the first grasslands begin that are nourished by the upper waters of the river Sirion. Seeing him she was mortally afraid and turned to flee; but in two swift leaps Huan overtook her. Speaking softly the deep tongue of the Lost Elves he bade her be not afeared, and "wherefore," said he, "do I see an Elfin maiden, and one most fair, wandering thus nigh to the places of the Prince of Evil Heart?

*

(22)   What is thy thought, O Huan?"

"Little counsel have I for thee," said he, "save that thou goest with all speed back to Artanor and thy father's halls, and I will accompany thee all the way, until those lands be reached that the magic of Melian the Queen does encompass." "That will I never do," said she, "while Beren liveth here, forgotten of his friends." "I thought that such would be thy answer," said he, "but if thou wilt still go forward with thy mad quest, then no counsel have I for thee save a desperate and a perilous one: we must make now all speed towards the ill places of Tiberth's abiding that are yet far off. I will guide thee thither by the most secret ways, and when we are come there thou must creep alone, if thou hast the heart, to the dwelling of that prince at an hour nigh noon when he and most of his household lie drowsing upon the terraces before his gates. There thou mayst perchance discover, if fortune is very kind, whether Beren be indeed within that ill place as thy mother said to thee. But lo, I will lie not far from the foot of the mount whereon Tiberth's hall is built, and thou must say to Tiberth so soon as thou seest him, be Beren there or be he not, that thou hast stumbled upon Huan of the Dogs lying sick of great wounds in a withered dale without his gates. Fear not overmuch, for herein wilt thou both do my pleasure and further thine own desires, as well as may be; nor do I think that when Tiberth hears thy tidings thou wilt be in any peril thyself for a time. Only do thou not direct him to the place that I shall show to thee; thou must offer to guide him thither thyself. Thus thou shalt get free again of his evil house, and shalt see what I contrive for the Prince of Cats." Then did Tinúviel shudder at the thought of what lay before, but she said that this rede would she sooner take than to return home, and they set forth straightway by secret pathways through the woods, and by winding trails over the bleak and stony lands that lay beyond.

At last on a day at morn they came to a wide dale hollowed like a bowl among the rocks. Deep were its sides, but nought grew there save low bushes of scanty leaves and withered grass. "This is the Withered Dale that I spake of," said Huan. "Yonder is the cave where the great

Here the typescript version of the *Tale of Tinúviel* ends, at the foot of a page. I think it is improbable that any more of this version was made.

NOTES

1 For earlier references to Olórë Mallë, the Way of Dreams, see I.18, 27; 211, 225.

2 The distinction made here between the Elves (who call the queen *Wendelin*) and, by implication, the Gnomes (who call her

Gwendeling) is even more explicit in the typescript version, p. 42 ('tis a tale of the *Gnomes*, wherefore I beg that thou fill not Eriol's ears with thy *Elfin* names') and p. 45 ('The Prince of Cats, whom the *Gnomes* have called Tiberth Bridhon Miaugion, but the *Elves* Tevildo'). See I. 50–1.

3   The manuscript as originally written read: 'Now Beren was a Gnome, son of a thrall of Melko's, some have said, that laboured in the darker places . . .' See note 4.

4   The manuscript as originally written read: 'I Beren of the Noldoli, son of Egnor the huntsman . . .' See note 3.

5   From this point, and continuing to the words 'forests of the south' on p. 21, the text is written on detached pages placed in the note-book. There is no rejected material corresponding to this passage. It is possible that it existed, and was removed from the book and lost; but, though the book is in a decayed state, it does not seem that any pages were removed here, and I think it more likely that my father simply found himself short of space, as he wrote over the original, erased, version, and (almost certainly) expanded it as he went.

6   The text as originally written read: 'came never back to Ellu, but plays . . .' (for *Ellu* see *Changes to Names* below). As a result of the interpolation 'but turned towards Palisor' Palisor is placed in the south of the world. In the tale of *The Coming of the Elves* (I.114) Palisor is called 'the midmost region' (see also the drawing of the 'World-Ship', I.84), and it seems possible that the word 'south' should have been changed; but it remains in the typescript (p. 47).

7   The *Tale of Turambar*, though composed after the *Tale of Tinúviel*, was in existence when *Tinúviel* was rewritten (see p. 69).

8   From 'amazed utterly' to 'if Tinúviel were not there' (p. 30) the text is written on an inserted page; see note 5 – here also the underlying textual situation is obscure.

9   A short passage of earlier text in pencil becomes visible here, ending: '. . . and Tinúviel grew to long sorely for Wendelin her mother and for the sight of Linwë and for Kapalen making music in pleasant glades.' *Kapalen* must be a name preceding *Tifanto*, itself preceding *Dairon* (see *Changes to Names* below).

10 *this Gnome*: original reading *this man*. This was a slip, but a significant slip (see p. 52), in all probability. It is possible that 'man' was used here, as occasionally elsewhere (e.g. p. 18 'as high as men could fashion their longest ladders', where the reference is to the Elves of Artanor), to mean 'male Elf', but in that case there would seem no reason to change it.

11 Struck out here in the manuscript: 'Beren of the Hills'.

12 'Mablung the heavy-handed, chief of the king's thanes, leaped up and grasped a spear' replaced the original reading 'Tifanto cast aside his pipe and grasped a spear'. Originally the name of Tinúviel's

brother was *Tifanto* throughout the tale. See notes 13–15, and the Commentary, p. 59.

13 *Mablung* replaced *Tifanto*, and again immediately below; see note 12.

14 'O King' replaced 'O father'; see note 12.

15 In this place *Mablung* was the form as first written; see the Commentary, p. 59.

16 It is essential to the narrative of the Coming of the Elves that the Solosimpi were the third and last of the three tribes; 'second' here can only be a slip, if a surprising one.

Changes made to names in
The Tale of Tinúviel

(i) Manuscript Version

Ilfiniol < *Elfriniol*. In the typescript text the name is *Ilfrin*. See pp. 201–2.

Tinwë Linto, Tinwelint In the opening passage of the tale (p. 8), where Ausir and Vëannë differ on the forms of Tinwelint's name, the MS is very confused and it is impossible to understand the succeeding stages. Throughout the tale, as originally written, Vëannë calls Tinwelint *Tinto Ellu* or *Ellu*, but in the argument at the beginning it is Ausir who calls him *Tinto Ellu* while Vëannë calls him *Tinto'ellon*. *(Tinto) Ellu* is certainly an 'Elvish' form, but it is corrected throughout the tale to the Gnomish *Tinwelint*, while Ausir's *Tinto Ellu* at the beginning is corrected to *Tinwë Linto*. (At the third occurrence of *Tinwë* in the opening passage the name as originally written was *Linwë*: see I.130.)

In the tales of *The Coming of the Elves* and *The Theft of Melko* in Part One *Ellu* is the name of the second lord of the Solosimpi chosen in Tinwelint's place (afterwards Olwë), but at both occurrences (I.120, 141) this is a later addition (I.130 note 5, 155). Many years later *Ellu* again became Thingol's name (Sindarin *Elu Thingol*, Quenya *Elwë Singollo*, in *The Silmarillion*).

Gwendeling As the tale was originally written, *Wendelin* was the name throughout (*Wendelin* is found in tales given in Part One, emended from *Tindriel*: I.106–7, 131). It was later changed throughout to the Gnomish form *Gwendeling* (found in the early Gnomish dictionary, I.273, itself changed later to *Gwedhiling*) except in the mouth of Ausir, who uses the 'Elvish' form *Wendelin* (p. 8).

Dairon < *Tifanto* throughout. For the change of *Tifanto* > *Mablung* at the end of the tale (notes 12–14 above) see the Commentary, p. 59, and for the name *Kapalen* preceding *Tifanto* see note 9.

Dor Lómin < *Aryador* (p. 11). In the tale of *The Coming of the*

Elves it is said (I.119) that Aryador was the name of Hisilómë among Men; for *Dor Lómin – Hisilómë* see I.112. At subsequent occurrences in this tale *Aryador* was not changed.

Angband was originally twice written, and in one of these cases it was changed to *Angamandi*, in the other (p. 35) allowed to stand; in all other instances *Angamandi* was the form first written. In the manuscript version of the tale Vëannë does not make consistent use of Gnomish or 'Elvish' forms: thus she says *Tevildo* (not *Tifil*), *Angamandi*, *Gwendeling* (< *Wendelin*), *Tinwelint* (< *Tinto* (*Ellu*)). In the typescript version, on the other hand, Vëannë says *Tiberth*, *Angband*, *Melian* (< *Gwenethlin*), *Thingol* (< *Tinwelint*).

Hirilorn, the Queen of Trees < *Golosbrindi, the Queen of the Forest* (p. 18); *Hirilorn* < *Golosbrindi* at subsequent occurrences.

Uinen < *Ónen* (or possibly *Únen*).

Egnor bo-Rimion < *Egnor go-Rimion*. In the tales previously given the patronymic prefix is *go-* (I.146, 155).

Tinwelint < *Tinthellon* (p. 35, the only case). Cf. *Tinto'ellon* mentioned above under *Tinwë Linto*.

i·Cuilwarthon < *i·Guilwarthon*.

(ii) Typescript Version

Tinúviel < *Tynwfiel* in the title and at every occurrence until the passage corresponding to MS version p. 11 'yet now did he see Tinúviel dancing in the twilight'; there and subsequently the form typed was *Tinúviel*.

Singoldo < *Tinwë Linto* (p. 41).

Melian < *Gwenethlin* at every occurrence until the passage corresponding to MS version p. 12 'the stateliness of Queen Gwendeling'; there and subsequently the form typed was *Melian*.

Thingol < *Tinwelint* at every occurrence until the passage corresponding to MS version p. 12 'by winding paths to the abode of Tinwelint'; there and subsequently the form typed was *Thingol*.

For *Egnor* > *Barahir* see p. 43.

Commentary on
The Tale of Tinúviel

§1. *The primary narrative*

In this section I shall consider only the conduct of the main story, and leave for the moment such questions as the wider history implied in it, Tinwelint's people and his dwelling, or the geography of the lands that appear in the story.

The story of Beren's coming upon Tinúviel in the moonlit glade in its earliest recorded form (pp. 11–12) was never changed in its central image; and it should be noticed that the passage in *The Silmarillion* (p. 165) is an extremely concentrated and exalted rendering of the scene: many elements not mentioned there were never in fact lost. In a very late reworking of the passage in the *Lay of Leithian** the hemlocks and the white moths still appear, and Daeron the minstrel is present when Beren comes to the glade. But there are nonetheless the most remarkable differences; and the chief of these is of course that Beren was here no mortal Man, but an Elf, one of the Noldoli, and the absolutely essential element of the story of Beren and Lúthien is not present. It will be seen later (pp. 71–2, 139) that this was not originally so, however: in the now lost (because erased) first form of the *Tale of Tinúviel* he had been a Man (it is for this reason that I have said that the reading *man* in the manuscript (see p. 33 and note 10), later changed to *Gnome*, is a 'significant slip'). Several years after the composition of the tale in the form in which we have it he became a Man again, though at that time (1925–6) my father appears to have hesitated long on the matter of the elvish or mortal nature of Beren.

In the tale there is, necessarily, a quite different reason for the hostility and distrust shown to Beren in Artanor (Doriath) – namely that 'the Elves of the woodland thought of the Gnomes of Dor Lómin as treacherous creatures, cruel and faithless' (see below, p. 65). It seems clear that at this time the history of Beren and his father (Egnor) was only very sketchily devised; there is in any case no hint of the story of the outlaw band led by his father and its betrayal by Gorlim the Unhappy (*The Silmarillion* pp. 162ff.) before the first form of the *Lay of Leithian*, where the story appears fully formed (the Lay was in being to rather beyond this point by the late summer of 1925). But an association of Beren's father (changed to Beren himself) with Úrin (Húrin) as 'brother in arms' is mentioned in the typescript version of the tale (pp. 44–5); according to the latest of the outlines for *Gilfanon's Tale* (I.240) 'Úrin and Egnor marched with countless battalions' (against the forces of Melko).

In the old story, Tinúviel had no meetings with Beren before the day when he boldly accosted her at last, and it was at that very time that she led him to Tinwelint's cave; they were not lovers, Tinúviel knew nothing of Beren but that he was enamoured of her dancing, and it seems that she brought him before her father as a matter of courtesy, the natural thing to do. The betrayal of Beren to Thingol by Daeron (*The Silmarillion* p. 166) therefore has no place in the old story – there is nothing to betray; and indeed it is not shown in the tale that Dairon knew anything

---

* The long unfinished poem in rhyming couplets in which is told the story of Beren and Lúthien Tinúviel; composed in 1925-31, but parts of it substantially rewritten many years later.

whatsoever of Beren before Tinúviel led him into the cave, beyond having once seen his face in the moonlight.

Despite these radical differences in the narrative structure, it is remarkable how many features of the scene in Tinwelint's hall (pp.12–13), when Beren stood before the king, endured, while all the inner significance was shifted and enlarged. To the beginning go back, for instance, Beren's abashment and silence, Tinúviel's answering for him, the sudden rising of his courage and uttering of his desire without preamble or hesitation. But the tone is altogether lighter and less grave than it afterwards became; in the jeering laughter of Tinwelint, who treats the matter as a jest and Beren as a benighted fool, there is no hint of what is explicit in the later story: 'Thus he wrought the doom of Doriath, and was ensnared within the curse of Mandos' (*The Silmarillion* p. 167). The Silmarils are indeed famous, and they have a holy power (p. 34), but the fate of the world is not bound up with them (*The Silmarillion* p. 67); Beren is an Elf, if of a feared and distrusted people, and his request lacks the deepest dimension of outrage; and he and Tinúviel are not lovers.

In this passage is the first mention of the Iron Crown of Melko, and the setting of the Silmarils in the Crown; and here again is a detail that was never lost: 'Never did this crown leave his head' (cf. *The Silmarillion* p. 81: 'That crown he never took from his head, though its weight became a deadly weariness').

But from this point Vëannë's story diverges in an altogether unexpected fashion from the later narrative. At no other place in the *Lost Tales* is the subsequent transformation more remarkable than in this, the precursor of the story of the capture of Beren and Felagund and their companions by Sauron the Necromancer, the imprisonment and death of all save Beren in the dungeons of Tol-in-Gaurhoth (the Isle of Werewolves in the river Sirion), and the rescue of Beren and overthrow of Sauron by Lúthien and Huan.

Most notably, what may be referred to as 'the Nargothrond Element' is entirely absent, and in so far as it already existed had as yet made no contact with the story of Beren and Tinúviel (for Nargothrond, not yet so named, at this period see pp. 81, 123–4). Beren has no ring of Felagund, he has no companions on his northward journey, and there is no relationship between (on the one hand) the story of his capture, his speech with Melko, and his dispatch to the house of Tevildo, and (on the other) the events of the later narrative whereby Beren and the band of Elves out of Nargothrond found themselves in Sauron's dungeon. Indeed, all the complex background of legend, of battles and rivalries, oaths and alliances, out of which the story of Beren and Lúthien arises in *The Silmarillion*, is very largely absent. The castle of the Cats 'is' the tower of Sauron on Tol-in-Gaurhoth, but only in the sense that it occupies the same 'space' in the narrative: beyond this there is no point in seeking even shadowy resemblances between the two establishments. The monstrous gormandising cats, their kitchens and their sunning terraces, and their engagingly Elvish-feline names (*Miaugion, Miaulë, Meoita*) all disappeared without trace. Did Tevildo? It would scarcely be true, I think, to say even that Sauron 'originated' in a cat: in the next phase of the legends the Necromancer (Thû) has no feline attributes. On the other hand it would be wrong to regard it as a simple matter of *replacement* (Thû stepping into the narrative place vacated by Tevildo) without any element of *transformation* of what was previously there. Tevildo's immediate successor is 'the Lord of Wolves', himself a werewolf, and he retains the Tevildo-trait of hating Huan more than any other creature in the world. Tevildo was 'an evil fay in beastlike shape' (p. 29); and the battle between the two great beasts, the hound against the werewolf (originally the hound against the demon in feline form) was never lost.

When the tale returns to Tinúviel in Artanor the situation is quite the reverse: for the story of her imprisonment in the house in Hirilorn and her escape from it never underwent any significant change. The passage in *The Silmarillion* (p. 172) is indeed very brief, but its lack of detail is due to compression rather than to omission based on dissatisfaction; the *Lay of Leithian*, from which the prose account in *The Silmarillion* directly derives, is in this passage so close, in point of narrative detail, to the *Tale of Tinúviel* as to be almost identical with it.

It may be observed that in this part of the story the earliest version had a strength that was diminished later, in that the duration of Tinúviel's imprisonment and her journey to Beren's rescue relates readily enough to that of Beren's captivity, which was intended by his captors to be unending; whereas in the later story there is a great deal of event and movement (with the addition of Lúthien's captivity in Nargothrond) to be fitted into the time when Beren was awaiting his death in the dungeon of the Necromancer.

While the strong element of 'explanatory' beast-fable (concerning cats and dogs) was to be entirely eliminated, and Tevildo Prince of Cats replaced by the Necromancer, Huan nonetheless remained from it as the great Hound of Valinor. His encounter with Tinúviel in the woods, her inability to escape from him, and indeed his love for her from the moment of their meeting (suggested in the tale, p. 23, explicit in *The Silmarillion* p. 173), were already present, though the context of their encounter and the motives of Huan were wholly different from the absence of 'the Nargothrond Element' (Felagund, Celegorm and Curufin).

In the story of the defeat of Tevildo and the rescue of Beren the germ of the later legend is clearly seen, though for the most part only in broad structural resemblances. It is curious to observe that the loud speaking of Tinúviel sitting perched on the sill of the kitchen hatch in the castle of the Cats, so that Beren might hear, is the precursor of her singing on the bridge of Tol-in-Gaurhoth the song that Beren heard in his dungeon (*The Silmarillion* p. 174). Tevildo's intention to hand her over to Melko remained in Sauron's similar purpose (*ibid.*); the killing of the cat

Oikeroi (p. 28) is the germ of Huan's fight with Draugluin – the skin of Huan's dead opponent is put to the same use in either case (pp. 30–1, *The Silmarillion* pp. 178–9); the battle of Tevildo and Huan was to become that of Huan and Wolf-Sauron, and with essentially the same outcome: Huan released his enemy when he yielded the mastery of his dwelling. This last is very notable: the utterance by Tinúviel of the spell which bound stone to stone in the evil castle (p. 29). Of course, when this was written the castle of Tevildo was an adventitious feature in the story – it had no previous history: it was an evil place through and through, and the spell (deriving from Melko) that Tevildo was forced to reveal was the secret of Tevildo's own power over his creatures as well as the magic that held the stones together. With the entry of Felagund into the developing legend and the Elvish watchtower on Tol Sirion (*Minas Tirith: The Silmarillion* pp. 120, 155–6) captured by the Necromancer, the spell is displaced: for it cannot be thought to be the work of Felagund, who built the fortress, since if it had been he would have been able to pronounce it in the dungeon and bring the place down over their heads – a less evil way for them to die. This element in the legend remained, however, and is fully present in *The Silmarillion* (p. 175), though since my father did not actually say there that Sauron told Huan and Lúthien what the words were, but only that he 'yielded himself', one may miss the significance of what happened:

> And she said: 'There everlastingly thy naked self shall endure the torment of his scorn, pierced by his eyes, unless thou yield to me the mastery of thy tower.'
>
> Then Sauron yielded himself, and Lúthien took the mastery of the isle and all that was there. . . .
>
> Then Lúthien stood upon the bridge, and declared her power: and the spell was loosed that bound stone to stone, and the gates were thrown down, and the walls opened, and the pits laid bare.

Here again the actual matter of the narrative is totally different in the early and late forms of the legend: in *The Silmarillion* 'many thralls and captives came forth in wonder and dismay . . . for they had lain long in the darkness of Sauron', whereas in the tale the inmates who emerged from the shaken dwelling (other than Beren and the apparently inconsequent figure of the blind slave-Gnome Gimli) were a host of cats, reduced by the breaking of Tevildo's spell to 'puny size'. (If my father had used in the tale names other than Huan, Beren, and Tinúviel, and in the absence of all other knowledge, including that of authorship, it would not be easy to demonstrate from a simple comparison between this part of the Tale and the story as told in *The Silmarillion* that the resemblances were more than superficial and accidental.)

A more minor narrative point may be noticed here. The typescript version would presumably have treated the fight of Huan and Tevildo somewhat differently, for in the manuscript Tevildo and his companion can flee up great trees (p. 28), whereas in the typescript nothing grew in the Withered Dale (where Huan was to lie feigning sick) save 'low bushes of scanty leaves' (p. 48).

In the remainder of the story the congruence between early and late forms is far closer. The narrative structure in the tale may be summarised thus:

- Beren is attired for disguise in the fell of the dead cat Oikeroi.
- He and Tinúviel journey together to Angamandi.
- Tinúviel lays a spell of sleep on Karkaras the wolf-ward of Angamandi.
- They enter Angamandi, Beren slinks in his beast-shape beneath the seat of Melko, and Tinúviel dances before Melko.
- All the host of Angamandi and finally Melko himself are cast into sleep, and Melko's iron crown rolls from his head.
- Tinúviel rouses Beren, who cuts a Silmaril from the crown, and the blade snaps.
- The sleepers stir, and Beren and Tinúviel flee back to the gates, but find Karkaras awake again.
- Karkaras bites off Beren's outthrust hand holding the Silmaril.
- Karkaras becomes mad with the pain of the Silmaril in his belly, for the Silmaril is a holy thing and sears evil flesh.
- Karkaras goes raging south to Artanor.
- Beren and Tinúviel return to Artanor; they go before Tinwelint and Beren declares that a Silmaril is in his hand.
- The hunting of the wolf takes place, and Mablung the Heavy-handed is one of the hunters.
- Beren is slain by Karkaras, and is borne back to the cavern of Tinwelint on a bier of boughs; dying he gives the Silmaril to Tinwelint.
- Tinúviel follows Beren to Mandos, and Mandos permits them to return into the world.

Changing the catskin of Oikeroi to the wolfskin of Draugluin, and altering some other names, this would do tolerably well as a précis of the story in *The Silmarillion*! But of course it is devised as a summary of similarities. There are major differences as well as a host of minor ones that do not appear in it.

Again, most important is the absence of 'the Nargothrond Element'. When this combined with the Beren legend it introduced Felagund as Beren's companion, Lúthien's imprisonment in Nargothrond by Celegorm and Curufin, her escape with Huan the hound of Celegorm, and the attack on Beren and Lúthien as they returned from Tol-in-Gaurhoth by Celegorm and Curufin, now fleeing from Nargothrond (*The Silmarillion* pp. 173–4, 176–8).

The narrative after the conclusion of the episode of 'the Thraldom of Beren' is conducted quite differently in the old story (pp. 30–1), in that here Huan is with Beren and Tinúviel; Tinúviel longs for her home, and Beren is grieved because he loves the life in the woods with the dogs, but he resolves the impasse by determining to obtain a Silmaril, and though Huan thinks their plan is folly he gives them the fell of Oikeroi, clad in which Beren sets out with Tinúviel for Angamandi. In *The Silmarillion* (p. 177) likewise, Beren, after long wandering in the woods with Lúthien (though not with Huan), resolves to set forth again on the quest of the Silmaril, but Lúthien's stance in the matter is different:

'You must choose, Beren, between these two: to relinquish the quest and your oath and seek a life of wandering upon the face of the earth; or to hold to your word and challenge the power of darkness upon its throne. But on either road I shall go with you, and our doom shall be alike.'

There then intervened the attack on Beren and Lúthien by Celegorm and Curufin, when Huan, deserting his master, joined himself to them; they returned together to Doriath, and when they got there Beren left Lúthien sleeping and went back northwards by himself, riding Curufin's horse. He was overtaken on the edge of Anfauglith by Huan bearing Lúthien on his back and bringing from Tol-in-Gaurhoth the skins of Draugluin and of Sauron's bat-messenger Thuringwethil (of whom in the old story there is no trace); attired in these Beren and Lúthien went to Angband. Huan is here their active counsellor.

The later legend is thus more full of movement and incident in this part than is the *Tale of Tinúviel* (though the final form was not achieved all at one stroke, as may be imagined); and in the *Silmarillion* form this is the more marked from the fact that the account is a compression and a summary of the long *Lay of Leithian*.*

In the *Tale of Tinúviel* the account of Beren's disguise is characteristically detailed: his instruction by Tinúviel in feline behaviour, his heat and discomfort inside the skin. Tinúviel's disguise as a bat has however not yet emerged, and whereas in *The Silmarillion* when confronted by

---

* Cf. Professor T. A. Shippey, *The Road to Middle-earth*, 1982, p. 193: 'In "Beren and Lúthien" as a whole there is too much plot. The other side of that criticism is that on occasion Tolkien has to be rather brisk with his own inventions. Celegorm wounds Beren, and the hound Huan turns on his master and pursues him; "returning he brought to Lúthien a herb out of the forest. With that leaf she staunched Beren's wound, and by her arts and her love she healed him. . . ." The motif of the healing herb is a common one, the centre for instance of the Breton *lai* of *Eliduc* (turned into *conte* by Marie de France). But in that it occupies a whole scene, if not a whole poem. In *The Silmarillion* it appears only to be dismissed in two lines, while Beren's wound is inflicted and healed in five. Repeatedly one has this sense of summary . . .' This sense is eminently justified! In the *Lay of Leithian* the wounding and the healing with the herb occupy some 64 lines. (Cf. my Foreword to *The Silmarillion*, p. 8.)

Carcharoth she 'cast back her foul raiment' and 'commanded him to sleep', here she used once more the magical misty robe spun of her hair: 'the black strands of her dark veil she cast in his eyes' (p. 31). The indifference of Karkaras to the false Oikeroi contrasts with Carcharoth's suspicion of the false Druagluin, of whose death he had heard tidings: in the old story it is emphasised that no news of the discomfiture of Tevildo (and the death of Oikeroi) had yet reached Angamandi.

The encounter of Tinúviel with Melko is given with far more detail than in *The Silmarillion* (here much compressed from its source); notable is the phrase (p. 32) 'he leered horribly, for his dark mind pondered some evil', forerunner of that in *The Silmarillion* (p. 180):

> Then Morgoth looking upon her beauty conceived in his thought an evil lust, and a design more dark than any that had yet come into his heart since he fled from Valinor.

We are never told anything more explicit.

Whether Melko's words to Tinúviel, 'Who art thou that flittest about my halls like a bat?', and the description of her dancing 'noiseless as a bat', were the germ of her later bat-disguise cannot be said, though it seems possible.

The knife with which Beren cut the Silmaril from the Iron Crown has a quite different provenance in the *Tale of Tinúviel*, being a kitchen-knife that Beren took from Tevildo's castle (pp. 29, 33); in *The Silmarillion* it was Angrist, the famous knife made by Telchar which Beren took from Curufin. The sleepers of Angamandi are here disturbed by the sound of the snapping of the knife-blade; in *The Silmarillion* it is the shard flying from the snapped knife and striking Morgoth's cheek that makes him groan and stir.

There is a minor difference in the accounts of the meeting with the wolf as Beren and Tinúviel fled out. In *The Silmarillion* 'Lúthien was spent, and she had not time nor strength to quell the wolf'; in the tale it seems that she might have done so if Beren had not been precipitate. Much more important, there appears here for the first time the conception of the holy power of the Silmarils that burns unhallowed flesh.*

The escape of Tinúviel and Beren from Angamandi and their return to Artanor (pp. 34–6) is treated quite differently in the *Tale of Tinúviel*. In *The Silmarillion* (pp. 182–3) they were rescued by the Eagles and set down on the borders of Doriath; and far more is made of the healing of Beren's wound, in which Huan plays a part. In the old story Huan comes to them later, after their long southward flight on foot. In both accounts there is a discussion between them as to whether or not they should return to her father's hall, but it is quite differently conducted – in the tale it is she who persuades Beren to return, in *The Silmarillion* it is Beren who persuades her.

* In an early note there is a reference to 'the sacred Silmarils': I.169, note 2.

There is a curious feature in the story of the Wolf-hunt (pp. 38–9) which may be considered here (see p. 50, notes 12–15). At first, it was Tinúviel's brother who took part in the hunt with Tinwelint, Beren, and Huan, and his name is here *Tifanto*, which was the name throughout the tale before its replacement by *Dairon*.* Subsequently 'Tifanto'–without passing through the stage of 'Dairon' – was replaced by 'Mablung the heavy-handed, chief of the king's thanes', who here makes his first appearance, as the fourth member of the hunt. But earlier in the tale it is told that Tifanto > Dairon, leaving Artanor to seek Tinúviel, became utterly lost, 'and came never back to Elfinesse' (p. 21), and the loss of Tifanto > Dairon is referred to again when Beren and Tinúviel returned to Artanor (pp. 36–7).

Thus on the one hand Tifanto was lost, and it is a grief to Tinúviel on her return to learn of it, but on the other he was present at the Wolf-hunt. *Tifanto* was then changed to *Dairon* throughout the tale, except in the story of the Wolf-hunt, where *Tifanto* was replaced by a new character, *Mablung*. This shows that *Tifanto* was removed from the hunt before the change of name to *Dairon*, but does not explain how, under the name *Tifanto*, he was both lost in the wilds and present at the hunt. Since there is nothing in the MS itself to explain this puzzle, I can only conclude that my father did, in fact, write at first that Tifanto was lost and never came back, and also that he took part in the Wolf-hunt; but observing this contradiction he introduced Mablung in the latter rôle (and probably did this even before the tale was completed, since at the last appearance of Mablung his name was written thus, not emended from *Tifanto*: see note 15). It was subsequent to this that *Tifanto* was emended, wherever it still stood, to *Dairon*.

In the tale the hunt is differently managed from the story in *The Silmarillion* (where, incidentally, Beleg Strongbow was present). It is curious that all (including, as it appears, Huan!) save Beren were asleep when Karkaras came on them ('in Beren's watch', p. 39). In *The Silmarillion* Huan slew Carcharoth and was slain by him, whereas here Karkaras met his death from the king's spear, and the boy Ausir tells at the end that Huan lived on to find Beren again at the time of 'the great deeds of the Nauglafring' (p. 41). Of Huan's destiny, that he should not die 'until he encountered the mightiest wolf that would ever walk the world', and of his being permitted 'thrice only ere his death to speak with words' (*The Silmarillion* p. 173), there is nothing here.

The most remarkable feature of the *Tale of Tinúviel* remains the fact that in its earliest extant form Beren was an Elf; and in this connection very notable are the words of the boy at the end (p. 40):

---

* The idea that Timpinen (Tinfang Warble) was the son of Tinwelint and sister of Tinúviel (see I.106, note 1) had been abandoned. Tifanto/Dairon is now named with Tinfang and Ivárë as 'the three most magic players of the Elves' (p. 10).

Yet said Mandos to those twain: 'Lo, O Elves, it is not to any life of perfect joy that I dismiss you, for such may no longer be found in all the world where sits Melko of the evil heart – and know ye that *ye will become mortal even as Men*, and when ye fare hither again it will be for ever, unless the Gods summon you indeed to Valinor.'

In the tale of *The Coming of the Valar and the Building of Valinor* there occurs the following passage (I.76; commentary I.90):

Thither [i.e. to Mandos] in after days fared the Elves of all the clans who were by illhap slain with weapons or did die of grief for those that were slain – and only so might the Eldar die, and then it was only for a while. There Mandos spake their doom, and there they waited in the darkness, dreaming of their past deeds, until such time as he appointed when they might again be born into their children, and go forth to laugh and sing again.

The same idea occurs in the tale of *The Music of the Ainur* (I.59). The peculiar dispensation of Mandos in the case of Beren and Tinúviel as here conceived is therefore that their whole 'natural' destiny as Elves was changed: having died as Elves might die (from wounds or from grief) they were not reborn as new beings, but returned from Mandos in their own persons – yet now 'mortal even as Men'. The earliest eschatology is too unclear to allow of a satisfactory interpretation of this 'mortality', and the passage in *The Building of Valinor* on the fates of Men (I.77) is particularly hard to understand (see the commentary on it, I.90ff.). But it seems possible that the words 'even as Men' in the address of Mandos to Beren and Tinúviel were included to stress the finality of whatever second deaths they might undergo; their departure would be as final as that of Men, there would be no second return in their own persons, and no reincarnation. They will remain in Mandos ('when ye fare hither again it will be for ever') – unless they are summoned by the Gods to dwell in Valinor. These last words should probably be related to the passage in *The Building of Valinor* concerning the fate of certain Men (I.77):

Few are they and happy indeed for whom at a season doth Nornorë the herald of the Gods set out. Then ride they with him in chariots or upon good horses down into the vale of Valinor and feast in the halls of Valmar, dwelling in the houses of the Gods until the Great End come.

§2.   *Places and peoples in the Tale of Tinúviel*

To consider first what can be learned of the geography of the Great Lands from this tale: the early 'dictionary' of the Gnomish language makes it clear that the meaning of *Artanor* was 'the Land Beyond', as it is interpreted in the text (p. 9). Several passages in the *Lost Tales* cast light on this expression. In an outline for Gilfanon's untold tale (I.240) the Noldoli exiled from Valinor

> now fought for the first time with the Orcs and captured the pass of the Bitter Hills; thus they escaped from the Land of Shadows . . . They entered the Forest of Artanor and the Region of the Great Plains . . .

(which latter, I suggested, may be the forerunner of the later Talath Dirnen, the Guarded Plain of Nargothrond). The tale to follow Gilfanon's, according to the projected scheme (I.241), was to be that of Tinúviel, and this outline begins: 'Beren son of Egnor wandered out of Dor Lómin [i.e. Hisilómë, see I.112] into Artanor . . .' In the present tale, it is said that Beren came 'through the terrors of the Iron Mountains until he reached the Lands Beyond' (p. 11), and also (p. 21) that some of the Dogs 'roamed the woods of Hisilómë or passing the mountainous places fared even at times into the region of Artanor and the lands beyond and to the south'. And finally, in the *Tale of Turambar* (p. 72) there is a reference to 'the road over the dark hills of Hithlum into the great forests of the Land Beyond where in those days Tinwelint the hidden king had his abode'.

It is quite clear, then, that Artanor, afterwards called Doriath (which appears in the title to the typescript text of the *Tale of Tinúviel*, together with an earlier form *Dor Athro*, p. 41), lay in the original conception in much the same relation to Hisilómë (the Land of Shadow(s), Dor Lómin, Aryador) as does Doriath to Hithlum (Hisilómë) in *The Silmarillion*: to the south, and divided from it by a mountain-range, the Iron Mountains or Bitter Hills.

In commenting on the tale of *The Theft of Melko and the Darkening of Valinor* I have noticed (I.158–9) that whereas in the *Lost Tales* Hisilómë is declared to be beyond the Iron Mountains, it is also said (in the *Tale of Turambar*, p. 77) that these mountains were so named from Angband, the Hells of Iron, which lay beneath 'their northernmost fastnesses', and that therefore there seems to be a contradictory usage of the term 'Iron Mountains' within the *Lost Tales* – 'unless it can be supposed that these mountains were conceived as a continuous range, the southerly extension (the later Mountains of Shadow) forming the southern fence of Hisilómë, while the northern peaks, being above Angband, gave the range its name'.

Now in the *Tale of Tinúviel* Beren, journeying north from Artanor, 'drew nigh to the lower hills and treeless lands that warned of the approach of the bleak Iron Mountains' (p. 14). These he had previously traversed, coming out of Hisilómë; but now 'he followed the Iron Mountains till he drew nigh to the terrible regions of Melko's abode'.

This seems to support the suggestion that the mountains fencing Hisilómë from the Lands Beyond were continuous with those above Angband; and we may compare the little primitive map (I.81), where the mountain range *f* isolates Hisilómë (*g*): see I.112, 135. The implication is that 'dim' or 'black' Hisilómë had no defence against Melko.

There appear now also the Mountains of Night (pp. 20, 46–7), and it seems clear that the great pinewoods of Taurfuin, the Forest of Night, grew upon those heights (in *The Silmarillion* Dorthonion 'Land of Pines', afterwards named Taur-nu-Fuin). Dairon was lost there, but Tinúviel, though she passed near, did not enter 'that dark region'. There is nothing to show that it was not placed then as it was later – to the east of Ered Wethrin, the Mountains of Shadow. It is also at least possible that the description (in the manuscript version only, p. 23) of Tinúviel, on departing from Huan, leaving 'the shelter of the trees' and coming to 'a region of long grass' is a first intimation of the great plain of Ard-galen (called after its desolation Anfauglith and Dor-nu-Fauglith), especially if this is related to the passage in the typescript version telling of Tinúviel's meeting with Huan 'in a little glade nigh to the forest's borders, where the first grasslands begin that are nourished by the upper waters of the river Sirion' (p. 47).

After their escape from Angamandi Huan found Beren and Tinúviel 'in that northward region of Artanor that was called afterward Nan Dumgorthin, the land of the dark idols' (p. 35). In the Gnomish dictionary *Nan Dumgorthin* is defined as 'a land of dark forest east of Artanor where on a wooded mountain were hidden idols sacrificed to by some evil tribes of renegade men' (*dum* 'secret, not to be spoken', *dumgort*, *dungort* 'an (evil) idol'). In the *Lay of the Children of Húrin* in alliterative verse Túrin and his companion Flinding (later Gwindor), fleeing after the death of Beleg Strongbow, came to this land:

> There the twain enfolded   phantom twilight
> and dim mazes   dark, unholy,
> in Nan Dungorthin   where nameless gods
> have shrouded shrines   in shadows secret,
> more old than Morgoth   or the ancient lords
> the golden Gods   of the guarded West.
> But the ghostly dwellers   of that grey valley
> hindered nor hurt them,   and they held their course
> with creeping flesh   and quaking limb.
> Yet laughter at whiles   with lingering echo,
> as distant mockery   of demon voices
> there harsh and hollow   in the hushed twilight
> Flinding fancied,   fell, unwholesome . . .

There are, I believe, no other references to the gods of Nan Dumgorthin. In the poem the land was placed west of Sirion; and finally, as Nan

Dungortheb 'the Valley of Dreadful Death', it becomes in *The Silmarillion* (pp. 81, 121) a 'no-land' between the Girdle of Melian and Ered Gorgoroth, the Mountains of Terror. But the description of it in the *Tale of Tinúviel* as a 'northward region of Artanor' clearly does not imply that it lay within the protective magic of Gwendeling, and it seems that this 'zone' was originally less distinctly bounded, and less extensive, than 'the Girdle of Melian' afterwards became. Probably *Artanor* was conceived at this time as a great region of forest in the heart of which was Tinwelint's cavern, and only his immediate domain was protected by the power of the queen:

> Hidden was his dwelling from the vision and knowledge of Melko by the magics of Gwendeling the fay, and she wove spells about the paths thereto that none but the Eldar might tread them easily, and so was the king secured from all dangers save it be treachery alone. (p. 9).

It seems, also, that her protection was originally by no means so complete and so mighty a wall of defence as it became. Thus, although Orcs and wolves disappeared when Beren and Tinúviel 'stepped within the circle of Gwendeling's magic that hid the paths from evil things and kept harm from the regions of the woodelves' (p. 35), the fear is expressed that even if Beren and Tinúviel reached the cavern of King Tinwelint 'they would but draw the chase behind them thither' (p. 34), and Tinwelint's people feared that Melko would 'upraise his strength and come utterly to crush them and Gwendeling's magic have not the strength to withhold the numbers of the Orcs' (p. 36).

The picture of Menegroth beside Esgalduin, accessible only by the bridge (*The Silmarillion* pp. 92–3) goes back to the beginning, though neither cave nor river are named in the tale. But (as will be seen more emphatically in later tales in this book) Tinwelint, the wood-fairy in his cavern, had a long elevation before him, to become ultimately Thingol of the Thousand Caves ('the fairest dwelling of any king that has ever been east of the Sea'). In the beginning, Tinwelint's dwelling was not a subterranean city full of marvels, silver fountains falling into basins of marble and pillars carved like trees, but a rugged cave; and if in the typescript version the cave comes to be 'vaulted immeasureable', it is still illuminated only by the dim and flickering light of torches (pp. 43, 46).

There have been earlier references in the *Lost Tales* to Tinwelint and the place of his dwelling. In a passage added to, but then rejected from, the tale of *The Chaining of Melko* (I.106, note 1) it is said that he was lost in Hisilómë and met Wendelin there; 'loving her he was content to leave his folk and dance for ever in the shadows'. In *The Coming of the Elves* (I.115) 'Tinwë abode not long with his people, and yet 'tis said lives still lord of the scattered Elves of Hisilómë'; and in the same tale (I.118–19) the 'Lost Elves' were still there 'long after when Men were shut in Hisilómë by Melko', and Men called them the Shadow Folk, and feared them. But in the *Tale of Tinúviel* the conception has changed. Tinwelint is now a king ruling, not in Hisilómë, but in Artanor.* (It is not said where it was that he came upon Gwendeling.)

In the account (manuscript version only, see pp. 9, 42) of Tinwelint's people there is mention of Elves 'who remained in the dark'; and this obviously refers to Elves who never left the Waters of Awakening. (Of course those who were lost on the march from Palisor also never left 'the dark' (i.e. they never came to the light of the Trees), but the distinction made in this sentence is not between the darkness and the light but between those who *remained* and those who *set out*). On the emergence of this idea in the course of the writing of the *Lost Tales* see I.234. Of Tinwelint's subjects 'the most were Ilkorindi', and they must be those who 'had been lost upon the march from Palisor' (earlier, 'the Lost Elves of Hisilómë').

Here, a major difference in essential conception between the old legend and the form in *The Silmarillion* is apparent. These Ilkorindi of Tinwelint's following ('eerie and strange beings' whose 'dark songs and chantings . . . faded in the wooded places or echoed in deep caves') are described in terms applicable to the wild Avari ('the Unwilling') of *The Silmarillion*; but they are of course actually the precursors of the Grey-elves of Doriath. The term *Eldar* is here equivalent to *Elves* ('all the Eldar both *those who remained in the dark* or had been lost upon the march from Palisor') and is not restricted to those who made, or at least embarked on, the Great Journey; all were Ilkorindi – Dark Elves – if they never passed over the Sea. The later significance of the Great Journey in conferring 'Eldarin' status was an aspect of the elevation of the Grey-elves of Beleriand, bringing about a distinction of the utmost importance within the category of the *Moriquendi* or 'Elves of the Darkness' – the *Avari* (who were not Eldar) and the *Úmanyar* (the Eldar who were 'not of Aman'): see the table 'The Sundering of the Elves' given in *The Silmarillion*. Thus:

	Lost Tales		Silmarillion	
	of Kôr	Avari		
Eldar	of the Great Lands (the Darkness): Ilkorindi	Eldar (of the Great Journey)	of Aman	of Middle-earth (Úmanyar)

But among Tinwelint's subjects there were also *Noldoli*, Gnomes. This matter is somewhat obscure, but at least it may be observed that the

* In the outlines for *Gilfanon's Tale* the 'Shadow Folk' of Hisilómë have ceased to be Elves and become 'fays' whose origin is unknown: I.237, 239.

manuscript and typescript versions of the *Tale of Tinúviel* do not envisage precisely the same situation.

The manuscript text is perhaps not perfectly explicit on the subject, but it is said (p. 9) that of Tinwelint's subjects '*the most* were Ilkorindi', and that before the rising of the Sun 'already were their numbers mingled with a many wandering Gnomes'. Yet Dairon fled from the apparition of Beren in the forest because 'all the Elves of the woodland thought of the Gnomes of Dor Lómin as treacherous creatures, cruel and faithless' (p. 11); and 'Dread and suspicion was between the Eldar and those of their kindred that had tasted the slavery of Melko, and in this did the evil deeds of the Gnomes at the Haven of the Swans revenge itself' (p. 11). The hostility of the Elves of Artanor to Gnomes was, then, specifically a hostility to the Gnomes of Hisilómë (Dor Lómin), who were suspected of being under the will of Melko (and this is probably a foreshadowing of the suspicion and rejection of Elves escaped from Angband described in *The Silmarillion* p. 156). In the manuscript it is said (p. 9) that *all* the Elves of the Great Lands (those who remained in Palisor, those who were lost on the march, and the Noldoli returned from Valinor) fell beneath the power of Melko, though many escaped and wandered in the wild; and as the manuscript text was first written (see p. 11 and note 3) Beren was 'son of a thrall of Melko's . . . that laboured in the darker places in the north of Hisilómë'. This conception seems reasonably clear, so far as it goes.

In the typescript version it is expressly stated that there were Gnomes 'in Tinwelint's service' (p. 43): the bridge over the forest river, leading to Tinwelint's door, was hung by them. It is not now stated that all the Elves of the Great Lands fell beneath Melko; rather there are named several centres of resistance to his power, in addition to Tinwelint/ Thingol in Artanor: Turgon of Gondolin, the Sons of Fëanor, and Egnor of Hisilómë (Beren's father) – one of the chiefest foes of Melko 'in all the kin of the Gnomes that still were free' (p. 44). Presumably this led to the exclusion in the typescript of the passage telling that the woodland Elves thought of the Gnomes of Dor Lómin as treacherous and faithless (see p. 43), while that concerning the distrust of those who had been Melko's slaves was retained. The passage concerning Hisilómë 'where dwelt Men, and thrall-Noldoli laboured, and few free-Eldar went' (p. 10) was also retained; but Hisilómë, in Beren's wish that he had never strayed out of it, becomes 'the wild free places of Hisilómë' (pp. 17, 45).

This leads to an altogether baffling question, that of the references to the Battle of Unnumbered Tears; and several of the passages just cited bear on it.

The story of 'The Travail of the Noldoli and the Coming of Mankind' that was to have been told by Gilfanon, but which after its opening pages most unhappily never got beyond the stage of outline projections, was to be followed by that of Beren and Tinúviel (see I. 241). After the Battle of Unnumbered Tears there is mention of the Thraldom of the Noldoli, the Mines of Melko, the Spell of Bottomless Dread, the shutting of Men in

Hisilómë, and *then* 'Beren son of Egnor wandered out of Dor Lómin into Artanor . . .' (In *The Silmarillion* the deeds of Beren and Lúthien preceded the Battle of Unnumbered Tears.)

Now in the *Tale of Tinúviel* there is a reference, in both versions, to the 'thrall-Noldoli' who laboured in Hisilómë and of Men dwelling there; and as the passage introducing Beren was first written in the manuscript his father was one of these slaves. It is said, again in both versions, that neither Tinwelint nor the most part of his people went to the battle, but that his lordship was greatly increased by fugitives from it (p. 9); and to the following statement that his dwelling was hidden by the magic of Gwendeling/Melian the typescript adds the word 'thereafter' (p. 43), i.e. after the Battle of Unnumbered Tears. In the changed passage in the typescript referring to Egnor he is one of the chiefest foes of Melko 'in all the kin of the Gnomes *that still were free*'.

All this seems to allow of only one conclusion: the events of the *Tale of Tinúviel* took place *after* the great battle; and this seems to be clinched by the express statement in the typescript: where the manuscript (p. 15) says that Melko 'sought ever to destroy the friendship and intercourse of Elves and Men', the second version adds (p. 44): '*lest they forget the Battle of Unnumbered Tears* and once more arise in wrath against him'.

It is very odd, therefore, that Vëannë should say at the beginning (in the manuscript only, p. 10 and see p. 43) that she will tell 'of things that happened in the halls of Tinwelint *after the arising of the Sun indeed but long ere the unforgotten Battle of Unnumbered Tears*'. (This in any case seems to imply a much longer period between the two events than is suggested in the outlines for *Gilfanon's Tale*: see I.242). This is repeated later (p. 17): 'it was a thing unthought . . . that any Elf . . . should fare untended to the halls of Melko, *even in those earlier days before the Battle of Tears* when Melko's power had not grown great . . .' But it is stranger still that this second sentence is retained in the typescript (p. 45). The typescript version has thus two inescapably contradictory statements:

Melko 'sought ever to destroy the friendship and intercourse of Elves and Men, lest they forget the Battle of Unnumbered Tears' (p. 44);

'Little love was there between the woodland Elves and the folk of Angband even in those days before the Battle of Unnumbered Tears' (p. 45).

Such a radical contradiction within a single text is in the highest degree unusual, perhaps unique, in all the writings concerned with the First Age. But I can see no way to explain it, other than simply accepting it as a radical contradiction; nor indeed can I explain those statements in both versions that the events of the tale took place *before* the battle, since virtually all indications point to the contrary.*

---

* In the *Tale of Turambar* the story of Beren and Tinúviel clearly and necessarily took place *before* the Battle of Unnumbered Tears (pp. 71–2, 140).

§3. Miscellaneous Matters

(i) Morgoth

Beren addresses Melko as 'most mighty Belcha Morgoth', which are said to be his names among the Gnomes (p. 44). In the Gnomish dictionary *Belcha* is given as the Gnomish form corresponding to *Melko* (see I.260), but *Morgoth* is not found in it: indeed this is the first and only appearance of the name in the *Lost Tales*. The element *goth* is given in the Gnomish dictionary with the meaning 'war, strife'; but if *Morgoth* meant at this period 'Black Strife' it is perhaps strange that Beren should use it in a flattering speech. A name-list made in the 1930s explains *Morgoth* as 'formed from his Orc-name *Goth* "Lord or Master" with *mor* "dark or black" prefixed', but it seems very doubtful that this etymology is valid for the earlier period. This name-list explains *Gothmog* 'Captain of Balrogs' as containing the same Orc-element ('Voice of *Goth* (Morgoth)'); but in the name-list to the tale of *The Fall of Gondolin* (p. 216) the name *Gothmog* is said to mean 'Strife-and-hatred' (*mog-* 'detest, hate' appears in the Gnomish dictionary), which supports the interpretation of *Morgoth* in the present tale as 'Black Strife'.*

(ii) Orcs and Balrogs

Despite the reference to 'the wandering bands of the goblins *and* the Orcs' (p. 14, retained in the typescript version), the terms are certainly synonymous in the *Tale of Turambar*. The Orcs are described in the present tale (*ibid.*) as 'foul broodlings of Melko'. In the second version (p. 44) wolf-rider Orcs appear.

Balrogs, mentioned in the tale (p. 15), have appeared in one of the outlines for *Gilfanon's Tale* (I.241); but they had already played an important part in the earliest of the *Lost Tales*, that of *The Fall of Gondolin* (see pp. 212–13).

(iii) Tinúviel's 'lengthening spell'

Of the 'longest things' named in this spell (pp. 19–20, 46) two, 'the sword of Nan' and 'the neck of Gilim the giant', seem now lost beyond recall, though they survived into the spell in the *Lay of Leithian*, where the sword of Nan is itself named, *Glend*, and Gilim is called 'the giant of

---

* Nothing is said in any text to suggest that Gothmog played such a role in relation to Morgoth as the interpretation 'Voice of *Goth*' implies, but nor is anything said to contradict it, and he was from the beginning an important figure in the evil realm and in especial relation to Melko (see p. 216). There is perhaps a reminiscence of 'the Voice of Morgoth' in 'the Mouth of Sauron', the Black Númenórean who was the Lieutenant of Barad-dûr (*The Return of the King* V. 10).

Eruman'. *Gilim* in the Gnomish dictionary means 'winter' (see I.260, entry *Melko*), which does not seem particularly appropriate: though a jotting, very difficult to read, in the little notebook used for memoranda in connection with the *Lost Tales* (see I.171) seems to say that Nan was a 'giant of summer of the South', and that he was like an elm.

The *Indravangs* (*Indrafangs* in the typescript) are the 'Longbeards'; this is said in the Gnomish dictionary to be 'a special name of the Nauglath or Dwarves' (see further the *Tale of the Nauglafring*, p. 247).

Karkaras (*Carcaras* in the typescript) 'Knife-fang' is named in the spell since he was originally conceived as the 'father of wolves, who guarded the gates of Angamandi in those days *and long had done so*' (p. 21). In *The Silmarillion* (p. 180) he has a different history: chosen by Morgoth 'from among the whelps of the race of Draugluin' and reared to be the death of Huan, he was set before the gates of Angband in that very time. In *The Silmarillion* (*ibid.*) Carcharoth is rendered 'the Red Maw', and this expression is used in the text of the tale (p. 34): 'both hand and jewel Karkaras bit off and took into his red maw'.

Glorund is the name of the dragon in the *Tale of Turambar* (*Glaurung* in *The Silmarillion*).

In the tale of *The Chaining of Melko* there is no suggestion that Tulkas had any part in the making of the chain (there in the form *Angaino*): I.100.

(iv)   *The influence of the Valar*

There is frequent suggestion that the Valar in some way exercised a direct influence over the minds and hearts of the distant Elves in the Great Lands. Thus it is said (p. 15) that the Valar must have inspired Beren's ingenious speech to Melko, and while this may be no more than a 'rhetorical' flourish, it is clear that Tinúviel's dream of Beren is meant to be accepted as 'a dream of the Valar' (p. 19). Again, 'the Valar set a new hope in her heart' (p. 47); and later in Vëannë's tale the Valar are seen as active 'fates', guiding the destinies of the characters — so the Valar 'brought' Huan to find Beren and Tinúviel in Nan Dumgorthin (p. 35), and Tinúviel says to Tinwelint that 'the Valar alone saved Beren from a bitter death' (p. 37).

II

TURAMBAR AND THE FOALÓKË

The *Tale of Turambar*, like that of *Tinúviel*, is a manuscript written in ink over a wholly erased original in pencil. But it seems certain that the *extant* form of *Turambar* preceded the *extant* form of *Tinúviel*. This can be deduced in more ways than one, but the order of composition is clearly exemplified in the forms of the name of the King of the Woodland Elves (Thingol). Throughout the manuscript of *Turambar* he was originally *Tintoglin* (and this appears also in the tale of *The Coming of the Elves*, where it was changed to *Tinwelint*, I.115, 131). A note on the manuscript at the beginning of the tale says: 'Tintoglin's name must be altered throughout to *Ellon* or *Tinthellon* = Q. *Ellu*', but the note was struck out, and all through the tale *Tintoglin* was in fact changed to *Tinwelint*.

Now in the *Tale of Tinúviel* the king's name was first given as *Ellu* (or *Tinto Ellu*), and once as *Tinthellon* (pp. 50–1); subsequently it was changed throughout to *Tinwelint*. It is clear that the direction to change *Tintoglin* to '*Ellon* or *Tinthellon* = Q. *Ellu*' belongs to the time when the *Tale of Tinúviel* was being, or had been, rewritten, and that the extant *Tale of Turambar* already existed.

There is also the fact that the rewritten *Tinúviel* was followed, at the same time of composition, by the first form of the 'interlude' in which Gilfanon appears (see I.203), whereas at the beginning of *Turambar* there is a reference to Ailios (who was replaced by Gilfanon) concluding the previous tale. On the different arrangement of the tale-telling at this point that my father subsequently introduced but failed to carry through see I.229–30. According to the earlier arrangement, Ailios told his tale on the first night of the feast of Turuhalmë or the Logdrawing, and Eltas followed with the *Tale of Turambar* on the second.

There is evidence that the *Tale of Turambar* was in existence at any rate by the middle of 1919. Humphrey Carpenter discovered a passage, written on a scrap of proof for the Oxford English Dictionary, in an early alphabet of my father's devising; and transliterating it he found it to be from this tale, not far from the beginning. He has told me that my father was using this version of the 'Alphabet of Rúmil' about June 1919 (see *Biography*, p. 100).

When then Ailios had spoken his fill the time for the lighting of candles was at hand, and so came the first day of Turuhalmë to an

end; but on the second night Ailios was not there, and being asked
by Lindo one Eltas began a tale, and said:

'Now all folk gathered here know that this is the story of
Turambar and the Foalókë, and it is,' said he, 'a favourite tale
among Men, and tells of very ancient days of that folk before the
Battle of Tasarinan when first Men entered the dark vales of
Hisilómë.

In these days many such stories do Men tell still, and more have
they told in the past especially in those kingdoms of the North that
once I knew. Maybe the deeds of other of their warriors have
become mingled therein, and many matters beside that are not in
the most ancient tale – but now I will tell to you the true and
lamentable tale, and I knew it long ere I trod Olórë Mallë in the
days before the fall of Gondolin.

In those days my folk dwelt in a vale of Hisilómë and that land
did Men name Aryador in the tongues they then used, but they
were very far from the shores of Asgon and the spurs of the Iron
Mountains were nigh to their dwellings and great woods of very
gloomy trees. My father said to me that many of our older men
venturing afar had themselves seen the evil worms of Melko and
some had fallen before them, and by reason of the hatred of our
people for those creatures and of the evil Vala often was the story
of Turambar and the Foalókë in their mouths – but rather after the
fashion of the Gnomes did they say Turumart and the Fuithlug.

For know that before the Battle of Lamentation and the ruin of
the Noldoli there dwelt a lord of Men named Úrin, and hearkening
to the summons of the Gnomes he and his folk marched with the
Ilkorindi against Melko, but their wives and children they left
behind them in the woodlands, and with them was Mavwin wife of
Úrin, and her son remained with her, for he was not yet war-high.
Now the name of that boy was Túrin and is so in all tongues, but
Mavwin do the Eldar call Mavoinë.

Now Úrin and his followers fled not from that battle as did most
of the kindreds of Men, but many of them were slain fighting to
the last, and Úrin was made captive. Of the Noldoli who fought
there all the companies were slain or captured or fled away in rout,
save that of Turondo (Turgon) only, and he and his folk cut a path
for themselves out of that fray and come not into this tale. Nonetheless the escape of that great company marred the complete
victory that otherwise had Melko won over his adversaries, and he
desired very greatly to discover whither they had fled; and this he
might not do, for his spies availed nothing, and no tortures at that

time had power to force treacherous knowledge from the captive Noldoli.

Knowing therefore that the Elves of Kôr thought little of Men, holding them in scant fear or suspicion for their blindness and lack of skill, he would constrain Úrin to take up his employ and go seek after Turondo as a spy of Melko. To this however neither threats of torture nor promises of rich reward would bring Úrin to con- 'sent, for he said: "Nay, do as thou wilt, for to no evil work of thine wilt thou ever constrain me, O Melko, thou foe of Gods and Men."

"Of a surety," said Melko in anger, "to no work of mine will I bid thee again, nor yet will I force thee thereto, but upon deeds of mine that will be little to thy liking shalt thou sit here and gaze, nor be able to move foot or hand against them." And this was the torture he devised for the affliction of Úrin the Steadfast, and setting him in a lofty place of the mountains he stood beside him and cursed him and his folk with dread curses of the Valar, putting a doom of woe and a death of sorrow upon them; but to Úrin he gave a measure of vision, so that much of those things that befell his wife and children he might see and be helpless to aid, for magic held him in that high place. "Behold!" said Melko, "the life of Túrin thy son shall be accounted a matter for tears wherever Elves or Men are gathered for the telling of tales"; but Úrin said: "At least none shall pity him for this, that he had a craven for father."

Now after that battle Mavwin got her in tears into the land of Hithlum or Dor Lómin where all Men must now dwell by the word of Melko, save some wild few that yet roamed without. There was Nienóri born to her, but her husband Úrin languished in the thraldom of Melko, and Túrin being yet a small boy Mavwin knew not in her distress how to foster both him and his sister, for Úrin's men had all perished in the great affray, and the strange men who dwelt nigh knew not the dignity of the Lady Mavwin, and all that land was dark and little kindly.

The next short section of the text was struck through afterwards and replaced by a rider on an attached slip. The rejected passage reads:

At that time the rumour [*written above*: memory] of the deeds of Beren Ermabwed had become noised much in Dor Lómin, wherefore it came into the heart of Mavwin, for lack of better counsel, to send Túrin to the court of Tintoglin,[1] begging him to foster this orphan for the memory of Beren, and to teach him the wisdom of fays and of Eldar; now Egnor[2] was akin to Mavwin and he was the father of Beren the One-handed.

The replacement passage reads:

Amended passage to fit better with the story of Tinúviel and the afterhistory of the Nauglafring:

The tale tells however that Úrin had been a friend of the Elves, and in this he was different from many of his folk. Now great had his friendship been with Egnor, the Elf of the greenwood, the huntsman of the Gnomes, and Beren Ermabwed son of Egnor he knew and had rendered him a service once in respect of Damrod his son; but the deeds of Beren of the One Hand in the halls of Tinwelint[3] were remembered still in Dor Lómin. Wherefore it came into the heart of Mavwin, for lack of other counsel, to send Túrin her son to the court of Tinwelint, begging him to foster this orphan for the memory of Úrin and of Beren son of Egnor.[4]

Very bitter indeed was that sundering, and for long [?time] Túrin wept and would not leave his mother, and this was the first of the many sorrows that befell him in life. Yet at length when his mother had reasoned with him he gave way and prepared him in anguish for that journey. With him went two old men, retainers aforetime of his father Úrin, and when all was ready and the farewells taken they turned their feet towards the dark hills, and the little dwelling of Mavwin was lost in the trees, and Túrin blind with tears could see her no more. Then ere they passed out of earshot he cried out: "O Mavwin my mother, soon will I come back to thee" – but he knew not that the doom of Melko lay between them.

Long and very weary and uncertain was the road over the dark hills of Hithlum into the great forests of the Land Beyond where in those days Tinwelint the hidden king had his abode; and Túrin son of Úrin[5] was the first of Men to tread that way, nor have many trodden it since. In perils were Túrin and his guardians of wolves and wandering Orcs that at that time fared even thus far from Angband as the power of Melko waxed and spread over the kingdoms of the North. Evil magics were about them, that often missing their way they wandered fruitlessly for many days, yet in the end did they win through and thanked the Valar therefor – yet maybe it was but part of the fate that Melko wove about their feet, for in after time Túrin would fain have perished as a child there in the dark woods.

Howso that may be, this was the manner of their coming to

Tinwelint's halls; for in the woodlands beyond the mountains they became utterly lost, until at length having no means of sustenance they were like to die, when they were discovered by a wood-ranger, a huntsman of the secret Elves, and he was called Beleg, for he was of great stature and girth as such was among that folk. Then Beleg led them by devious paths through many dark and lonely forestlands to the banks of that shadowed stream before the cavernous doors of Tinwelint's halls. Now coming before that king they were received well for the memory of Úrin the Steadfast, and when also the king heard of the bond tween Úrin and Beren the One-handed[6] and of the plight of that lady Mavwin his heart became softened and he granted her desire, nor would he send Túrin away, but rather said he: "Son of Úrin, thou shalt dwell sweetly in my woodland court, nor even so as a retainer, but behold as a second child of mine shalt thou be, and all the wisdoms of Gwedheling and of myself shalt thou be taught."

After a time therefore when the travellers had rested he despatched the younger of the two guardians of Túrin back unto Mavwin, for such was that man's desire to die in the service of the wife of Úrin, yet was an escort of Elves sent with him, and such comfort and magics for the journey as could be devised, and moreover these words did he bear from Tinwelint to Mavwin: "Behold O Lady Mavwin wife of Úrin the Steadfast, not for love nor for fear of Melko but of the wisdom of my heart and the fate of the Valar did I not go with my folk to the Battle of Unnumbered Tears, who now am become a safety and a refuge for all who fearing evil may find the secret ways that lead to the protection of my halls. Perchance now is there no other bulwark left against the arrogance of the Vala of Iron, for men say Turgon is not slain, but who knoweth the truth of it or how long he may escape? Now therefore shall thy son Túrin be fostered here as my own child until he is of age to succour thee – then, an he will, he may depart." More too he bid the Lady Mavwin, might she o'ercome the journey, fare back also to his halls, and dwell there in peace; but this when she heard she did not do, both for the tenderness of her little child Nienóri, and for that rather would she dwell poor among Men than live sweetly as an almsguest even among the woodland Elves. It may be too that she clung to that dwelling that Úrin had set her in ere he went to the great war, hoping still faintly for his return, for none of the messengers that had borne the lamentable tidings from that field might say that he was dead, reporting only that none knew where he might be – yet in truth those messengers were few and half-distraught, and now the years were slowly passing since the last blow fell on that most grievous day. Indeed in after days she yearned to look again upon Túrin, and maybe in the end, when Nienóri had grown, had cast aside her pride and fared over the hills, had not these become impassable for the might and great magic of Melko, who hemmed all Men in Hithlum and slew such as dared beyond its walls.

Thus came to pass the dwelling of Túrin in the halls of Tinwelint; and with him was suffered to dwell Gumlin the aged who had fared with him out of Hithlum, and had no heart or strength for the returning. Very much joy had he in that sojourn, yet did the sorrow of his sundering from Mavwin fall never quite away from him; great waxed his strength of body and the stoutness of his feats got him praise wheresoever Tinwelint was held as lord, yet he was a silent boy and often gloomy, and he got not love easily and fortune did not follow him, for few things that he desired greatly came to him and many things at which he laboured went awry. For nothing however did he grieve so much as the ceasing of all messengers between Mavwin and himself, when after a few years as has been told the hills became untraversable and the ways were shut. Now Túrin was seven years old when he fared to the woodland Elves, and seven years he dwelt there while tidings came ever and anon to him from his mother, so that he heard how his sister Nienóri grew to a slender maid and very fair, and how things grew better in Hithlum and his mother more in peace; and then all words ceased, and the years passed.

To ease his sorrow and the rage of his heart, that remembered always how Úrin and his folk had gone down in battle against Melko, Túrin was for ever ranging with the most warlike of the folk of Tinwelint far abroad, and long ere he was grown to first manhood he slew and took hurts in frays with the Orcs that prowled unceasingly upon the confines of the realm and were a menace to the Elves. Indeed but for his prowess much hurt had that folk sustained, and he held the wrath of Melko from them for many years, and after his days they were harassed sorely, and in the end must have been cast into thraldom had not such great and dread events befallen that Melko forgot them.

Now about the courts of Tinwelint there dwelt an Elf called Orgof, and he, as were the most of that king's folk, was an Ilkorin, yet he had Gnome-blood also. Of his mother's side he was nearly akin to the king himself, and was in some favour being a good hunter and an Elf of prowess, yet was he somewhat loose with his tongue and overweening by reason of his favour with the king; yet of nothing was he so fain as of fine raiment and of jewels and of gold and silver ornament, and was ever himself clad most bravely. Now Túrin lying continually in the woods and travailing in far and lonely places grew to be uncouth of raiment and wild of locks, and Orgof made jest of him whensoever the twain sat at the king's board; but Túrin said never a word to his foolish jesting, and indeed at no time did he give much heed to words that were spoken to him, and the eyes beneath his shaggy brows oftentimes looked as to a great distance – so that he seemed to see far things and to listen to sounds of the woodland that others heard not.

On a time Túrin sate at meat with the king, and it was that day twelve years since he had gazed through his tears upon Mavwin standing before the doors and weeping as he made his way among the trees, until their stems had taken her from his sight, and he was moody, speaking curt answers to those that sat nigh him, and most of all to Orgof.

But this fool would not give him peace, making a laugh of his rough clothes and tangled hair, for Túrin had then come new from a long abiding in the woods, and at length he drew forth daintily a comb of gold that he had and offered it to Túrin; and having drunk well, when Túrin deigned not to notice him he said: "Nay, an thou knowst not how to use a comb, hie thee back to thy mother, for she perchance will teach thee – unless in sooth the women of Hithlum be as ugly as their sons and as little kempt." Then a fierce anger born of his sore heart and these words concerning the lady Mavwin blazed suddenly in Túrin's breast, so that he seized a heavy drinking-vessel of gold that lay by his right hand and unmindful of his strength he cast it with great force in Orgof's teeth, saying: "Stop thy mouth therewith, fool, and prate no more." But Orgof's face was broken and he fell back with great weight, striking his head upon the stone of the floor and dragging upon him the table and all its vessels, and he spake nor prated again, for he was dead.

Then all men rose in silence, but Túrin, gazing aghast upon the body of Orgof and the spilled wine upon his hand, turned on his heel and strode into the night; and some that were akin to Orgof drew their weapons half from their sheaths, yet none struck, for the king gave no sign but stared stonily upon the body of Orgof, and very great amaze was in his face. But Túrin laved his hands in the stream without the doors and burst there into tears, saying:

"Lo! Is there a curse upon me, for all I do is ill, and now is it so turned that I must flee the house of my fosterfather an outlaw guilty of blood – nor look upon the faces of any I love again." And in his heart he dared not return to Hithlum lest his mother be bitterly grieved at his disgrace, or perchance he might draw the wrath of the Elves behind him to his folk; wherefore he got himself far away, and when men came to seek him he might not be found.

Yet they did not seek his harm, although he knew it not, for Tinwelint despite his grief and the ill deed pardoned him, and the most of his folk were with him in that, for Túrin had long held his peace or returned courtesy to the folly of Orgof, though stung often enough thereby, for that Elf being not a little jealous was used to barb his words; and now therefore the near kinsmen of Orgof were constrained by fear of Tinwelint and by many gifts to accept the king's doom.

Yet Túrin in unhappiness, believing the hand of all against him and the heart of the king become that of a foe, crept to the uttermost bounds of that woodland realm. There he hunted for his subsistence, being a good shot with the bow, yet he rivalled not the Elves at that, for rather at the wielding of the sword was he mightier than they. To him gathered a few wild spirits, and amongst them was Beleg the huntsman, who had rescued Gumlin and Túrin in the woods aforetime. Now in many adventures were those twain together, Beleg the Elf and Túrin the Man, which are not now told or remembered but which once were sung in many a place. With beast and with goblin they warred and fared at times into far places unknown to the Elves, and the fame of the hidden hunters of the marches began to be heard among Orcs and Elves, so that perchance Tinwelint would soon have become aware of the place of Túrin's abiding, had not upon a time all that band of Túrin's fallen into desperate encounter with a host of Orcs who outnumbered them three times. All were there slain save Túrin and Beleg, and Beleg escaped with wounds, but Túrin was overborne and bound, for such was the will of Melko that he be brought to him alive; for behold, dwelling in the halls of Linwë[7] about which had that fay Gwedheling the queen woven much magic and mystery and such power of spells as can come only from Valinor, whence indeed long time agone she once had brought them, Túrin had been lost out of his sight, and he feared lest he cheat the doom that was devised for him. Therefore now he purposed to entreat him grievously before the eyes of Úrin; but Úrin had called upon the Valar of the West, being taught much concerning them by the

Eldar of Kôr – the Gnomes he had encountered – and his words came, who shall say how, to Manwë Súlimo upon the heights of Taniquetil, the Mountain of the World. Nonetheless was Túrin dragged now many an evil league in sore distress, a captive of the pitiless Orcs, and they made slow journeying, for they followed ever the line of dark hills toward those regions where they rise high and gloomy and their heads are shrouded in black vapours. There are they called Angorodin or the Iron Mountains, for beneath the roots of their northernmost fastnesses lies Angband, the Hells of Iron, most grievous of all abodes – and thither were they now making laden with booty and with evil deeds.

Know then that in those days still was Hithlum and the Lands Beyond full of the wild Elves and of Noldoli yet free, fugitives of the old battle; and some wandered ever wearily, and others had secret and hidden abodes in caves or woodland fastnesses, but Melko sought untiringly after them and most pitilessly did he entreat them of all his thralls did he capture them. Orcs and dragons and evil fays were loosed against them and their lives were full of sorrow and travail, so that those who found not in the end the realms of Tinwelint nor the secret stronghold of the king of the city of stone* perished or were enslaved.

Noldoli too there were who were under the evil enchantments of Melko and wandered as in a dream of fear, doing his ill bidding, for the spell of bottomless dread was on them and they felt the eyes of Melko burn them from afar. Yet often did these sad Elves both thrall and free hear the voice of Ulmo in the streams or by the sea-marge where the waters of Sirion mingled with the waves; for Ulmo, of all the Valar, still thought of them most tenderly and designed with their slender aid to bring Melko's evil to ruin. Then remembering the blessedness of Valinor would they at times cast away their fear, doing good deeds and aiding both Elves and Men against the Lord of Iron.

Now was it that it came into the heart of Beleg the hunter of the Elves to seek after Túrin so soon as his own hurts were healed. This being done in no great number of days, for he had a skill of healing, he made all speed after the band of Orcs, and he had need of all his craft as tracker to follow that trail, for a band of the goblins of Melko go cunningly and very light. Soon was he far beyond any regions known to him, yet for love of Túrin he pressed on, and in this did he show courage greater than the most of that

* Gondolin.

woodland folk, and indeed there are none who may now measure the depth of fear and anguish that Melko set in the hearts of Men and of Elves in those sad days. Thus did it fall out that Beleg became lost and benighted in a dark and perilous region so thick with pines of giant growth that none but the goblins might find a track, having eyes that pierced the deepest gloom, yet were many even of these lost long time in those regions; and they were called by the Noldoli Taurfuin, the Forest of Night. Now giving himself up for lost Beleg lay with his back to a mighty tree and listened to the wind in the gaunt tops of the forest many fathoms above him, and the moaning of the night airs and the creaking of the branches was full of sorrow and foreboding, and his heart became utterly weary.

On a sudden he noticed a little light afar among the trees steady and pale as it were of a glowworm very bright, yet thinking it might scarce be glowworm in such a place he crept towards it. Now the Noldoli that laboured in the earth and aforetime had skill of crafts in metals and gems in Valinor were the most valued of the thralls of Melko, and he suffered them not to stray far away, and so it was that Beleg knew not that these Elves had little lanterns of strange fashion, and they were of silver and of crystal and a flame of a pale blue burnt forever within, and this was a secret and the jewel-makers among them alone knew it nor would they reveal it even to Melko, albeit many jewels and many magic lights they were constrained to make for him.

Aided by these lamps the Noldoli fared much at night, and seldom lost a path had they but once trodden it before. So it was that drawing near Beleg beheld one of the hill-gnomes stretched upon the needles beneath a great pine asleep, and his blue lantern stood glimmering nigh his head. Then Beleg awakened him, and that Elf started up in great fear and anguish, and Beleg learned that he was a fugitive from the mines of Melko and named himself Flinding bo-Dhuilin of an ancient house of the Gnomes. Now falling into talk Flinding was overjoyed to have speech with a free Noldo, and told many tales of his flight from the uttermost fastness of the mines of Melko; and at length said he: "When I thought myself all but free, lo, I strayed at night unwarily into the midmost of an Orc-camp, and they were asleep and much spoil and weighted packs they had, and many captive Elves I thought I descried: and one there was that lay nigh to a trunk to which he was bound most grievously, and he moaned and cried out bitterly against Melko, calling on the names of Úrin and Mavwin; and though at that time

being a craven from long captivity I fled heedlessly, now do I
marvel much, for who of the thralls of Angband has not known of
Úrin the Steadfast who alone of Men defies Melko chained in
torment upon a bitter peak?"

Then was Beleg in great eagerness and sprang to his feet shouting: "'Tis Túrin, fosterson of Tinwelint, even he whom I seek,
who was the son of Úrin long ago. – Nay, lead me to this camp, O
son of Duilin, and soon shall he be free," but Flinding was much
afeared, saying: "Softer words, my Beleg, for the Orcs have ears of
cats, and though a day's march lies between me and that encampment who knows whether they be not followed after."

Nonetheless hearing the story of Túrin from Beleg, despite his
dread he consented to lead Beleg to that place, and long ere the sun
rose on the day or its fainting beams crept into that dark forest they
were upon the road, guided by the dancing light of Flinding's
swinging lamp. Now it happened that in their journeying their
paths crossed that of the Orcs who now were renewing their
march, but in a direction other than that they had for long pursued, for now fearing the escape of their prisoner they made for a
place where they knew the trees were thinner and a track ran for
many a league easy to pursue; wherefore that evening, or ever they
came to the spot that Flinding sought, they heard a shouting and a
rough singing that was afar in the woods but drawing near; nor did
they hide too soon ere the whole of that Orc-band passed nigh to
them, and some of the captains were mounted upon small horses,
and to one of these was Túrin tied by the wrists so that he must
trot or be dragged cruelly. Then did Beleg and Flinding follow
timorously after as dusk fell on the forest, and when that band
encamped they lurked near until all was quiet save the moaning of
the captives. Now Flinding covered his lamp with a pelt and they
crept near, and behold the goblins slept, for it was not their wont
to keep fire or watch in their bivouacs, and for guard they trusted
to certain fierce wolves that went always with their bands as dogs
with Men, but slept not when they camped, and their eyes shone
like points of red light among the trees. Now was Flinding in sore
dread, but Beleg bid him follow, and the two crept between the
wolves at a point where there was a great gap between them, and as
the luck of the Valar had it Túrin was lying nigh, apart from the
others, and Beleg came unseen to his side and would cut his
bonds, when he found his knife had dropped from his side in his
creeping and his sword he had left behind without the camp.
Therefore now, for they dare not risk the creeping forth and back

again, do Beleg and Flinding both stout men essay to carry him sleeping soundly in utter weariness stealthily from the camp, and this they did, and it has ever been thought a great feat, and few have done the like in passing the wolf guards of the goblins and despoiling their camps.

Now in the woods at no great distance from the camp they laid him down, for they might not bear him further, seeing that he was a Man and of greater stature than they;[8] but Beleg fetched his sword and would cut his bonds forthwith. The bonds about his wrists he severed first and was cutting those upon the ankles when blundering in the dark he pricked Túrin's foot deeply, and Túrin awoke in fear. Now seeing a form bend over him in the gloom sword in hand and feeling the smart of his foot he thought it was one of the Orcs come to slay him or to torment him – and this they did often, cutting him with knives or hurting him with spears; but now Túrin feeling his hand free leapt up and flung all his weight suddenly upon Beleg, who fell and was half-crushed, lying speechless on the ground; but Túrin at the same time seized the sword and struck it through Beleg's throat or ever Flinding might know what had betid. Then Túrin leapt back and shouting out curses upon the goblins bid them come and slay him or taste of his sword, for he fancied himself in the midst of their camp, and thought not of flight but only of selling his life dear. Now would he have made at Flinding, but that Gnome sprang back, dropping his lamp, so that its cover slipped and the light of it shone forth, and he called out in the tongue of the Gnomes that Túrin should hold his hand and slay not his friends – then did Túrin hearing his speech pause, and as he stood, by the light of the lamp he saw the white face of Beleg lying nigh his feet with pierced throat, and he stood as one stricken to stone, and such was the look upon his face that Flinding dared not speak for a long while. Indeed little mind had he for words, for by that light had he also seen the fate of Beleg and was very bitter in heart. At length however it seemed to Flinding that the Orcs were astir, and so it was, for the shouts of Túrin had come to them; wherefore he said to Túrin: "The Orcs are upon us, let us flee," but Túrin answered not, and Flinding shook him, bidding him gather his wits or perish, and then Túrin did as he was bid but yet as one dazed, and stooping he raised Beleg and kissed his mouth.

Then did Flinding guide Túrin as well as he might swiftly from those regions, and Túrin wandered with him following as he led, and at length for a while they had shaken off pursuit and could breathe again. Now then did Flinding have space to tell Túrin all he knew and of his meeting with Beleg, and the floods of Túrin's tears were loosed, and he wept bitterly, for Beleg had been his comrade often in many deeds; and this was the third anguish that befell Túrin, nor did he lose the mark of that sorrow utterly in all his life; and long he wandered with Flinding caring little whither he went, and but for that Gnome soon would he have been recaptured or lost, for he thought only of the stark face of Beleg the huntsman, lying in the dark forest slain by his hand even as he cut the bonds of thraldom from him.

In that time was Túrin's hair touched with grey, despite his few years. Long time however did Túrin and the Noldo journey together, and by reason of the magic of that lamp fared by night and hid by day and were lost in the hills, and the Orcs found them not.

Now in the mountains there was a place of caves above a stream, and that stream ran down to feed the river Sirion, but grass grew before the doors of the caves, and these were cunningly concealed by trees and such magics as those scattered bands that dwelt therein remembered still. Indeed at this time this place had grown to be a strong dwelling of the folk and many a fugitive swelled them, and there the ancient arts and works of the Noldoli came once more to life albeit in a rude and rugged fashion.

There was smithying in secret and forging of good weapons, and even fashioning of some fair things beside, and the women spun once more and wove, and at times was gold quarried privily in places nigh, where it was found, so that deep in those caverns might vessels of beauty be seen in the flame of secret lights, and old songs were faintly sung. Yet did the dwellers in the caves flee always before the Orcs and never give battle unless compelled by mischance or were they able to so entrap them that all might be slain and none escape alive; and this they did of policy that no tidings reach Melko of their dwelling nor might he suspect any numerous gathering of folk in those parts.

This place however was known to the Noldo Flinding who fared with Túrin; indeed he was once of that people long since, before the Orcs captured him and he was held in thraldom. Thither did he now wend being sure that the pursuit came no longer nigh them, yet went he nonetheless by devious ways, so that it was long ere they drew nigh to that region, and the spies and watchers of the Rodothlim (for so were that folk named) gave warning of their approach, and the folk withdrew before them, such as were abroad from their dwelling. Then they closed their doors and hoped that the strangers might not discover their caves, for they feared and mistrusted all unknown folk of whatever race, so evil were the lessons of that dreadful time.

Now then Flinding and Túrin dared even to the caves' mouths, and perceiving that these twain knew now the paths thereto the Rodothlim sallied and made them prisoners and drew them within their rocky halls, and they were led before the chief, Orodreth. Now the free Noldoli at that time feared much those of their kin who had tasted thraldom, for compelled by fear and torture and spells much treachery had they wrought; even thus did the evil deeds of the Gnomes at Cópas Alqalunten find vengeance,' setting Gnome against Gnome, and the Noldoli cursed the day that ever they first hearkened to the deceit of Melko, rueing utterly their departure from the blessed realm of Valinor.

Nonetheless when Orodreth heard the tale of Flinding and knew it to be true he welcomed him with joy back among the folk, yet was that Gnome so changed by the anguish of his slavery that few knew him again; but for Flinding's sake Orodreth hearkened to the tale of Túrin, and Túrin told of his travails and named Úrin as his sire, nor had the Gnomes yet forgot that name. Then was the heart of Orodreth made kind and he bade them dwell among the Rodothlim and be faithful to him. So came the sojourn of Túrin among the people of the caves, and he dwelt with Flinding bo-Dhuilin and laboured much for the good of the folk, and slew many a wandering Orc, and did doughty deeds in their defence. In return much did he learn of new wisdom from them, for memories of Valinor burnt yet deep in their wild hearts, and greater still was their wisdom than that of such Eldar as had seen never the blest faces of the Gods.

Among that people was a very fair maiden and she was named Failivrin, and her father was Galweg; and this Gnome had a liking for Túrin and aided him much, and Túrin was often with him in ventures and good deeds. Now many a tale of these did Galweg make beside his hearth and Túrin was often at his board, and the heart of Failivrin became moved at the sight of him, and wondered often at his gloom and sadness, pondering what sorrow lay locked in his breast, for Túrin went not gaily being weighted with the death of Beleg that he felt upon his head, and he suffered not his heart to be moved, although he was glad of her sweetness; but he deemed himself an outlawed man and one burdened with a heavy doom of ill. Therefore did Failivrin become sorrowful and wept in secret, and she grew so pale that folk marvelled at the whiteness and delicacy of her face and her bright eyes that shone therein.

Now came a time when the Orc-bands and the evil things of Melko drew ever nigher to the dwelling of this folk, and despite the good spells that ran in the stream beneath it seemed like that their abode would remain no longer hidden. It is said however that during all this time the dwelling of Túrin in the caves and his deeds among the Rodothlim were veiled from Melko's eyes, and that he infested not the Rodothlim for Túrin's sake nor out of design, but rather it was the ever increasing numbers of these creatures and their growing power and fierceness that brought them so far afield. Nonetheless the blindness and ill-fortune that he wove of old clung yet to Túrin, as may be seen.

Each day grew the brows of the chiefs of the Rodothlim more dark, and dreams came to them[10] bidding them arise and depart swiftly and secretly, seeking, if it might be, after Turgon, for with him might yet salvation be found for the Gnomes. Whispers too there were in the stream at eve, and those among them skilled to hear such voices added their foreboding at the councils of the folk. Now at these councils had Túrin won him a place by dint of many valorous deeds, and he gainsaid their fears, trusting in his strength, for he lusted ever for war with the creatures of Melko, and he upbraided the men of the folk, saying: "Lo! Ye have weapons of great excellence of workmanship, and yet are the most of them clean of your foes' blood. Remember ye the Battle of Uncounted Tears and forget not your folk that there fell, nor seek ever to flee, but fight and stand."

Now despite the wisdom of their wisest such bitter words confused their counsels and delayed them, and there were no few of the stout-hearted that found hope in them, being sad at the thought of abandoning those places where they had begun to make an abiding place of peace and goodliness; but Túrin begged Orodreth for a sword, and he had not wielded a sword since the slaying of Beleg, but rather had he been contented with a mighty club. Now then Orodreth let fashion for him a great sword, and it was made by magic to be utterly black save at its edges, and those were shining bright and sharp as but Gnome-steel may be. Heavy it was, and was sheathed in black, and it hung from a sable belt, and Túrin named it Gurtholfin the Wand of Death; and often that blade leapt in his hand of its own lust, and it is said that at times it spake dark words to him. Therewith did he now range the hills, and slew unceasingly, so that Blacksword of the Rodothlim became a name of terror to the Orcs, and for a great season all evil was fended from the caverns of the Gnomes. Hence comes that name of Túrin's among the Gnomes, calling him Mormagli or Mormakil according to their speech, for these names signify black sword.

The greater however did Túrin's valour become so grew the love of Failivrin more deep, and did men murmur against him in his absence she spake for him, and sought ever to minister to him, and her he treated ever courteously and happily, saying he had found a fair sister in the Gnome-lands. By Túrin's deeds however was the ancient counsel of the Rodothlim set aside and their abode made known far and wide, nor was Melko ignorant of it, yet many of the Noldoli now fled to them and their strength waxed and Túrin was held in great honour among them. Then were days of great happiness and for a while men lived openly again and might fare far abroad from their homes in safety, and many boasted of the salvation of the Noldoli, while Melko gathered in secret his great hordes. These did he loose suddenly upon them at unawares, and they gathered their warriors in great haste and went against him, but behold, an army of Orcs descended upon them, and wolves, and Orcs mounted upon wolves; and a great worm was with them whose scales were polished bronze and whose breath was a mingled fire and smoke, and his name was Glorund.[11] All the men of the Rodothlim fell or were taken in that battle, for the foe was numberless, and that was the most bitter affray since the evil field of Nínin-Udathriol.* Orodreth was there sorely hurt and Túrin bore him out of the fight ere yet all was ended, and with the aid of Flinding whose wounds were not great[12] he got him to the caves.

There died Orodreth, reproaching Túrin that he had ever withstood his wise counsels, and Túrin's heart was bitter at the ruin of the folk that was set to his account.[13] Then leaving Lord Orodreth dead Túrin went to the places of Galweg's abiding, and there was Failivrin weeping bitterly at the tidings of her father's death, but Túrin sought to comfort her, and for the pain of her heart and the sorrow of her father's death and of the ruin of her folk she swooned upon his breast and cast her arms about

---

* At the bottom of the manuscript page is written:

'*Nieriltasinwa*   the battle of unnumbered tears
Glorund   Laurundo or *Undolaurë*'

Later *Glorund* and *Laurundo* were emended to *Glorunt* and *Laurunto*.

him. So deep was the ruth of Túrin's heart that in that hour he deemed he loved her very dearly; yet were now he and Flinding alone save for a few aged carles and dying men, and the Orcs having despoiled the field of dead were nigh upon them.

Thus stood Túrin before the doors with Gurtholfin in hand, and Flinding was beside him; and the Orcs fell on that place and ransacked it utterly, dragging out all the folk that lurked therein and all their goods, whatsoever of great or little worth might there lie hid. But Túrin denied the entrance of Galweg's dwelling to them, and they fell thick about him, until a company of their archers standing at a distance shot a cloud of arrows at him. Now he wore chainmail such as all the warriors of the Gnomes have ever loved and still do wear, yet it turned not all those ill shafts, and already was he sore hurt when Flinding fell pierced suddenly through the eye; and soon too had he met his death – and his weird had been the happier thereby – had not that great drake coming now upon the sack bidden them cease their shooting; but with the power of his breath he drove Túrin from those doors and with the magic of his eyes he bound him hand and foot.

Now those drakes and worms are the evillest creatures that Melko has made, and the most uncouth, yet of all are they the most powerful, save it be the Balrogs only. A great cunning and wisdom have they, so that it has been long said amongst Men that whosoever might taste the heart of a dragon would know all tongues of Gods or Men, of birds or beasts, and his ears would catch whispers of the Valar or of Melko such as never had he heard before. Few have there been that ever achieved a deed of such prowess as the slaying of a drake, nor might any even of such doughty ones taste their blood and live, for it is as a poison of fires that slays all save the most godlike in strength. Howso that may be, even as their lord these foul beasts love lies and lust after gold and precious things with a great fierceness of desire, albeit they may not use nor enjoy them.

Thus was it that this *lókë* (for so do the Eldar name the worms of Melko) suffered the Orcs to slay whom they would and to gather whom they listed into a very great and very sorrowful throng of women, maids, and little children, but all the mighty treasure that they had brought from the rocky halls and heaped glistering in the sun before the doors he coveted for himself and forbade them set finger on it, and they durst not withstand him, nor could they have done so an they would.

In that sad band stood Failivrin in horror, and she stretched out her arms towards Túrin, but Túrin was held by the spell of the drake, for that beast had a foul magic in his glance, as have many others of his kind, and he turned the sinews of Túrin as it were to stone, for his eye held Túrin's eye so that his will died, and he could not stir of his own purpose, yet might he see and hear.

Then did Glorund taunt Túrin nigh to madness, saying that lo! he had cast away his sword nor had the heart to strike a blow for his friends — now Túrin's sword lay at his feet whither it had slipped from his unnervéd grasp. Great was the agony of Túrin's heart thereat, and the Orcs laughed at him, and of the captives some cried bitterly against him. Even now did the Orcs begin to drive away that host of thralls, and his heart broke at the sight, yet he moved not; and the pale face of Failivrin faded afar, and her voice was borne to him crying: "O Túrin Mormakil, where is thy heart; O my beloved, wherefore dost thou forsake me?" So great then became Túrin's anguish that even the spell of that worm might not restrain it, and crying aloud he reached for the sword at his feet and would wound the drake with it, but the serpent breathed a foul and heated breath upon him, so that he swooned and thought that it was death.

A long time thereafter, and the tale telleth not how long, he came to himself, and he was lying gazing at the sun before the doors, and his head rested against a heap of gold even as the ransackers had left it. Then said the drake, who was hard by: "Wonderest thou not wherefore I have withheld death from thee, O Túrin Mormakil, who wast once named brave?" Then Túrin remembered all his griefs and the evil that had fallen upon him, and he said: "Taunt me not, foul worm, for thou knowest I would die; and for that alone, methinks, thou slayest me not."

But the drake answered saying: "Know then this, O Túrin son of Úrin, that a fate of evil is woven about thee, and thou mayst not untangle thy footsteps from it whitherever thou goest. Yea indeed, I would not have thee slain, for thus wouldst thou escape very bitter sorrows and a weird of anguish." Then Túrin leaping suddenly to his feet and avoiding that beast's baleful eye raised aloft his sword and cried: "Nay, from this hour shall none name me Túrin if I live. Behold, I will name me a new name and it shall be Turambar!" Now this meaneth Conqueror of Fate, and the form of the name in the Gnome-speech is Turumart. Then uttering these words he made a second time at the drake, thinking indeed to force the drake to slay him and to conquer his fate by death, but the dragon laughed, saying: "Thou fool! An I would, I had slain thee long since and could do so here and now, and if I will not thou canst not do battle with me waking, for my eye can cast once more the binding spell upon thee that thou stand as stone. Nay, get thee gone, O Turambar Conqueror of Fate! First thou must meet thy doom an thou wouldst o'ercome it." But Turambar was filled with shame and anger, and perchance he had slain himself, so great was his madness, although thus might he not hope that ever his spirit would be freed from the dark glooms of Mandos or stray into the pleasant paths of Valinor;[14] but amidst his misery he bethought him of Failivrin's pallid face and he bowed his head, for the thought came into his heart to seek back through all the woods after her sad footsteps even be it to Angamandi and the Hills of Iron. Maybe in that desperate venture he had found a kindly and swift death or perchance an ill one, and maybe he had rescued Failivrin and found happiness, yet not thus was he fated to earn the name he had taken anew, and the drake reading his mind suffered him not thus lightly to escape his tide of ill.

"Hearken to me, O son of Úrin," said he; "ever wast thou a coward at heart, vaunting thyself falsely before men. Perchance thou thinkest it a gallant deed to go follow after a maiden of strange kin, recking little of thine own that suffer now terrible things? Behold, Mavwin who loves thee long has eagerly awaited thy return, knowing that thou hast found manhood a while ago, and she looks for thy succour in vain, for little she knows that her son is an outlaw stained with the blood of his comrades, a defiler of his lord's table. Ill do men entreat her, and behold the Orcs infest now those parts of Hithlum, and she is in fear and peril and her daughter Nienóri thy sister with her."

Then was Turambar aflame with sorrow and with shame for the lies of that worm were barbed with truth, and for the spell of his eyes he believed all that was said. Therefore his old desire to see once more Mavwin his mother and to look upon Nienóri whom he had never seen since his first days[15] grew hot within him, and with a heart torn with sorrow for the fate of Failivrin he turned his feet towards the hills seeking Dor Lómin, and his sword was sheathed. And truly is it said: "Forsake not for anything thy friends – nor believe those who counsel thee to do so" – for of his abandoning of Failivrin in danger that he himself could see came the very direst evil upon him and all he loved; and indeed his heart was confounded and wavered, and he left those places in uttermost shame and weariness. But the dragon gloated upon the hoard and lay coiled upon it, and the fame of that great treasure of golden vessels and of unwrought gold that lay by the caves above the stream fared far and wide about; yet the great worm slept before it, and evil thoughts he had as he pondered the planting of his cunning lies and the sprouting thereof and their growth and fruit, and fumes of smoke went up from his nostrils as he slept.

On a time therefore long afterward came Turambar with great travail into Hisilómë, and found at length the place of the abode of his mother, even the one whence he had been sundered as a child, but behold, it was roofless and the tilth about it ran wild. Then his heart smote him, but he learned of some that dwelt nigh that lighting on better days the Lady Mavwin had departed some years agone to places not far distant where was a great and prosperous dwelling of men, for that region of Hisilómë was fertile and men tilled the land somewhat and many had flocks and herds, though for the most part in the dark days after the great battle men feared to dwell in settled places and ranged the woods and hunted or fished, and so it was with those kindreds about the waters of Asgon whence after arose Tuor son of Peleg.

Hearing these words however Turambar was amazed, and questioned them concerning the wandering into those regions of Orcs and other fierce folk of Melko, but they shook their heads, and said that never had such creatures come hither deep into the land of Hisilómë.[16] "If thou wishest for Orcs then go to the hills that encompass our land about," said they, "and thou wilt not search long. Scarce may the wariest fare in and out so constant is their watch, and they infest the rocky gates of the land that the Children of Men be penned for ever in the Land of Shadows; but men say 'tis the will of Melko that they trouble us not here – and yet it seems to us that thou hast come from afar, and at this we marvel, for long is it since one from other lands might tread this way." Then Turambar was in perplexity at this and he doubted the deceit of the dragon's words, yet he went now in hope to the dwelling of men and the house of his mother, and coming upon homesteads of men he was easily directed thither. Now men looked strangely at his questioning, and indeed they had reason, yet were such as he spoke to in great awe and wonder at him and shrank back from speech with him, for his garb was of the wild woods and his hair was long and his face haggard and drawn as with unquenchable sorrows, and therein burnt fiercely his dark eyes beneath dark brows. A collar of fine gold he wore and his mighty sword was at his side, and men marvelled much at him;

and did any dare to question him he named himself Turambar son of the weary forest,* and that seemed but the more strange to them.

Now came he to the dwelling of Mavwin, and behold it was a fair house, but none dwelt there, and grass was high in the gardens, and there were no kine in the byres nor horses in the sheds, and the pastures about were silent and empty. Only the swallows had dwelling beneath the timbers of the eaves and these made a noise and a bustle as if departure for autumn was at hand, and Turambar sat before the carven doors and wept. And one who was passing on to other dwellings, for a track passed nigh to that homestead, espied him, and coming asked him his grief, and Turambar said that it was bitter for a son sundered for many years from his home to give up all that was dear and dare the dangers of the infested hills to find only the halls of his kindred empty when he returned at last.

"Nay, then this is a very trick of Melko's," said the other, "for of a truth here dwelt the Lady Mavwin wife of Úrin, and yet is she gone two years past very secretly and suddenly, and men say that she seeks her son who is lost, and that her daughter Nienóri goes with her, but I know not the story. This however I know, and many about here do likewise, and cry shame thereon, for know that the guardianship of all her goods and land she gave to Brodda, a man whom she trusted, and he is lord of these regions by men's consent and has to wife a kinswoman of hers. But now she is long away he has mingled her herds and flocks, small as they were, with his mighty ones, branding them with his own marks, yet the dwelling and stead of Mavwin he suffereth to fall to ruin, and men think ill of it but move not, for the power of Brodda has grown to be great."

Then Turambar begged him to set his feet upon the paths to Brodda's halls, and the man did as he desired, so that Turambar striding thither came upon them just as night fell and men sat to meat in that house. Great was the company that night and the light of many torches fell upon them, but the Lady Airin was not there, for men drank overmuch at Brodda's feasts and their songs were fierce and quarrels blazed about the hall, and those things she loved not. Now Turambar smote upon the gates and his heart was black and a great wrath was in him, for the words of the stranger before his mother's doors were bitter to him.

* A note on the manuscript referring to this name reads: '*Turumart go-Dhrauthodauros* [emended to *bo-Dhrauthodavros*] or *Turambar Rúsitaurion*.'

Then did some open to his knocking and Turambar strode into that hall, and Brodda bade him be seated and ordered wine and meats to be set before him, but Turambar would neither eat nor drink, so that men looking askance upon his sullenness asked him who he might be. Then Turambar stepping out into the midst of them before the high place where Brodda sat said: "Behold, 1 am Turambar son of the forest", and men laughed thereat, but Turambar's eyes were full of wrath. Then said Brodda in doubt: "What wilt thou of me, O son of the wild forest?" But Turambar said: "Lord Brodda, I am come to repay thy stewardship of others' goods," and silence fell in that place; but Brodda laughed, saying again: "But who art thou?" And thereupon Turambar leapt upon the high place and ere Brodda might foresee the act he drew Gurtholfin and seizing Brodda by the locks all but smote his head from off his body, crying aloud: "So dieth the rich man who addeth the widow's little to his much. Lo, men die not all in the wild woods, and am I not in truth the son of Úrin, who having sought back unto his folk findeth an empty hall despoiled." Then was there a great uproar in that hall, and indeed though he was burdened overmuch with his many griefs and wellnigh distraught, yet was this deed of Turambar violent and unlawful. Some were there nonetheless that would not unsheathe their weapons, saying that Brodda was a thief and died as one, but many there were that leapt with swords against Turambar and he was hard put to it, and one man he slew, and it was Orlin. Then came Airin of the long hair in great fear into the halls and at her voice men stayed their hands; but great was her horror when she saw the deeds that were done, and Turambar turned his face away and might not look upon her, for his wrath was grown cold and he was sick and weary.

But she hearing the tale said: "Nay, grieve not for me, son of Úrin, but for thyself; for my lord was a hard lord and cruel and unjust, and men might say somewhat in thy defence, yet behold thou hast slain him now at his board being his guest, and Orlin thou hast slain who is of thy mother's kin; and what shall be thy doom?" At those words some were silent and many shouted "death", but Airin said that it was not wholly in accord with the laws of that place, "for," said she, "Brodda was slain wrongfully, yet just was the wrath of the slayer, and Orlin too did he slay in defence, though it were in the hall of a feast. Yet now I fear that this man must get him swiftly from among us nor ever set foot upon these lands again, else shall any man slay him; but those lands and goods that were Úrin's shall Brodda's kin hold, save only do Mavwin and Nienóri return ever from their wandering, yet even so may Túrin son of Úrin inherit nor part nor parcel of them ever." Now this doom seemed just to all save Turambar, and they marvelled at the equity of Airin whose lord lay slain, and they guessed not at the horror of her life aforetime with that man; but Turambar cast his sword upon the floor and bade them slay him, yet they would not for the words of Airin whom they loved, and Airin suffered it not for the love of Mavwin, hoping yet to join those twain mother and son in happiness, and her doom she had made to satisfy men's anger and save Túrin from death. "Nay," said she, "three days do I give thee to get thee out of the land, wherefore go!" and Turambar lifting his sword wiped it, saying: "Would I were clean of his blood," and he went forth into the night. In the folly of his heart now did he deem himself cut off in truth for ever from Mavwin his mother, thinking that never again would any he loved be fain to look upon him. Then did he thirst for news of his mother and sister and of none might he ask, but wandered back over the hills knowing only that they sought him still perchance in the forests of the Lands Beyond, and no more did he know for a long while.

Of his wanderings thereafter has no tale told, save that after much roaming his sorrow grew dulled and his heart dead, until at last in places very far away many a journey beyond the river of the Rodothlim he fell in with some huntsmen of the woods, and these were Men. Some of that company were thanes of Úrin, or sons of them, and they had wandered darkly ever since that Battle of Tears, but now did Turambar join their number, and built his life anew so well as he might. Now that people had houses in a more smiling region of the woods in lands that were not utterly far from Sirion or the grassy hills of that river's middle course, and they were hardy men and bowed not to Melko, and Turambar got honour among them.

Now is it to tell that far other had matters fallen out with Mavwin than the Foalókë had said to Túrin, for her days turning to better she had peace and honour among the men of those regions. Nonetheless her grief at the loss of her son by reason of the cutting off of all messengers deepened only with the years, albeit Nienóri grew to a most fair and slender maid. At the time of Túrin's flight from the halls of Tinwelint she was already twelve[17] years old and tall and beautiful.

Now the tale tells not the number of days that Turambar

sojourned with the Rodothlim but these were very many, and during that time Nienóri grew to the threshold of womanhood, and often was there speech between her and her mother of Túrin that was lost. In the halls of Tinwelint too the memory of Túrin lived still, and there still abode Gumlin, now decrepit in years, who aforetime had been the guardian of Túrin's childhood upon that first journey to the Lands Beyond. Now was Gumlin white-haired and the years were heavy on him, but he longed sorely for a sight once more of the folk of Men and of the Lady Mavwin his mistress. On a time then Gumlin learnt of the withdrawal from the hills of the greater number of those Orc-bands and other fierce beings of Melko's that had for so long made them impassable to Elves and Men. Now for a space were the hills and the paths that led over them far and wide free of his evil, for Melko had at that time a great and terrible project afoot, and that was the destruction of the Rodothlim and of many dwellings of the Gnomes beside, that his spies had revealed,[18] yet all the folk of those regions breathed the freer for a while, though had they known all perchance they had not done so.

Then Gumlin the aged fell to his knees before Tinwelint and begged that he suffer him to depart homeward, that he might see his mistress of old ere death took him to the halls of Mandos — if indeed that lady had not fared thither before him. Then the king[19] said yea, and for his journey he gave him two guides for the succouring of his age; yet those three, Gumlin and the woodland Elves, made a very hard journey, for it was late winter, and yet would Gumlin by no means abide until spring should come.

Now as they drew nigh to that region of Hisilómë where aforetime Mavwin had dwelt and nigh where she dwelt yet a great snow fell, as happened oft in those parts on days that should rather have been ones of early spring. Therein was Gumlin whelmed, and his guides seeking aid came unawares upon Mavwin's house, and calling for aid of her were granted it. Then by the aid of the folk of Mavwin was Gumlin found and carried to the house and warmed back to life, and coming to himself at length he knew Mavwin and was very joyful.

Now when he was in part healed he told his tale to Mavwin, and as he recounted the years and the doughtiest of the feats of Túrin she was glad, but great was her sorrow and dismay at the tidings of his sundering from Linwë[20] and the manner of it, and going from Gumlin she wept bitterly. Indeed for long and since ever she knew that Túrin, an he lived, had grown to manhood she had wondered that he sought not back to her, and often dread had filled her heart lest attempting this he had perished in the hills; but now the truth was bitter to bear and she was desolate for a great while, nor might Nienóri comfort her.

Now by reason of the unkindness of the weather those guides that had brought Gumlin out of Tinwelint's realms abode as her guests until spring came, but with spring's first coming Gumlin died.

Then arose Mavwin and going to several of the chiefs of those places she besought their aid, telling them the tale of Túrin's fate as Gumlin had told it to her. But some laughed, saying she was deceived by the babblings of a dying man, and the most said that she was distraught with grief, and that it would be a fool's counsel to seek beyond the hills a man who had been lost for years agone: "nor," said they, "will we lend man or horse to such a quest, for all our love for thee, O Mavwin wife of Úrin."

Then Mavwin departed in tears but railed not at them, for she had scant hope in her plea and knew that wisdom was in their words. Nonetheless being unable to rest she came now to those guides of the Elves, who chafed already to be away beneath the sun; and she said to them: "Lead me now to your lord," and they would dissuade her, saying that the road was no road for a woman's feet to tread; yet she did not heed them. Rather did she beg of her friend whose name was Airin Faiglindra* (long-tressed) and was wed to Brodda a lord of that region, and rich and powerful, that Nienóri might be taken under the guardianship of her husband and all her goods thereto. This did Airin obtain of Brodda without great pleading, and when she knew this she would take farewell of her daughter; but her plan availed little, for Nienóri stood before her mother and said: "Either thou goest not, O Mavwin my mother, or go we both," nor would anything turn her from those words. Therefore in the end did both mother and daughter make them ready for that sore journey, and the guides murmured much thereat. Yet it so happened that the season which followed that bitter winter was very kindly, and despite the forebodings of the guides the four passed the hills and made their long journey with no greater evils than hunger and thirst.

Coming therefore at length before Tinwelint Mavwin cast herself down and wept, begging pardon for Túrin and compassion and aid for herself and Nienóri; but Tinwelint bade her arise and

* In the margin is written *Firilanda*.

seat herself beside Gwedheling his queen, saying: "Long years ago was Túrin thy son forgiven, aye, even as he left these halls, and many a weary search have we made for him. No outlawry of mine was it that took him from this realm, but remorse and bitterness drew him to the wilds, and there, methinks, evil things o'ertook him, or an he lives yet I fear me it is in bondage to the Orcs." Then Mavwin wept again and implored the king to give her aid, for she said: "Yea verily I would fare until the flesh of my feet were worn away, if haply at the journey's end I might see the face of Túrin son of Úrin my well-beloved." But the king said that he knew not whither she might seek her son save in Angamandi, and thither he might not send any of his lieges, not though his heart were full of ruth for the sorrow of Úrin's folk. Indeed Tinwelint spoke but as he believed just, nor meant he to add to Mavwin's sorrow save only to restrain her from so mad and deadly a quest, but Mavwin hearing him spake no word more, and going from him went out into the woods and suffered no one to stay her, and only Nienóri followed her whithersoever she went.

Now the folk of Tinwelint looked with pity on those twain and with kindness, and secretly they watched them, and unbeknown kept much harm from them, so that the wandering ladies of the woods became familiar among them and dear to many, yet were they a sight of ruth, and folk swore hatred to Melko and his works who saw them pass. Thus came it that after many moons Mavwin fell in with a band of wandering Gnomes, and entering into discourse with them the tale was told to her of the Rodothlim, such as those Gnomes knew of it, and of the dwelling of Túrin among them. Of the whelming of that abode of folk by the hosts of Melko and by the dragon Glorund they told too, for those deeds were then new and their fame went far and wide. Now Túrin they named not by name, calling him Mormakil, a wild man who fled from the face of Tinwelint and escaped thereafter from the hands of the Orcs.

Then was the heart of Mavwin filled with hope and she questioned them more, but the Noldoli said that they had not heard that any came alive out of that ransacking save such as were haled to Angamandi, and then again was Mavwin's hope dashed low. Yet did she nonetheless get her back to the king's halls, and telling her tale besought his aid against the Foalókë. Now it was Mavwin's thought that perchance Túrin dwelt yet in the thraldom of the dragon and it might fall to them in some manner to liberate him, or again should the prowess of the king's men suffice then might they slay the worm in vengeance for his evils, and so at his death might he speak words of knowledge concerning the fate of Túrin, were he indeed no longer nigh the caverns of the Rodothlim. Of the mighty hoard that that worm guarded Mavwin recked little, but she spake much of it to Tinwelint, even as the Noldoli had spoken of it to her. Now the folk of Tinwelint were of the woodlands and had scant wealth, yet did they love fair and beauteous things, gold and silver and gems, as do all the Eldar but the Noldoli most of all; nor was the king of other mind in this, and his riches were small, save it be for that glorious Silmaril that many a king had given all his treasury contained if he might possess it.

Therefore did Tinwelint answer: "Now shalt thou have aid, O Mavwin most steadfast, and, openly I say it to thee, it is not for hope of freeing Túrin thereby that I grant it to thee, for such hope I do not see in this tale, but rather the death of hope. Yet it is a truth that I have need and desire of treasury, and it may be that such shall come to me by this venture; yet half of the spoil shalt thou have O Mavwin for the memory of Úrin and Túrin, or else shalt thou ward it for Nienóri thy daughter." Then said Mavwin: "Nay, give me but a woodman's cot and my son," and the king answered: "That I cannot, for I am but a king of the wild Elves, and no Vala of the western isles."

Then Tinwelint gathered a picked band of his warriors and hunters and told them his bidding, and it seemed that the name of the Foalókë was known already among them, and there were many who could guide the band unto the regions of his dwelling, yet was that name a terror to the stoutest and the places of his abode a land of accursed dread. Now the ancient dwellings of the Rodothlim were not utterly distant from the realm of Tinwelint, albeit far enough, but the king said to Mavwin: "Bide now and Nienóri also with me, and my men shall fare against the drake, and all that they do and find in those places will they faithfully report," – and his men said: "Yea, we will do thy bidding, O King," but fear stood in their eyes.

Then Mavwin seeing it said: "Yea, O King, let Nienóri my daughter bide indeed at the feet of Gwedheling the Queen, but I who care not an I die or live will go look upon the dragon and find my son"; and Tinwelint laughed, yet Gwedheling and Nienóri fearing that she spake no jest pled earnestly with her. But she was as adamant, fearing lest this her last hope of rescuing Túrin come to nought through the terror of Tinwelint's men, and none might move her. "Of love, I know," said she, "come all the words ye

speak, yet give me rather a horse to ride and if ye will a sharp knife
for my own death at need, and let me be gone." Now these words
struck amazement into those Elves that heard, for indeed the
wives and daughters of Men in those days were hardy and their
youth lasted a great span, yet did this seem a madness to all.

Madder yet did it seem when Nienóri, seeing the obstinacy of
her mother, said before them all: "Then I too will go; whither my
mother Mavwin goeth thither more easily yet shall I, Nienóri
daughter of Úrin, fare"; but Gwedheling said to the king that he
allow it not, for she was a fay and perchance foresaw dimly what
might be.

Then had Mavwin ended the dispute and departed from the
king's presence into the woods, had not Nienóri caught at her robe
and stayed her, and so did all plead with Mavwin, till at length it
was agreed that the king send a strong party against the Foalókë
and that Nienóri and Mavwin ride with them until the regions of
the beast be found. Then should they seek a high place whence
they might see something of the deeds yet in safety and secrecy,
while the warriors crept upon the worm to slay it. Now of this high
place a woodsman told, and often had he gazed therefrom upon
the dwelling of the worm afar. At length was that band of dragon-
slayers got ready, and they were mounted upon goodly horses
swift and sure-going, albeit few of those beasts were possessed by
the folk of the woods. Horses too were found for Nienóri and for
Mavwin, and they rode at the head of the warriors, and folk
marvelled much to see their bearing, for the men of Úrin and those
amongst whom Nienóri was nurtured were much upon horses,
and both knave and maid among them rode even in tender years.

After many days' going came now that cavalcade within view of
a place that once had been a fair region, and through it a swift river
ran over a rocky bed, and of one side was the brink of it high and
tree-grown and of the other the land was more level and fertile and
broad-swelling, but beyond the high bank of the river the hills
drew close. Thither as they looked they saw that the land had
become all barren and was blasted for a great distance about the
ancient caverns of the Rodothlim, and the trees were crushed to
the earth or snapped. Toward the hills a black heath stretched and
the lands were scored with the great slots that that loathly worm
made in his creeping.

Many are the dragons that Melko has loosed upon the world and
some are more mighty than others. Now the least mighty — yet
were they very great beside the Men of those days — are cold as is

the nature of snakes and serpents, and of them a many having wings go with the uttermost noise and speed; but the mightier are hot and very heavy and slow-going, and some belch flame, and fire flickereth beneath their scales, and the lust and greed and cunning evil of these is the greatest of all creatures: and such was the Foalókë whose burning there set all the places of his habitation in waste and desolation. Already greater far had this worm waxen than in the days of the onslaught upon the Rodothlim, and greater too was his hoarded treasure, for Men and Elves and even Orcs he slew, or enthralled that they served him, bringing him food to slake his lust [?on] precious things, and spoils of their harryings to swell his hoard.

Now was that band aghast as they looked upon that region from afar, yet they prepared them for battle, and drawing lots sent one of their number with Nienóri and Mavwin to that high place[21] upon the confines of the withered land that had been named, and it was covered with trees, and might be reached by hidden paths. Even as those three rode thither and the warriors crept stealthily toward the caves, leaving their horses that were already in a sweat of fear, behold the Foalókë came from his lair, and sliding down the bank lay across the stream, as often was his wont. Straightway great fog and steams leapt up and a stench was mingled therein, so that that band was whelmed in vapours and well-nigh stifled, and they crying to one another in the mist displayed their presence to the worm; and he laughed aloud. At that most awful of all sounds of beasts they fled wildly in the mists, and yet they could not discover their horses, for these in an extremity of terror broke loose and fled.

Then Nienóri hearing far cries and seeing the great mist roll toward them from the river turned back with her mother to the place of sundering, and there alighting waited in great doubt. Suddenly came that blind mist upon them as they stood, and with it came flying madly the dim horses of the huntsmen. Then their own catching their terror trampled to death that Elf who was their escort as he caught at the flying bridles, and wild with fear they sped to the dark woods and never more bore Man or Elf upon their saddles; but Mavwin and Nienóri were left alone and succourless upon the borders of the places of fear. Very perilous indeed was their estate, and long they groped in the mist and knew not where they were nor saw they ever any of the band again, and only pale voices seemed to pass them by afar crying out as in dread, and then all was silent. Now did they cling together and being weary stumbled on heedless whither their steps might go, till on a sudden the sun gleamed thin above them, and hope returned to them; and behold the mists lifted and the airs became clearer and they stood not far from the river. Even now it smoked as it were hot, and behold the Foalókë lay there and his eyes were upon them.

No word did he speak nor did he move, but his baleful eye held their gaze until the strength seemed to leave their knees and their minds grew dim. Then did Nienóri drag herself by a might of will from that influence for a while, and "Behold," she cried, "O serpent of Melko, what wilt thou with us – be swift to say or do, for know that we seek not thee nor thy gold but one Túrin who dwelt here upon a time." Then said the drake, and the earth quaked at him: "Thou liest – glad had ye been at my death, and glad thy band of cravens who now flee gibbering in the woods might they have despoiled me. Fools and liars, liars and cravens, how shall ye slay or despoil Glorund the Foalókë, who ere his power had waxen slew the hosts of the Rodothlim and Orodreth their lord, devouring all his folk."

"Yet perchance," said Nienóri, "one Túrin got him from that fray and dwells still here beneath thy bonds, an he has not escaped thee and is now far hence," and this she said at a venture, hoping against hope, but said the evil one: "Lo! the names of all who dwelt here before the taking of the caves of my wisdom I know, and I say to thee that none who named himself Túrin went hence alive." And even so was Túrin's boast subtly turned against him, for these beasts love ever to speak thus, doubly playing with cunning words.[22]

"Then was Túrin slain in this evil place," said Mavwin, but the dragon answered: "Here did the name of Túrin fade for ever from the earth – but weep not, woman, for it was the name of a craven that betrayed his friends." "Foul beast, cease thy evil sayings," said Mavwin; "slayer of my son, revile not the dead, lest thine own bane come upon thee." "Less proud must be thy words, O Mavwin, an thou wilt escape torment or thy daughter with thee," did that drake answer, but Mavwin cried: "O most accursed, lo! I fear thee not. Take me an thou wilt to thy torments and thy bondage, for of a truth I desired thy death, but suffer only Nienóri my daughter to go back to the dwellings of Men: for she came hither constrained by me, and knowing not the purposes of our journey."

"Seek not to cajole me, woman," sneered that evil one. "Liever would I keep thy daughter and slay thee or send thee back to thy hovels, but I have need of neither of you." With those words he opened full his evil eyes, and a light shone in them, and Mavwin and Nienóri quaked beneath them and a swoon came upon their minds, and them seemed that they groped in endless tunnels of darkness, and there they found not one another ever again, and calling only vain echoes answered and there was no glimmer of light.

When however after a time that she remembered not the blackness left the mind of Nienóri, behold the river and the withered places of the Foalókë were no more about her, but the deep woodlands, and it was dusk. Now she seemed to herself to awake from dreams of horror nor could she recall them, but their dread hung dark behind her mind, and her memory of all past things was dimmed. So for a long while she strayed lost in the woods, and haply the spell alone kept life in her, for she hungered bitterly and was athirst, and by fortune it was summer, for her garments became torn and her feet unshod and weary, and often she wept, and she went she knew not whither.

Now on a time in an opening in the wood she descried a campment as it were of Men, and creeping nigh by reason of hunger to espy it she saw that they were creatures of a squat and unlovely stature that dwelt there, and most evil faces had they, and their voices and their laughter was as the clash of stone and metal. Armed they were with curved swords and bows of horn, and she was possessed with fear as she looked upon them, although she knew not that they were Orcs, for never had she seen those evil ones before. Now did she turn and flee, but was espied, and one let fly a shaft at her that quivered suddenly in a tree beside her as she ran, and others seeing that it was a woman young and fair gave chase whooping and calling hideously. Now Nienóri ran as best she might for the density of the wood, but soon was she spent and capture and dread thraldom was very near, when one came crashing through the woods as though in answer to her lamentable cries.

Wild and black was his hair yet streaked with grey, and his face was pale and marked as with deep sorrows of the past, and in his hand he bare a great sword whereof all but the very edge was black. Therewith he leapt against the following Orcs and hewed them, and they soon fled, being taken aback, and though some shot arrows at random amidst the trees they did little scathe, and five of them were slain.

Then sat Nienóri upon a stone and for weariness and the

lessened strain of fear sobs shook her and she could not speak; but her rescuer stood beside her awhile and marvelled at her fairness and that she wandered thus lonely in the woods, and at length he said: "O sweet maiden of the woods, whence comest thou, and what may be thy name?"

"Nay, these things I know not," said she. "Yet methinks I stray very far from my home and folk, and many very evil things have fallen upon me in the way, whereof nought but a cloud hangs upon my memory — nay, whence I am or whither I go I know not" — and she wept afresh, but that man spake, saying: "Then behold, I will call thee Níniel, or little one of tears," and thereat she raised her face towards his, and it was very sweet though marred with weeping, and she said with a look of wonderment: "Nay, not Níniel, not Níniel." Yet more might she not remember, and her face filled with distress, so that she cried: "Nay, who art thou, warrior of the woods; why troublest thou me?" "Turambar am I called," said he, "and no home nor kindred have I nor any past to think on, but I wander for ever," and again at that name that maiden's wonder stirred.

"Now," said Turambar, "dry thy tears, O Níniel, for thou hast come upon such safety as these words afford. Lo, one am I now of a small folk of the forest, and a sweet dwelling in a clearing have we far from hence, but today as thy fortune would we fared a-hunting, — aye, and Orc-harrying too, for we are hard put to it to fend those evil ones from our homes."

Then did Níniel (for thus Turambar called her ever, and she learnt to call it her name) fare away with him to his comrades, and they asking little got them upon horses, and Turambar set Níniel before him, and thus they fared as swift as they might from the danger of the Orcs.

Now at the time of the affray of Turambar with the pursuing Orcs was half the day already spent, yet were they already leagues upon their way ere they dismounted once more, and it was then early night. Already at the sunset had it seemed to Níniel that the woods were lighter and less gloomy and the air less evil-laden than behind. Now did they make a camp in a glade and the stars shone clear above where the tree-roof was thin, but Níniel lay a little apart and they gave her many fells to keep her from the night chills, and thus she slept more softly than for many a night and the breezes kissed her face, but Turambar told his comrades of the meeting in the wood and they wondered who she might be or how she came wandering thither as one under a spell of blind forgetfulness.

Next day again they pressed on and so for many journeys more beside until at length weary and fain for rest they came one noon to a woodland stream, and this they followed for some way until, behold, they came to a place where it might be forded by reason of its shallowness and of the rocks that stood up in its course; but on their right it dived in a great fall and fell into a chasm, and Turambar pointing said: "Now are we nigh to home, for this is the fall of the Silver Bowl," but Níniel not knowing why was filled with a dread and could not look upon the loveliness of that foaming water. Now soon came they to places of thinner trees and to a slope whereon but few grew save here and there an ancient oak of great girth, and the grass about their feet was soft, for the clearing had been made many years and was very wide. There stood also a cluster of goodly houses of timber, and a tilth was about them and trees of fruit. To one of these houses that was adorned with strange rude carvings, and flowers bloomed bright about it, did Turambar lead now Níniel. "Behold," said he, "my abode–there an thou listest thou shalt abide for now, but methinks it is a lonely hall, and there be houses of this folk beside where there are maidens and womenfolk, and there wouldst thou liever and better be." So came it afterward that Nienóri dwelt with the wood-rangers,* and after a while entered the house of Bethos, a stout man who had fought though then but a boy in the Battle of Unnumbered Tears. Thence did he escape, but his wife was a Noldo-maiden, as the tale telleth, and very fair, and fair also were his sons and daughters save only his eldest son Tamar Lamefoot.

Now as the days passed Turambar grew to love Níniel very greatly indeed, and all the folk beside loved her for her great loveliness and sweetness, yet was she ever half-sorrowful and often distraught of mind, as one that seeks for something mislaid that soon she must discover, so that folk said: "Would that the Valar would lift the spell that lies upon Níniel." Nonetheless for the most part she was happy indeed among the folk and in the house of Bethos, and each day she grew ever fairer, and Tamar Lamefoot who was held of little account loved her though in vain.

Now came days when life once more seemed to contain joy to Turambar, and the bitterness of the past grew dim and far away, and a fresh love was in his heart. Then did he think to put his fate

---

* In the margin, apparently with reference to the word 'wood-rangers', is written Vettar.

for ever from him and live out his life there in the woodland homes
with children about him, and looking upon Níniel he desired to
wed her. Then did he often press his suit with her, yet though he
was a man of valiance and renown she delayed him, saying nor yea
nor no, yet herself she knew not why, for it seemed to her heart
that she loved him deeply, fearing for him were he away, and
knowing happiness when he was nigh.

Now it was a custom of that folk to obey a chief, and he was
chosen by them from their stoutest men, and that office did he
hold until of his own will he laid it down again being sick or gone in
years, or were he slain. And at that time Bethos was their chief;
but he was slain by evil luck in a foray not long after — for despite
his years he still rode abroad — and it fell out that a new captain
must be chosen. In the end then did they name Turambar, for his
lineage, in that it was known among them that he was son of Úrin,
was held in esteem among those stout rebels against Melko,
whereas[23] he had beside become a very mighty man in all deeds and
one of wisdom great beyond his years, by reason of his far wanderings and his dealings with the Elves.

Seeing therefore the love of their new chief for Níniel and
thinking they knew that she loved him also in return, those men
began to say how they would lief see their lord wed, and that it was
folly to delay for no good cause; but this word came to the ears of
Níniel, and at length she consented to be the wife of Turambar,
and all were fain thereat. A goodly feast was made and there was
song and mirth, and Níniel became lady of the woodland-rangers
and dwelt thereafter in Turambar's house. There great was their
happiness, though there lay at times a chill foreboding upon
Níniel's heart, but Turambar was in joy and said in his heart:
"'Twas well that I did name myself Turambar, for lo! I have
overcome the doom of evil that was woven about my feet." The
past he laid aside and to Níniel he spoke not overmuch of bygone
things, save of his father and mother and the sister he had not
seen, but always was Níniel troubled at such talk and he knew not
why.[24] But of his flight from the halls of Tinwelint and the death of
Beleg and of his seeking back to Hisilómë he said never a word,
and the thought of Failivrin lay locked in his deepest heart well-
nigh forgotten.

Naught ever might Níniel tell him of her days before, and did he
ask her distress was written on her face as though he troubled the
surface of dark dreams, and he grieved at times thereat, but it
weighed not much upon him.

Now fare the days by and Níniel and Turambar dwell in peace,
but Tamar Lamefoot wanders the woods thinking the world an ill
and bitter place, and he loved Níniel very greatly nor might he
stifle his love. But behold, in those days the Foalókë waxed fat,
and having many bands of Noldoli and of Orcs subject to him he
thought to extend his dominion far and wide. Indeed in many
places in those days these beasts of Melko's did in like manner,
setting up kingdoms of terror of their own that flourished beneath
the evil mantle of Melko's lordship. So it was that the bands of
Glorund the drake harried the folk of Tinwelint very grievously,
and at length there came some nigh even to those woods and glades
that were beloved of Turambar and his folk.

Now those woodmen fled not but dealt stoutly with their foes,
and the wrath of Glorund the worm was very great when tidings
were brought to him of a brave folk of Men that dwelt far beyond
the river and that his marauders might not subdue them. It is told
indeed that despite the cunning of his evil designs he did not yet
know where was the dwelling of Turambar or of Nienóri; and of
truth in those days it seemed that fortune smiled on Turambar
awhile, for his people waxed and they became prosperous, and
many escaped even from uttermost Hisilómë and came unto him,
and store of wealth and good things he gathered, for all his
battles brought him victory and booty. Like a king and queen did
Turambar and Níniel become, and there was song and mirth in
those glades of their dwelling, and much happiness in their halls.
And Níniel conceived.[25]

Much of this did spies report to the Foalókë, and his wrath was
terrible. Moreover his greed was mightily kindled, so that after
pondering much he set a guard that he might trust to watch his
dwelling and his treasury, and the captain of these was Mîm the
dwarf.[26] Then leaving the caves and the places of his sleep he
crossed the streams and drew into the woods, and they blazed
before his face. Tidings of this came swiftly to Turambar, but he
feared not as yet nor indeed heeded the tale much, for it was a very
great way from the home of the woodmen to the caverns of the
worm. But now sank Níniel's heart, and though she knew not
wherefore a weight of dread and sorrow lay upon her, and seldom
after the coming of that word did she smile, so that Turambar
wondered and was sad.

Now draweth the Foalókë during that time through the deep
woods and a path of desolation lies behind, and yet in his creeping
a very great while passes, until, behold, suddenly a party of the

woodmen come upon him unawares sleeping in the woods among the broken trees. Of these several were overcome by the noxious breath of the beast and after were slain; but two making their utmost speed brought tidings to their lord that the tale aforetime had not been vain, and indeed now was the drake crept even within the confines of his realm; and so saying they fell fainting before his feet.

Now the place where the dragon lay was low-lying and a little hill there was, not far distant, islanded among the trees but itself not much wooded, whence might be espied albeit afar off much of that region now torn by the passage of the drake. A stream there was too that ran through the forest in that part between the drake and the dwellings of the woodmen, but its course ran very nigh to the dragon and it was a narrow stream with banks deep-cloven and o'erhung with trees. Wherefore Turambar purposed now to take his stoutest men to that knoll and watch if they could the dragon's movements in secret, that perchance they might fall upon him at some disadvantage and contrive to slay him, for in this lay their best hope. This band he suffered not to be very great, and the rest at his bidding took arms and scoured about, fearing that hosts of the Orcs were come with the worm their lord. This indeed was not so, and he came alone trusting in his overwhelming power.

Now when Turambar made ready to depart then Níniel begged to ride beside him and he consented, for he loved her and it was his thought that if he fell and the drake lived then might none of that people be saved, and he would liever have Níniel by him, hoping perchance to snatch her at the least from the clutches of the worm, by death at his own or one of his liege's hands.

So rode forth together Turambar and Níniel, as that folk knew them, and behind were a score of good men. Now the distance to that knoll among the woods they compassed in a day's journey, and after them though it were against the bidding and counsel of Turambar there stole a great concourse of his folk, even women and children. The lure of a strange dread held them, and some thought to see a great fight, and others went with the rest thinking little, nor did any think to see what in the end their eyes saw; and they followed not far behind, for Turambar's party went slowly and warily. When first then Turambar suffered her to ride beside him Níniel was blither than for long she had been, and she brightened the foreboding of those men's hearts; but soon they came to a place not far from the foot of the knoll, and there her heart sank, and indeed a gloom fell upon all.

Yet very fair was that place, for here flowed that same stream that further down wound past the dragon's lair in a deep bed cloven deep into the earth; and it came rushing cold from the hills beyond the woodmen's homes, and it fell over a great fall where the water-worn rock jutted smooth and grey from amid the grass. Now this was the head of that force which the woodmen named the Silver Bowl, and aforetime Turambar and Níniel had passed it by, faring home first from the rescuing of Níniel. The height of that fall was very great and the waters had a loud and musical voice, splashing into a silver foam far below where they had worn a great hollow in the rocks; and this hollow was o'ershadowed by trees and bushes, but the sun gleamed through upon the spray; and about the head of the fall there was an open glade and a green sward where grew a wealth of flowers, and men loved that spot.

Here did Níniel of a sudden weep, and casting herself upon Turambar begged him tempt not fate but rather fly with her and all his folk, leading them into distant lands. But looking at her he said: "Nay, Níniel mine, nor thou nor I die this day, nor yet tomorrow, by the evil of the dragon or by the foemen's swords," but he knew not the fulfilment of his words; and hearing them Níniel quelled her weeping and was very still. Having therefore rested a while here those warriors afterward climbed the hill and Níniel fared with them. Afar off they might see from its summit a wide tract where all the trees were broken and the lands were hurt[27] and scorched and the earth black, yet nigh the edge of the trees that were still unharmed, and that was not far from the lip of the deep river-chasm, there arose a thin smoke of great blackness, and men said: "There lieth the worm."

Then were counsels of many a kind spoken upon that hill-top, and men feared to go openly against the dragon by day or by night or whether he waked or slept, and seeing their dread Turambar gave them a rede, and it was taken, and these were his words: "Well have ye said, O huntsmen of the woods, that not by day or by night shall men hope to take a dragon of Melko unawares, and behold this one hath made a waste about him, and the earth is beaten flat so that none may creep near and be hidden. Wherefore whoso hath the heart shall come with me and we will go down the rocks to the foot of the fall, and so gaining the path of the stream perchance we may come as nigh to the drake as may be. Then must we climb if we are able up under the near bank and so wait, for methinks the Foalókë will rest not much longer ere he draweth on towards our dwellings. Thus must he either cross this deep stream or turn far out of his ways, for he is grown too mighty to creep along its bed. Now I think not that he will turn aside, for it is but a ditch, a narrow rut filled with trickling water, to the great Foalókë of the golden caves. If however he belie my counsel and come not on by this path, some few of you must take courage in your hearts, striving to decoy him warily back across the stream, that there we who lie hid may give him his bane stabbing from beneath, for the armour of these vile worms is of little worth upon their bellies."

Now of that band were there but six that stood forward readily to go with Turambar, and he seeing that said that he had thought there were more than six brave men among his folk, yet after that he would not suffer any of the others to go with him, saying that better were the six without the hindrance of the fearful. Then did Turambar take farewell of Níniel and they kissed upon the hilltop, and it was then late afternoon, but Níniel's heart went as to stone with grief; and all that company descended to the head of Silver Bowl, and there she beheld her lord climb to the fall's bottom with his six companions. Now when he was vanished far below she spake bitterly to those who had dared not to go, and they for shame answered not but crept back unto the hill-top and gazed out towards the dragon's lair, and Níniel sat beside the water looking before her, and she wept not but was in anguish.

None stayed beside her save Tamar alone who had fared unbidden with that company, and he had loved her since first she dwelt in Bethos' halls, and once had thought to win her ere Turambar took her. The lameness of Tamar was with him from childhood, yet was he both wise and kindly, though held of little account among those folk, to whom strength was safety and valour the greatest pride of men. Now however did Tamar bear a sword, and many had scoffed at him for that, yet he took joy at the chance of guarding Níniel, albeit she noticed him not.

Now is it to tell that Turambar reached the place of his design after great labour in the rocky bed of the stream, and with his men clambered with difficulty up the steep side of that ravine. Just below the lip of it they were lodged in certain overhanging trees, and not far off they might hear the great breathing of the beast, and some of his companions fell in dread.

Already had darkness come and all the night they clung there, and there was a strange flickering where the dragon lay and dread noises and a quaking if he stirred, and when dawn came Turambar saw that he had but three companions, and he cursed the others for their cravenhood, nor doth any tale tell whither those unfaithful ones fled. On this day did all come to pass as Turambar had thought, for the drake bestirring himself drew slowly to the chasm's edge and turned not aside, but sought to overcreep it and come thus at the homes of the woodmen. Now the terror of his oncoming was very great, for the earth shook, and those three feared lest the trees that upheld them should loosen their roots and fall into the rocky stream below. The leaves too of those trees that grew nigh were shrivelled in the serpent's breath, yet were they not hurt because of the shelter of the bank.

At length did the drake reach the stream-edge and the sight of his evil head and dripping jaws was utterly hideous, and these they saw clearly and were in terror lest he too espy them, for he crossed not over at the spot where Turambar had chosen to lie hid because of the narrowness here of the chasm and its lesser depth. Rather he began to heave himself now across the ravine a little below them, and so slipping from their places Turambar and his men reached as swiftly as might be the stream's bed and came beneath the belly of the worm. Here was the heat so great and so vile the stench that his men were taken with a sore dread and durst not climb the bank again. Then in his wrath Turambar would have turned his sword against them, but they fled, and so was it that alone he scaled the wall until he came close beneath the dragon's body, and he reeled by reason of the heat and of the stench and clung to a stout bush.

Then abiding until a very vital and unfended spot was within stroke, he heaved up Gurtholfin his black sword and stabbed with all his strength above his head, and that magic blade of the Rodothlim went into the vitals of the dragon even to the hilt, and the yell of his death-pain rent the woods and all that heard it were aghast.

Then did that drake writhe horribly and the huge spires of his contortions were terrible to see, and all the trees he brake that stood nigh to the place of his agony. Almost had he crossed the chasm when Gurtholfin pierced him, and now he cast himself upon its farther bank and laid all waste about him, and lashed and coiled and made a yelling and a bellowing such that the stoutest blenched and turned to flee. Now those afar thought that this was the fearsome noise of battle betwixt the seven, Turambar and his comrades,[28] and little they hoped ever to see any of them return, and Níniel's heart died within her at the sounds; but below in the ravine those three cravens who had watched Turambar from afar fled now in terrror back towards the fall, and Turambar clung nigh to the lip of the chasm white and trembling, for he was spent.

At length did those noises of horror cease, and there arose a great smoking, for Glorund was dying. Then in utter hardihood did Turambar creep out alone from his hiding, for in the agony of the Foalókë his sword was dragged from his hand ere he might withdraw it, and he cherished Gurtholfin beyond all his possessions, for all things died, or man or beast, whom once its edges bit. Now Turambar saw where the dragon lay, and he was stretched out stiff upon his side, and Gurtholfin stood yet in his belly; but he breathed still.

Nonetheless Turambar creeping up set his foot upon his body and withdrew Gurtholfin hardly with all his strength, and as he did so he said in the triumph of his heart: "Now do we meet again, O Glorund, thou and I, Turambar, who was once named brave";[29] but even as he spake the evil blood spouted from that wound upon his hand and burnt it, and it was withered, so that for the sudden pain he cried aloud. Then the Foalókë opening his dread eyes looked upon him, and he fell in a swoon beside the drake and his sword was under him.

Thus did the day draw on and there came no tidings to the hill-top, nor could Níniel longer bear her anguish but arose and made as to leave that glade above the waterfall, and Tamar Lamefoot said: "What dost thou seek to do?" but she: "I would seek my lord and lay me in death beside him, for methinks he is dead", and he sought to dissuade her but without avail. And even as evening fell that fair lady crept through the woods and she would not that Tamar should follow her, but seeing that he did so she fled blindly through the trees, tearing her clothes and marring her face in places of thorny undergrowth, and Tamar being lame could not keep up with her. So fell night upon the woods and all was still, and a great dread for Níniel fell upon Tamar, so that he cursed his weakness and his heart was bitter, yet did he cease not to follow so swiftly as he might, and losing sight of her he bent his course towards that part of the forest nigh to the ravine where had been fought the worm's last fight, for indeed that might be perceived by the watchers on the hill. Now rose a bright moon when the night was old, and Tamar, wandering often alone far and wide from the woodmen's homes, knew those places, and came at last to the edge of that desolation that the dragon had made in his agony; but the moonlight was very bright, and staying among the bushes near the edge of that place Tamar heard and saw all that there betid.

Behold now Níniel had reached those places not long before

him, and straightway did she run fearless into the open for love of
her lord, and so found him lying with his withered hand in a swoon
across his sword; but the beast that lay hugely stretched beside she
heeded not at all, and falling beside Turambar she wept, and
kissed his face, and put salve upon his hand, for such she had
brought in a little box when first they sallied forth, fearing that
many hurts would be gotten ere men wended home.

Yet Turambar woke not at her touch, nor stirred, and she cried
aloud, thinking him now surely dead: "O Turambar, my lord,
awake, for the serpent of wrath is dead and I alone am near!" But
lo! at those words the drake stirred his last, and turning his baleful
eyes upon her ere he shut them for ever said: "O thou Nienóri
daughter of Mavwin, I give thee joy that thou hast found thy
brother at the last, for the search hath been weary – and now is he
become a very mighty fellow and a stabber of his foes unseen"; but
Nienóri sat as one stunned, and with that Glorund died, and with
his death the veil of his spells fell from her, and all her memory
grew crystal clear, neither did she forget any of those things that had
befallen her since first she fell beneath the magic of the worm; so
that her form shook with horror and anguish. Then did she start to
her feet, standing wanly in the moon, and looking upon Turambar
with wide eyes thus spake she aloud: "Then is thy doom spent at
last. Well art thou dead, O most unhappy," but distraught with
her woe suddenly she fled from that place and fared wildly away as
one mad whithersoever her feet led her.

But Tamar whose heart was numbed with grief and ruth followed
as he might, recking little of Turambar, for wrath at the fate of
Nienóri filled all his heart. Now the stream and the deep chasm lay
across her path, but it so chanced that she turned aside ere she
came to its banks and followed its winding course through stony
and thorny places until she came once again to the glade at the
head of the great roaring fall, and it was empty as the first grey
light of a new day filtered through the trees.

There did she stay her feet and standing spake as to herself: "O
waters of the forest whither do ye go? Wilt thou take Nienóri,
Nienóri daughter of Úrin, child of woe? O ye white foams, would
that ye might lave me clean – but deep, deep must be the waters
that would wash my memory of this nameless curse. O bear me
hence, far far away, where are the waters of the unremembering
sea. O waters of the forest whither do ye go?" Then ceasing
suddenly she cast herself over the fall's brink, and perished where
it foams about the rocks below; but at that moment the sun arose

above the trees and light fell upon the waters, and the waters roared unheeding above the death of Nienóri.

Now all this did Tamar behold, and to him the light of the new sun seemed dark, but turning from those places he went to the hill-top and there was already gathered a great concourse of folk, and among them were those three that had last deserted Turambar, and they made a story for the ears of the folk. But Tamar coming stood suddenly before them, and his face was terrible to see, so that a whisper ran among them: "He is dead"; but others said: "What then has befallen the little Níniel?" – but Tamar cried aloud: "Hear, O my people, and say if there is a fate like unto the one I tell unto thee, or a woe so heavy. Dead is the drake, but at his side lieth also Turambar dead, even he who was first called Túrin son of Úrin,[30] and that is well; aye very well," and folk murmured, wondering at his speech, and some said that he was mad. But Tamar said: "For know, O people, that Níniel the fair beloved of you all and whom I love dearer than my heart is dead, and the waters roar above her, for she has leapt o'er the falls of Silver Bowl desiring never more to see the light of day. Now endeth all that evil spell, now is the doom of the folk of Úrin terribly fulfilled, for she that ye called Níniel was even Nienóri daughter of Úrin, and this did she know or ever she died, and this did she tell to the wild woods, and their echo came to me."

At those words did the hearts of all who stood there break for sorrow and for dread, yet did none dare to go to the place of the anguish of that fair lady, for a sad spirit abideth there yet and none sets foot upon its sward; but a great remorse pierced the hearts of those three cravens, and creeping from the throng they went to seek their lord's body, and behold they found him stirring and alive, for when the dragon died the swoon had left him, and he slept a deep sleep of weariness, yet now was he awakening and was in pain. Even as those three stood by he spake and said "Níniel", and at that word they hid their faces for ruth and horror, and could not look upon his face, but afterward they roused him, and behold he was very fain of his victory; yet suddenly marking his hand he said: "Lo! one has been that has tended my hurt with skill – who think ye that it was?" – but they answered him not, for they guessed. Now therefore was Turambar borne weary and hurt back among his folk, and one sped before and cried that their lord lived, but men knew not if they were glad; and as he came among them many turned aside their faces to hide their hearts' perplexity and their tears, and none durst speak.

But Turambar said to those that stood nigh: "Where is Níniel, my Níniel – for I had thought to find her here in gladness – yet if she has returned rather to my halls then is it well", but those that heard could no longer restrain their weeping, and Turambar rose crying: "What new ill is this – speak, speak, my people, and torment me not!" But one said: "Níniel alas is dead my lord," but Turambar cried out bitterly against the Valar and his fate of woe, and at last another said: "Aye, she is dead, for she fell even into the depths of Silver Bowl," but Tamar who stood by muttered: "Nay, she cast herself thither." Then Turambar catching those words seized him by the arm and cried: "Speak, thou club-foot, speak, say what meaneth thy foul speech, or thou shalt lose thy tongue," for his misery was terrible to see.

Now was Tamar's heart in a great turmoil of pain for the dread things that he had seen and heard, and the long hopelessness of his love for Níniel, so did rage against Turambar kindle suddenly within him, and shaking off his touch he said: "A maid thou foundest in the wild woods and gave her a jesting name, that thou and all the folk called her Níniel, the little one of tears. Ill was that jest, Turambar, for lo! she has cast herself away blind with horror and with woe, desiring never to see thee again, and the name she named herself in death was Nienóri daughter of Úrin, child of woe, nor may all the waters of the Silver Bowl as they drop into the deep shed the full tale of tears o'er Níniel."

Then Turambar with a roar took his throat and shook him, saying: "Thou liest – thou evil son of Bethos" – but Tamar gasped "Nay, accursed one; so spake Glorund the drake, and Níniel hearing knew that it was true." But Turambar said: "Then go commune in Mandos with thy Glorund," and he slew him before the face of the people, and fared after as one mad, shouting "He lieth, he lieth"; and yet being free now of blindness and of dreams in his deep heart he knew that it was true and that now his weird was spent at last.

So did he leave the folk behind and drive heedless through the woods calling ever the name of Níniel, till the woods rang most dismally with that word, and his going led him by circuitous ways ever to the glade of Silver Bowl, and none had dared to follow him. There shone the sun of afternoon, and lo, were all the trees grown sere although it was high summer still, and noise there was as of dying autumn in the leaves. Withered were all the flowers and the grass, and the voice of the falling water was sadder than tears for the death of the white maiden Nienóri daughter of Úrin that there had been. There stood Turambar spent at last, and there he drew his sword, and said: "Hail, Gurtholfin, wand of death, for thou art all men's bane and all men's lives fain wouldst thou drink, knowing no lord or faith save the hand that wields thee if it be strong. Thee only have I now – slay me therefore and be swift, for life is a curse, and all my days are creeping foul, and all my deeds are vile, and all I love is dead." And Gurtholfin said: "That will I gladly do, for blood is blood, and perchance thine is not less sweet than many a one's that thou hast given me ere now"; and Turambar cast himself then upon the point of Gurtholfin, and the dark blade took his life.

But later some came timidly and bore him away and laid him in a place nigh, and raised a great mound over him, and thereafter some drew a great rock there with a smooth face, and on it were cut strange signs such as Turambar himself had taught them in dead days, bringing that knowledge from the caves of the Rodothlim, and that writing said:

> Turambar slayer of Glorund the Worm
> who also was Túrin Mormakil
> Son of Úrin of the Woods

and beneath that was carven the word "Níniel" (or child of tears); but she was not there, nor where the waters have laid her fair form doth any man know.'

Now thereupon did Eltas cease his speaking, and suddenly all who hearkened wept; but he said thereto: 'Yea, 'tis an unhappy tale, for sorrow hath fared ever abroad among Men and doth so still, but in the wild days were very terrible things done and suffered; and yet hath Melko seldom devised more cruelty, nor do I know a tale that is more pitiful.'

Then after a time some questioned him concerning Mavwin and Úrin and after happenings, and he said: 'Now of Mavwin hath no sure record been preserved like unto the tale of Túrin Turambar her son, and many things are said and some of them differ from one another; but this much can I tell to ye, that after those dread deeds the woodfolk had no heart for their abiding place and departed to other valleys of the wood, and yet did a few linger sadly nigh their old homes; and once came an aged dame wandering through the woods, and she chanced upon that carven rock. To her did one of those woodmen read the meaning of the signs, and he told her all the tale as he remembered it – but she was silent, and nor spoke nor moved. Then said he: "Thy heart is heavy, for it is a tale to move all men to tears." But she said: "Ay, sad indeed is my heart, for I am Mavwin, mother of those twain," and that man perceived that not yet had that long tale of sorrow reached its ending – but Mavwin arose and went out into the woods crying in anguish, and for long time she haunted that spot so that the woodman and his folk fled and came never back, and none may say whether indeed it was Mavwin that came there or her dark shade that sought not back to Mandos by reason of her great unhappiness.[31]

Yet it is said that all these dread happenings Úrin saw by the magic of Melko, and was continually tempted by that Ainu to yield to his will, and he would not; but when the doom of his folk was utterly fulfilled then did Melko think to use Úrin in another and more subtle way, and he released him from that high and bitter place where he had sat through many years in torment of heart. But Melko went to him and spoke evilly of the Elves to him, and especially did he accuse Tinwelint[32] of weakness and cravenhood. "Never can I comprehend," said he, "wherefore it is that there be still great and wise Men who trust to the friendship of the Elves, and becoming fools enough to resist my might do treble their folly in looking for sure help therein from Gnomes or Fairies. Lo, O Úrin, but for the faint heart of Tinwelint of the woodland how could my designs have come to pass, and perchance now had Nienóri lived and Mavwin thy wife had wept not, being glad for the recovery of her son. Go therefore, O foolish one, and return to eat the bitter bread of almsgiving in the halls of thy fair friends."

Then did Úrin bowed with years and sorrow depart unmolested from Melko's realms and came unto the better lands, but ever as he went he pondered Melko's saying and the cunning web of woven truth and falsity clouded his heart's eye, and he was very bitter in spirit. Now therefore he gathered to him a band of wild Elves,[33] and they were waxen a fierce and lawless folk that dwelt not with their kin, who thrust them into the hills to live or die as they might. On a time therefore Úrin led them to the caves of the Rodothlim, and behold the Orcs had fled therefrom at the death of Glorund, and one only dwelt there still, an old misshapen dwarf who sat ever on the pile of gold singing black songs of enchantment to himself. But none had come nigh till then to despoil him, for the terror of the drake lived longer than he, and none had ventured thither again for dread of the very spirit of Glorund the worm.[34] Now therefore when those Elves approached the dwarf stood before the doors of the cave that was once the abode of Galweg, and he cried: "What will ye with me, O outlaws of the hills?" But Úrin answered: "We come to take what is not thine." Then said that dwarf, and his name was Mîm: "O Úrin, little did I think to see thee, a lord of Men, with such a rabble. Hearken now to the words of Mîm the fatherless, and depart, touching not this gold no more than were it venomous fires. For has not Glorund lain long years upon it, and the evil of the drakes of Melko is on it, and no good can it bring to Man or Elf, but I, only I, can ward it, Mîm the dwarf, and by many a dark spell have I bound it to myself." Then Úrin wavered, but his men were wroth at that, so that he bid them seize it all, and Mîm stood by and watched, and he broke forth into terrible and evil curses. Thereat did Úrin smite him, saying: "We came but to take what was not thine – now for thy evil words we will take what is thine as well, even thy life."

But Mîm dying said unto Úrin: "Now Elves and Men shall rue this deed, and because of the death of Mîm the dwarf shall death follow this gold so long as it remain on Earth, and a like fate shall every part and portion share with the whole." And Úrin shuddered, but his folk laughed.

Now Úrin caused his followers to bear this gold to the halls of Tinwelint, and they murmured at that, but he said: "Are ye become as the drakes of Melko, that would lie and wallow in gold and seek no other joy? A sweeter life shall ye have in the court of that king of greed, an ye bear such treasury to him, than all the gold of Valinor can get you in the empty woods."

Now his heart was bitter against Tinwelint, and he desired to have a vengeance on him, as may be seen. So great was that hoard that great though Úrin's company might be scarce could they bear it to the caves of Tinwelint the king, and some 'tis said was left behind and some was lost upon the way, and evil has followed its finders for ever.

Yet in the end that laden host came to the bridge before the doors, and being asked by the guards Úrin said: "Say to the king that Úrin the Steadfast is come bearing gifts," and this was done. Then Úrin let bear all that magnificence before the king, but it was hidden in sacks or shut in boxes of rough wood; and Tinwelint greeted Úrin with joy and with amaze and bid him thrice welcome, and he and all his court arose in honour of that lord of Men; but Úrin's heart was blind by reason of his tormented years and of the lies of Melko, and he said: "Nay, O King, I do not desire to hear such words – but say only, where is Mavwin my wife, and knowest

thou what death did Nienóri my daughter die?" And Tinwelint
said that he knew not.

Then did Úrin fiercely tell that tale, and the king and all his folk
about him hid their faces for great ruth, but Úrin said: "Nay,[35] had
you such a heart as have the least of Men, never would they have
been lost; but lo, I bring you now a payment in full for the troubles
of your puny band that went against Glorund the drake, and
deserting gave up my dear ones to his power. Gaze, O Tinwelint,
sweetly on my gifts, for methinks the lustre of gold is all your heart
contains."

Then did men cast down that treasury at the king's feet, un-
covering it so that all that court were dazzled and amazed – but
Úrin's men understood now what was forward and were little
pleased. "Behold the hoard of Glorund," said Úrin, "bought by
the death of Nienóri with the blood of Túrin slayer of the worm.
Take it, O craven king, and be glad that some Men be brave to win
thee riches."

Then were Úrin's words more than Tinwelint could endure,
and he said: "What meanest thou, child of Men, and wherefore
upbraidest thou me?[36] Long did I foster thy son and forgave him
the evil of his deeds, and afterward thy wife I succoured, giving
way against my counsel to her wild desires. Melko it is that hates
thee and not I. Yet what is it to me – and wherefore dost thou of
the uncouth race of Men endure to upbraid a king of the Eldalië?
Lo! in Palisor my life began years uncounted before the first of
Men awoke. Get thee gone, O Úrin, for Melko hath bewitched
thee, and take thy riches with thee" – but he forebore to slay or to
bind Úrin in spells, remembering his ancient valiance in the
Eldar's cause.

Then Úrin departed, but would not touch the gold, and stricken
in years he reached Hisilómë and died among Men, but his words
living after him bred estrangement between Elves and Men. Yet it
is said that when he was dead his shade fared into the woods
seeking Mavwin, and long those twain haunted the woods about
the fall of Silver Bowl bewailing their children. But the Elves of
Kôr have told, and they know, that at last Úrin and Mavwin fared
to Mandos, and Nienóri was not there nor Túrin their son.
Turambar indeed had followed Nienóri along the black pathways
to the doors of Fui, but Fui would not open to them, neither
would Vefántur. Yet now the prayers of Úrin and Mavwin came
even to Manwë, and the Gods had mercy on their unhappy fate, so
that those twain Túrin and Nienóri entered into Fôs'Almir, the

bath of flame, even as Urwendi and her maidens had done in ages past before the first rising of the Sun, and so were all their sorrows and stains washed away, and they dwelt as shining Valar among the blessed ones, and now the love of that brother and sister is very fair; but Turambar indeed shall stand beside Fionwë in the Great Wrack, and Melko and his drakes shall curse the sword of Mormakil.'

And so saying Eltas made an end, and none asked further.

NOTES

1 The passage was rejected before the change of *Tintoglin* to *Tinwelint*; see p. 69.

2 Above the name *Egnor* is written 'Damrod the Gnome'; see Commentary, pp. 139–40.

3 Here and immediately below the name as first written was *Tinthellon*; this rider must belong to the same time as the note on the MS directing that *Tintoglin* be changed to *Ellon* or *Tinthellon* (p. 69). See note 32.

4 Associated with this replacement is a note on the manuscript reading: 'If Beren be a Gnome (as now in the story of Tinúviel) the references to Beren must be altered.' In the rejected passage Egnor father of Beren 'was akin to Mavwin', i.e. Egnor was a Man. See notes 5 and 6, and the Commentary, p. 139.

5 'Túrin son of Úrin': original reading 'Beren Ermabwed'. See notes 4 and 6.

6 Original reading 'and when also the king heard of the kinship between Mavwin and Beren'. See notes 4 and 5.

7 *Linwë (Tinto)* was the king's original 'Elvish' name, and belongs to the same 'layer' of names as *Tintoglin* (see I.115, 131). Its retention here (not changed to *Tinwë*) is clearly a simple oversight. See notes 19 and 20.

8 Original reading 'seeing that he was a Man of great size'.

9 With this passage cf. that in the *Tale of Tinúviel* p. 11, which is closely similar. That the passage in *Turambar* is the earlier (to be presumed in any case) is shown by the fact that that in *Tinúviel* is only relevant if Beren is a Gnome, not a Man (see note 4).

10 'dreams came to them': original reading 'dreams the Valar sent to them'.

11 'and his name was Glorund' was added later, as were the subsequent occurrences of the name on pp. 86, 94, 98; but from the first on p. 103 onwards *Glorund* appears in the manuscript as first written.

12 'with the aid of Flinding whose wounds were not great': original reading 'with the aid of a lightly wounded man'. All the subsequent references to Flinding in this passage were added.

13   Original reading 'Túrin's heart was bitter, and so it was that he and
     that other alone returned from that battle'. – In the phrase 'reproach-
     ing Túrin that he had ever withstood his wise counsels' 'ever' means
     'always': Túrin had always resisted Orodreth's counsels.

14   Original reading 'although all folk at that time held such a deed
     grievous and cowardly'.

15   Original reading 'and to look upon Nienóri again'. This was emended
     to 'and to look upon Nienóri whom he had never seen'. The words
     'since his first days' were added still later.

16   The following passage was struck out, apparently at the time of
     writing:

>   "Indeed," said they, "it is the report of men of travel and rangers
>   of the hills that for many and many moons have even the farthest
>   marches been free of them and unwonted safe, and so have many
>   men fared out of Hisilómë to the Lands Beyond." And this was
>   the truth that during the life of Turambar as an exile from the
>   court of Tintoglin or hidden amongst the Rothwarin Melko had
>   troubled Hisilómë little and the paths thereto.

     (*Rothwarin* was the original form throughout, replaced later by
     Rodothlim.) See p. 92, where the situation described in the rejected
     passage is referred to the earlier time (before the destruction of the
     Rodothlim) when Mavwin and Nienóri left Hisilómë.

17   Original reading 'twice seven'. When Túrin fled from the land of
     Tinwelint it was exactly 12 years since he had left his mother's house
     (p. 75), and Nienóri was born before that, but just how long before
     is not stated.

18   After 'a great and terrible project afoot' the original reading was 'the
     story of which entereth not into this tale'. I do not know whether this
     means that when my father first wrote here of Melko's 'project' he
     did not have the destruction of the Rodothlim in mind.

19   'the king': original reading 'Linwë'. See note 7.

20   *Linwë*: an oversight. See note 7.

21   'that high place': original reading 'a hill'.

22   This sentence, 'And even so was Túrin's boast . . .', was added in
     pencil later. The reference is to Túrin's naming himself *Turambar* –
     'from this hour shall none name me Túrin if I live', p. 86.

23   This sentence, from 'for his lineage . . .' to approximately this point,
     is very lightly struck through. On the opposite page of the MS is
     hastily scribbled: 'Make Turambar never tell new folk of his lineage
     (will bury the past) – this avoids chance (as cert.) of Níniel hearing
     his lineage from any.' See Commentary, p. 131.

24   Against this sentence there is a pencilled question-mark in the
     margin. See note 23 and the Commentary, p. 131.

25   'And Níniel conceived' was added in pencil later. See Commentary,
     p. 135.

26 'and the captain of these was Mîm the dwarf' added afterwards in pencil. See Commentary p. 137.

27 The word *tract* may be read as *track*, and the word *hurt* (but with less probability) as *burnt*.

28 As it stands this sentence can hardly mean other than that the people thought that the men were fighting among themselves; but why should they think such a thing? More likely, my father inadvertently missed out the end of the sentence: 'betwixt the seven, Turambar and his comrades, and the dragon.'

29 Turambar refers to Glorund's words to him before the caves of the Rodothlim: 'O Túrin Mormakil, who wast once named brave' (p. 86).

30 These words, from 'even he who . . .', were added later in pencil. *Úrin* may also be read as *Húrin*.

31 From this point to the end of Eltas' tale the original text was struck through, and is followed in the manuscript book by two brief narrative outlines, these being rejected also. The text given here (from 'Yet it is said . . .') is found on slips placed in the book. For the rejected material see the Commentary, pp. 135–7.

32 Throughout the final portion of the text (that written on slips, see note 31) the king's name was first written *Tinthellon*, not *Tintoglin* (see note 3).

33 'Elves': original reading 'men'. The same change was made below ('Now therefore when those Elves approached'), and a little later 'men' was removed in two places ('his folk laughed', 'Úrin caused his followers to bear the gold', p. 114); but several occurrences of 'men' were retained, possibly through oversight, though 'men' is used of Elves very frequently in the *Tale of Turambar* (e.g. 'Beleg and Flinding both stout men', p. 80).

34 This sentence, from 'But none had come nigh . . .', was added later in pencil.

35 This sentence, from 'Then did Úrin fiercely . . .', was added later, replacing 'Then said Úrin: "Yet had you such a heart . . ."'

36 This sentence, from "What meanest thou . . .", replaces the original reading "Begone, and take thy filth with thee."

Changes made to names in
The Tale of Turambar

Fuithlug < *Fothlug* < *Fothlog*
Nienóri At the first occurrence (p. 71) my father originally wrote *Nyenòre (Nienor)*. Afterwards he struck out *Nyenòre*, removed the brackets round *Nienor*, and added *-i*, giving *Nienori*. At subsequent occurrences the name was written both *Nienor* and

Nienóri, but *Nienor* was changed to *Nienóri* later throughout the earlier part of the tale. Towards the end, and in the text written on slips that concludes it, the form is *Nienor*. I have given *Nienóri* throughout.

Tinwelint < *Tinthellon* (p. 72, twice). See p. 69 and note 3. *Tinwelint* < *Tinthellon* also in the concluding portion of the text, see note 32.

Tinwelint < *Tintoglin* throughout the tale, except as just noted (where *Tinwelint* < *Tinthellon* in passages added later); see p. 69.

Gwedheling < *Gwendeling* at all occurrences (*Gwendeling* unchanged at p. 76, but this is obviously an oversight: I read *Gwedheling* in the text). In the Gnomish dictionary the form *Gwendeling* was changed to *Gwedhiling*; see p. 50.

Flinding bo-Dhuilin < *Flinding go-Dhuilin* This change, made at the occurrence on p. 78, was not made at p. 82, but this was clearly because the form was missed, and I read *bo-Dhuilin* in both cases; the same change from *go-* to *bo-* in the *Tale of Tinúviel*, see p. 51. The form *Dhuilin* is taken by the name when the patronymic is prefixed (cf. *Duilin* p. 79).

Rodothlim < *Rothwarin* at every occurrence.

Gurtholfin < *Gortholfin* at the first occurrences, but from p. 90 *Gurtholfin* was the form first written.

Commentary on
The Tale of Turambar

§1. *The primary narrative*

In commenting on this long tale it is convenient to break it into short sections. In the course of this commentary I frequently refer to the long (though incomplete) prose narrative, the *Narn i Hîn Húrin*, given in *Unfinished Tales* pp. 57 ff., often in preference to the briefer account in *The Silmarillion*, chapter XXI; and in reference to the former I cite '*Narn*' and the page-number in *Unfinished Tales*.

(i) *The capture of Úrin and Túrin's childhood in Hisilómë* (pp. 70–2).

At the outset of the tale, it would be interesting to know more of the teller, Eltas. He is a puzzling figure: he seems to be a Man (he says that 'our people' called Turambar *Turumart* 'after the fashion of the Gnomes') living in Hisilómë after the days of Turambar but before the fall of Gondolin, and he 'trod Olórë Mallë', the Path of Dreams. Is he then a child, one of 'the children of the fathers of the fathers of Men', who 'found Kôr and remained with the Eldar for ever' (*The Cottage of Lost Play*, I.19–20)?

The opening passage agrees in almost all essentials with the ultimate form of the story. Thus there go back to the beginning of the 'tradition' (or at least to its earliest extant form) the departure of Húrin to the Battle of Unnumbered Tears at the summons of the Noldor, while his wife (Mavwin = Morwen) and young son Túrin remained behind; the great stand of Húrin's men, and Húrin's capture by Morgoth; the reason for Húrin's torture (Morgoth's wish to learn the whereabouts of Turgon) and the mode of it, and Morgoth's curse; the birth of Nienor shortly after the great battle.

That Men were shut in Hisilómë (or Hithlum, the Gnomish form, which here first appears, equated with Dor Lómin, p. 71) after the Battle of Unnumbered Tears is stated in *The Coming of the Elves* (I.118) and in the last of the outlines for *Gilfanon's Tale* (I.241); later on this was transformed into the confinement of the treacherous Easterling Men in Hithlum (*The Silmarillion* p. 195), and their ill-treatment of the survivors of the House of Hador became an essential element in the story of Túrin's childhood. But in the *Tale of Turambar* the idea is already present that 'the strange men who dwelt nigh knew not the dignity of the Lady Mavwin'. It is not in fact clear where Úrin dwelt: it is said here that after the battle 'Mavwin got her in tears into the land of Hithlum or Dor Lómin where all Men must now dwell', which can only mean that she went there, on account of Melko's command, from wherever she had dwelt with Úrin before; on the other hand, a little later in the tale (p. 73), and in apparent contradiction to this, Mavwin would not accept the invitation of Tinwelint to come to Artanor partly because (it is suggested) 'she clung to that dwelling that Úrin had set her in *ere he went to the great war*'.

In the later story Morwen resolved to send Túrin away from fear that he would be enslaved by the Easterlings (*Narn* p. 70), whereas here all that is said is that Mavwin 'knew not in her distress how to foster both him and his sister' (which presumably reflects her poverty). This in turn reflects a further difference, namely that here Nienóri was born before Túrin's departure (but see p. 131); in the later legend he and his companions left Dor-lómin in the autumn of the Year of Lamentation and Nienor was born early in the following year – thus he had never seen her, even as an infant.

An important underlying difference is the absence in the tale of the motive that Húrin had himself visited Gondolin, a fact known to Morgoth and the reason for his being taken alive (*The Silmarillion* pp. 158–9, 196–7); this element in the story arose much later, when the founding of Gondolin was set far back and long before the Battle of Unnumbered Tears.

(ii)   *Túrin in Artanor* (pp. 72–6)

From the original story of Túrin's journey the two old men who accom-

panied him, one of whom returned to Mavwin while the older remained
with Túrin, were never lost; and the cry of Túrin as they set out
reappears in the *Narn* (p. 73): 'Morwen, Morwen, when shall I see you
again?'

Beleg was present from the beginning, as was the meaning of his name:
'he was called Beleg *for* he was of great stature' (see I.254, entry *Haloisi
velikë*, and the Appendix to *The Silmarillion*, entry *beleg*); and he
plays the same rôle in the old story, rescuing the travellers starving in the
forest and taking them to the king.

In the later versions there is no trace of the remarkable message sent by
Tinwelint to Mavwin, and indeed his curiously candid explanation, that
he held aloof from the Battle of Unnumbered Tears because in his
wisdom he foresaw that Artanor could become a refuge if disaster befell,
is hardly in keeping with his character as afterwards conceived. There
were of course quite other reasons for his conduct (*The Silmarillion*
p. 189). On the other hand, Mavwin's motives for not herself leaving
Hithlum remained unchanged (see the passage in the *Narn*, p. 70, where
the word 'almsguest' is an echo of the old tale); but the statement is
puzzling that Mavwin might, when Nienóri was grown, have put aside
her pride and passed over the mountains, had they not become impassable
– clearly suggesting that she never left Hithlum. Perhaps the meaning is,
however, that she might have made the journey *earlier* (while Túrin was
still in Artanor) than she in fact did (when for a time the ways became
easier, but Túrin had gone).

The character of Túrin as a boy reappears in every stroke of the
description in the *Narn* (p. 77):

> It seemed that fortune was unfriendly to him, so that often what he
> designed went awry, and what he desired he did not gain; neither did
> he win friendship easily, for he was not merry, and laughed seldom,
> and a shadow lay on his youth.

(It is a notable point that is added in the tale: 'at no time did he give
much heed to words that were spoken to him'). And the ending of all
word between Túrin and his mother comes about in the same way –
increased guard on the mountains (*Narn* p. 78).

While the story of Túrin and Saeros as told in *The Silmarillion*, and in
far more detail in the *Narn*, goes back in essentials to the *Tale of
Turambar*, there are some notable differences – the chief being that as
the story was first told Túrin's tormentor was slain outright by the
thrown drinking-cup. The later complications of Saeros' treacherous
assault on Túrin the following day and his chase to the death, of the trial
of Túrin in his absence for this deed and of the testimony of Nellas (this
last only in the *Narn*) are entirely absent, necessarily; nor does Mablung
appear – indeed it seems clear that Mablung first emerged at the end of
the *Tale of Tinúviel* (see p. 59). Some details survived (as the comb

which Orgof/Saeros offered tauntingly to Túrin, *Narn* p. 80), while others were changed or neglected (as that it was the anniversary of Túrin's departure from his home − though the figure of twelve years agrees with the later story, and that the king was present in the hall, contrast *Narn* p. 79). But the taunt that roused Túrin to murderous rage remained essentially the same, in that it touched on his mother; and the story was never changed that Túrin came into the hall tousled and roughly clad, and that he was mocked for this by his enemy.

Orgof is not greatly distinct from Saeros, if less developed. He was in the king's favour, proud, and jealous of Túrin; in the later story he was a Nandorin Elf while here he is an Ilkorin with some Gnomish blood (for Gnomes in Artanor see p. 65), but doubtless some peculiarity in his origin was part of the 'tradition'. In the old story he is explicitly a fop and a fool, and he is not given the motives of hatred for Túrin that are ascribed to him in the *Narn* (p. 77).

Though far simpler in narrative, the essential element of Túrin's ignorance of his pardon was present from the outset. The tale provides an explanation, not found later, of why Túrin did not, on leaving Artanor, return to Hithlum; cf. the *Narn* p. 87: 'to Dor-lómin he did not dare, for it was closely beset, and one man alone could not hope at that time, as he thought, to come through the passes of the Mountains of Shadow.'

Túrin's prowess against the Orcs during his sojourn in Artanor is given a more central or indeed unique importance in the tale ('he held the wrath of Melko from them for many years') especially as Beleg, his companion-in-arms in the later versions, is not here mentioned (and in this passage the power of the queen to withstand invasion of the kingdom seems again (see p. 63) less than it afterwards became).

(iii)   *Túrin and Beleg* (pp. 76–81)

That part of the Túrin saga following on his days in Artanor/Doriath underwent a large development later ('Túrin among the Outlaws'), and indeed my father never brought this part of the story to finality. In the oldest version there is a much more rapid development of the plot: Beleg joins Túrin's band, and the destruction of the band and capture of Túrin by the Orcs follows (in terms of the narrative) almost immediately. There is no mention of 'outlaws' but only of 'wild spirits', no long search for Túrin by Beleg, no capture and maltreatment of Beleg by the band, and no betrayal of the camp by a traitor (the part ultimately taken by Mîm the Dwarf). Beleg indeed (as already noticed) is not said to have been Túrin's companion in the earlier time, before the slaying of Orgof, and they only take up together after Túrin's self-imposed exile.

Beleg is called a Noldo (p. 78), and if this single reference is to be given full weight (and there seems no reason not to: it is explicit in the *Tale of Tinúviel* that there were Noldoli in Artanor, and Orgof had Gnomish blood) then it is to be observed that Beleg as originally conceived was an Elf of Kôr. He is not here marked out as a great bowman (neither his name Cúthalion 'Strongbow' nor his great bow Belthronding appear); he is described at his first appearance (p. 73) as 'a wood-ranger, a huntsman of the secret Elves', but not as the chief of the marchwardens of the realm.

But from the capture of Túrin to the death of Beleg the old tale was scarcely changed afterwards in any really important respect, though altered in many details: such as Beleg's shooting of the wolf-sentinels silently in the darkness in the later story, and the flash of lightning that illuminated Beleg's face – but the blue-shining lamps of the Noldor appear again in much later writings: one was borne by the Elves Gelmir and Arminas who guided Tuor through the Gate of the Noldor on his journey to the sea (see *Unfinished Tales* pp. 22, 51 note 2). In my father's painting (probably dating from 1927 or 1928) of the meeting between Beleg and Flinding in Taur-nu-Fuin (reproduced in *Pictures by J. R. R. Tolkien*, no. 37) Flinding's lamp is seen beside him. The plot of the old story is very precisely contrived in such details as the reason for the carrying of Túrin, still sleeping, out of the Orc-camp, and for Beleg's using his sword, rather than a knife, to cut Túrin's bonds; perhaps also in the crushing of Beleg by Túrin so that he was winded and could not speak his name before Túrin gave him his death-blow.

The story of Túrin's madness after the slaying of Beleg, the guidance of Gwindor, and the release of Túrin's tears at Eithel Ivrin, is here in embryo. Of the peculiar nature of Beleg's sword there is no suggestion.

(iv)   *Túrin among the Rodothlim; Túrin and Glorund* (pp. 81–8)

In this passage is found (so far as written record goes, for it is to be remembered that a wholly erased text underlies the manuscript) the origin of Nargothrond, as yet unnamed. Among many remarkable features the chief is perhaps that Orodreth was there before Felagund, Lord of Caves, with whom in the later legend Nargothrond was identified, as its founder and deviser. (In *The Silmarillion* Orodreth was one of Finrod Felagund's brothers (the sons of Finarfin), to whom Felagund gave the command of Minas Tirith on Tol Sirion after the making of Nargothrond (p. 120), and Orodreth became King of Nargothrond after Felagund's death.) In the tale this cave-dwelling of exiled Noldoli is a simpler and rougher place, and (as is suggested) short-lived against the overwhelming power of Melko; but, as so often, there were many features that were never altered, even though in a crucial respect the history of Nargothrond was to be greatly modified by contact with the legend of Beren and Tinúviel. Thus the site was from the start 'above a stream' (the later Narog) that 'ran down to feed the river Sirion', and as is seen later (p. 96) the bank of the river on the side of the caves was higher and the hills drew close: cf. *The Silmarillion* p. 114: 'the caves under the

High Faroth in its steep western shore'. The policy of secrecy and refusal of open war pursued by the Elves of Nargothrond was always an essential element (cf. *The Silmarillion* pp. 168, 170),* as was the overturning of that policy by the confidence and masterfulness of Túrin (though in the tale there is no mention of the great bridge that he caused to be built). Here, however, the fall of the redoubt is perhaps more emphatically attributed to Túrin, his coming there seen more simply as a curse, and the disaster as more inevitably proceeding from his unwisdom: at least in the fragments of this part of the *Narn* (pp. 155–7) Túrin's case against Gwindor, who argued for the continuation of secrecy, is seemingly not without substance, despite the outcome. But the essential story is the same: Túrin's policy revealed Nargothrond to Morgoth, who came against it with overwhelming strength and destroyed it.

In relation to the earliest version the roles of Flinding (Gwindor), Failivrin (Finduilas),† and Orodreth were to undergo a remarkable set of transferences. In the old tale Flinding had been of the Rodothlim before his capture and imprisonment in Angband, just as afterwards Gwindor came from Nargothrond (but with a great development in his story, see *The Silmarillion* pp. 188, 191–2), and on his return was so changed as to be scarcely recognisable (I pass over such enduring minor features as the taking of Túrin and Flinding/Gwindor prisoner on their coming to the caves). The beautiful Failivrin is already present, and her unrequited love for Túrin, but the complication of her former relation with Gwindor is quite absent, and she is not the daughter of Orodreth the King but of one Galweg (who was to disappear utterly). Flinding is not shown as opposed to Túrin's policies; and in the final battle he aids Túrin in bearing Orodreth out of the fight. Orodreth dies (after being carried back to the caves) reproaching Túrin for what he has brought to pass – as does Gwindor dying in *The Silmarillion* (p. 213), with the added bitterness of his relation with Finduilas. But Failivrin's father Galweg is slain in the battle, as is Finduilas' father Orodreth in *The Silmarillion*. Thus in the evolution of the legend Orodreth took over the rôle of Galweg, while Gwindor took over in part the rôle of Orodreth.

As I have noticed earlier, there is no mention in the tale of any peculiarity attaching to Beleg's sword, and though the Black Sword is already present it was made for Túrin on the orders of Orodreth, and its blackness and its shining pale edges were of its first making (see *The Silmarillion* pp. 209–10). Its power of speech ('it is said that at times it spake dark words to him') remained afterwards in its dreadful words to Túrin before his death (*Narn* p. 145) – a motive that appears already

---

* From the first of these passages it seems that when Beren came to Nargothrond the 'secret' policy was already pursued under Felagund; but from the second it seems that it came into being from the potent rhetoric of Curufin after Beren went there.

† In *The Silmarillion* she is named Finduilas, and the name Faelivrin 'which is the gleam of the sun on the pools of Ivrin' was given to her by Gwindor (pp. 209–10).

in the tale, p. 112; and Túrin's name derived from the sword (here *Mormagli*, *Mormakil*, later *Mormegil*) was already devised. But of Túrin's disguising of his true name in Nargothrond there is no suggestion: indeed it is explicitly stated that he said who he was.

Of Gelmir and Arminas and the warning they brought to Nargothrond from Ulmo (*Narn* pp. 159–62) the germ can perhaps be seen in the 'whispers in the stream at eve', which undoubtedly implies messages from Ulmo (see p. 77).

The dragon Glorund is named in the 'lengthening spell' in the *Tale of Tinúviel* (pp. 19, 46), but the actual name was only introduced in the course of the writing of the *Tale of Turambar* (see note 11). There is no suggestion that he had played any previous part in the history, or indeed that he was the first of his kind, the Father of Dragons, with a long record of evil already before the Sack of Nargothrond. Of great interest is the passage in which the nature of the dragons of Melko is defined: their evil wisdom, their love of lies and gold (which 'they may not use or enjoy'), and the knowledge of tongues that Men say would come from eating a dragon's heart (with evident reference to the legend in the Norse Edda of Sigurd Fafnisbane, who was enabled to understand, to his own great profit, the speech of birds when he ate the heart of the dragon Fafnir, roasting it on a spit).

The story of the sack of Nargothrond is somewhat differently treated in the old story, although the essentials were to remain of the driving away of Failivrin/Finduilas among the captives and of the powerlessness of Túrin to aid her, being spellbound by the dragon. Minor differences (such as the later arrival of Glorund on the scene: in *The Silmarillion* Túrin only came back to Nargothrond after Glaurung had entered the caves and the sack was 'well nigh achieved') and minor agreements (such as the denial of the plunder to the Orcs) may here be passed over; most interesting is the account of Túrin's words with the dragon. Here the whole issue of Túrin's escaping or not escaping his doom is introduced, and it is significant that he takes the name *Turambar* at this juncture, whereas in the later legend he takes it when he joins the Woodmen in Brethil, and less is made of it. The old version is far less powerfully and concisely expressed, and the dragon's words are less subtle and ingeniously untrue. Here too the moral is very explicitly pointed, that Túrin *should not* have abandoned Failivrin 'in danger that he himself could see' – does this not suggest that, even under the dragon's spell as he was, there was a weakness (a 'blindness', see p. 83) in Túrin which the dragon touched? As the story is told in *The Silmarillion* the moral would seem uncalled for: Túrin was opposed by an adversary too powerful for his mind and will.

There is here a remarkable passage in which suicide is declared a sin, depriving such a one of all hope 'that ever his spirit would be freed from the dark glooms of Mandos or stray into the pleasant paths of Valinor'. This seems to go with the perplexing passage in the tale of *The Coming of the Valar and the Building of Valinor* concerning the fates of Men: see p. 60.

Finally, it is strange that in the old story the gold and treasure was carried out from the caves by the Orcs and remained there (it 'lay by the caves above the stream'), and the dragon most uncharacteristically 'slept before it' in the open. In *The Silmarillion* Glaurung 'gathered all the hoard and riches of Felagund and heaped them, and lay upon them in the innermost hall'.

(v)   *Túrin's return to Hithlum* (pp. 88–91)

In this passage the case is much as in previous parts of the tale: the large structure of the story was not greatly changed afterwards, but there are many important differences nonetheless.

In the *Tale of Turambar* it is clear that the house of Mavwin was not imagined as standing near to the hills or mountains that formed the barrier between Hithlum and the Lands Beyond: Túrin was told that never did Orcs 'come hither deep into the land of Hisilómë', in contrast to the *Narn* (p. 68), where 'Húrin's house stood in the south-east of Dor-lómin, and the mountains were near; Nen Lalaith indeed came down from a spring under the shadow of Amon Darthir, over whose shoulder there was a steep pass'. The removal of Mavwin from one house to another in Hithlum, visited in turn by Túrin as he sought for her, was afterwards rejected, to the improvement of the story. Here Túrin comes back to his old home in the late summer, whereas in *The Silmarillion* the fall of Nargothrond took place in the late autumn ('the leaves fell from the trees in a great wind as they went, for the autumn was passing to a dire winter,' p. 213) and Túrin came to Dor-lómin in the Fell Winter (p. 215).

The names Brodda and Airin (later spelled Aerin) remained; but Brodda is here the lord of the land, and Airin plays a more important part in the scene in the hall, dealing justice with vigour and wisdom, than she does later. It is not said here that she had been married by force, though her life with Brodda is declared to have been very evil; but of course the situation in the later narratives is far more clear-cut – the Men of Hithlum were 'Easterlings', 'Incomers' hostile to the Elves and the remnant of the House of Hador, whereas in the early story no differentiation is made among them, and indeed Brodda was 'a man whom Mavwin trusted'. The motive of Brodda's ill-treatment of Mavwin is already present, but only to the extent that he embezzled her goods after her departure; in the *Narn* it seems from Aerin's words to Túrin (p. 107) that the oppression of Morwen by Brodda and others was the cause of her going at last to Doriath. In the brief account in *The Silmarillion* (p. 215) it is not indeed made explicit that Brodda in particular deserved Túrin's hatred.

Túrin's conduct in the hall is in the tale essentially simpler: the true story has been told to him by a passer-by, he enters to exact vengeance on Brodda for thieving Mavwin's goods, and he does so with dispatch. As

told in the *Narn*, where Túrin's eyes are only finally opened to the
deception that has been practised upon him by the words of Aerin, who is
present in the hall, his rage is more passionate, crazed, and bitter, and
indeed more comprehensible: and the moral observation that Túrin's
deed was 'violent and unlawful' is not made. The story of Airin's judgement on these doings, made in order to save Túrin, was afterwards
removed; and Túrin's solitary departure was expanded, with the addition
also of the firing of Brodda's hall by Aerin (*Narn* p. 109).

Some details survived all the changes: in the *Narn* Túrin still seizes
Brodda by the hair, and just as in the tale his rage suddenly expired after
the deed of violence ('his wrath was grown cold'), so in the *Narn* 'the fire
of his rage was as ashes'. It may be noticed here that while in the old story
Túrin does not rename himself so often, his tendency to do so is already
present.

The story of how Túrin came among the Woodmen and delivered
them from Orcs is not found in the *Tale of Turambar*; nor is there any
mention of the Mound of Finduilas near the Crossings of Teiglin nor any
account of her fate.

(vi)   *The return of Gumlin to Hithlum and the departure of*
Mavwin and Nienóri to Artanor (pp. 91–3)

In the later story the elder of Túrin's guardians (Gumlin in the tale,
Grithnir in the *Narn*) plays no part after his bringing Túrin to Doriath:
it is only said that he stayed there till he died (*Narn* p. 74); and Morwen
had no tidings out of Doriath before leaving her home – indeed she only
learnt that Túrin had left Thingol's realm when she got there (*The
Silmarillion* p. 211; cf. Aerin's words in the *Narn*, p. 107: 'She looked to
find her son there awaiting her.') This whole section of the tale does no
more than explain with what my father doubtless felt (since he afterwards
rejected it almost in its entirety) to be unnecessary complication why
Mavwin went to Tinwelint. I think it is clear, however, that the difference
between the versions here depends on the different views of Mavwin's
(Morwen's) condition in Hithlum. In the old story she is not suffering
hardship and oppression; she trusts Brodda to the extent of entrusting
not only her goods to him but even her daughter, and is said indeed to
have 'peace and honour among the men of those regions'; the chieftains
speak of the love they bear her. A motive for her departure is found in the
coming of Gumlin and the news he brings of Túrin's flight from the lands
of Tinwelint. In the later story, on the other hand, Brodda's character as
tyrant and oppressor is extended, and it is Morwen's very plight at his
hands that leads her to depart. (The news that came to Túrin in Doriath
that 'Morwen's plight was eased' (*Narn* p. 77, cf. *The Silmarillion*
p. 199) is probably a survival from the old story; nothing is said in the
later narratives to explain how this came about, and ceased.) In either
case her motive for leaving is coupled with the fact of the increased safety

of the lands; but whereas in the later story the reason for this was the prowess of the Black Sword of Nargothrond, in the tale it was the 'great and terrible project' of Melko that was afoot – the assault on the caves of the Rodothlim (see note 18).

It is curious that in this passage Airin and Brodda are introduced as if for the first time. It is perhaps significant that the part of the tale extending from the dragon's words 'Hearken to me, O son of Úrin . . .' on p. 87 to '. . . fell to his knees before Tinwelint' on p. 92 was written in a separate part of the manuscript book: possibly this replaced an earlier text in which Brodda and Airin did not appear. But many such questions arise from the earliest manuscripts, and few can now be certainly unravelled.

(vii)   *Mavwin and Nienóri in Artanor and their meeting
with Glorund* (pp. 93–9)

The next essential step in the development of the plot – the learning by Mavwin/Morwen of Túrin's sojourn in Nargothrond – is more neatly and naturally handled in *The Silmarillion* (p. 217) and the *Narn* (p. 112), where news is brought to Thingol by fugitives from the sack, in contrast to the *Tale of Turambar*, where Mavwin and Nienóri only learn of the destruction of the Elves of the Caves from a band of Noldoli while themselves wandering aimlessly in the forest. It is odd that these Noldoli did not name Túrin by his name but only as the *Mormakil*: it seems that they did not know who he was, but they knew enough of his history to make his identity plain to Mavwin. As noted above, Túrin declared his name and lineage to the Elves of the Caves. In the later narrative, on the other hand, Túrin did conceal it in Nargothrond, calling himself Agarwaen, but all those who brought news of the fall to Doriath 'declared that it was known to many in Nargothrond ere the end that the Mormegil was none other than Túrin son of Húrin of Dor-lómin'.

As often, unneeded complication in the early story was afterwards cleared away: thus the elaborate argumentation needed to get Tinwelint's warriors and Mavwin and Nienóri on the road together is gone from *The Silmarillion* and the *Narn*. In the tale the ladies and the Elvish warriors all set off together with the full intention that the former shall watch developments from a high place (afterwards Amon Ethir, the Hill of Spies); in the later story Morwen simply rides off, and the party of Elves, led by Mablung, follows after her, with Nienor among them in disguise.

Particularly notable is the passage in the tale in which Mavwin holds out the great gold-hoard of the Rodothlim as a bait to Tinwelint, and Tinwelint unashamedly admits that (as a wild Elf of the woods) it is this, not any hope of aiding Túrin, that moves him to send out a party. The majesty, power, and pride of Thingol rose with the development of the conception of the Grey-elves of Beleriand; as I have said earlier (p. 63) 'In the beginning, Tinwelint's dwelling was not a subterranean city full of marvels . . . but a rugged cave', and here he is seen planning a foray to augment his slender wealth in precious things – a far cry from the description of his vast treasury in the *Narn* (p. 76):

> Now Thingol had in Menegroth deep armouries filled with great wealth of weapons: metal wrought like fishes' mail and shining like water in the moon; swords and axes, shields and helms, wrought by Telchar himself or by his master Gamil Zirak the old, or by elven-wrights more skilful still. For some things he had received in gift that came out of Valinor and were wrought by Fëanor in his mastery, than whom no craftsman was greater in all the days of the world.

Great as are the differences from the later legend in the encounter with the dragon, the stinking vapours raised by his lying in the river as the cause of the miscarriage of the plan, the maddened flight of the horses, and the enspelling of Nienor so that all memory of her past was lost, are already present. Most striking perhaps of the many differences is the fact that Mavwin was present at the conversation with Glorund; and of these speeches there is no echo in the *Narn* (pp. 118–19), save that Nienor's naming of Túrin as the object of their quest revealed her identity to the dragon (this is explicit in the *Narn*, and may probably be surmised from the tale). The peculiar tone of Glaurung in the later narrative, sneering and curt, knowing and self-possessed, and unfathomably wicked, can be detected already in the words of Glorund, but as he evolved he gained immeasurably in dread by becoming more laconic.

The chief difference of structure lies in the total absence of the 'Mablung-element' from the tale, nor is there any foreshadowing of it. There is no suggestion of an exploration of the sacked dwellings in the dragon's absence (indeed he does not, as it appears, go any distance from them); the purpose of the expedition from Artanor was expressly warlike ('a strong party against the Foalókë', 'they prepared them for battle'), since Tinwelint had hopes of laying hands on the treasure, whereas afterwards it became purely a scouting foray, for Thingol 'desired greatly to know more of the fate of Nargothrond' (*Narn* p. 113).

A curious point is that though Mavwin and Nienóri were to be stationed on the tree-covered 'high place' that was afterward called the Hill of Spies, and where they were in fact so stationed in *The Silmarillion* and the *Narn*, it seems that in the old story they never got there, but were ensnared by Glorund where he lay in, or not far from, the river. Thus the 'high place' had in the event almost no significance in the tale.

(viii) *Turambar and Níniel* (pp. 99–102)

In the later legend Nienor was found by Mablung after her enspelling by Glaurung, and with three companions he led her back towards the borders of Doriath. The chase after Nienor by the band of Orcs (*Narn* p. 120) is present in the tale, but it does not have its later narrative function of leading to Nienor's flight and loss by Mablung and the other Elves (who do not appear): rather it leads directly to her rescue by Turambar, now dwelling among the Woodmen. In the *Narn* (p. 122) the Woodmen of Brethil did indeed come past the spot where they found her on their return from a foray against Orcs; but the circumstances of her finding are altogether different, most especially since there is in the tale no mention of the Haudh-en-Elleth, the Mound of Finduilas.

An interesting detail concerns Nienor's response to Turambar's naming her *Níniel*. In *The Silmarillion* and the *Narn* 'she shook her head, but said: Níniel'; in the present text she said: 'Not Níniel, not Níniel.' One has the impression that in the old story what impressed her darkened mind was only the resemblance of *Níniel* to her own forgotten name *Nienóri* (and of *Turambar* to *Túrin*), whereas in the later she both denied and in some way accepted the name *Níniel*.

An original element in the legend is the Woodmen's bringing of Níniel to a place ('Silver Bowl') where there was a great waterfall (afterwards Dimrost, the Rainy Stair, where the stream of Celebros 'fell towards Teiglin'): and these falls were near to the dwellings of the Woodmen – but the place where they found Níniel was much further off in the forest (several days' journey) than were the Crossings of Teiglin from Dimrost. When she came there she was filled with dread, a foreboding of what was to happen there afterwards, and this is the origin of her shuddering fit in the later narratives, from which the place was renamed Nen Girith, the Shuddering Water (see *Narn* p. 149, note 24).

The utter darkness imposed on Níniel's mind by the dragon's spell is less emphasized in the tale, and there is no suggestion that she needed to relearn her very language; but it is interesting to observe the recurrence in a changed context of the simile of 'one that seeks for something mislaid': in the *Narn* (p. 123) Níniel is said to have taken great delight in the relearning of words, 'as one that finds again treasures great and small that were mislaid'.

The lame man, here called Tamar, and his vain love of Níniel already appear; unlike his later counterpart Brandir he was not the chief of the Woodmen, but he was the son of the chief. He was also Half-elven! Most extraordinary is the statement that the wife of Bethos the chieftain and mother of Tamar was an Elf, a woman of the Noldoli: this is mentioned in passing, as if the great significance and rarity of the union of Elf and Mortal had not yet emerged – but in a Name-list associated with the tale of *The Fall of Gondolin* Eärendel is said to be 'the only being that is half of the kindred of the Eldalië and half of Men' (p. 215).*

---

* In a later rewriting of a passage in that tale (p. 164 and note 22) it is said of Tuor and Idril of Gondolin: 'Thus was first wed a child of Men with a daughter of Elfinesse, nor was Tuor the last.'

The initial reluctance of Níniel to receive Turambar's suit is given no explanation in the tale: the implication must be that some instinct, some subconscious appreciation of the truth, held her back. In *The Silmarillion* (p. 220)

> for that time she delayed in spite of her love. For Brandir foreboded he knew not what, and sought to restrain her, rather for her sake than his own or rivalry with Turambar; and he revealed to her that Turambar was Túrin son of Húrin, and though she knew not the name a shadow fell upon her mind.

In the final version as in the oldest, the Woodmen knew who Turambar was. My father's scribbled directions for the alteration of the story cited in note 23 ('Make Turambar never tell new folk of his lineage . . .') are puzzling: for since Níniel had lost all memory of her past she would not know the names Túrin son of Húrin even if it were told to her that Turambar was he. It is however possible that when my father wrote this he imagined Níniel's lost knowledge of herself and her family as being nearer the surface of her mind, and capable of being brought back by hearing the names – in contrast to the later story where she did not consciously recognise the name of Túrin even when Brandir told it to her. Clearly the question-mark against the reference in the text of the tale to Turambar's speaking to Níniel 'of his father and mother and the sister he had not seen' and Níniel's distress at his words (see note 24) depends on the same train of thought. The statement here that Turambar had never seen his sister is at variance with what is said earlier in the tale, that he did not leave Hithlum until after Nienóri's birth (p. 71); but my father was uncertain on this point, as is clearly seen from the succession of readings, changed back and forth between the two ideas, given in note 15.

(ix) *The slaying of Glorund* (pp. 103–8)

In this section I follow the narrative of the tale as far as Túrin's swoon when the dying dragon opened his eyes and looked at him. Here the later story runs very close to the old, but there are many interesting differences.

In the tale Glorund is said to have had bands of both Orcs and Noldoli subject to him, but only the Orcs remained afterwards; cf. the *Narn* p. 125:

> Now the power and malice of Glaurung grew apace, and he waxed fat [cf. 'the Foalókë waxed fat'], and he gathered Orcs to him, and ruled as a dragon-King, and all the realm of Nargothrond that had been was laid under him.

The mention in the tale that Tinwelint's people were 'grievously harried' by Glorund's bands suggests once again that the magic of the Queen was no very substantial protection; while the statement that 'at length there came some [Orcs] nigh even to those woods and glades that were beloved of Turambar and his folk' seems at variance with Turambar's saying to Níniel earlier that 'we are hard put to it to fend those evil ones from our homes' (p. 100). There is no mention here of Turambar's pledge to Níniel that he would go to battle only if the homes of the Woodmen were assailed (*Narn* pp. 125–6); and there is no figure corresponding to Dorlas of the later versions. Tamar's character, briefly described (p. 106), is in accord so far as it goes with what is later told of Brandir, but the relationship of Brandir to Níniel, who called him her brother (*Narn* p. 124), had not emerged. The happiness and prosperity of the Woodmen under Turambar's chieftainship is much more strongly emphasized in the tale (afterwards he was not indeed the chieftain, at least not in name); and it leads in fact to Glorund's greed as a motive for his assault on them.

The topographical indications in this passage, important to the narrative, are readily enough accommodated to the later accounts, with one major exception: it is clear that in the old story the stream of the waterfall that fell down to the Silver Bowl was the same as that which ran through the gorge where Turambar slew Glorund:

Here flowed that same stream that further down wound past the dragon's lair [*lair* = the place where he was lying] in a deep bed cloven deep into the earth (p. 105).

Thus Turambar and his companions, as he said,

will go down the rocks to the foot of the fall, and so gaining the path of the stream perchance we may come as nigh to the drake as may be (*ibid.*).

In the final story, on the other hand, the falling stream (Celebros) was a tributary of Teiglin; cf. the *Narn* p. 127:

Now the river Teiglin . . . flowed down from Ered Wethrin swift as Narog, but at first between low shores, until after the Crossings, gathering power from other streams, it clove a way through the feet of the highlands upon which stood the Forest of Brethil. Thereafter it ran in deep ravines, whose great sides were like walls of rock, but pent at the bottom the waters flowed with great force and noise. And right in the path of Glaurung there lay now one of these gorges, by no means the deepest, but the narrowest, just north of the inflow of Celebros.

The pleasant place ('a green sward where grew a wealth of flowers') survived; cf. the *Narn* p. 123: 'There was a wide greensward at the head of the falls, and birches grew about it.' So also did the 'Silver Bowl', though the name was lost: 'the stream [Celebros] went over a lip of worn stone, and fell down by many foaming steps into a rocky bowl far below' (*Narn, ibid.*; cf. the tale p. 105: 'it fell over a great fall where the water-worn rock jutted smooth and grey from amid the grass'). The 'little hill' or 'knoll', 'islanded among the trees', from which Turambar and his companions looked out is not so described in the *Narn*, but the picture of a high place and lookout near the head of the falls remained, as may be seen from the statement in the *Narn* (p. 123) that from Nen Girith 'there was a wide view towards the ravines of Teiglin'; later (*Narn* p. 128) it is said that it was Turambar's intention to 'ride to the high fall of Nen Girith . . . whence he could look far across the lands'. It seems certain, then, that the old image never faded, and was only a little changed.

While in both old and late accounts a great concourse of the people follow Turambar to the head of the falls against his bidding, in the late his motive for commanding them not to come is explicit: they are to remain in their homes and prepare for flight. Here on the other hand Níniel rides with Turambar to the head of Silver Bowl and says farewell to him there. But a detail of the old story survived: Turambar's words to Níniel 'Nor thou nor I die this day, nor yet tomorrow, by the evil of the dragon or by the foemen's swords' are closely paralleled by his words to her in the *Narn* (p. 129): 'Neither you nor I shall be slain by this Dragon, nor by any foe of the North'; and in the one account Níniel 'quelled her weeping and was very still', while in the other she 'ceased to weep and fell silent'. The situation is generally simpler in the tale, in that the Woodmen are scarcely characterised; Tamar is not as Brandir the titular head of the people, and this motive for bitterness against Turambar is absent, nor is there a Dorlas to insult him or a Hunthor to rebuke Dorlas. Tamar is however present with Níniel at the same point in the story, having girded himself with a sword: 'and many scoffed at him for that', just as it is afterwards said of Brandir that he had seldom done so before (*Narn* p. 132).

Turambar here set out from the head of the falls with six companions, all of whom proved in the end fainthearted, whereas later he had only two, Dorlas and Hunthor, and Hunthor remained staunch, though killed by a falling stone in the gorge. But the result is the same, in that Turambar must climb the further cliff of the gorge alone. Here the dragon remained where he lay near the brink of the cliff all night, and only moved with the dawn, so that his death and the events that immediately followed it took place by daylight. But in other respects the killing of the dragon remained even in many details much as it was originally written, more especially if comparison is made with the *Narn* (p. 134), where there reappears the need for Turambar and his companion(s) to move from their first station in order to come up directly under the belly of the beast (this is passed over in *The Silmarillion*).

Two notable points in this section remain to be mentioned; both are afterthoughts pencilled into the manuscript. In the one we meet for the first time Mîm the Dwarf as the captain of Glorund's guard over his treasure during his absence – a strange choice for the post, one would think. On this matter see p. 137 below. In the other it is said that Níniel conceived a child by Turambar, which, remarkably enough, is not said in the text as originally written; on this see p. 135.

(x)   *The deaths of Túrin and Nienóri* (pp. 108–12)

In the conclusion of the story the structure remained the same from the old tale to the *Narn*: the moonlight, the tending of Turambar's burnt hand, the cry of Níniel that stirred the dragon to his final malice, the accusation by the dragon that Turambar was a stabber of foes unseen, Turambar's naming Tamar/Brandir 'Club-foot' and sending him to consort with the dragon in death, the sudden withering of the leaves at the place of Nienor's leap as if it were already the end of autumn, the invocation of Nienor to the waters and of Turambar to his sword, the raising of Túrin's mound and the inscription in 'strange signs' upon it. Many other features could be added. But there are also many differences; here I refer only to some of the most important.

Mablung being absent from the old story, it is only Turambar's intuition ('being free now of blindness' – the blindness that Melko 'wove of old', p. 83)* that informs him that Tamar was telling the truth. The slaying of Glaurung and all its aftermath is in the late story compassed in the course of a single night and the morning of the next day, whereas in the tale it is spread over two nights, the intervening day, and the morning of the second. Turambar is carried back to the people on the hill-top by the three deserters who had left him in the ravine, whereas in the late story he comes himself. (Of the slaying of Dorlas by Brandir there is no trace in the tale, and the taking of a sword by Tamar has no issue.)

Particularly interesting is the result of the changing of the place where Túrin and Nienóri died. In the tale there is only one river, and Níniel follows the stream up through the woods and casts herself over the falls of Silver Bowl (in the place afterwards called Nen Girith), and here too, in the glade above the falls, Turambar slew himself; in the developed story her death-leap was into the ravine of Teiglin at Cabed-en-Aras, the Deer's Leap, near the spot where Turambar lay beside Glaurung, and here Turambar's death took place also. Thus Níniel's sense of dread when she first came to Silver Bowl with the Woodmen who rescued her

---

* Cf. his words to Mablung in the *Narn*, p. 144: 'For see, I am blind! Did you not know? Blind, blind, groping since childhood in a dark mist of Morgoth!'

(p. 101) foreboded her own death in that place, but in the changed story there is less reason for a foreknowledge of evil to come upon her there. But while the place was changed, the withering of the leaves remained, and the awe of the scene of their deaths, so that none would go to Cabed-en-Aras after, as they would not set foot on the grass above Silver Bowl.

The most remarkable feature of the earliest version of the story of Turambar and Níniel is surely that as my father first wrote it he did *not* say that she had conceived a child by him (note 25); and thus there is nothing in the old story corresponding to Glaurung's words to her: 'But the worst of all his deeds thou shalt feel in thyself' (*Narn* p. 138). The fact that above all accounts for Nienor's utter horror and despair was added to the tale later.

In concluding this long analysis of the *Tale of Turambar* proper the absence of place-names in the later part of it may be remarked. The dwelling of the Rodothlim is not named, nor the river that flowed past it; no name is given to the forest where the Woodmen dwelt, to their village, or even to the stream of such central importance at the end of the story (contrast Nargothrond, Narog, Tumhalad, Amon Ethir, Brethil, Amon Obel, Ephel Brandir, Teiglin, Celebros of the later narratives).

§2. *The further narrative of Eltas (after the death of Túrin)*

My father struck out the greater part of this continuation, allowing it to stand only as far as the words 'by reason of her great unhappiness' on p. 113 (see note 31). From the brief passage that was retained it is seen that the story of Morwen's coming to the stone on Túrin's mound goes back to the beginning, though in the later story she met Húrin there (*The Silmarillion*, p. 229).

The rejected part continues as follows:

Yet it is said also that when the doom of his folk was utterly fulfilled then was Úrin released by Melko, and bowed with age he fared back into the better lands. There did he gather some few to him, and they went and found the caverns of the Rothwarin [*earlier form for* Rodothlim, *see p.* 119] empty, and none guarded them, and a mighty treasury lay there still for none had found it, in that the terror of the drake lived longer than he and none had ventured thither again. But Úrin let bear the gold even before Linwë [i.e. Tinwelint], and casting it before his feet bade him bitterly to take his vile reward, naming him a craven by whose faint heart had much evil fallen to his house that might never have been; and in this began a new estrangement between Elves and Men, for Linwë was wroth at Úrin's words and bid him begone, for said he: "Long did I foster Túrin thy son and forgave him the evil of his deeds, and afterward thy wife I succoured, giving way against my counsel to her wild desires. Yet what is it to me – and wherefore dost thou, O son of the uncouth race of Men, endure to upbraid a king of the Eldalië, whose life began in Palisor ages uncounted before Men were born?" And then Úrin would have gone, but his men were not willing to leave the gold there, and a dissension arose between them and the Elves, and of this grew bitter blows, and Tintoglin [i.e. Tinwelint] might not stay them.

There then was Úrin's band slain in his halls, and they stained with their blood the dragon's hoard; but Úrin escaped and cursed that gold with a dread curse so that none might enjoy it, and he that held any part of it found evil and death to come of it. But Linwë hearing that curse caused the gold to be cast into a deep pool of the river before his doors, and not for very long did any see it again save for the Ring of Doom [*emended to:* the Necklace of the Dwarves], and that tale belongs not here, although therein did the evil of the worm Glorund find its last fulfilment.

(The last phrase is an addition to the text.) The remainder of this rejected narrative, concerning the final fates of Úrin and Mavwin and their children, is essentially the same as in the replacement text given on p. 115 ('Then Úrin departed . . .') and need not be given.

Immediately following the rejected narrative there is a short outline headed 'Story of the Nauglafring or the Necklace of the Dwarves', and this also was struck through. Here there is no mention of Úrin at all, but it is told that the Orcs (emended from *Gongs*, see I.245 note 10) who guarded the treasury of Glorund went in search of him when he did not come back to the caves, and in their absence Tintoglin (i.e. Tinwelint), learning of Glorund's death, sent Elves to steal the hoard of the Rothwarin (i.e. Rodothlim). The Orcs returning cursed the thieves, and they cursed the gold also.

Linwë (i.e. Tinwelint) guarded the gold, and he had a great necklace made by certain Úvanimor (Nautar or Nauglath). (*Úvanimor* have been defined in an earlier tale as 'monsters, giants, and ogres', see I.75, 236; *Nauglath* are Dwarves, I.236). In this Necklace the Silmaril was set; but the curse of the gold was on him, and he defrauded them of part of their reward. The Nauglath plotted, and got aid of Men; Linwë was slain in a raid, and the gold carried away.

There follows another rejected outline, headed 'The Necklace of the Dwarves', and this combines features of the preceding outline with features of the rejected ending of Eltas' narrative (pp. 135–6). Here Úrin gathers a band of Elves and Men who are wild and fierce, and they go to the caves, which are lightly guarded because the 'Orqui' (i.e. Orcs) are abroad seeking Glorund. They carry off the treasure, and the Orcs returning curse it. Úrin casts the treasure before the king and reproaches him (saying that he might have sent a greater company to the caves to secure the treasure, if not to aid Mavwin in her distress); 'Tintoglin would not touch it and bid Úrin hold what he had won, but Úrin would depart with bitter words'. Úrin's men were not willing to leave it, and they sneaked back; there was an affray in the king's halls, and much blood was spilt on the gold. The outline concludes thus:

The Gongs sack Linwë's halls and Linwë is slain and the gold is carried far away. Beren Ermabwed falls upon them at a crossing of Sirion and the treasure is cast into the water, and with it the Silmaril of Fëanor. The Nauglath that dwell nigh dive after the gold but only one mighty necklace of gold (and that Silmaril is on it) do they find. This becomes a mark of their king.

These two outlines are partly concerned with the story of the Nauglafring and show my father pondering that story before he wrote it; there is no need to consider these elements here. It is evident that he was in great doubt as to the further course of the story after the release of Úrin – what happened to the dragon's hoard? Was it guarded or unguarded, and if guarded by whom? How did it come at last into Tinwelint's hands? Who cursed it, and at what point in the story? If it was Úrin and his band that seized it, were they Men or Elves or both?

In the final text, written on slips placed in the manuscript book and given above pp. 113–16, these questions were resolved thus: Úrin's band was at first Men, then changed to Elves (see note 33); the treasure was guarded by the dwarf Mîm, whom Úrin slew, and it was he who cursed the gold as he died; Úrin's band became a baggage-train to carry the treasure to Tinwelint in sacks and wooden boxes (and they got it to the bridge before the king's door in the heart of the forest without, apparently, any difficulty). In this text there is no hint of what happened to the treasure after Úrin's departure (because the *Tale of the Nauglafring* begins at that point).

Subsequent to the writing of the *Tale of Turambar* proper, my father inserted Mîm into the text at an earlier point in the story (see pp. 103, 118 note 26), making him the captain of the guard appointed by Glorund to watch the treasure in his absence; but whether this was written in before or after the appearance of Mîm at the end (pp. 113–14) – whether it represents a different idea, or is an explanation of how Mîm came to be there – I cannot say.

In *The Silmarillion* (pp. 230–2) the story is wholly changed, in that the treasure remained in Nargothrond, and Húrin after the slaying of Mîm (for a far better reason than that in the early narrative) brought nothing from it to Doriath save the Necklace of the Dwarves.

Of the astonishing feature at the end of Eltas' narrative (pp. 115–16) of the 'deification' of Túrin Turambar and Nienóri (and the refusal of the Gods of Death to open their doors to them) it must be said that nowhere is there any explanation given – though in much later versions of the mythology Túrin Turambar appears in the Last Battle and smites Morgoth with his black sword. The purifying bath into which Túrin and Nienóri entered, called *Fôs'Almir* in the final text, was in the rejected text named *Fauri*; in the *Tale of the Sun and Moon* it has been described (I. 187), but is there given other names: *Tanyasalpë, Faskalanúmen*, and *Faskalan*.

There remains one further scrap of text to be considered. The second of the rejected outlines given above (pp. 136–7) was written in ink over a pencilled outline that was *not* erased, and I have been able to disinter a good deal of it from beneath the later writing. The two passages have nothing to do with each other; for some reason my father did not trouble in this case to erase earlier writing. The underlying text, so far as I can make it out, reads:

> Tirannë and Vainóni fall in with the evil magician Kurúki who gives them a baneful drink. They forget their names and wander distraught in the woods. Vainóni is lost. She meets Turambar who saves her from Orcs and aids in her search for her mother. They are wed and live in happiness. Turambar becomes lord of rangers of the woods and a harrier of the Orcs. He goes to seek out the Foalókë which ravages his land. The treasure-heap – and flight of his band. He slays the Foalókë and is wounded. Vainóni succours him, but the dragon in dying tells her all, lifting the veil Kurúki has set over them. Anguish of Turambar and Vainóni. She flees into the woods and casts herself over a waterfall. Madness of Turambar who dwells alone . . . .´Úrin escapes from Angamandi and seeks Tirannë. Turambar flees from him and falls upon his sword. . . . . Úrin builds a cairn and . . . . doom of Melko. Tirannë dies of grief and Úrin reaches Hisilómë. . . . .
> Purification of Turambar and Vainóni who fare shining about the world and go with the hosts of Tulkas against Melko.

Detached jottings follow this, doubtless written at the same time:

> Úrin escapes. Tirannë learns of Túrin. Both wander distraught . . . in the wood.
> Túrin leaves Linwë for in a quarrel he slew one of Linwë's kin (accidentally).
> Introduce Failivrin element into the story?
> Turambar unable to fight because of Foalókë's eyes. Sees Failivrin depart.

This can only represent some of my father's very earliest meditations on the story of Túrin Turambar. (That it appears in the notebook at the *end* of the fully-written Tale may seem surprising, but he clearly used these books in a rather eccentric way.) Nienóri is here called *Vainóni*, and Mavwin *Tirannë*; the spell of forgetfulness is here laid by a magician named *Kurúki*, although it is the dragon who lifts the veil that the magician set over them. Túrin's two encounters with the dragon seem to have emerged from an original single one.

As I have mentioned before, the *Tale of Turambar*, like others of the *Lost Tales*, is written in ink over a wholly erased pencilled text, and the extant form of the tale is such that it could only be derived from a rougher draft preceding it; but the underlying text is so completely erased that there is no clue as to what stage it had reached in the development of the legend. It may well be – I think it is extremely probable – that in this outline concerning Vainóni, Tirannë, and Kurúki we glimpse by an odd chance a 'layer' in the Túrin-saga older even than the erased text underlying the extant version.

§3.   *Miscellaneous Matters*

(i)   *Beren*

The rejected passage given on p. 71, together with the marginal note 'If Beren be a Gnome (as now in the story of Tinúviel) the references to Beren must be altered' (note 4), is the basis for my assertion (p. 52) that in the earliest, now lost, form of the *Tale of Tinúviel* Beren was a Man. I have shown, I hope, that the extant form of the *Tale of Turambar* preceded the extant form of the *Tale of Tinúviel* (p. 69). Beren was a Man, *and akin to Mavwin*, when the extant *Turambar* was written; he became a Gnome in the extant *Tinúviel*; and this change was then written into *Turambar*. What the replacement passage on p. 72 does is to change the relation of Egnor and Beren from kinship with Úrin's wife to friendship with Úrin. (A correction to the typescript version of *Tinúviel*, p. 45, is later: making the comradeship of Úrin with Beren rather than with Egnor.) Two further changes to the text of Turambar consequent on the change in Beren from Man to Elf are given in notes 5 and 6. – It is interesting to observe that in the developed genealogy of *The Silmarillion*, when Beren was of course again a Man, he was also again akin to Morwen: for Beren was first cousin to Morwen's father Baragund.

In the rejected passage on p. 71 my father wrote against the name Egnor 'Damrod the Gnome' (note 2), and in the amended passage he wrote that Úrin had known Beren 'and had rendered him a service once in respect of Damrod his son'. There is no clue anywhere as to what this service may have been; but in the second of the 'schemes' for *The Book of Lost Tales* (see I.233–4) the outline for the *Tale of the Nauglafring* refers to the son of Beren and Tinúviel, the father of Elwing, by the name *Daimord*, although in the actual tale as written the son is as he was to remain *Dior*. Presumably *Daimord* is to be equated with *Damrod*.

I cannot explain the insertion of 'Damrod the Gnome' against 'Egnor' in the rejected passage — possibly it was no more than a passing idea, to give the name *Damrod* to Beren's father.

It may be noticed here that both the rejected and the replacement passages make it very clear that the events of the story of Beren and Tinúviel took place *before* the Battle of Unnumbered Tears; see pp. 65–6.

(ii)   *The Battle of Tasarinan*

It is said at the beginning of the present tale (p. 70) that it 'tells of very ancient days of that folk [Men] before the Battle of Tasarinan when first Men entered the dark vales of Hisilómë'.

On the face of it this offers an extreme contradiction, since it is said many times that Men were shut in Hisilómë at the time of the Battle of Unnumbered Tears, and the *Tale of Turambar* takes place — must take place — after that battle. The solution lies, however, in an ambiguity in the sentence just cited. My father did not mean that this was a tale of Men in ancient days of that folk before they entered Hisilómë; he meant 'this is a tale of the ancient days *when* Men first entered Hisilómë — long before the Battle of Tasarinan'.

Tasarinan is the Land of Willows, *Nan-tathren* in *The Silmarillion*; the early word-lists or dictionaries give the 'Elvish' form *tasarin* 'willow' and the Gnomish *tathrin*.* The Battle of Tasarinan took place long after, in the course of the great expedition from Valinor for the release of the enslaved Noldoli in the Great Lands. See pp. 219–20.

(iii)   *The geography of the Tale of Turambar*

The passage describing the route of the Orcs who captured Túrin (p. 77) seems to give further support to the idea that 'the mountains fencing Hisilómë from the Lands Beyond were continuous with those above Angband' (p. 62); for it is said here that the Orcs 'followed ever the line of dark hills toward those regions where they rise high and gloomy and their heads are shrouded in black vapours', and '*there* are they called Angorodin or the Iron Mountains, for beneath the roots of their northernmost fastnesses lies Angband'.

The site of the caves of the Rodothlim, agreeing well with what is said later of Nargothrond, has been discussed already (p. 123), as has the topography of the Silver Bowl and the ravine in which Turambar slew Glorund, in relation to the later Teiglin, Celebros, and Nen Girith (pp. 132–3). There are in addition some indications in the tale of how the caves of the Rodothlim related to Tinwelint's kingdom and to the land

---

* *Tasarinan* survived as the Quenya name without change: 'the willow-meads of Tasarinan' in Treebeard's song in *The Two Towers*, III.4.

where the Woodmen dwelt. It is said (p. 95) that 'the dwellings of the Rodothlim were not utterly distant from the realm of Tinwelint, albeit far enough'; while the Woodmen dwelt 'in lands that were not utterly far from Sirion or the grassy hills of that river's middle course' (p. 91), which may be taken to agree tolerably with the situation of the Forest of Brethil. The region where they lived is said in the same passage to have been 'very far away many a journey beyond the river of the Rodothlim', and Glorund's wrath was great when he heard of 'a brave folk of Men that dwelt far beyond the river' (p. 103); this also can be accommodated quite well to the developed geographical conception – Brethil was indeed a good distance beyond the river (Narog) for one setting out from Nargothrond.

My strong impression is that though the geography of the west of the Great Lands *may* have been still fairly vague, it already had, in many important respects, the same essential structure and relations as those seen on the map accompanying *The Silmarillion*.

(iv)   *The influence of the Valar*

As in the *Tale of Tinúviel* (see p. 68), in the *Tale of Turambar* also there are several references to the power of the Valar in the affairs of Men and Elves in the Great Lands – and to prayers, both of thanksgiving and request, addressed to them: thus Túrin's guardians 'thanked the Valar' that they accomplished the journey to Artanor (p. 72), and more remarkably, Úrin 'called upon the Valar of the West, being taught much concerning them by the Eldar of Kôr – the Gnomes he had encountered – and his words came, who shall say how, to Manwë Súlimo upon the heights of Taniquetil' (p. 77). (Úrin was already an 'Elf-friend', instructed by the Noldoli; cf. the replacement passage on p. 72.) Was his prayer 'answered'? Possibly this is the meaning of the very strange expression 'as the luck of the Valar had it' (p. 79), when Flinding and Beleg found Túrin lying near the point where they entered the Orc-camp.*

Dreams sent by the Valar came to the chieftains of the Rodothlim, though this was changed later and the reference to the Valar removed (p. 83 and note 10); the Woodmen said 'Would that the Valar would lift the spell that lies upon Níniel' (p. 101); and Túrin 'cried out bitterly against the Valar and his fate of woe' (p. 111).

An interesting reference to the Valar (and their power) occurs in Tinwelint's reply (p. 95) to Mavwin's words 'Give me but a woodman's cot and my son'. The king said: 'That I cannot, for I am but a king of the wild Elves, *and no Vala of the western isles.*' In the small part of *Gilfanon's Tale* that was actually written it is told (I.231) of the Dark Elves who remained in Palisor that they said that 'their brethren had gone

---

* The Gnomish dictionary has the entry: *gwalt* '**good** luck – any providential occurrence or thought: "the luck of the Valar", *i·walt ne Vanion*' (I.272).

westward to the Shining Isles. There, said they, do the Gods dwell, and they called them the Great Folk of the West, and thought they dwelt on firelit islands in the sea.'

(v)   Túrin's age

According to the *Tale of Turambar*, when Túrin left Mavwin he was seven years old, and it was after he had dwelt among the woodland Elves for seven years that all tidings from his home ceased (p. 74); in the *Narn* the corresponding years are eight and nine, and Túrin was seventeen, not fourteen, when 'his grief was renewed' (pp. 68, 76–7). It was exactly twelve years to the day of his departure from Mavwin when he slew Orgof and fled from Artanor (p. 75), when he was nineteen; in the *Narn* (p. 79) it was likewise twelve years since he left Hithlum when he hunted Saeros to his death, but he was twenty.

'The tale tells not the number of days that Turambar sojourned with the Rodothlim but these were very many, and during that time Nienóri grew to the threshold of womanhood' (pp. 91–2). Nienóri was seven years younger than Túrin: she was twelve when he fled from Artanor (*ibid.*). He cannot then have dwelt among the Rodothlim for more than (say) five or six years; and it is said that when he was chosen chieftain of the Woodmen he possessed 'wisdom great beyond his years'.

Bethos, chieftain of the Woodmen before Túrin, 'had fought *though then but a boy* in the Battle of Unnumbered Tears' (p. 101), but he was killed in a foray, since '*despite his years* he still rode abroad'. But it is impossible to relate Bethos' span (from 'a boy' at the Battle of Unnumbered Tears to his death on a foray at an age sufficiently ripe to be remarked on) to Túrin's; for the events after the destruction of the Rodothlim, culminating in Túrin's rescue of Níniel after her first encounter with Glorund, cannot cover any great length of time. What is clear and certain is that in the old story Túrin died when still a very young man. According to the precise dating provided in much later writing, he was 35 years old at his death.

(vi)   The stature of Elves and Men

The Elves are conceived to be of slighter build and stature than Men: so Beleg 'was of great stature and girth *as such was among that folk*' (p. 73), and Túrin 'was a Man and of greater stature than they', i.e. Beleg and Flinding (p. 80) – this sentence being an emendation from 'he was a Man of great size' (note 8). See on this matter I. 32, 235.

(vii)   Winged Dragons

At the end of *The Silmarillion* (p. 252) Morgoth 'loosed upon his foes the last desperate assault that he had prepared, and out of the pits of Angband there issued the winged dragons, that had not before been seen'. The suggestion is that winged dragons were a refinement of Morgoth's original design (embodied in Glaurung, Father of Dragons who went upon his belly). According to the *Tale of Turambar* (pp. 96–7), on the other hand, among Melko's many dragons some were smaller, cold like snakes, and of these many were flying creatures; while others, the mightier, were hot and heavy, fire-dragons, and these were unwinged. As already noted (p. 125) there is no suggestion in the tale that Glorund was the first of his kind.

III

THE FALL OF GONDOLIN

At the end of Eltas' account of Úrin's visit to Tinwelint and of the strange fates of Úrin and Mavwin, Túrin and Nienóri (p. 116), the manuscript written on loose sheets in fact continues with a brief interlude in which the further course of the tale-telling is discussed in Mar Vanwa Tyaliéva.

And so saying Eltas made an end, and none asked further. But Lindo bid all thank him for his tale, and thereto he said: 'Nay, if you will, there is much yet to tell concerning the gold of Glorund, and how the evil of that worm found its last fulfilment – but behold, that is the story of the Nauglafring or the Necklace of the Dwarves and must wait a while – and other stories of lighter and more happy things I have to tell if you would liefer listen to them.'

Then arose many voices begging Eltas to tell the tale of the Nauglafring on the morrow, but he said: 'Nay! For who here knows the full tale of Tuor and the coming of Eärendel, or who was Beren Ermabwed, and what were his deeds, for such things is it better to know rightly first.' And all said that Beren Ermabwed they knew well, but of the coming of Eärendel little enough had ever been told.

'And great harm is that,' said Lindo, 'for it is the greatest of the stories of the Gnomes, and even in this house is Ilfiniol son of Bronweg, who knows those deeds more truly than any that are now on Earth.'

About that time Ilfiniol the Gong-warden entered indeed, and Lindo said to him: 'Behold, O Littleheart son of Bronweg, it is the desire of all that you tell us the tales of Tuor and of Eärendel as soon as may be.' And Ilfiniol was fain of that, but said he: 'It is a mighty tale, and seven times shall folk fare to the Tale-fire ere it be rightly told; and so twined is it with those stories of the Nauglafring and of the Elf-march[1] that I would fain have aid in that telling of Ailios here and of Meril the Lady of the Isle, for long is it since she sought this house.'

Therefore were messengers sent on the next day to the *korin*[2] of high elms, and they said that Lindo and Vairë would fain see the face of their lady among them, for they purposed to make a festival and to hold a great telling of Elfin tales, ere Eriol their guest fared awhile to Tavrobel. So was it that for three days that room heard no more tales and the folk of Vanwa Tyaliéva made great preparations, but on the fourth night Meril fared there amid her company of maidens, and full of light and mirth was that place; but after the evening meat a great host sat before Tôn a Gwedrin,[3] and the maidens of Meril sang the most beautiful songs that island knew.[4]

And of those one did afterward Heorrenda turn to the language of his folk, and it is thus.[5]

But when those songs had fallen into silence then said Meril, who sate in the chair of Lindo: 'Come now, O Ilfiniol, begin thou the tale of tales, and tell it more fully than thou hast ever done.'

Then said Littleheart son of Bronweg . . . (Tale of Gondolin). [sic]

This then is the *Link* between the *Tale of Turambar* and *The Fall of Gondolin* (an earlier 'preface' to the tale is given below). It seems that my father hesitated as to which tale was to follow *Turambar* (see note 4), but decided that it was time to introduce *The Fall of Gondolin*, which had been in existence for some time.

In this *Link*, Ailios (later Gilfanon) is present ('I would fain have aid . . . of Ailios here') at the end of Eltas' tale of Turambar, but at the beginning of Eltas' tale (p. 70) it is expressly said that he was not present that night. On the proposal that Eriol should 'fare awhile' to Tavrobel (as the guest of Gilfanon) see I. 175.

The fact that Eltas speaks of the tale of Beren Ermabwed as if he did not know that it had only recently been told in Mar Vanwa Tyaliéva is no doubt to be explained by that tale not having been told before the Tale-fire (see pp. 4–7).

The teller of the tale of *The Fall of Gondolin*, Littleheart the Gong-warden of Mar Vanwa Tyaliéva, has appeared several times in the *Lost Tales*, and his Elvish name(s) have many different forms (see under *Changes made to names* at the end of the text of the tale). In *The Cottage of Lost Play* he is said (I. 15) to be 'ancient beyond count', and to have 'sailed in Wingilot with Eärendel in that last voyage wherein they sought for Kôr'; and in the *Link* to *The Music of the Ainur* (I. 46) he 'had a weather-worn face and blue eyes of great merriment, and was very slender and small, nor might one say if he were fifty or ten thousand'. He is a Gnome, the son of Bronweg/Voronwë (Voronwë of *The Silmarillion*) (I. 48, 94).

The texts of 'The Fall of Gondolin'

The textual history of *The Fall of Gondolin*, if considered in detail, is extremely complex; but though I will set it out here, as I understand it, there is no need in fact for it to complicate the reading of the tale.

In the first place, there is a very difficult manuscript contained in two school exercise-books, where the title of the tale is *Tuor and the Exiles of Gondolin (which bringeth in the great tale of Eärendel)*. (This is the only title actually found in the early texts, but my father always later referred to it as *The Fall of Gondolin*.) This manuscript is (or rather, was) the original text of the tale, dating from 1916–17 (see I.203 and *Unfinished Tales* p. 4), and I will call it here for convenience *Tuor A*. My father's treatment of it subsequently was unlike that of *Tinúviel* and *Turambar* (where the original text was erased and a new version written in its place); in this tale he did not set down a complete new text, but allowed a good deal of the old to stand, at least in the earlier part of it: as the revision progressed the rewriting in ink over the top of the pencilled text did become almost continuous, and though the pencil was not erased the ink effectively obliterates it. But even after the second version becomes continuous there are several places where the old narrative was not over-written but merely struck through, and remains legible. Thus, while *Tuor A* is on the same footing as *Tinúviel* and *Turambar* (and others of the *Lost Tales*) in that it is a later revision, a second version, my father's method in *Gondolin* allows it to be seen that here at least the revision was by no means a complete recasting (still less a re-imagining); for if those passages in the later parts of the tale which can still be compared in the two versions shew that he was following the old fairly closely, the same is quite probably true in those places where no comparison can be made.

From *Tuor A*, as it was *when all changes had been made to it* (i.e. when it was in the form that it has now), my mother made a fair copy (*Tuor B*), which considering the difficulty of the original is extremely exact, with only very occasional errors of transcription. I have said in *Unfinished Tales* (p. 5) that this copy was made 'apparently in 1917', but this now seems to me improbable.* Such conceptions as the Music of the Ainur, which is referred to by later addition in *Tuor A* (p. 163), *may* of course have been in my father's mind a good while before he wrote that tale in Oxford while working on the Dictionary (I.45), but it seems more likely that the revision of *Tuor A* (and therefore also *Tuor B* copied from it after its revision) belongs to that period also.

Subsequently my father took his pencil to *Tuor B*, emending it fairly heavily, though mostly in the earlier part of the tale, and almost entirely

---

* Humphrey Carpenter in his *Biography* (p. 92) says that the tale 'was written out during Tolkien's convalescence at Great Haywood early in 1917', but he is doubtless referring to the original pencilled text of *Tuor A*.

for stylistic rather than narrative reasons; but these emendations, as will be seen, were not all made at the same time. Some of them are written out on separate slips, and of these several have on their reverse sides parts of an etymological discussion of certain Germanic words for the Butcher-bird or Shrike, material which appears in the Oxford Dictionary in the entry *Wariangle*. Taken with the fact that one of the slips with this material on the reverse clearly contains a direction for the shortening of the tale when delivered orally (see note 21), it is virtually certain that a good deal of the revision of *Tuor B* was made before my father read it to the Essay Club of Exeter College in the spring of 1920 (see *Unfinished Tales* p. 5).

That not all the emendations to *Tuor B* were made at the same time is shown by the existence of a typescript (*Tuor C*), without title, which extends only so far as 'your hill of vigilance against the evil of Melko' (p. 161). This was taken from *Tuor B* when some changes had been made to it, but not those which I deduce to have been made before the occasion when it was read aloud. An odd feature of this text is that blanks were left for many of the names, and only some were filled in afterwards. Towards the end of it there is a good deal of independent variation from *Tuor B*, but it is all of a minor character and none has narrative significance. I conclude that this was a side-branch that petered out.

The textual history can then be represented thus:

Tuor A (original 1916-17 text in pencil)
↓
heavily revised and in the later parts entirely overwritten
↓
Tuor B (fair copy)
↓
minor stylistic revisions (and changes to names)

                              ↓
                                Tuor C (typescript; does not
                                extend far; minor stylistic
                                changes)
↓
further alterations mainly on inserted
slips (and further changes to names)
before reading it at Exeter College in
1920
      (the text in this book)

Since the narrative itself underwent very little change of note in the course of this history (granted that substantial parts of the original text *Tuor A* are almost entirely illegible), the text that follows here is that of *Tuor B* in its final form, with some interesting earlier readings given in the Notes. It seems that my father did not check the fair copy *Tuor B* against the original, and did not in every case pick up the errors of transcription it contains; when he did, he emended them anew, according to the sense, and not by reference back to *Tuor A*. In a very few cases I have gone back to *Tuor A* where this is clearly correct (as 'a wall of water rose nigh to the cliff-top', p. 151, where *Tuor B* and the typescript *Tuor C* have 'high to the cliff-top').

Throughout the typescript Tuor is called *Tûr*. In *Tuor B* the name is sometimes emended from *Tuor* to *Tûr* in the earlier part of the tale (it appears as *Tûr* in the latest revisions), but by no means in every case. My father apparently decided to change the name but ultimately decided against it; and I give *Tuor* throughout.

An interesting document accompanies the Tale: this is a substantial though incomplete list of names (with explanations) that occur in it, now in places difficult or impossible to read. The names are given in alphabetical order but go only as far as L. Linguistic information from this list is incorporated in the Appendix on Names, but the head-note to the list may be cited here:

> Here is set forth by Eriol at the teaching of Bronweg's son Elfrith [*emended from* Elfriniel] or Littleheart (and he was so named for the youth and wonder of his heart) those names and words that are used in these tales from either the tongue of the Elves of Kôr as at that time spoken in the Lonely Isle, or from that related one of the Noldoli their kin whom they wrested from Melko.
>
> Here first are they which appear in *The Tale of Tuor and the Exiles of Gondolin*, first among these those ones in the Gnome-speech.

In *Tuor A* appear two versions (one struck out) of a short 'preface' to the tale by Littleheart which does not appear in *Tuor B*. The second version reads:

> Then said Littleheart son of Bronweg: 'Now the story that I tell is of the Noldoli, who were my father's folk, and belike the names will ring strange in your ears and familiar folk be called by names not before heard, for the Noldoli speak a curious tongue sweet still to my ears though not maybe to all the Eldar. Wise folk see it as close kin to Eldarissa, but it soundeth not so, and I know nought of such lore. Wherefore will I utter to you the right Eldar names where there be such, but in many cases there be none.
>   Know then,' said he, 'that

The earlier version (headed 'Link between *Tuor* and tale before') begins in the same way but then diverges:

> . . . and it is sweet to my ears still, though lest it be not so to all else of Eldar and Men here gathered I will use no more of it than I must, and that is in the names of those folk and things whereof the tale tells but

for which, seeing they passed away ere ever the rest of the Eldar came from Kôr, the Elves have no true names. Know then,' said he, 'that Tuor

This 'preface' thus connects to the opening of the tale. There here appears, in the second version, the name *Eldarissa* for the language of the *Eldar* or *Elves*, as opposed to *Noldorissa* (a term found in the Name-list); on the distinction involved see I.50–1. With Littleheart's words here compare what Rúmil said to Eriol about him (I.48):

'"Tongues and speeches," they will say, "one is enough for me" – and thus said Littleheart the Gong-warden once upon a time: "Gnome-speech," said he, "is enough for me – did not that one Eärendel and Tuor and Bronweg my father (that mincingly ye miscall Voronwë) speak it and no other?" Yet he had to learn the Elfin in the end, or be doomed either to silence or to leave Mar Vanwa Tyaliéva . . .'

After these lengthy preliminaries I give the text of the Tale.

★

Tuor and the Exiles of Gondolin
(which bringeth in the great tale of Eärendel)

Then said Littleheart son of Bronweg: 'Know then that Tuor was a man who dwelt in very ancient days in that land of the North called Dor Lómin or the Land of Shadows, and of the Eldar the Noldoli know it best.

Now the folk whence Tuor came wandered the forests and fells and knew not and sang not of the sea; but Tuor dwelt not with them, and lived alone about that lake called Mithrim, now hunting in its woods, now making music beside its shores on his rugged harp of wood and the sinews of bears. Now many hearing of the power of his rough songs came from near and far to hearken to his harping, but Tuor left his singing and departed to lonely places. Here he learnt many strange things and got knowledge of the wandering Noldoli, who taught him much of their speech and lore; but he was not fated to dwell for ever in those woods.

Thereafter 'tis said that magic and destiny led him on a day to a cavernous opening down which a hidden river flowed from Mithrim. And Tuor entered that cavern seeking to learn its secret, but the waters of Mithrim drove him forward into the heart of the rock and he might not win back into the light. And this, 'tis said, was the will of Ulmo Lord of Waters at whose prompting the Noldoli had made that hidden way.

Then came the Noldoli to Tuor and guided him along dark passages amid the mountains until he came out in the light once more, and saw that the river flowed swiftly in a ravine of great depth with sides unscalable. Now Tuor desired no more to return but went ever forward, and the river led him always toward the west.[6]

The sun rose behind his back and set before his face, and where the water foamed among many boulders or fell over falls there were at times rainbows woven across the ravine, but at evening its smooth sides would glow in the setting sun, and for these reasons Tuor called it Golden Cleft or the Gully of the Rainbow Roof, which is in the speech of the Gnomes Glorfalc or Cris Ilbranteloth.

Now Tuor journeyed here for three days,[7]drinking the waters of the secret river and feeding on its fish; and these were of gold and blue and silver and of many wondrous shapes. At length the ravine widened, and ever as it opened its sides became lower and more rough, and the bed of the river more impeded with boulders against which the waters foamed and spouted. Long times would Tuor sit and gaze at the splashing water and listen to its voice, and then he would rise and leap onward from stone to stone singing as he went; or as the stars came out in the narrow strip of heaven above the gully he would raise echoes to answer the fierce twanging of his harp.

One day after a great journey of weary going Tuor at deep evening heard a cry, and he might not decide of what creature it came. Now he said: "It is a fay-creature", now, "Nay, 'tis but some small beast that waileth among the rocks"; or again it seemed to him that an unknown bird piped with a voice new to his ears and strangely sad – and because he had not heard the voice of any bird in all his wandering down Golden Cleft he was glad of the sound although it was mournful. On the next day at an hour of the morning he heard the same cry above his head, and looking up beheld three great white birds beating back up the gully on strong wing, and uttering cries like to the ones he had heard amid the dusk. Now these were the gulls, the birds of Ossë.[8]

In this part of that riverway there were islets of rock amid the currents, and fallen rocks fringed with white sand at the gully-side, so that it was ill-going, and seeking a while Tuor found a spot where he might with labour scale the cliffs at last. Then came a fresh wind against his face, and he said: "This is very good and like the drinking of wine," but he knew not that he was near the confines of the Great Sea.

As he went along above the waters that ravine again drew together and the walls towered up, so that he fared on a high cliff-top, and there came a narrow neck, and this was full of noise. Then Tuor looking downward saw the greatest of marvels, for it seemed that a flood of angry water would come up the narrows and flow back against the river to its source, but that water which had come down from distant Mithrim would still press on, and a wall of water rose nigh to the cliff-top, and it was crowned with foam and twisted by the winds. Then the waters of Mithrim were overthrown and the incoming flood swept roaring up the channel and whelmed the rocky islets and churned the white sand – so that Tuor fled and was afraid, who did not know the ways of the sea; but the Ainur put it into his heart to climb from the gully when he did, or had he been whelmed in the incoming tide, and that was a fierce one by reason of a wind from the west. Then Tuor found himself in a rugged country bare of trees, and swept by a wind coming from the set of the sun, and all the shrubs and bushes leaned to the dawn because of that prevalence of that wind. And here for a while he wandered till he came to the black cliffs by the sea and saw the ocean and its waves for the first time, and at that hour the sun sank beyond the rim of Earth far out to sea, and he stood on the cliff-top with outspread arms, and his heart was filled with a longing very great indeed. Now some say that he was the first of Men to reach the Sea and look upon it and know the desire it brings; but I know not if they say well.

In those regions he set up his abode, dwelling in a cove sheltered by great sable rocks, whose floor was of white sand, save when the high flood partly overspread it with blue water; nor did foam or froth come there save at times of the direst tempest. There long he sojourned alone and roamed about the shore or fared over the rocks at the ebb, marvelling at the pools and the great weeds, the dripping caverns and the strange sea-fowl that he saw and came to know; but the rise and fall of the water and the voice of the waves was ever to him the greatest wonder and ever did it seem a new and unimaginable thing.

Now on the quiet waters of Mithrim over which the voice of the duck or moorhen would carry far he had fared much in a small boat with a prow fashioned like to the neck of a swan, and this he had lost on the day of his finding the hidden river. On the sea he adventured not as yet, though his heart was ever egging him with a strange longing thereto, and on quiet evenings when the sun went down beyond the edge of the sea it grew to a fierce desire.

Timber he had that came down the hidden river; a goodly wood it was, for the Noldoli hewed it in the forests of Dor Lómin and floated it to him of a purpose. But he built not as yet aught save a dwelling in a sheltered place of his cove, which tales among the Eldar since name Falasquil. This by slow labour he adorned with fair carvings of the beasts and trees and flowers and birds that he knew about the waters of Mithrim, and ever among them was the Swan the chief, for Tuor loved this emblem and it became the sign of himself, his kindred and folk thereafter. There he passed a very great while until the loneliness of the empty sea got into his heart, and even Tuor the solitary longed for the voice of Men. Herewith the Ainur[9] had something to do: for Ulmo loved Tuor.

One morning while casting his eye along the shore – and it was then the latest days of summer – Tuor saw three swans flying high and strong from the northward. Now these birds he had not before seen in these regions, and he took them for a sign, and said: "Long has my heart been set on a journey far from here; lo! now at length I will follow these swans." Behold, the swans dropped into the water of his cove and there swimming thrice about rose again and winged slowly south along the coast, and Tuor bearing his harp and spear followed them.

'Twas a great day's journey Tuor put behind him that day; and he came ere evening to a region where trees again appeared, and the manner of the land through which he now fared differed greatly from those shores about Falasquil. There had Tuor known mighty cliffs beset with caverns and great spoutholes, and deep-walled coves, but from the cliff-tops a rugged land and flat ran bleakly back to where a blue rim far to the east spake of distant hills. Now however did he see a long and sloping shore and stretches of sand, while the distant hills marched ever nearer to the margin of the sea, and their dark slopes were clad with pine or fir and about their feet sprang birches and ancient oaks. From the feet of the hills fresh torrents rushed down narrow chasms and so found the shores and the salt waves. Now some of these clefts Tuor might not overleap, and often was it ill-going in these places, but still he laboured on, for the swans fared ever before him, now circling suddenly, now speeding forward, but never coming to earth, and the rush of their strong-beating wings encouraged him.

'Tis told that in this manner Tuor fared onward for a great

number of days, and that winter marched from the north somewhat speedier than he for all his tirelessness. Nevertheless came he
without scathe of beast or weather at a time of first spring to a river
mouth. Now here was the land less northerly and more kindly
than about the issuing of Golden Cleft, and moreover by a trend of
the coast was the sea now rather to the south of him than to the
west, as he could mark by the sun and stars; but he had kept his
right hand always to the sea.

This river flowed down a goodly channel and on its banks were
rich lands: grasses and moist meadow to the one side and tree-
grown slopes of the other; its waters met the sea sluggishly and
fought not as the waters of Mithrim in the north. Long tongues of
land lay islanded in its course covered with reeds and bushy
thicket, until further to seaward sandy spits ran out; and these
were places beloved by such a multitude of birds as Tuor had
nowhere yet encountered. Their piping and wailing and whistling
filled the air; and here amid their white wings Tuor lost sight of
the three swans, nor saw he them again.

Then did Tuor grow for a season weary of the sea, for the
buffeting of his travel had been sore. Nor was this without Ulmo's
devising, and that night the Noldoli came to him and he arose
from sleep. Guided by their blue lanterns he found a way beside
the river border, and strode so mightily inland that when dawn
filled the sky to his right hand lo! the sea and its voice were far
behind him, and the wind came from before him so that its odour
was not even in the air. Thus came he soon to that region that has
been called Arlisgion "the place of reeds", and this is in those lands
that are to the south of Dor Lómin and separated therefrom by the
Iron Mountains whose spurs run even to the sea. From those
mountains came this river, and of a great clearness and marvellous
chill were its waters even at this place. Now this is a river most
famous in the histories of Eldar and Noldoli and in all tongues is it
named Sirion. Here Tuor rested awhile until driven by desire he
arose once more to journey further and further by many days'
marches along the river borders. Full spring had not yet brought
summer when he came to a region yet more lovely. Here the song
of small birds shrilled about him with a music of loveliness, for
there are no birds that sing like the songbirds of the Land of
Willows; and to this region of wonder he had now come. Here the
river wound in wide curves with low banks through a great plain of
the sweetest grass and very long and green; willows of untold age
were about its borders, and its wide bosom was strewn with

waterlily leaves, whose flowers were not yet in the earliness of the year, but beneath the willows the green swords of the flaglilies were drawn, and sedges stood, and reeds in embattled array. Now there dwelt in these dark places a spirit of whispers, and it whispered to Tuor at dusk and he was loth to depart; and at morn for the glory of the unnumbered buttercups he was yet more loth, and he tarried.

Here saw he the first butterflies and was glad of the sight; and it is said that all butterflies and their kindred were born in the valley of the Land of Willows. Then came the summer and the time of moths and the warm evenings, and Tuor wondered at the multitude of flies, at their buzzing and the droning of the beetles and the hum of bees; and to all these things he gave names of his own, and wove the names into new songs on his old harp; and these songs were softer than his singing of old.

Then Ulmo grew in dread lest Tuor dwell for ever here and the great things of his design come not to fulfilment. Therefore he feared longer to trust Tuor's guidance to the Noldoli alone, who did service to him in secret, and out of fear of Melko wavered much. Nor were they strong against the magic of that place of willows, for very great was its enchantment. Did not even after the days of Tuor Noldorin and his Eldar come there seeking for Dor Lómin and the hidden river and the caverns of the Gnomes' imprisonment; yet thus nigh to their quest's end were like to abandon it? Indeed sleeping and dancing here, and making fair music of river sounds and the murmur of grass, and weaving rich fabrics of gossamer and the feathers of winged insects, they were whelmed by the goblins sped by Melko from the Hills of Iron and Noldorin made bare escape thence. But these things were not as yet.

Behold now Ulmo leapt upon his car before the doorway of his palace below the still waters of the Outer Sea; and his car was drawn by narwhal and sealion and was in fashion like a whale; and amidst the sounding of great conches he sped from Ulmonan. So great was the speed of his going that in days, and not in years without count as might be thought, he reached the mouth of the river. Up this his car might not fare without hurt to its water and its banks; therefore Ulmo, loving all rivers and this one more than most, went thence on foot, robed to the middle in mail like the scales of blue and silver fishes; but his hair was a bluish silver and his beard to his feet was of the same hue, and he bore neither helm nor crown. Beneath his mail fell the skirts of his kirtle of shimmering greens, and of what substance these were woven is not known, but whoso looked into the depths of their subtle colours seemed to behold the faint movements of deep waters shot with the stealthy lights of phosphorescent fish that live in the abyss. Girt was he with a rope of mighty pearls, and he was shod with mighty shoes of stone.

Thither he bore too his great instrument of music; and this was of strange design, for it was made of many long twisted shells pierced with holes. Blowing therein and playing with his long fingers he made deep melodies of a magic greater than any other among musicians hath ever compassed on harp or lute, on lyre or pipe, or instruments of the bow. Then coming along the river he sate among the reeds at twilight and played upon his thing of shells; and it was nigh to those places where Tuor tarried. And Tuor hearkened and was stricken dumb. There he stood knee-deep in the grass and heard no more the hum of insects, nor the murmur of the river borders, and the odour of flowers entered not into his nostrils; but he heard the sound of waves and the wail of sea-birds, and his soul leapt for rocky places and the ledges that reek of fish, for the splash of the diving cormorant and those places where the sea bores into the black cliffs and yells aloud.

Then Ulmo arose and spake to him and for dread he came near to death, for the depth of the voice of Ulmo is of the uttermost depth: even as deep as his eyes which are the deepest of all things. And Ulmo said: "O Tuor of the lonely heart, I will not that thou dwell for ever in fair places of birds and flowers; nor would I lead thee through this pleasant land,[10] but that so it must be. But fare now on thy destined journey and tarry not, for far from hence is thy weird set. Now must thou seek through the lands for the city of the folk called Gondothlim or the dwellers in stone, and the Noldoli shall escort thee thither in secret for fear of the spies of Melko. Words I will set to your mouth there, and there you shall abide awhile. Yet maybe thy life shall turn again to the mighty waters; and of a surety a child shall come of thee than whom no man shall know more of the uttermost deeps, be it of the sea or of the firmament of heaven." Then spake Ulmo also to Tuor some of his design and desire, but thereof Tuor understood little at that time and feared greatly.

Then Ulmo was wrapped in a mist as it were of sea air in those inland places, and Tuor, with that music in his ears, would fain return to the regions of the Great Sea; yet remembering his bidding turned and went inland along the river, and so fared till day. Yet he that has heard the conches of Ulmo hears them call him till death, and so did Tuor find.

When day came he was weary and slept till it was nigh dusk again, and the Noldoli came to him and guided him. So fared he many days by dusk and dark and slept by day, and because of this it came afterwards that he remembered not over well the paths that he traversed in those times. Now Tuor and his guides held on untiring, and the land became one of rolling hills and the river wound about their feet, and there were many dales of exceeding pleasantness; but here the Noldoli became ill at ease. "These," said they, "are the confines of those regions which Melko infesteth with his Goblins, the people of hate. Far to the north — yet alas not far enough, would they were ten thousand leagues — lie the Mountains of Iron where sits the power and terror of Melko, whose thralls we are. Indeed in this guiding of thee we do in secret from him, and did he know all our purposes the torment of the Balrogs would be ours."

Falling then into such fear the Noldoli soon after left him and he fared alone amid the hills, and their going proved ill afterwards, for "Melko has many eyes", 'tis said, and while Tuor fared with the Gnomes they took him twilight ways and by many secret tunnels through the hills. But now he became lost, and climbed often to the tops of knolls and hills scanning the lands about. Yet he might not see signs of any dwelling of folk, and indeed the city of the Gondothlim was not found with ease, seeing that Melko and his spies had not even yet discovered it. 'Tis said nonetheless that at this time those spies got wind thus that the strange foot of Man had been set in those lands, and that for that Melko doubled his craft and watchfulness.

Now when the Gnomes out of fear deserted Tuor, one Voronwë or Bronweg followed afar off despite his fear, when chiding availed not to enhearten the others. Now Tuor had fallen into a great weariness and was sitting beside the rushing stream, and the sea-longing was about his heart, and he was minded once more to follow this river back to the wide waters and the roaring waves. But this Voronwë the faithful came up with him again, and standing by his ear said: "O Tuor, think not but that thou shalt again one day see thy desire; arise now, and behold, I will not leave thee. I am not of the road-learned of the Noldoli, being a craftsman and maker of things made by hand of wood and of metal, and I joined not the band of escort till late. Yet of old have I heard whispers and sayings said in secret amid the weariness of thraldom, concerning a city where Noldoli might be free could they find the hidden way thereto; and we twain may without a doubt[11] find the road to the City of Stone, where is that freedom of the Gondothlim."

Know then that the Gondothlim were that kin of the Noldoli who alone escaped Melko's power when at the Battle of Unnumbered Tears he slew and enslaved their folk[12] and wove spells about them and caused them to dwell in the Hells of Iron, faring thence at his will and bidding only.

Long time did Tuor and Bronweg[13] seek for the city of that folk, until after many days they came upon a deep dale amid the hills. Here went the river over a very stony bed with much rush and noise, and it was curtained with a heavy growth of alders; but the walls of the dale were sheer, for they were nigh to some mountains which Voronwë knew not. There in the green wall that Gnome found an opening like a great door with sloping sides, and this was cloaked with thick bushes and long-tangled undergrowth; yet Voronwë's piercing sight might not be deceived. Nonetheless 'tis said that such a magic had its builders set about it (by aid of Ulmo whose power ran in that river even if the dread of Melko fared upon its banks) that none save of the blood of the Noldoli might light on it thus by chance; nor would Tuor have found it ever but for the steadfastness of that Gnome Voronwë.[14] Now the Gondothlim made their abode thus secret out of dread of Melko; yet even so no few of the braver Noldoli would slip down the river Sirion from those mountains, and if many perished so by Melko's evil, many finding this magic passage came at last to the City of Stone and swelled its people.

Greatly did Tuor and Voronwë rejoice to find this gate, yet entering they found there a way dark, rough-going, and circuitous; and long time they travelled faltering within its tunnels. It was full of fearsome echoes, and there a countless stepping of feet would come behind them, so that Voronwë became adread, and said: "It is Melko's goblins, the Orcs of the hills." Then would they run, falling over stones in the blackness, till they perceived it was but the deceit of the place. Thus did they come, after it seemed a measureless time of fearful groping, to a place where a far light glimmered, and making for this gleam they came to a gate like that by which they had entered, but in no way overgrown. Then they passed into the sunlight and could for a while see nought, but instantly a great gong sounded and there was a clash of armour, and behold, they were surrounded by warriors in steel.

Then they looked up and could see, and lo! they were at the foot of steep hills, and these hills made a great circle wherein lay a wide plain, and set therein, not rightly at the midmost but rather nearer to that place where they stood, was a great hill with a level top, and upon that summit rose a city in the new light of the morning.

Then Voronwë spake to the Guard of the Gondothlim, and his speech they comprehended, for it was the sweet tongue of the Gnomes.[15] Then spake Tuor also and questioned where they might be, and who might be the folk in arms who stood about, for he was somewhat in amaze and wondered much at the goodly fashion of their weapons. Then 'twas said to him by one of that company: "We are the guardians of the issue of the Way of Escape. Rejoice that ye have found it, for behold before you the City of Seven Names where all who war with Melko may find hope."

Then said Tuor: "What be those names?" And the chief of the Guard made answer: "'Tis said and 'tis sung: 'Gondobar am I called and Gondothlimbar, City of Stone and City of the Dwellers in Stone; Gondolin the Stone of Song and Gwarestrin am I named, the Tower of Guard, Gar Thurion or the Secret Place, for I am hidden from the eyes of Melko; but they who love me most greatly call me Loth, for like a flower am I, even Lothengriol the flower that blooms on the plain.' Yet," said he, "in our daily speech we speak and we name it mostly Gondolin." Then said Voronwë: "Bring us thither, for we fain would enter," and Tuor said that his heart desired much to tread the ways of that fair city.

Then said the chief of the Guard that they themselves must abide here, for there were yet many days of their moon of watch to pass, but that Voronwë and Tuor might pass on to Gondolin; and moreover that they would need thereto no guide, for "Lo, it stands fair to see and very clear, and its towers prick the heavens above the Hill of Watch in the midmost plain." Then Tuor and his companion fared over the plain that was of a marvellous level, broken but here and there by boulders round and smooth which lay amid a sward, or by pools in rocky beds. Many fair pathways lay across that plain, and they came after a day's light march to the foot of the Hill of Watch (which is in the tongue of the Noldoli Amon Gwareth). Then did they begin to ascend the winding stairways which climbed up to the city gate; nor might any one reach that city save on foot and espied from the walls. As the westward gate was golden in the last sunlight did they come to the long stair's head, and many eyes gazed[16] upon them from the battlements and towers.

But Tuor looked upon the walls of stone, and the uplifted towers, upon the glistering pinnacles of the town, and he looked upon the stairs of stone and marble, bordered by slender balustrades and cooled by the leap of threadlike waterfalls seeking the plain from the fountains of Amon Gwareth, and he fared as one in some dream of the Gods, for he deemed not such things were seen by men in the visions of their sleep, so great was his amaze at the glory of Gondolin.

Even so came they to the gates, Tuor in wonder and Voronwë in great joy that daring much he had both brought Tuor hither in the will of Ulmo and had himself thrown off the yoke of Melko for ever. Though he hated him no wise less, no longer did he dread that Evil One[17] with a binding terror (and of a sooth that spell which Melko held over the Noldoli was one of bottomless dread, so that he seemed ever nigh them even were they far from the Hells of Iron, and their hearts quaked and they fled not even when they could; and to this Melko trusted often).

Now is there a sally from the gates of Gondolin and a throng comes about these twain in wonder, rejoicing that yet another of the Noldoli has fled hither from Melko, and marvelling at the stature and the gaunt limbs of Tuor, his heavy spear barbed with fish bone and his great harp. Rugged was his aspect, and his locks were unkempt, and he was clad in the skins of bears. 'Tis written that in those days the fathers of the fathers of Men were of less stature than Men now are, and the children of Elfinesse of greater growth, yet was Tuor taller than any that stood there. Indeed the Gondothlim were not bent of back as some of their unhappy kin became, labouring without rest at delving and hammering for Melko, but small were they and slender and very lithe.[18] They were swift of foot and surpassing fair; sweet and sad were their mouths, and their eyes had ever a joy within quivering to tears; for in those times the Gnomes were exiles at heart, haunted with a desire for their ancient home that faded not. But fate and unconquerable eagerness after knowledge had driven them into far places, and now were they hemmed by Melko and must make their abiding as fair as they might by labour and by love.

How it came ever that among Men the Noldoli have been confused with the Orcs who are Melko's goblins, I know not, unless it be that certain of the Noldoli were twisted to the evil of Melko and mingled among these Orcs, for all that race were bred by Melko of the subterranean heats and slime. Their hearts were of granite and their bodies deformed; foul their faces which smiled not, but their laugh that of the clash of metal, and to nothing were they more fain than to aid in the basest of the purposes of Melko. The greatest hatred was between them and the Noldoli, who named them Glamhoth, or folk of dreadful hate.

Behold, the armed guardians of the gate pressed back the thronging folk that gathered about the wanderers, and one among them spake saying: "This is a city of watch and ward, Gondolin on Amon Gwareth, where all may be free who are of true heart, but none may be free to enter unknown. Tell me then your names." But Voronwë named himself Bronweg of the Gnomes, come hither[19] by the will of Ulmo as guide to this son of Men; and Tuor said: "I am Tuor son of Peleg son of Indor of the house of the Swan of the sons of the Men of the North who live far hence, and I fare hither by the will of Ulmo of the Outer Oceans."

Then all who listened grew silent, and his deep and rolling voice held them in amaze, for their own voices were fair as the plash of fountains. Then a saying arose among them: "Lead him before the king."

Then did the throng return within the gates and the wanderers with them, and Tuor saw they were of iron and of great height and strength. Now the streets of Gondolin were paved with stone and wide, kerbed with marble, and fair houses and courts amid gardens of bright flowers were set about the ways, and many towers of great slenderness and beauty builded of white marble and carved most marvellously rose to the heaven. Squares there were lit with fountains and the home of birds that sang amid the branches of their aged trees, but of all these the greatest was that place where stood the king's palace, and the tower thereof was the loftiest in the city, and the fountains that played before the doors shot twenty fathoms and seven in the air and fell in a singing rain of crystal: therein did the sun glitter splendidly by day, and the moon most magically shimmered by night. The birds that dwelt there were of the whiteness of snow and their voices sweeter than a lullaby of music.

On either side of the doors of the palace were two trees, one that bore blossom of gold and the other of silver, nor did they ever fade, for they were shoots of old from the glorious Trees of Valinor that lit those places before Melko and Gloomweaver withered them: and those trees the Gondothlim named Glingol and Bansil.

Then Turgon king of Gondolin robed in white with a belt of gold, and a coronet of garnets was upon his head, stood before his doors and spake from the head of the white stairs that led thereto. "Welcome, O Man of the Land of Shadows. Lo! thy coming was set in our books of wisdom, and it has been written that there would come to pass many great things in the homes of the Gondothlim whenso thou faredst hither."

Then spake Tuor, and Ulmo set power in his heart and majesty in his voice. "Behold, O father of the City of Stone, I am bidden by him who maketh deep music in the Abyss, and who knoweth the mind of Elves and Men, to say unto thee that the days of Release draw nigh. There have come to the ears of Ulmo whispers of your dwelling and your hill of vigilance against the evil of Melko, and he is glad: but his heart is wroth and the hearts of the Valar are angered who sit in the mountains of Valinor and look upòn the world from the peak of Taniquetil, seeing the sorrow of the thraldom of the Noldoli and the wanderings of Men; for Melko ringeth them in the Land of Shadows beyond hills of iron. Therefore have I been brought by a secret way to bid you number your hosts and prepare for battle, for the time is ripe."

Then spake Turgon: "That will I not do, though it be the words of Ulmo and all the Valar. I will not adventure this my people against the terror of the Orcs, nor emperil my city against the fire of Melko."

Then spake Tuor: "Nay, if thou dost not now dare greatly then will the Orcs dwell for ever and possess in the end most of the mountains of the Earth, and cease not to trouble both Elves and Men, even though by other means the Valar contrive hereafter to release the Noldoli; but if thou trust now to the Valar, though terrible the encounter, then shall the Orcs fall, and Melko's power be minished to a little thing."

But Turgon said that he was king of Gondolin and no will should force him against his counsel to emperil the dear labour of long ages gone; but Tuor said, for thus was he bidden by Ulmo who had feared the reluctance of Turgon: "Then am I bidden to say that men of the Gondothlim repair swiftly and secretly down the river Sirion to the sea, and there build them boats and go seek back to Valinor: lo! the paths thereto are forgotten and the highways faded from the world, and the seas and mountains are about it, yet still dwell there the Elves on the hill of Kôr and the Gods sit in Valinor, though their mirth is minished for sorrow and fear of Melko, and they hide their land and weave about it inaccessible magic that no evil come to its shores. Yet still might thy messengers win there and turn their hearts that they rise in wrath and smite Melko, and destroy the Hells of Iron that he has wrought beneath the Mountains of Darkness."

Then said Turgon: "Every year at the lifting of winter have messengers repaired swiftly and by stealth down the river that is called Sirion to the coasts of the Great Sea, and there builded them boats whereto have swans and gulls been harnessed or the strong wings of the wind, and these have sought back beyond the moon and sun to Valinor; but the paths thereto are forgotten and the highways faded from the world, and the seas and mountains are about it, and they that sit within in mirth reck little of the dread of Melko or the sorrow of the world, but hide their land and weave about it inaccessible magic, that no tidings of evil come ever to their ears. Nay, enough of my people have for years untold gone out to the wide waters never to return, but have perished in the deep places or wander now lost in the shadows that have no paths; and at the coming of next year no more shall fare to the sea, but rather will we trust to ourselves and our city for the warding off of Melko; and thereto have the Valar been of scant help aforetime."

Then Tuor's heart was heavy, and Voronwë wept; and Tuor sat by the great fountain of the king and its splashing recalled the music of the waves, and his soul was troubled by the conches of Ulmo and he would return down the waters of Sirion to the sea. But Turgon, who knew that Tuor, mortal as he was, had the favour of the Valar, marking his stout glance and the power of his voice sent to him and bade him dwell in Gondolin and be in his favour, and abide even within the royal halls if he would.

Then Tuor, for he was weary, and that place was fair, said yea; and hence cometh the abiding of Tuor in Gondolin. Of all Tuor's deeds among the Gondothlim the tales tell not, but 'tis said that many a time would he have stolen thence, growing weary of the concourses of folk, and thinking of empty forest and fell or hearing afar the sea-music of Ulmo, had not his heart been filled with love for a woman of the Gondothlim, and she was a daughter of the king.

Now Tuor learnt many things in those realms taught by Voronwë whom he loved, and who loved him exceeding greatly in return; or else was he instructed by the skilled men of the city and the wise men of the king. Wherefore he became a man far mightier than aforetime and wisdom was in his counsel; and many things became clear to him that were unclear before, and many things known that are still unknown to mortal Men. There he heard concerning that city of Gondolin and how

unstaying labour through ages of years had not sufficed to its
building and adornment whereat folk[20] travailed yet; of the delving of that hidden tunnel he heard, which the folk named the Way
of Escape, and how there had been divided counsels in that
matter, yet pity for the enthralled Noldoli had prevailed in the end
to its making; of the guard without ceasing he was told, that
was held there in arms and likewise at certain low places in the
encircling mountains, and how watchers dwelt ever vigilant on
the highest peaks of that range beside builded beacons ready
for the fire; for never did that folk cease to look for an onslaught
of the Orcs did their stronghold become known.

Now however was the guard of the hills maintained rather by
custom than necessity, for the Gondothlim had long ago with
unimagined toil levelled and cleared and delved all that plain
about Amon Gwareth, so that scarce Gnome or bird or beast or
snake could approach but was espied from many leagues off, for
among the Gondothlim were many whose eyes were keener than
the very hawks of Manwë Súlimo Lord of Gods and Elves who
dwells upon Taniquetil; and for this reason did they call that
vale Tumladin or the valley of smoothness. Now this great work
was finished to their mind, and folk were the busier about the
quarrying of metals and the forging of all manner of swords and
axes, spears and bills, and the fashioning of coats of mail,
byrnies and hauberks, greaves and vambraces, helms and shields.
Now 'twas said to Tuor that already the whole folk of Gondolin
shooting with bows without stay day or night might not expend
their hoarded arrows in many years, and that yearly their fear of
the Orcs grew the less for this.

There learnt Tuor of building with stone, of masonry and the
hewing of rock and marble; crafts of weaving and spinning,
broidure and painting, did he fathom, and cunning in metals.
Musics most delicate he there heard; and in these were they who
dwelt in the southern city the most deeply skilled, for there played
a profusion of murmuring founts and springs. Many of these
subtleties Tuor mastered and learned to entwine with his songs to
the wonder and heart's joy of all who heard. Strange stories of the
Sun and Moon and Stars, of the manner of the Earth and its
elements, and of the depths of heaven, were told to him; and the
secret characters of the Elves he learnt, and their speeches and old
tongues, and heard tell of Ilúvatar, the Lord for Always, who
dwelleth beyond the world, of the great music of the Ainur about
Ilúvatar's feet in the uttermost deeps of time, whence came the

making of the world and the manner of it, and all therein and their governance.[21]

Now for his skill and his great mastery over all lore and craft whatsoever, and his great courage of heart and body, did Tuor become a comfort and stay to the king who had no son; and he was beloved by the folk of Gondolin. Upon a time the king caused his most cunning artificers to fashion a suit of armour for Tuor as a great gift, and it was made of Gnome-steel overlaid with silver; but his helm was adorned with a device of metals and jewels like to two swan-wings, one on either side, and a swan's wing was wrought on his shield; but he carried an axe rather than a sword, and this in the speech of the Gondothlim he named Dramborleg, for its buffet stunned and its edge clove all armour.

A house was built for him upon the southern walls, for he loved the free airs and liked not the close neighbourhood of other dwellings. There it was his delight often to stand on the battlements at dawn, and folk rejoiced to see the new light catch the wings of his helm — and many murmured and would fain have backed him into battle with the Orcs, seeing that the speeches of those two, Tuor and Turgon, before the palace were known to many; but this matter went not further for reverence of Turgon, and because at this time in Tuor's heart the thought of the words of Ulmo seemed to have grown dim and far off.

Now came days when Tuor had dwelt among the Gondothlim many years. Long had he known and cherished a love for the king's daughter, and now was his heart full of that love. Great love too had Idril for Tuor, and the strands of her fate were woven with his even from that day when first she gazed upon him from a high window as he stood a way-worn suppliant before the palace of the king. Little cause had Turgon to withstand their love, for he saw in Tuor a kinsman of comfort and great hope. Thus was first wed a child of Men with a daughter of Elfinesse, nor was Tuor the last. Less bliss have many had than they, and their sorrow in the end was great. Yet great was the mirth of those days when Idril and Tuor were wed before the folk in Gar Ainion, the Place of the Gods, nigh to the king's halls. A day of merriment was that wedding to the city of Gondolin, and of [22] the greatest happiness to Tuor and Idril. Thereafter dwelt they in joy in that house upon the walls that looked out south over Tumladin, and this was good to the hearts of all in the city save Meglin alone. Now that Gnome was come of an ancient house, though now were its numbers less than others, but he himself was nephew to the king by his mother the king's sister Isfin; and that tale of Isfin and Eöl may not here be told.[23]

Now the sign of Meglin was a sable Mole, and he was great among quarrymen and a chief of the delvers after ore; and many of these belonged to his house. Less fair was he than most of this goodly folk, swart and of none too kindly mood, so that he won small love, and whispers there were that he had Orc's blood in his veins, but I know not how this could be true. Now he had bid often with the king for the hand of Idril, yet Turgon finding her very loth had as often said nay, for him seemed Meglin's suit was caused as much by the desire of standing in high power beside the royal throne as by love of that most fair maid. Fair indeed was she and brave thereto; and the people called her Idril of the Silver Feet* in that she went ever barefoot and bareheaded, king's daughter as she was, save only at pomps of the Ainur; and Meglin gnawed his anger seeing Tuor thrust him out.

In these days came to pass the fulfilment of the time of the desire of the Valar and the hope of [the] Eldalië, for in great love Idril bore to Tuor a son and he was called Eärendel. Now thereto there are many interpretations both among Elves and Men, but belike it was a name wrought of some secret tongue among the Gondothlim[24] and that has perished with them from the dwellings of the Earth.

Now this babe was of greatest beauty; his skin of a shining white and his eyes of a blue surpassing that of the sky in southern lands – bluer than the sapphires of the raiment of Manwë;[25] and the envy of Meglin was deep at his birth, but the joy of Turgon and all the people very great indeed.

Behold now many years have gone since Tuor was lost amid the foothills and deserted by those Noldoli; yet many years too have gone since to Melko's ears came first those strange tidings – faint were they and various in form – of a Man wandering amid the dales of the waters of Sirion. Now Melko was not much afraid of the race of Men in those days of his great power, and for this reason did Ulmo work through one of this kindred for the better deceiving of Melko, seeing that no Valar and scarce any of the Eldar or Noldoli might stir unmarked of his vigilance. Yet nonetheless foreboding smote that ill heart at the tidings, and he got together a mighty army of spies: sons of the Orcs were there with

* Faintly pencilled above in *Tuor B: Idril Talceleb.*

eyes of yellow and green like cats that could pierce all glooms and see through mist or fog or night; snakes that could go everywhither and search all crannies or the deepest pits or the highest peaks, listen to every whisper that ran in the grass or echoed in the hills; wolves there were and ravening dogs and great weasels full of the thirst of blood whose nostrils could take scent moons old through running water, or whose eyes find among shingle footsteps that had passed a lifetime since; owls came and falcons whose keen glance might descry by day or night the fluttering of small birds in all the woods of the world, and the movement of every mouse or vole or rat that crept or dwelt throughout the Earth. All these he summoned to his Hall of Iron, and they came in multitudes. Thence he sent them over the Earth to seek this Man who had escaped from the Land of Shadows, but yet far more curiously and intently to search out the dwelling of the Noldoli that had escaped his thraldom; for these his heart burnt to destroy or to enslave.

Now while Tuor dwelt in happiness and in great increase of knowledge and might in Gondolin, these creatures through the years untiring nosed among the stones and rocks, hunted the forests and the heaths, espied the airs and lofty places, tracked all paths about the dales and plains, and neither let nor stayed. From this hunt they brought a wealth of tidings to Melko – indeed among many hidden things that they dragged to light they discovered that Way of Escape whereby Tuor and Voronwë entered aforetime. Nor had they done so save by constraining some of the less stout of the Noldoli with dire threats of torment to join in that great ransacking; for because of the magic about that gate no folk of Melko unaided by the Gnomes could come to it. Yet now they had pried of late far into its tunnels and captured within many of the Noldoli creeping there to flee from thraldom. They had scaled too the Encircling Hills* at certain places and gazed upon the beauty of the city of Gondolin and the strength of Amon Gwareth from afar; but into the plain they could not win for the vigilance of its guardians and the difficulty of those mountains. Indeed the Gondothlim were mighty archers, and bows they made of a marvel of power. Therewith might they shoot an arrow into heaven seven times as far as could the best bowman among Men shoot at a mark upon the ground; and they would have suffered no falcon to hover long over their plain or snake to crawl therein; for they liked not creatures of blood, broodlings of Melko.

* Pencilled above in *Tuor B: Heborodin*.

Now in those days was Eärendel one year old when these ill
tidings came to that city of the spies of Melko and how they
encompassed the vale of Tumladin around. Then Turgon's heart
was saddened, remembering the words of Tuor in past years
before the palace doors; and he caused the watch and ward to be
thrice strengthened at all points, and engines of war to be devised
by his artificers and set upon the hill. Poisonous fires and hot
liquids, arrows and great rocks, was he prepared to shoot down on
any who would assail those gleaming walls; and then he abode as
well content as might be, but Tuor's heart was heavier than the
king's, for now the words of Ulmo came ever to his mind, and their
purport and gravity he understood more deeply than of old; nor
did he find any great comfort in Idril, for her heart boded more
darkly even than his own.

Know then that Idril had a great power of piercing with her
thought the darkness of the hearts of Elves and Men, and the
glooms of the future thereto – further even than is the common
power of the kindreds of the Eldalië; therefore she spake thus on a
day to Tuor: "Know, my husband, that my heart misgives me for
doubt of Meglin, and I fear that he will bring an ill on this fair
realm, though by no means may I see how or when – yet I dread
lest all that he knows of our doings and preparations become in
some manner known to the Foe, so that he devise a new means of
whelming us, against which we have thought of no defence. Lo! I
dreamed on a night that Meglin builded a furnace, and coming at
us unawares flung therein Eärendel our babe, and would after
thrust in thee and me; but that for sorrow at the death of our fair
child I would not resist."

And Tuor answered: "There is reason for thy fear, for neither is
my heart good towards Meglin; yet is he the nephew of the king
and thine own cousin, nor is there charge against him, and I see
nought to do but to abide and watch."

But Idril said: "This is my rede thereto: gather thou in deep
secret those delvers and quarrymen who by careful trial are found
to hold least love for Meglin by reason of the pride and arrogance
of his dealings among them. From these thou must choose trusty
men to keep watch upon Meglin whenso he fares to the outer hills,
yet I counsel thee to set the greater part of those in whose secrecy
thou canst confide at a hidden delving, and to devise with their aid
– howsoever cautious and slow that labour be – a secret way from
thy house here beneath the rocks of this hill unto the vale below.
Now this way must not lead toward the Way of Escape, for my

heart bids me trust it not, but even to that far distant pass, the Cleft of Eagles in the southern mountains; and the further this delving reach thitherward beneath the plain so much the better would I esteem it – yet let all this labour be kept dark save from a few."

Now there are none such delvers of earth or rock as the Noldoli (and this Melko knows), but in those places is the earth of a great hardness; and Tuor said: "The rocks of the hill of Amon Gwareth are as iron, and only with much travail may they be cloven; yet if this be done in secret then must great time and patience be added; but the stone of the floor of the Vale of Tumladin is as forgéd steel, nor may it be hewn without the knowledge of the Gondothlim save in moons and years."

Idril said then: "Sooth this may be, but such is my rede, and there is yet time to spare." Then Tuor said that he might not see all its purport, "but 'better is any plan than a lack of counsel', and I will do even as thou sayest".

Now it so chanced that not long after Meglin went to the hills for the getting of ore, and straying in the mountains alone was taken by some of the Orcs prowling there, and they would do him evil and terrible hurt, knowing him to be a man of the Gondothlim. This was however unknown of Tuor's watchers. But evil came into the heart of Meglin, and he said to his captors: "Know then that I am Meglin son of Eöl who had to wife Isfin sister of Turgon king of the Gondothlim." But they said: "What is that to us?" And Meglin answered: "Much is it to you; for if you slay me, be it speedy or slow, ye will lose great tidings concerning the city of Gondolin that your master would rejoice to hear." Then the Orcs stayed their hands, and said they would give him life if the matters he opened to them seemed to merit that; and Meglin told them of all the fashion of that plain and city, of its walls and their height and thickness, and the valour of its gates; of the host of men at arms who now obeyed Turgon he spake, and the countless hoard of weapons gathered for their equipment, of the engines of war and the venomous fires.

Then the Orcs were wroth, and having heard these matters were yet for slaying him there and then as one who impudently enlarged the power of his miserable folk to the mockery of the great might and puissance of Melko; but Meglin catching at a straw said: "Think ye not that ye would rather pleasure your master if ye bore to his feet so noble a captive, that he might hear my tidings of himself and judge of their verity?"

Now this seemed good to the Orcs, and they returned from the mountains about Gondolin to the Hills of Iron and the dark halls of Melko; thither they haled Meglin with them, and now was he in a sore dread. But when he knelt before the black throne of Melko in terror of the grimness of the shapes about him, of the wolves that sat beneath that chair and of the adders that twined about its legs, Melko bade him speak. Then told he those tidings, and Melko hearkening spake very fair to him, that the insolence of his heart in great measure returned.

Now the end of this was that Melko aided by the cunning of Meglin devised a plan for the overthrow of Gondolin. For this Meglin's reward was to be a great captaincy among the Orcs – yet Melko purposed not in his heart to fulfil such a promise – but Tuor and Eärendel should Melko burn, and Idril be given to Meglin's arms – and such promises was that evil one fain to redeem. Yet as meed of treachery did Melko threaten Meglin with the torment of the Balrogs. Now these were demons with whips of flame and claws of steel by whom he tormented those of the Noldoli who durst withstand him in anything – and the Eldar have called them Malkarauki. But the rede that Meglin gave to Melko was that not all the host of the Orcs nor the Balrogs in their fierceness might by assault or siege hope ever to overthrow the walls and gates of Gondolin even if they availed to win unto the plain without. Therefore he counselled Melko to devíse out of his sorceries a succour for his warriors in their endeavour. From the greatness of his wealth of metals and his powers of fire he bid him make beasts like snakes and dragons of irresistible might that should overcreep the Encircling Hills and lap that plain and its fair city in flame and death.

Then Meglin was bidden fare home lest at his absence men suspect somewhat; but Melko wove about him the spell of bottomless dread, and he had thereafter neither joy nor quiet in his heart. Nonetheless he wore a fair mask of good liking and gaiety, so that men said: "Meglin is softened", and he was held in less disfavour; yet Idril feared him the more. Now Meglin said: "I have laboured much and am minded to rest, and to join in the dance and the song and the merrymakings of the folk", and he went no more quarrying stone or ore in the hills: yet in sooth he sought herein to drown his fear and disquiet. A dread possessed him that Melko was ever at hand, and this came of the spell; and he durst never again wander amid the mines lest he again fall in with the Orcs and be bidden once more to the terrors of the halls of darkness.

Now the years fare by, and egged by Idril Tuor keepeth ever at his secret delving; but seeing that the leaguer of spies hath grown thinner Turgon dwelleth more at ease and in less fear. Yet these years are filled by Melko in the utmost ferment of labour, and all the thrall-folk of the Noldoli must dig unceasingly for metals while Melko sitteth and deviseth fires and calleth flames and smokes to come from the lower heats, nor doth he suffer any of the Noldoli to stray ever a foot from their places of bondage. Then on a time Melko assembled all his most cunning smiths and sorcerers, and of iron and flame they wrought a host of monsters such as have only at that time been seen and shall not again be till the Great End. Some were all of iron so cunningly linked that they might flow like slow rivers of metal or coil themselves around and above all obstacles before them, and these were filled in their innermost depths with the grimmest of the Orcs with scimitars and spears; others of bronze and copper were given hearts and spirits of blazing fire, and they blasted all that stood before them with the terror of their snorting or trampled whatso escaped the ardour of their breath; yet others were creatures of pure flame that writhed like ropes of molten metal, and they brought to ruin whatever fabric they came nigh, and iron and stone melted before them and became as water, and upon them rode the Balrogs in hundreds; and these were the most dire of all those monsters which Melko devised against Gondolin.

Now when the seventh summer had gone since the treason of Meglin, and Eärendel was yet of very tender years thóugh a valorous child, Melko withdrew all his spies, for every path and corner of the mountains was now known to him; yet the Gondothlim thought in their unwariness that Melko would no longer seek against them, perceiving their might and the impregnable strength of their dwelling.

But Idril fell into a dark mood and the light of her face was clouded, and many wondered thereat; yet Turgon reduced the watch and ward to its ancient numbers, and to somewhat less, and as autumn came and the gathering of fruits was over folk turned with glad hearts to the feasts of winter: but Tuor stood upon the battlements and gazed upon the Encircling Hills.

Now behold, Idril stood beside him, and the wind was in her hair, and Tuor thought that she was exceeding beautiful, and stooped to kiss her; but her face was sad, and she said: "Now come the days when thou must make choice," and Tuor knew not what she said. Then drawing him within their halls she said to him how

her heart misgave her for fear concerning Eärendel her son, and
for boding that some great evil was nigh, and that Melko would be
at the bottom of it. Then Tuor would comfort her, but might not,
and she questioned him concerning the secret delving, and he said
how it now led a league into the plain, and at that was her heart
somewhat lightened. But still she counselled that the delving be
pressed on, and that henceforth should speed weigh more than
secrecy, "because now is the time very near". And another rede
she gave him, and this he took also, that certain of the bravest and
most true among the lords and warriors of the Gondothlim be
chosen with care and told of that secret way and its issue. These
she counselled him to make into a stout guard and to give them his
emblem to wear that they become his folk, and to do thus under
pretext of the right and dignity of a great lord, kinsman to the
king. "Moreover," said she, "I will get my father's favour to that."
In secret too she whispered to folk that if the city came to its last
stand or Turgon be slain that they rally about Tuor and her son,
and to this they laughed a yea, saying however that Gondolin
would stand as long as Taniquetil or the Mountains of Valinor.

Yet to Turgon she spoke not openly, nor suffered Tuor to do so,
as he desired, despite their love and reverence for him – a great and
a noble and a glorious king he was – seeing that he trusted in
Meglin and held with blind obstinacy his belief in the impregnable
might of the city and that Melko sought no more against it,
perceiving no hope therein. Now in this he was ever strengthened
by the cunning sayings of Meglin. Behold, the guile of that
Gnome was very great, for he wrought much in the dark, so
that folk said: "He doth well to bear the sign of a sable
mole"; and by reason of the folly of certain of the quarrymen,
and yet more by reason of the loose words of certain among his
kin to whom word was somewhat unwarily spoken by Tuor, he
gathered a knowledge of the secret work and laid against that
a plan of his own.

So winter deepened, and it was very cold for those regions, so
that frost fared about the plain of Tumladin and ice lay on its
pools; yet the fountains played ever on Amon Gwareth and the
two trees blossomed, and folk made merry till the day of terror
that was hidden in the heart of Melko.

In these ways that bitter winter passed, and the snows lay
deeper than ever before on the Encircling Hills; yet in its time a
spring of wondrous glory melted the skirts of those white mantles
and the valley drank the waters and burst into flowers. So came

and passed with revelry of children the festival of Nost-na-Lothion or the Birth of Flowers, and the hearts of the Gondothlim were uplifted for the good promise of the year; and now at length is that great feast Tarnin Austa or the Gates of Summer near at hand. For know that on a night it was their custom to begin a solemn ceremony at midnight, continuing it even till the dawn of Tarnin Austa broke, and no voice was uttered in the city from midnight till the break of day, but the dawn they hailed with ancient songs. For years uncounted had the coming of summer thus been greeted with music of choirs, standing upon their gleaming eastern wall; and now comes even the night of vigil and the city is filled with silver lamps, while in the groves upon the new-leaved trees lights of jewelled colours swing, and low musics go along the ways, but no voice sings until the dawn.

The sun has sunk beyond the hills and folk array them for the festival very gladly and eagerly – glancing in expectation to the East. Lo! even when she had gone and all was dark, a new light suddenly began, and a glow there was, but it was beyond the northward heights,[26] and men marvelled, and there was a thronging of the walls and battlements. Then wonder grew to doubt as that light waxed and became yet redder, and doubt to dread as men saw the snow upon the mountains dyed as it were with blood. And thus it was that the fire-serpents of Melko came upon Gondolin.

Then came over the plain riders who bore breathless tidings from those who kept vigil on the peaks; and they told of the fiery hosts and the shapes like dragons, and said: "Melko is upon us." Great was the fear and anguish within that beauteous city, and the streets and byeways were filled with the weeping of women and the wailing of children, and the squares with the mustering of soldiers and the ring of arms. There were the gleaming banners of all the great houses and kindreds of the Gondothlim. Mighty was the array of the house of the king and their colours were white and gold and red, and their emblems the moon and the sun and the scarlet heart.[27] Now in the midmost of these stood Tuor above all heads, and his mail of silver gleamed; and about him was a press of the stoutest of the folk. Lo! all these wore wings as it were of swans or gulls upon their helms, and the emblem of the White Wing was upon their shields. But the folk of Meglin were drawn up in the same place, and sable was their harness, and they bore no sign or emblem, but their round caps of steel were covered with moleskin, and they fought with axes two-headed like mattocks. There Meglin prince of Gondobar gathered many warriors of dark countenance and lowering gaze about him, and a ruddy glow shone upon their faces and gleamed about the polished surfaces of their accoutrement. Behold, all the hills to the north were ablaze, and it was as if rivers of fire ran down the slopes that led to the plain of Tumladin, and folk might already feel the heat thereof.

And many other kindreds were there, the folk of the Swallow and the Heavenly Arch, and from these folk came the greatest number and the best of the bowmen, and they were arrayed upon the broad places of the walls. Now the folk of the Swallow bore a fan of feathers on their helms, and they were arrayed in white and dark blue and in purple and black and showed an arrowhead on their shields. Their lord was Duilin, swiftest of all men to run and leap and surest of archers at a mark. But they of the Heavenly Arch being a folk of uncounted wealth were arrayed in a glory of colours, and their arms were set with jewels that flamed in the light now over the sky. Every shield of that battalion was of the blue of the heavens and its boss a jewel built of seven gems, rubies and amethysts and sapphires, emeralds, chrysoprase, topaz, and amber, but an opal of great size was set in their helms. Egalmoth was their chieftain, and wore a blue mantle upon which the stars were broidered in crystal, and his sword was bent – now none else of the Noldoli bore curved swords – yet he trusted rather to the bow, and shot therewith further than any among that host.

There too were the folk of the Pillar and of the Tower of Snow, and both these kindreds were marshalled by Penlod, tallest of Gnomes. There were those of the Tree, and they were a great house, and their raiment was green. They fought with iron-studded clubs or with slings, and their lord Galdor was held the most valiant of all the Gondothlim save Turgon alone. There stood the house of the Golden Flower who bare a rayed sun upon their shield, and their chief Glorfindel bare a mantle so broidered in threads of gold that it was diapered with celandine as a field in spring; and his arms were damascened with cunning gold.

Then came there from the south of the city the people of the Fountain, and Ecthelion was their lord, and silver and diamonds were their delight; and swords very long and bright and pale did they wield, and they went into battle to the music of flutes. Behind them came the host of the Harp, and this was a battalion of brave warriors; but their leader Salgant was a craven, and he fawned upon Meglin. They were dight with tassels of silver and tassels of gold, and a harp of silver shone in their blazonry upon a field of black; but Salgant bore one of gold, and he alone rode into battle of all the sons of the Gondothlim, and he was heavy and squat.

Now the last of the battalions was furnished by the folk of the Hammer of Wrath, and of these came many of the best smiths and craftsmen, and all that kindred reverenced Aulë the Smith more than all other Ainur. They fought with great maces like hammers, and their shields were heavy, for their arms were very strong. In older days they had been much recruited by Noldoli who escaped from the mines of Melko, and the hatred of this house for the works of that evil one and the Balrogs his demons was exceeding great. Now their leader was Rog, strongest of the Gnomes, scarce second in valour to that Galdor of the Tree. The sign of this people was the Stricken Anvil, and a hammer that smiteth sparks about it was set on their shields, and red gold and black iron was their delight. Very numerous was that battalion, nor had any amongst them a faint heart, and they won the greatest glory of all those fair houses in that struggle against doom; yet were they ill-fated, and none ever fared away from that field, but fell about Rog and vanished from the Earth; and with them much craftsmanship and skill has been lost for ever.[28]

This was the fashion and the array of the eleven houses of the Gondothlim with their signs and emblems, and the bodyguard of Tuor, the folk of the Wing, was accounted the twelfth. Now is the face of that chieftain grim and he looks not to live long – and there in his house upon the walls Idril arrays herself in mail, and seeks Eärendel. And that child was in tears for the strange lights of red that played about the walls of the chamber where he slept; and tales that his nurse Meleth had woven him concerning fiery Melko at times of his waywardness came to him and troubled him. But his mother coming set about him a tiny coat of mail that she had let fashion in secret, and at that time he was glad and exceeding proud, and he shouted for pleasure. Yet Idril wept, for much had she cherished in her heart the fair city and her goodly house, and the love of Tuor and herself that had dwelt therein; but now she saw its destroying nigh at hand, and feared that her contriving would fail against this overwhelming might of the terror of the serpents.

It was now four hours still from middle night, and the sky was red in the north and in the east and west; and those serpents of iron had reached the levels of Tumladin, and those fiery ones were among the lowest slopes of the hills, so that the guards were taken and set in evil torment by the Balrogs that scoured all about, saving only to the furthest south where was Cristhorn the Cleft of Eagles.

Then did King Turgon call a council, and thither fared Tuor and Meglin as royal princes; and Duilin came with Egalmoth and Penlod the tall, and Rog strode thither with Galdor of the Tree and golden Glorfindel and Ecthelion of the voice of music. Thither too fared Salgant atremble at the tidings, and other nobles beside of less blood but better heart.

Then spake Tuor and this was his rede, that a mighty sally be made forthwith, ere the light and heat grew too great in the plain; and many backed him, being but of different minds as to whether the sally should be made by the entire host with the maids and wives and children amidmost, or by diverse bands seeking out in many directions; and to this last Tuor leaned.

But Meglin and Salgant alone held other counsel and were for holding to the city and seeking to guard those treasures that lay within. Out of guile did Meglin speak thus, fearing lest any of the Noldoli escape the doom that he had brought upon them for the saving of his skin, and he dreaded lest his treason become known and somehow vengeance find him in after days. But Salgant spake both echoing Meglin and being grievously afraid of issuing from the city, for he was fain rather to do battle from an impregnable fortress than to risk hard blows upon the field.

Then the lord of the house of the Mole played upon the one weakness of Turgon, saying: "Lo! O King, the city of Gondolin contains a wealth of jewels and metals and stuffs and of things wrought by the hands of the Gnomes to surpassing beauty, and all these thy lords – more brave meseems than wise – would abandon to the Foe. Even should victory be thine upon the plain thy city will be sacked and the Balrogs get hence with a measureless booty"; and Turgon groaned, for Meglin had known his great love for the wealth and loveliness of that burg[29] upon Amon Gwareth. Again said Meglin, putting fire in his voice: "Lo! Hast thou for nought laboured through years uncounted at the building of walls of impregnable thickness and in the making of gates whose valour may not be overthrown; is the power of the hill Amon Gwareth become as lowly as the deep vale, or the hoard of weapons that lie upon it and its unnumbered arrows of so little worth that in the hour of peril thou wouldst cast all aside and go naked into the open against enemies of steel and fire, whose trampling shakes the earth and the Encircling Mountains ring with the clamour of their footsteps?"

And Salgant quaked to think of it and spake noisily, saying: "Meglin speaks well, O King, hear thou him." Then the king took the counsel of those twain though all the lords said otherwise, nay rather the more for that: therefore at his bidding does all that folk abide now the assault upon their walls. But Tuor wept and left the king's hall, and gathering the men of the Wing went through the streets seeking his home; and by that hour was the light great and lurid and there was stifling heat and a black smoke and stench arose about the pathways to the city.

And now came the Monsters across the valley and the white towers of Gondolin reddened before them; but the stoutest were in dread seeing those dragons of fire and those serpents of bronze and iron that fare already about the hill of the city; and they shot unavailing arrows at them. Then is there a cry of hope, for behold, the snakes of fire may not climb the hill for its steepness and for its glassiness, and by reason of the quenching waters that fall upon its sides; yet they lie about its feet and a vast steam arises where the streams of Amon Gwareth and the flames of the serpents drive together. Then grew there such a heat that women became faint and men sweated to weariness beneath their mail, and all the springs of the city, save only the fountain of the king, grew hot and smoked.

But now Gothmog lord of Balrogs, captain of the hosts of Melko, took counsel and gathered all his things of iron that could coil themselves around and above all obstacles before them. These he bade pile themselves before the northern gate; and behold, their great spires reached even to its threshold and thrust at the towers and bastions about it, and by reason of the exceeding heaviness of their bodies those gates fell, and great was the noise thereof: yet the most of the walls around them still stood firm. Then the engines and the catapults of the king poured darts and boulders and molten metals on those ruthless beasts, and their hollow bellies clanged beneath the buffeting, yet it availed not for they might not be broken, and the fires rolled off them. Then were the topmost opened about their middles, and an innumerable host of the Orcs, the goblins of hatred, poured therefrom into the breach; and who shall tell of the gleam of their scimitars or the flash of the broad-bladed spears with which they stabbed?

Then did Rog shout in a mighty voice, and all the people of the Hammer of Wrath and the kindred of the Tree with Galdor the valiant leapt at the foe. There the blows of their great hammers and the dint of their clubs rang to the Encircling Mountains and the Orcs fell like leaves; and those of the Swallow and the Arch poured arrows like the dark rains of autumn upon them, and both

Orcs and Gondothlim fell thereunder for the smoke and the confusion. Great was that battle, yet for all their valour the Gondothlim by reason of the might of ever increasing numbers were borne slowly backwards till the goblins held part of the northernmost city.

At this time is Tuor at the head of the folk of the Wing struggling in the turmoil of the streets, and now he wins through to his house and finds that Meglin is before him. Trusting in the battle now begun about the northern gate and in the uproar in the city, Meglin had looked to this hour for the consummation of his designs. Learning much of the secret delving of Tuor (yet only at the last moment had he got this knowledge and he could not discover all) he said nought to the king or any other, for it was his thought that of a surety that tunnel would go in the end toward the Way of Escape, this being the most nigh to the city, and he had a mind to use this to his good, and to the ill of the Noldoli. Messengers by great stealth he despatched to Melko to set a guard about the outer issue of that Way when the assault was made; but he himself thought now to take Eärendel and cast him into the fire beneath the walls, and seizing Idril he would constrain her to guide him to the secrets of the passage, that he might win out of this terror of fire and slaughter and drag her withal along with him to the lands of Melko. Now Meglin was afeared that even the secret token which Melko had given him would fail in that direful sack, and was minded to help that Ainu to the fulfilment of his promises of safety. No doubt had he however of the death of Tuor in that great burning, for to Salgant he had confided the task of delaying him in the king's halls and egging him straight thence into the deadliest of the fight – but lo! Salgant fell into a terror unto death, and he rode home and lay there now aquake on his bed; but Tuor fared home with the folk of the Wing.

Now Tuor did this, though his valour leapt to the noise of war, that he might take farewell of Idril and Eärendel, and speed them with a bodyguard down the secret way ere he returned himself to the battle throng to die if must be: but he found a press of the Mole-folk about his door, and these were the grimmest and least good-hearted of folk that Meglin might get in that city. Yet were they free Noldoli and under no spell of Melko's like their master, wherefore though for the lordship of Meglin they aided not Idril, no more would they touch of his purpose despite all his curses.

Now then Meglin had Idril by the hair and sought to drag her to the battlements out of cruelty of heart, that she might see the fall of Eärendel to the flames; but he was cumbered by that child, and she fought, alone as she was, like a tigress for all her beauty and slenderness. There he now struggles and delays amid oaths while that folk of the Wing draw nigh – and lo! Tuor gives a shout so great that the Orcs hear it afar and waver at the sound of it. Like a crash of tempest the guard of the Wing were amid the men of the Mole, and these were stricken asunder. When Meglin saw this he would stab Eärendel with a short knife he had; but that child bit his left hand, that his teeth sank in, and he staggered, and stabbed weakly, and the mail of the small coat turned the blade aside; and thereupon Tuor was upon him and his wrath was terrible to see. He seized Meglin by that hand that held the knife and broke the arm with the wrench, and then taking him by the middle leapt with him upon the walls, and flung him far out. Great was the fall of his body, and it smote Amon Gwareth three times ere it pitched in the midmost of the flames; and the name of Meglin has gone out in shame from among Eldar and Noldoli.

Then the warriors of the Mole being more numerous than those few of the Wing, and loyal to their lord, came at Tuor, and there were great blows, but no man might stand before the wrath of Tuor, and they were smitten and driven to fly into what dark holes they might, or flung from the walls. Then Tuor and his men must get them to the battle of the Gate, for the noise of it has grown very great, and Tuor has it still in his heart that the city may stand; yet with Idril he left there Voronwë against his will and some other swordsmen to be a guard for her till he returned or might send tidings from the fray.

Now was the battle at that gate very evil indeed, and Duilin of the Swallow as he shot from the walls was smitten by a fiery bolt of the Balrogs who leapt about the base of Amon Gwareth; and he fell from the battlements and perished. Then the Balrogs continued to shoot darts of fire and flaming arrows like small snakes into the sky, and these fell upon the roofs and gardens of Gondolin till all the trees were scorched, and the flowers and grass burned up, and the whiteness of those walls and colonnades was blackened and seared: yet a worse matter was it that a company of those demons climbed upon the coils of the serpents of iron and thence loosed unceasingly from their bows and slings till a fire began to burn in the city to the back of the main army of the defenders.

Then said Rog in a great voice: "Who now shall fear the Balrogs for all their terror? See before us the accursed ones who for ages have tormented the children of the Noldoli, and who now set a fire at our backs with their shooting. Come ye of the Hammer of Wrath and we will smite them for their evil." Thereupon he lifted his mace, and its handle was long; and he made a way before him by the wrath of his onset even unto the fallen gate: but all the people of the Stricken Anvil ran behind like a wedge, and sparks came from their eyes for the fury of their rage. A great deed was that sally, as the Noldoli sing yet, and many of the Orcs were borne backward into the fires below; but the men of Rog leapt even upon the coils of the serpents and came at those Balrogs and smote them grievously, for all they had whips of flame and claws of steel, and were in stature very great. They battered them into nought, or catching at their whips wielded these against them, that they tore them even as they had aforetime torn the Gnomes; and the number of Balrogs that perished was a marvel and dread to the hosts of Melko, for ere that day never had any of the Balrogs been slain by the hand of Elves or Men.

Then Gothmog Lord of Balrogs gathered all his demons that were about the city and ordered them thus: a number made for the *i*olk of the Hammer and gave before them, but the greater company rushing upon the flank contrived to get to their backs, higher upon the coils of the drakes and nearer to the gates, so that Rog might not win back save with great slaughter among his folk. But Rog seeing this essayed not to win back, as was hoped, but with all his folk fell on those whose part was to give before him; and they fled before him now of dire need rather than of craft. Down into the plain were they harried, and their shrieks rent the airs of Tumladin. Then that house of the Hammer fared about smiting and hewing the astonied bands of Melko till they were hemmed at the last by an overwhelming force of the Orcs and the Balrogs, and a fire-drake was loosed upon them. There did they perish about Rog hewing to the last till iron and flame overcame them, and it is yet sung that each man of the Hammer of Wrath took the lives of seven foemen to pay for his own. Then did dread fall more heavily still upon the Gondothlim at the death of Rog and the loss of his battalion, and they gave back further yet into the city, and Penlod perished there in a lane with his back to the wall, and about him many of the men of the Pillar and many of the Tower of Snow.

Now therefore Melko's goblins held all the gate and a great part of the walls on either side, whence numbers of the Swallow and those of the Rainbow were thrust to doom; but within the city they had won a great space reaching nigh to the centre, even to the Place of the Well that adjoined the Square of the Palace. Yet about those ways and around the gate their dead were piled in uncounted heaps, and they halted therefore and took counsel, seeing that for the valour of the Gondothlim they had lost many more than they had hoped and far more than those defenders. Fearful too they were for that slaughter Rog had done amid the Balrogs, because of those demons they had great courage and confidence of heart.

Now then the plan that they made was to hold what they had won, while those serpents of bronze and with great feet for trampling climbed slowly over those of iron, and reaching the walls there opened a breach wherethrough the Balrogs might ride upon the dragons of flame: yet they knew this must be done with speed, for the heats of those drakes lasted not for ever, and might only be plenished from the wells of fire that Melko had made in the fastness of his own land.

But even as their messengers were sped they heard a sweet music that was played amid the host of the Gondothlim and they feared what it might mean; and lo! there came Ecthelion and the people of the Fountain whom Turgon till now had held in reserve, for he watched the most of that affray from the heights of his tower. Now marched these folk to a great playing of their flutes, and the crystal and silver of their array was most lovely to see amid the red light of the fires and the blackness of the ruins.

Then on a sudden their music ceased and Ecthelion of the fair voice shouted for the drawing of swords, and before the Orcs might foresee his onslaught the flashing of those pale blades was amongst them. 'Tis said that Ecthelion's folk there slew more of the goblins than fell ever in all the battles of the Eldalië with that race, and that his name is a terror among them to this latest day, and a warcry to the Eldar.

Now it is that Tuor and the men of the Wing fare into the fight and range themselves beside Ecthelion and those of the Fountain, and the twain strike mighty blows and ward each many a thrust from the other, and harry the Orcs so that they win back almost to the gate. But there behold a quaking and a trampling, for the dragons labour mightily at beating a path up Amon Gwareth and at casting down the walls of the city; and already there is a gap therein and a confusion of masonry where the ward-towers have fallen in ruin. Bands of the Swallow and of the Arch of Heaven there fight bitterly amid the wreck or contest the walls to east and west with the foe; but even as Tuor comes nigh driving the Orcs, one of those brazen snakes heaves against the western wall and a great mass of it shakes and falls, and behind comes a creature of fire and Balrogs upon it. Flames gust from the jaws of that worm and folk wither before it, and the wings of the helm of Tuor are blackened, but he stands and gathers about him his guard and all of the Arch and Swallow he can find, whereas on his right Ecthelion rallies the men of the Fountain of the South.

Now the Orcs again take heart from the coming of the drakes, and they mingle with the Balrogs that pour about the breach, and they assail the Gondothlim grievously. There Tuor slew Othrod a lord of the Orcs cleaving his helm, and Balcmeg he hewed asunder, and Lug he smote with his axe that his limbs were cut from beneath him at the knee, but Ecthelion shore through two captains of the goblins at a sweep and cleft the head of Orcobal their chiefest champion to his teeth; and by reason of the great doughtiness of those two lords they came even unto the Balrogs. Of those demons of power Ecthelion slew three, for the brightness of his sword cleft the iron of them and did hurt to their fire, and they writhed; yet of the leap of that axe Dramborleg that was swung by the hand of Tuor were they still more afraid, for it sang like the rush of eagle's wings in the air and took death as it fell, and five of them went down before it.

But so it is that few cannot fight always against the many, and Ecthelion's left arm got a sore rent from a whip of the Balrog's and his shield fell to earth even as that dragon of fire drew nigh amid the ruin of the walls. Then Ecthelion must lean on Tuor, and Tuor might not leave him, though the very feet of the trampling beast were upon them, and they were like to be overborne: but Tuor hewed at a foot of the creature so that flame spouted forth, and that serpent screamed, lashing with its tail; and many of both Orcs and Noldoli got their death therefrom. Now Tuor gathered his might and lifted Ecthelion, and amid a remnant of the folk got thereunder and escaped the drake; yet dire was the killing of men that beast had wrought, and the Gondothlim were sorely shaken.

Thus it was that Tuor son of Peleg gave before the foe, fighting as he yielded ground, and bore from that battle Ecthelion of the Fountain, but the drakes and the foemen held half the city and all the north of it. Thence marauding bands fared about the streets and did much ransacking, or slew in the dark men and women and children, and many, if occasion let, they bound and led back and flung in the iron chambers amid the dragons of iron, that they might drag them afterward to be thralls of Melko.

Now Tuor reached the Square of the Folkwell by a way entering from the north, and found there Galdor denying the western entry by the Arch of Inwë to a horde of the goblins, but about him was now but a few of those men of the Tree. There did Galdor become the salvation of Tuor, for he fell behind his men stumbling beneath Ecthelion over a body that lay in the dark, and the Orcs had taken them both but for the sudden rush of that champion and the dint of his club.

There were the scatterlings of the guard of the Wing and of the houses of the Tree and the Fountain, and of the Swallow and the Arch, welded to a good battalion, and by the counsel of Tuor they gave way out of that Place of the Well, seeing that the Square of the King that lay next was the more defensible. Now that place had aforetime contained many beautiful trees, both oak and poplar, around a great well of vast depth and great purity of water; yet at that hour it was full of the riot and ugliness of those hideous people of Melko, and those waters were polluted with their carcases.

Thus comes the last stout gathering of those defenders in the Square of the Palace of Turgon. Among them are many wounded and fainting, and Tuor is weary for the labours of the night and the weight of Ecthelion who is in a deadly swoon. Even as he led that battalion in by the Road of Arches from the north-west (and they had much ado to prevent any foe getting behind their backs) a noise arose at the eastward of the square, and lo! Glorfindel is driven in with the last of the men of the Golden Flower.

Now these had sustained a terrible conflict in the Great Market to the east of the city, where a force of Orcs led by Balrogs came on them at unawares as they marched by a circuitous way to the fight about the gate. This they did to surprise the foe upon his left flank, but were themselves ambuscaded; there fought they bitterly for hours till a fire-drake new-come from the breach overwhelmed them, and Glorfindel cut his way out very hardly and with few men; but that place with its stores and its goodly things of fine workmanship was a waste of flames.

The story tells that Turgon had sent the men of the Harp to their aid because of the urgency of messengers from Glorfindel, but Salgant concealed this bidding from them, saying they were to garrison the square of the Lesser Market to the south where he dwelt, and they fretted thereat. Now however they brake from Salgant and were come before the king's hall; and that was very timely, for a triumphant press of foemen was at Glorfindel's heels. On these the men of the Harp unbidden fell with great eagerness and utterly redeemed the cravenhood of their lord, driving the enemy back into the market, and being leaderless fared even over wrathfully, so that many of them were trapped in the flames or sank before the breath of the serpent that revelled there.

Tuor now drank of the great fountain and was refreshed, and loosening Ecthelion's helm gave him to drink, splashing his face that his swoon left him. Now those lords Tuor and Glorfindel clear the square and withdraw all the men they may from the entrances and bar them with barriers, save as yet on the south. Even from that region comes now Egalmoth. He had had charge of the engines on the wall; but long since deeming matters to call rather for handstrokes about the streets than shooting upon the battlements he gathered some of the Arch and of the Swallow about him, and cast away his bow. Then did they fare about the city dealing good blows whenever they fell in with bands of the enemy. Thereby he rescued many bands of captives and gathered no few wandering and driven men, and so got to the King's Square with hard fighting; and men were fain to greet him for they had feared him dead. Now are all the women and children that had gathered there or been brought in by Egalmoth stowed in the king's halls, and the ranks of the houses made ready for the last. In that host of survivors are some, be it however few, of all the kindreds save of the Hammer of Wrath alone; and the king's house is as yet untouched. Nor is this any shame, for their part was ever to bide fresh to the last and defend the king.

But now the men of Melko have assembled their forces, and seven dragons of fire are come with Orcs about them and Balrogs upon them down all the ways from north, east, and west, seeking the Square of the King. Then there was carnage at the barriers, and Egalmoth and Tuor went from place to place of the defence, but Ecthelion lay by the fountain; and that stand was the most stubborn-valiant that is remembered in all the songs or in any tale. Yet at long last a drake bursts the barrier to the north – and there had once been the issue of the Alley of Roses and a fair place to see or to walk in, but now there is but a lane of blackness and it is filled with noise.

Tuor stood then in the way of that beast, but was sundered from Egalmoth, and they pressed him backward even to the centre of the square nigh the fountain. There he became weary from the strangling heat and was beaten down by a great demon, even Gothmog lord of Balrogs, son of Melko. But lo! Ecthelion, whose face was of the pallor of grey steel and whose shield-arm hung limp at his side, strode above him as he fell; and that Gnome drave at the demon, yet did not give him his death, getting rather a wound to his sword-arm that his weapon left his grasp. Then leapt Ecthelion lord of the Fountain, fairest of the Noldoli, full at Gothmog even as he raised his whip, and his helm that had a spike upon it he drave into that evil breast, and he twined his legs about his foeman's thighs; and the Balrog yelled and fell forward; but those two dropped into the basin of the king's fountain which was very deep. There found that creature his bane; and Ecthelion sank steel-laden into the depths, and so perished the lord of the Fountain after fiery battle in cool waters.[30]

Now Tuor had arisen when the assault of Ecthelion gave him space, and seeing that great deed he wept for his love of that fair Gnome of the Fountain, but being wrapped in battle he scarce cut his way to the folk about the palace. There seeing the wavering of the enemy by reason of the dread of the fall of Gothmog the marshal of the hosts, the royal house laid on and the king came down in splendour among them and hewed with them, that they swept again much of the square, and of the Balrogs slew even two score, which is a very great prowess indeed: but greater still did they do, for they hemmed in one of the Fire-drakes for all his flaming, and forced him into the very waters of the fountain that he perished therein. Now this was the end of that fair water; and its pools turned to steam and its spring was dried up, and it shot no more into the heaven, but rather a vast column of vapour arose to the sky and the cloud therefrom floated over all the land.

Then dread fell on all for the doom of the fountain, and the square was filled with mists of scalding heat and blinding fogs, and the people of the royal house were killed therein by heat and by the foe and by the serpents and by one another: but a body of them saved the king, and there was a rally of men beneath Glingol and Bansil.

Then said the king: "Great is the fall of Gondolin", and men shuddered, for such were the words of Amnon the prophet of old;[31] but Tuor speaking wildly for ruth and love of the king cried: "Gondolin stands yet, and Ulmo will not suffer it to perish!" Now were they at that time standing, Tuor by the Trees and the king upon the Stairs, as they had stood aforetime when Tuor spake the embassy of Ulmo. But Turgon said: "Evil have I brought upon the Flower of the Plain in despite of Ulmo, and now he leaveth it to wither in the fire. Lo! hope is no more in my heart for my city of loveliness, but the children of the Noldoli shall not be worsted for ever."

Then did the Gondothlim clash their weapons, for many stood

nigh, but Turgon said: "Fight not against doom, O my children! Seek ye who may safety in flight, if perhaps there be time yet: but let Tuor have your lealty." But Tuor said: "Thou art king"; and Turgon made answer: "Yet no blow will I strike more", and he cast his crown at the roots of Glingol. Then did Galdor who stood there pick it up, but Turgon accepted it not, and bare of head climbed to the topmost pinnacle of that white tower that stood nigh his palace. There he shouted in a voice like a horn blown among the mountains, and all that were gathered beneath the Trees and the foemen in the mists of the square heard him: "Great is the victory of the Noldoli!" And 'tis said that it was then middle night, and that the Orcs yelled in derision.

Then did men speak of a sally, and were of two minds. Many held that it were impossible to burst through, nor might they even so get over the plain or through the hills, and that it were better therefore to die about the king. But Tuor might not think well of the death of so many fair women and children, were it at the hands of their own folk in the last resort, or by the weapons of the enemy, and he spake of the delving and of the secret way. Therefore did he counsel that they beg Turgon to have other mind, and coming among them lead that remnant southward to the walls and the entry of that passage; but he himself burnt with desire to fare thither and know how Idril and Eärendel might be, or to get tidings hence to them and bid them begone speedily, for Gondolin was taken. Now Tuor's plan seemed to the lords desperate indeed – seeing the narrowness of the tunnel and the greatness of the company that must pass it – yet would they fain take this rede in their straits. But Turgon hearkened not, and bid them fare now ere it was too late, and "Let Tuor," said he, "be your guide and your chieftain. But I Turgon will not leave my city, and will burn with it." Then sped they messengers again to the tower, saying: "Sire, who are the Gondothlim if thou perish? Lead us!" But he said: "Lo! I abide here"; and a third time, and he said: "If I am king, obey my behests, and dare not to parley further with my commands." After that they sent no more and made ready for the forlorn attempt. But the folk of the royal house that yet lived would not budge a foot, but gathered thickly about the base of the king's tower. "Here," said they, "we will stay if Turgon goes not forth"; and they might not be persuaded.

Now was Tuor torn sorely between his reverence for the king and the love for Idril and his child, wherewith his heart was sick; yet already serpents fare about the square trampling upon dead and dying, and the foe gathers in the mists for the last onslaught; and the choice must be made. Then because of the wailing of the women in the halls of the palace and the greatness of his pity for that sad remainder of the peoples of Gondolin, he gathered all that rueful company, maids, children and mothers, and setting them amidmost marshalled as well as he might his men around them. Deepest he set them at flank and at rear, for he purposed falling back southward fighting as best he might with the rearguard as he went; and thus if it might so be to win down the Road of Pomps to the Place of the Gods ere any great force be sent to circumvent him. Thence was it his thought to go by the Way of Running Waters past the Fountains of the South to the walls and to his home; but the passage of the secret tunnel he doubted much. Thereupon espying his movement the foe made forthwith a great onslaught upon his left flank and his rear – from east and north – even as he began to withdraw; but his right was covered by the king's hall and the head of that column drew already into the Road of Pomps.

Then some of the hugest of the drakes came on and glared in the fog, and he must perforce bid the company to go at a run, fighting on the left at haphazard; but Glorfindel held the rear manfully and many more of the Golden Flower fell there. So it was that they passed the Road of Pomps and reached Gar Ainion, the Place of the Gods; and this was very open and at its middle the highest ground of all the city. Here Tuor looks for an evil stand and it is scarce in his hope to get much further; but behold, the foe seems already to slacken and scarce any follow them, and this is a wonder. Now comes Tuor at their head to the Place of Wedding, and lo! there stands Idril before him with her hair unbraided as on that day of their marriage before; and great is his amaze. By her stood Voronwë and none other, but Idril saw not even Tuor, for her gaze was set back upon the Place of the King that now lay somewhat below them. Then all that host halted and looked back whither her eyes gazed and their hearts stood still; for now they saw why the foe pressed them so little and the reason of their salvation. Lo! a drake was coiled even on the very steps of the palace and defiled their whiteness; but swarms of the Orcs ransacked within and dragged forth forgotten women and children or slew men that fought alone. Glingol was withered to the stock and Bansil was blackened utterly, and the king's tower was beset. High up could they descry the form of the king, but about the base a serpent of iron spouting flame lashed and rowed with his tail, and

Balrogs were round him; and there was the king's house in great anguish, and dread cries carried up to the watchers. So was it that the sack of the halls of Turgon and that most valiant stand of the royal house held the mind of the foe, so that Tuor got thence with his company, and stood now in tears upon the Place of the Gods.

Then said Idril: "Woe is me whose father awaiteth doom even upon his topmost pinnacle; but seven times woe whose lord hath gone down before Melko and will stride home no more!" – for she was distraught with the agony of that night.

Then said Tuor: "Lo! Idril, it is I, and I live; yet now will I get thy father hence, be it from the Hells of Melko!" With that he would make down the hill alone, maddened by the grief of his wife; but she coming to her wits in a storm of weeping clasped his knees saying: "My lord! My lord!" and delayed him. Yet even as they spake a great noise and a yelling rose from that place of anguish. Behold, the tower leapt into a flame and in a stab of fire it fell, for the dragons crushed the base of it and all who stood there. Great was the clangour of that terrible fall, and therein passed Turgon King of the Gondothlim, and for that hour the victory was to Melko.

Then said Idril heavily: "Sad is the blindness of the wise"; but Tuor said: "Sad too is the stubbornness of those we love – yet 'twas a valiant fault," then stooping he lifted and kissed her, for she was more to him than all the Gondothlim; but she wept bitterly for her father. Then turned Tuor to the captains, saying: "Lo, we must get hence with all speed, lest we be surrounded"; and forthwith they moved onward as swiftly as they might and got them far from thence ere the Orcs tired of sacking the palace and rejoicing at the fall of the tower of Turgon.

Now are they in the southward city and meet but scattered bands of plunderers who fly before them; yet do they find fire and burning everywhere for the ruthlessness of that enemy. Women do they meet, some with babes and some laden with chattels, but Tuor would not let them bear away aught save a little food. Coming now at length to a greater quiet Tuor asked Voronwë for tidings, in that Idril spake not and was well-nigh in a swoon; and Voronwë told him of how she and he had waited before the doors of the house while the noise of those battles grew and shook their hearts; and Idril wept for lack of tidings from Tuor. At length she had sped the most part of her guard down the secret way with Eärendel, constraining them to depart with imperious words, yet was her grief great at that sundering. She herself would bide, said she, nor seek to live after her lord; and then she fared about gathering womenfolk and wanderers and speeding them down the tunnel, and smiting marauders with her small band; nor might they dissuade her from bearing a sword.

At length they had fallen in with a band somewhat too numerous, and Voronwë had dragged her thence but by the luck of the Gods, for all else with them perished, and their foe burned Tuor's house; yet found not the secret way. "Therewith," said Voronwë, "thy lady became distraught of weariness and grief, and fared into the city wildly to my great fear – nor might I get her to sally from the burning."

About the saying of these words were they come to the southern walls and nigh to Tuor's house, and lo! it was cast down and the wreckage was asmoke; and thereat was Tuor bitterly wroth. But there was a noise that boded the approach of Orcs, and Tuor despatched that company as swiftly as might be down that secret way.

Now is there great sorrow upon that staircase as those exiles bid farewell to Gondolin; yet are they without much hope of further life beyond the hills, for how shall any slip from the hand of Melko?

Glad is Tuor when all have passed the entrance and his fear lightens; indeed by the luck of the Valar only can all those folk have got therein unspied of the Orcs. Some now are left who casting aside their arms labour with picks from within and block up the entry of the passage, faring then after the host as they might; but when that folk had descended the stairway to a level with the valley the heat grew to a torment for the fire of the dragons that were about the city; and they were indeed nigh, for the delving was there at no great depth in the earth. Boulders were loosened by the tremors of the ground and falling crushed many, and fumes were in the air so that their torches and lanterns went out. Here they fell over bodies of some that had gone before and perished, and Tuor was in fear for Eärendel; and they pressed on in great darkness and anguish. Nigh two hours were they in that tunnel of the earth, and towards its end it was scarce finished, but rugged at the sides and low.[32]

Then came they at the last lessened by wellnigh a tithe to the tunnel's opening, and it debouched cunningly in a large basin where once water had lain, but it was now full of thick bushes. Here were gathered no small press of mingled folk whom Idril and Voronwë sped down the hidden way before them, and they were weeping softly in weariness and sorrow, but Eärendel was not there. Thereat were Tuor and Idril in anguish of heart.[33] Lamentation was there too among all those others, for amidmost of the plain about them loomed afar the hill of Amon Gwareth crowned with flames, where had stood the gleaming city of their home. Fire-drakes are about it and monsters of iron fare in and out of its gates, and great is that sack of the Balrogs and Orcs. Somewhat of comfort has this nonetheless for the leaders, for they judge the plain to be nigh empty of Melko's folk save hard by the city, for thither have fared all his evil ones to revel in that destruction.

"Now," therefore said Galdor, "we must get as far hence toward the Encircling Mountains as may be ere dawn come upon us, and that giveth no great space of time, for summer is at hand."[34] Thereat rose a dissension, for a number said that it were folly to make for Cristhorn as Tuor purposed. "The sun," say they, "will be up long ere we win the foothills, and we shall be whelmed in the plain by those drakes and those demons. Let us fare to Bad Uthwen, the Way of Escape, for that is but half the journeying, and our weary and our wounded may hope to win so far if no further."

Yet Idril spake against this, and persuaded the lords that they trust not to the magic of that way that had aforetime shielded it from discovery: "for what magic stands if Gondolin be fallen?" Nonetheless a large body of men and women sundered from Tuor and fared to Bad Uthwen, and there into the jaws of a monster who by the guile of Melko at Meglin's rede sat at the outer issue that none came through. But the others, led by one Legolas Greenleaf of the house of the Tree, who knew all that plain by day or by dark, and was night-sighted, made much speed over the vale for all their weariness, and halted only after a great march. Then was all the Earth spread with the grey light of that sad dawn which looked no more on the beauty of Gondolin; but the plain was full of mists – and that was a marvel, for no mist or fog came there ever before, and this perchance had to do with the doom of the fountain of the king. Again they rose, and covered by the vapours fared long past dawn in safety, till they were already too far away for any to descry them in those misty airs from the hill or from the ruined walls.

Now the Mountains or rather their lowest hills were on that side seven leagues save a mile from Gondolin, and Cristhorn the Cleft of Eagles two leagues of upward going from the beginning of the Mountains, for it was at a great height; wherefore they had yet two leagues and part of a third to traverse amid the spurs and foothills, and they were very weary.[35] By now the sun hung well above a saddle in the eastern hills, and she was very red and great; and the mists nigh them were lifted, but the ruins of Gondolin were utterly hidden as in a cloud. Behold then at the clearing of the airs they saw, but a few furlongs off, a knot of men that fled on foot, and these were pursued by a strange cavalry, for on great wolves rode Orcs, as they thought, brandishing spears. Then said Tuor: "Lo! there is Eärendel my son; behold, his face shineth as a star in the waste,[36] and my men of the Wing are about him, and they are in sore straits." Forthwith he chose fifty of the men that were least weary, and leaving the main company to follow he fared over the plain with that troop as swiftly as they had strength left. Coming now to carry of voice Tuor shouted to the men about Eärendel to stand and flee not, for the wolfriders were scattering them and slaying them piecemeal, and the child was upon the shoulders of one Hendor, a house-carle of Idril's, and he seemed like to be left with his burden. Then they stood back to back and Hendor and Eärendel amidmost; but Tuor soon came up, though all his troop were breathless.

Of the wolfriders there were a score, and of the men that were about Eärendel but six living; therefore had Tuor opened his men into a crescent of but one rank, and hoped so to envelop the riders, lest any escaping bring tidings to the main foe and draw ruin upon the exiles. In this he succeeded, so that only two escaped, and therewithal wounded and without their beasts, wherefore were their tidings brought too late to the city.

Glad was Eärendel to greet Tuor, and Tuor most fain of his child; but said Eärendel: "I am thirsty, father, for I have run far – nor had Hendor need to bear me." Thereto his father said nought, having no water, and thinking of the need of all that company that he guided; but Eärendel said again: "'Twas good to see Meglin die so, for he would set arms about my mother – and I liked him not; but I would travel in no tunnels for all Melko's wolfriders." Then Tuor smiled and set him upon his shoulders. Soon after this the main company came up, and Tuor gave Eärendel to his mother who was in a great joy; but Eärendel would not be borne in her arms, for he said: "Mother Idril, thou art weary, and warriors in mail ride not among the Gondothlim, save it be old Salgant!" and his mother laughed amid her sorrow; but Eärendel said: "Nay, where is Salgant?" – for Salgant had told him quaint tales or played drolleries with him at times, and Eärendel had much laughter of the old Gnome in those days when he came many a day to the house of Tuor, loving the good wine and fair repast he there received. But none could say where Salgant was, nor can they now. Mayhap he was whelmed by fire upon his bed; yet some have it that he was taken captive to the halls of Melko and made his buffoon – and this is an ill fate for a noble of the good race of the Gnomes. Then was Eärendel sad at that, and walked beside his mother in silence.

Now came they to the foothills and it was full morning but still grey, and there nigh to the beginning of the upward road folk stretched them and rested in a little dale fringed with trees and with hazel-bushes, and many slept despite their peril, for they were utterly spent. Yet Tuor set a strict watch, and himself slept not. Here they made one meal of scanty food and broken meats; and Eärendel quenched his thirst and played beside a little brook. Then said he to his mother: "Mother Idril, I would we had good Ecthelion of the Fountain here to play to me on his flute, or make me willow-whistles! Perchance he has gone on ahead?" But Idril said nay, and told what she had heard of his end. Then said Eärendel that he cared not ever to see the streets of Gondolin again, and he wept bitterly; but Tuor said that he would not again see those streets, "for Gondolin is no more".

Thereafter nigh to the hour of sundown behind the hills Tuor bade the company arise, and they pressed on by rugged paths. Soon now the grass faded and gave way to mossy stones, and trees fell away, and even the pines and firs grew sparse. About the set of the sun the way so wound behind a shoulder of the hills that they might not again look toward Gondolin. There all that company turned, and lo! the plain is clear and smiling in the last light as of old; but afar off as they gazed a great flare shot up against the darkened north – and that was the fall of the last tower of Gondolin, even that which had stood hard by the southern gate, and whose shadow fell oft across the walls of Tuor's house. Then sank the sun, and they saw Gondolin no more.

Now the pass of Cristhorn, that is the Eagles' Cleft, is one of dangerous going, and that host had not ventured it by dark, lanternless and without torches, and very weary and cumbered with women and children and sick and stricken men, had it not been for their great fear of Melko's scouts, for it was a great company and might not fare very secretly. Darkness gathered rapidly as they approached that high place, and they must string out into a long and straggling line. Galdor and a band of men spear-armed went ahead, and Legolas was with them, whose eyes were like cats' for the dark, yet could they see further. Thereafter followed the least weary of the women supporting the sick and the wounded that could go on foot. Idril was with these, and Eärendel who bore up well, but Tuor was in the midmost behind them with all his men of the Wing, and they bare some who were grievously hurt, and Egalmoth was with him, but he had got a hurt in that sally from the square. Behind again came many women with babes, and girls, and lamed men, yet was the going slow enough for them. At the rearmost went the largest band of men battle-whole, and there was Glorfindel of the golden hair.

Thus were they come to Cristhorn, which is an ill place by reason of its height, for this is so great that spring nor summer come ever there, and it is very cold. Indeed while the valley dances in the sun, there all the year snow dwells in those bleak places, and even as they came there the wind howled, coming from the north behind them, and it bit sorely. Snow fell and whirled in wind-eddies and got into their eyes, and this was not good, for there the path is narrow, and of the right or westerly hand a sheer wall rises nigh seven chains from the way, ere it bursts atop into jagged pinnacles where are many eyries. There dwells Thorndor King of Eagles, Lord of the Thornhoth, whom the Eldar named Sorontur. But of the other hand is a fall not right sheer yet dreadly steep, and it has long teeth of rock up-pointing so that one may climb down – or fall maybe – but by no means up. And from that deep is no escape at either end any more than by the sides, and Thorn Sir runs at bottom. He falls therein from the south over a great precipice but with a slender water, for he is a thin stream in those heights, and he issues to the north after flowing but a rocky mile above ground down a narrow passage that goes into the mountain, and scarce a fish could squeeze through with him.

Galdor and his men were come now to the end nigh to where Thorn Sir falls into the abyss, and the others straggled, for all Tuor's efforts, back over most of the mile of the perilous way between chasm and cliff, so that Glorfindel's folk were scarce come to its beginning, when there was a yell in the night that echoed in that grim region. Behold, Galdor's men were beset in the dark suddenly by shapes leaping from behind rocks where they had lain hidden even from the glance of Legolas. It was Tuor's thought that they had fallen in with one of Melko's ranging companies, and he feared no more than a sharp brush in the dark, yet he sent the women and sick around him rearward and joined his men to Galdor's, and there was an affray upon the perilous path. But now rocks fell from above, and things looked ill, for they did grievous hurt; but matters seemed to Tuor yet worse when the noise of arms came from the rear, and tidings were said to him by a man of the Swallow that Glorfindel was ill bested by men from behind, and that a Balrog was with them.

Then was he sore afraid of a trap, and this was even what had in truth befallen; for watchers had been set by Melko all about the encircling hills. Yet so many did the valour of the Gondothlim draw off to the assault ere the city could be taken that these were but thinly spread, and were at the least here in the south. Nonetheless one of these had espied the company as they started the upward going from the dale of hazels, and as many bands were got together against them as might be, and devised to fall upon the exiles to front and rear even upon the perilous way of Cristhorn. Now Galdor and Glorfindel held their own despite the surprise of assault, and many of the Orcs were struck into the abyss; but the falling of the rocks was like to end all their valour, and the flight from Gondolin to come to ruin. The moon about that hour rose above the pass, and the gloom somewhat lifted, for his pale light filtered into dark places; yet it lit not the path for the height of the walls. Then arose Thorndor, King of Eagles, and he loved not Melko, for Melko had caught many of his kindred and chained them against sharp rocks to squeeze from them the magic words whereby he might learn to fly (for he dreamed of contending even against Manwë in the air); and when they would not tell he cut off their wings and sought to fashion therefrom a mighty pair for his use, but it availed not.

Now when the clamour from the pass rose to his great eyrie he said: "Wherefore are these foul things, these Orcs of the hills, climbed near to my throne; and why do the sons of the Noldoli cry out in the low places for fear of the children of Melko the accursed? Arise O Thornhoth, whose beaks are of steel and whose talons swords!"

Thereupon there was a rushing like a great wind in rocky places, and the Thornhoth, the people of the Eagles, fell on those Orcs who had scaled above the path, and tore their faces and their hands and flung them to the rocks of Thorn Sir far below. Then were the Gondothlim glad, and they made in after days the Eagle a sign of their kindred in token of their joy, and Idril bore it, but Eärendel loved rather the Swan-wing of his father. Now unhampered Galdor's men bore back those that opposed them, for they were not very many and the onset of the Thornhoth affrighted them much; and the company fared forward again, though Glorfindel had fighting enough in the rear. Already the half had passed the perilous way and the falls of Thorn Sir, when that Balrog that was with the rearward foe leapt with great might on certain lofty rocks that stood into the path on the left side upon the lip of the chasm, and thence with a leap of fury he was past Glorfindel's men and among the women and the sick in front, lashing with his whip of flame. Then Glorfindel leapt forward upon him and his golden armour gleamed strangely in the moon, and he hewed at that demon that it leapt again upon a great boulder and Glorfindel after. Now there was a deadly combat upon that high rock above the folk; and these, pressed behind and hindered ahead, were grown so close that well nigh all could see, yet was it over ere Glorfindel's men could leap to his side. The ardour of Glorfindel drave that Balrog from point to point, and his mail fended him from its whip and claw. Now had he beaten a heavy swinge upon its iron helm, now hewn off the creature's whip-arm at the elbow. Then sprang the Balrog in the torment of his pain and fear full at Glorfindel, who stabbed like a dart of a snake; but he found only a shoulder, and was grappled, and they swayed to a fall upon the crag-top. Then Glorfindel's left hand sought a dirk, and this he thrust up that it pierced the Balrog's belly nigh his own face (for that demon was double his stature); and it shrieked, and fell backwards from the rock, and falling clutched Glorfindel's yellow locks beneath his cap, and those twain fell into the abyss.

Now was this a very grievous thing, for Glorfindel was most dearly beloved – and lo! the dint of their fall echoed about the hills, and the abyss of Thorn Sir rang. Then at the death-cry of the Balrog the Orcs before and behind wavered and were slain or fled far away, and Thorndor himself, a mighty bird, descended to the abyss and brought up the body of Glorfindel; but the Balrog lay, and the water of Thorn Sir ran black for many a day far below in Tumladin.

Still do the Eldar say when they see good fighting at great odds of power against a fury of evil: "Alas! 'Tis Glorfindel and the Balrog", and their hearts are still sore for that fair one of the Noldoli. Because of their love, despite the haste and their fear of the advent of new foes, Tuor let raise a great stone-cairn over Glorfindel just there beyond the perilous way by the precipice of Eagle-stream, and Thorndor has let not yet any harm come thereto, but yellow flowers have fared thither and blow ever now

about that mound in those unkindly places; but the folk of the
Golden Flower wept at its building and might not dry their tears.

Now who shall tell of the wanderings of Tuor and the exiles of
Gondolin in the wastes that lie beyond the mountains to the south
of the vale of Tumladin? Miseries were theirs and death, colds and
hungers, and ceaseless watches. That they won ever through those
regions infested by Melko's evil came from the great slaughter and
damage done to his power in that assault, and from the speed and
wariness with which Tuor led them; for of a certain Melko knew of
that escape and was furious thereat. Ulmo had heard tidings in the
far oceans of the deeds that were done, but he could not yet aid
them for they were far from waters and rivers – and indeed they
thirsted sorely, and they knew not the way.

But after a year and more of wandering, in which many a time
they journeyed long tangled in the magic of those wastes only to
come again upon their own tracks, once more the summer came,
and nigh to its height[37] they came at last upon a stream, and
following this came to better lands and were a little comforted.
Here did Voronwë guide them, for he had caught a whisper of
Ulmo's in that stream one late summer's night – and he got ever
much wisdom from the sound of waters. Now he led them even till
they came down to Sirion which that stream fed, and then both
Tuor and Voronwë saw that they were not far from the outer issue
of old of the Way of Escape, and were once more in that deep
dale of alders. Here were all the bushes trampled and the trees
burnt, and the dale-wall scarred with flame, and they wept, for
they thought they knew the fate of those who sundered aforetime
from them at the tunnel-mouth.

Now they journeyed down that river but were again in fear from
Melko, and fought affrays with his Orc-bands and were in peril
from the wolfriders, but his firedrakes sought not at them, both
for the great exhaustion of their fires in the taking of Gondolin,
and the increasing power of Ulmo as the river grew. So came they
after many days – for they went slowly and got their sustenance
very hardly – to those great heaths and morasses above the Land of
Willows, and Voronwë knew not those regions. Now here goes
Sirion a very great way under earth, diving at the great cavern of
the Tumultuous Winds, but running clear again above the Pools
of Twilight, even where Tulkas[38] after fought with Melko's self.
Tuor had fared over these regions by night and dusk after Ulmo
came to him amid the reeds, and he remembered not the ways. In

places that land is full of deceits and very marshy; and here the host had long delay and was vexed by sore flies, for it was autumn still, and agues and fevers fared amongst them, and they cursed Melko.

Yet came they at last to the great pools and the edges of that most tender Land of Willows; and the very breath of the winds thereof brought rest and peace to them, and for the comfort of that place the grief was assuaged of those who mourned the dead in that great fall. There women and maids grew fair again and their sick were healed, and old wounds ceased to pain; yet they alone who of reason feared their folk living still in bitter thraldom in the Hells of Iron sang not, nor did they smile.

Here they abode very long indeed, and Eärendel was a grown boy ere the voice of Ulmo's conches drew the heart of Tuor, that his sea-longing returned with a thirst the deeper for years of stifling; and all that host arose at his bidding, and got them down Sirion to the Sea.

Now the folk that had passed into the Eagles' Cleft and who saw the fall of Glorfindel had been nigh eight hundreds – a large wayfaring, yet was it a sad remnant of so fair and numerous a city. But they who arose from the grasses of the Land of Willows in years after and fared away to sea, when spring set celandine in the meads and they had held sad festival in memorial of Glorfindel, these numbered but three hundreds and a score of men and man-children, and two hundreds and three score of women and maid-children. Now the number of women was few because of their hiding or being stowed by their kinsfolk in secret places in the city. There they were burned or slain or taken and enthralled, and the rescue-parties found them too seldom; and it is the greatest ruth to think of this, for the maids and women of the Gondothlim were as fair as the sun and as lovely as the moon and brighter than the stars. Glory dwelt in that city of Gondolin of the Seven Names, and its ruin was the most dread of all the sacks of cities upon the face of Earth. Nor Bablon, nor Ninwi, nor the towers of Trui, nor all the many takings of Rûm that is greatest among Men, saw such terror as fell that day upon Amon Gwareth in the kindred of the Gnomes; and this is esteemed the worst work that Melko has yet thought of in the world.

Yet now those exiles of Gondolin dwelt at the mouth of Sirion by the waves of the Great Sea. There they take the name of Lothlim, the people of the flower, for Gondothlim is a name too sore to their hearts; and fair among the Lothlim Eärendel grows in the house of his father,[39] and the great tale of Tuor is come to its waning.'

Then said Littleheart son of Bronweg: 'Alas for Gondolin.'

And no one in all the Room of Logs spake or moved for a great while.

NOTES

1 Not of course the great journey to the Sea from the Waters of Awakening, but the expedition of the Elves of Kôr for the rescue of the Gnomes (see I.26).

2 A *korin* is defined in *The Cottage of Lost Play* (I.16) as 'a great circular hedge, be it of stone or of thorn or even of trees, that encloses a green sward'; Meril-i-Turinqi dwelt 'in a great *korin* of elms'.

3 *Tôn a Gwedrin* is the Tale-fire.

4 There is here a direction: 'See hereafter the Nauglafring', but this is struck out.

5 On Heorrenda see pp. 290ff, 323. A small space is left after the words 'it is thus' to mark the place of the poem in Old English that was to be inserted, but there is no indication of what it was to be.

(In the following notes 'the original reading' refers to the text of Tuor A, *and of* Tuor B *before the emendation in question. It does not imply that the reading of* Tuor A *was, or was not, found in the original pencilled text (in the great majority of cases this cannot be said).)*

6 This passage, beginning with the words 'And Tuor entered that cavern . . .' on p. 149, is a late replacement written on a slip (see p. 147). The original passage was largely similar in meaning, but contained the following:

Now in delving that riverway beneath the hills the Noldoli worked unknown to Melko who in those deep days held them yet hidden and thralls beneath his will. Rather were they prompted by Ulmo who strove ever against Melko; and through Tuor he hoped to devise for the Gnomes release from the terror of the evil of Melko.

7 'three days': 'three years' all texts, but 'days?' pencilled above 'years' in *Tuor B*.

8 The 'evolution' of sea-birds through Ossë is described in the tale of *The Coming of the Elves*, I.123; but the sentence here derives from the original pencilled text of *Tuor A*.

9 In the typescript *Tuor C* a blank was left here (see p. 147) and subsequently filled in with 'Ulmo', not 'Ainur'.

10   The original reading was: 'Thou Tuor of the lonely heart the Valar
     will not to dwell for ever in fair places of birds and flowers; nor
     would they lead thee through this pleasant land . . .'
11   *Tuor C* adds here: 'with Ulmo's aid'.
12   The reference to the Battle of Unnumbered Tears is a later addition
     to *Tuor B*. The original reading was: 'who alone escaped Melko's
     power when he caught their folk . . .'
13   In *Tuor A* and *B Voronwë* is used throughout, but this phrase, with
     the form *Bronweg*, is an addition to *Tuor B* (replacing the original
     'Now after many days these twain found a deep dale').
14   The typescript *Tuor C* has here:

> . . . that none, were they not of the blood of the Noldoli, might
> light on it, neither by chance nor agelong search. Thus was
> it secure from all ill hap save treachery alone, and never would
> Tûr have won thereto but for the steadfastness of that Gnome
> Voronwë.

In the next sentence *Tuor C* has 'yet even so no few of the bolder of
the Gnomes enthralled would slip down the river Sirion from the
fell mountains'.

15   The original reading was: 'his speech they comprehended, though
     somewhat different was the tongue of the free Noldoli by those days
     to that of the sad thralls of Melko.' The typescript *Tuor C* has: 'they
     comprehended him for they were Noldoli. Then spake Tûr also in
     the same tongue . . .'
16   The original reading was: 'It was early morn when they drew near
     the gates and many eyes gazed . . .' But when Tuor and Voronwë
     first saw Gondolin it was 'in the new light of the morning' (p. 158),
     and it was 'a day's light march' across the plain; hence the change
     made later to *Tuor B*.
17   'Evil One': original reading 'Ainu'.
18   This passage, from 'Rugged was his aspect . . .', is a replacement on
     a separate slip; the original text was:

> Tuor was goodly in countenance but rugged and unkempt
> of locks and clad in the skins of bears, yet his stature
> was not overgreat among his own folk, but the Gondothlim,
> though not bent as were no few of their kin who laboured at
> ceaseless delving and hammering for Melko, were small and
> slender and lithe.

In the original passage Men are declared to be of their nature taller
than the Elves of Gondolin. See pp. 142, 220.

19   'come hither': 'escaped from Melko' *Tuor C*.
20   'folk': original reading 'men'. This is the only place where 'men' in
     reference to Elves is changed. The use is constant in *The Fall of
     Gondolin*, and even occurs once in an odd-sounding reference to

the hosts of Melko: 'But now the men of Melko have assembled their forces' (p. 183).

21 The passage ending here and beginning with the words 'Then Tuor's heart was heavy . . .' on p. 162 was bracketed by my father in *Tuor B*, and on a loose slip referring to this bracketed passage he wrote:

> (If nec[essary]): Then is told how Idril daughter of the king added her words to the king's wisdom so that Turgon bid Tuor rest himself awhile in Gondolin, and being forewise prevailed on him [to] abide there in the end. How he came to love the daughter of the king, Idril of the Silver Feet, and how he was taught deeply in the lore of that great folk and learned of its history and the history of the Elves. How Tuor grew in wisdom and mighty in the counsels of the Gondothlim.

The only narrative difference here from the actual text lies in the introduction of the king's daughter Idril as an influence on Tuor's decision to remain in Gondolin. The passage is otherwise an extremely abbreviated summary of the account of Tuor's instruction in Gondolin, with omission of what is said in the text about the preparations of the Gondothlim against attack; but I do not think that this was a proposal for shortening the written tale. Rather, the words 'If necessary' suggest strongly that my father had in mind only a reduction for oral delivery – and that was when it was read to the Exeter College Essay Club in the spring of 1920; see p. 147. Another proposed shortening is given in note 32.

22 This passage, beginning 'Great love too had Idril for Tuor . . .', was written on a separate slip and replaced the original text as follows:

> The king hearing of this, and finding that his child Idril, whom the Eldar speak of as Irildë, loved Tuor in return, he consented to their being wed, seeing that he had no son, and Tuor was like to make a kinsman of strength and consolation. There were Idril and Tuor wed before the folk in that Place of the Gods, Gar Ainion, nigh the king's palace; and that was a day of mirth to the city of Gondolin, but of (&c.)

The replacement states that the marriage of Tuor and Idril was the first but not the last of the unions of Man and Elf, whereas it is said in the Name-list to *The Fall of Gondolin* that Eärendel was 'the only being that is half of the kindred of the Eldalië and half of Men' (see p. 215).

23 The phrase 'and that tale of Isfin and Eöl may not here be told' was added to *Tuor B*. See p. 220.

24 Original reading: 'a name wrought of the tongue of the Gondothlim'.

25 The sapphires given to Manwë by the Noldoli are referred to in the

tale of *The Coming of the Elves*, I.128. The original pencilled text
of *Tuor A* can be read here: 'bluer than the sapphires of Súlimo'.

26   The passage ending here and beginning with 'In these ways that
bitter winter passed . . .' is inserted on a separate sheet in *Tuor B*
(but is not part of the latest layer of emendation); it replaces a much
shorter passage going back to the primary text of *Tuor A*:

> Now on midwinter's day at early even the sun sank betimes
> beyond the mountains, and lo! when she had gone a light
> arose beyond the hills to the north, and men marvelled (&c.)

See notes 34 and 37.

27   The Scarlet Heart: the heart of Finwë Nólemë, Turgon's father,
was cut out by Orcs in the Battle of Unnumbered Tears, but it was
regained by Turgon and became his emblem; see I.241 and note 11.

28   This passage describing the array and the emblems of the houses of
the Gondothlim was relatively very little affected by the later
revision of *Tuor A*; the greater part of it is in the original pencilled
text, which was allowed to stand, and all the names appear to be
original.

29   The word 'burg' is used in the Old English sense of a walled and
fortified town.

30   The death of Ecthelion in the primary text of *Tuor A* is legible; the
revision introduced a few changes of wording, but no more.

31   This sentence, from 'and men shuddered', was added to *Tuor B*. On
the prophecy see I.172.

32   *Tuor B* is bracketed from 'Now comes Tuor at their head to the Place
of Wedding' on p. 186 to this point, and an inserted slip relating to
this bracketing reads:

> How Tuor and his folk came upon Idril wandering distraught in
> the Place of the Gods. How Tuor and Idril from that high place
> saw the sack of the King's Hall and the ruin of the King's Tower
> and the passing of the king, for which reason the foe followed not
> after. How Tuor heard tidings of Voronwë that Idril had sent
> Eärendel and her guard down the hidden way, and fared into the
> city in search of her husband; how in peril from the enemy they
> had rescued many that fled and sent them down the secret way.
> How Tuor led his host with the luck of the Gods to the mouth of
> that passage, and how all descended into the plain, sealing the
> entrance utterly behind them. How the sorrowful company issued
> into a dell in the vale of Tumladin.

This is simply a summary of the text as it stands; I suppose it was a
cut proposed for the recitation of the tale if that seemed to be taking
too long (see note 21).

33   This passage, from 'Here were gathered . . .', replaced in *Tuor B* the
original reading: 'Here they are fain to rest, but finding no signs of

Eärendel and his escort Tuor is downcast, and Idril weeps.' This was rewritten partly for narrative reasons, but also to put it into the past tense. In the next sentence the text was emended from 'Lamentation is there . . .' and 'about them looms . . .' But the sentence following ('Fire-drakes are about it . . .') was left untouched; and I think that it was my father's intention, only casually indicated and never carried through, to reduce the amount of 'historical present' in the narrative.

34   'for summer is at hand': the original reading was 'albeit it is winter'. See notes 26 and 37.

35   The original reading was:

> Now the Mountains were on that side seven leagues save a mile from Gondolin, and Cristhorn the Cleft of Eagles another league of upward going from the beginning of the Mountains; wherefore they were now yet two leagues and part of a third from the pass, and very weary thereto.

36   'Behold, his face shineth as a star in the waste' was added to *Tuor B*.

37   This passage, from 'But after a year and more of wandering . . .', replaced the original reading 'But after a half-year's wandering, nigh midsummer'. This emendation depends on the changing of the time of the attack on Gondolin from midwinter to the 'Gates of Summer' (see notes 26 and 34). Thus in the revised version summer is retained as the season when the exiles came to the lands about Sirion, but they spent a whole year and more, rather than a half-year, to reach them.

38   'even where Tulkas': original reading: 'even where Noldorin and Tulkas'. See pp. 278–9.

39   The original pencilled text of *Tuor A* had 'Fair among the Lothlim grows Eärendel in Sornontur the house of Tuor'. The fourth letter of this name could as well be read as a *u*.

Changes made to names in
The Fall of Gondolin

Ilfiniol   < *Elfriniol* in the first three occurrences of the name in the initial linking passage, *Ilfiniol* so written at the fourth.

(In *The Cottage of Lost Play* (I.15) the Gong-warden of Mar Vanwa Tyaliéva is named only *Littleheart*; in the *Link* to *The Music of the Ainur* his Elvish name is *Ilverin* < *Elwenildo* (I.46, 52); and in the *Link* to the *Tale of Tinúviel* he is *Ilfiniol* < *Elfriniol* as here, while the typescript has *Ilfrin* (p. 7).

In the head-note to the Name-list to *The Fall of Gondolin* he is *Elfrith* < *Elfriniel*, and this is the only place where the meaning of the name 'Littleheart' is explained (p. 148); the Name-list has an entry '*Elf* meaneth "heart" (as Elfin *Elben*): *Elfrith* is Littleheart' (see I.255, entry *Ilverin*). In another projected list of names, abandoned after only a couple of entries had been made, we meet again the form *Elfrith*, and also *Elbenil* > *Elwenil*.

This constant changing of name is to be understood in relation to swiftly changing phonological ideas and formulations, but even so is rather extraordinary.)

In the following notes it is to be understood, for brevity's sake, that names in Tuor B *(before emendation) are found in the same form in* Tuor A; *e.g.* 'Mithrim < Asgon *in* Tuor B' *implies that* Tuor A *has* Asgon *(unchanged).*

Tuor Although sometimes emended to *Tûr* in *Tuor B*, and invariably written *Tûr* in the typescript *Tuor C*, I give *Tuor* throughout; see p. 148.

Dor Lómin This name was so written from the first in *Tuor B*. *Tuor A* has, at the first three occurrences, *Aryador* > *Mathusdor*; at the fourth, *Aryador* > *Mathusdor* > *Dor Lómin*.

Mithrim < *Asgon* throughout *Tuor B*; *Tuor C* has *Asgon* unchanged.

Glorfalc or Cris Ilbranteloth (p. 150) *Tuor A* has *Glorfalc or Teld Quing Ilon*; *Tuor B* as written had no Elvish names, *Glorfalc or Cris Ilbranteloth* being a later addition.

Ainur As in the first draft of *The Music of the Ainur* (I.61) the original text of *Tuor A* had *Ainu* plural.

Falasquil At both occurrences (p. 152) in *Tuor A* this replaces the original name now illegible but beginning with *Q*; in *Tuor B* my mother left blanks and added the name later in pencil; in *Tuor C* blanks are left in the typescript and not filled in.

Arlisgion This name was added later to *Tuor B*.

Orcs *Tuor A* and *B* had *Orqui* throughout; my father emended this in *Tuor B* to *Orcs*, but not consistently, and in the later part of the tale not at all. In one place only (p. 193, in Thorndor's speech) both texts have *Orcs* (also *Orc-bands* p. 195). As with the name *Tuor/Tûr* I give throughout the form that was to prevail.

At the only occurrence of the singular the word is written with a *k* in both *Tuor A* and *B* ('Ork's blood', p. 165).

Gar Thurion < *Gar Furion* in *Tuor B* (*Gar Furion* in *Tuor C*).

Loth < *Lôs* in *Tuor B* (*Lôs* in *Tuor C*).

Lothengriol < *Lósengriol* in *Tuor B* (*Lósengriol* in *Tuor C*).

Taniquetil At the occurrence on p. 161 there was added in the original text of *Tuor A*: (*Danigwiel*), but this was struck out.

Kôr Against this name (p. 161) is pencilled in *Tuor B*: *Tûn*. See I. 222, II. 292.

Gar Ainion < *Gar Ainon* in *Tuor B* (p. 164; at the occurrence on p. 186 not emended, but I read *Gar Ainion* in both places).

Nost-na-Lothion < *Nost-na-Lossion* in *Tuor B*.

Duilin At the first occurrence (p. 173) < *Duliglin* in the original text of *Tuor A*.

Rog In *Tuor A* spelt *Rôg* in the earlier occurrences, *Rog* in the later; in *Tuor B* spelt *Rôg* throughout but mostly emended later to *Rog*.

Dramborleg At the occurrence on p. 181 < *Drambor* in the original text of *Tuor A*.

Bansil At the occurrence on p. 184 only, *Bansil* > *Banthil* in *Tuor B*.

Cristhorn From the first occurrence on p. 189 written *Cristhorn* (not *Cris Thorn*) in *Tuor A*; *Cris Thorn Tuor B* throughout.

Bad Uthwen < *Bad Uswen* in *Tuor B*. The original reading in *Tuor A* was (apparently) *Bad Usbran*.

Sorontur < *Ramandur* in *Tuor B*.

Bablon, Ninwi, Trui, Rûm The original text of *Tuor A* had *Babylon*, *Nineveh*, *Troy*, and (probably) *Rome*. These were changed to the forms given in the text, except *Nineveh* > *Ninwë*, changed to *Ninwi* in *Tuor B*.

Commentary on
The Fall of Gondolin

§1. The primary narrative

As with the *Tale of Turambar* I break my commentary on this tale into sections. I refer frequently to the much later version (which extends only to the coming of Tuor and Voronwë to sight of Gondolin across the plain) printed in *Unfinished Tales* pp. 17–51 ('Of Tuor and his Coming to Gondolin'); this I shall call here 'the later *Tuor*'.

(i) *Tuor's journey to the Sea and the visitation*
of Ulmo (pp. 149–56)

In places the later *Tuor* (the abandonment of which is one of the saddest facts in the whole history of incompletion) is so close in wording to *The Fall of Gondolin*, written more than thirty years before, as to make it almost certain that my father had it in front of him, or at least had recently reread it. Striking examples from the late version (pp. 23–4) are: 'The sun rose behind his back and set before his face, and where the water foamed among the boulders or rushed over sudden falls, at morning and evening rainbows were woven across the stream'; 'Now he said: "It is a fay-voice," now: "Nay, it is a small beast that is wailing in the waste"'; '[Tuor] wandered still for some days in a rugged country bare of trees; and it was swept by a wind from the sea, and all that grew there, herb or bush, leaned ever to the dawn because of the prevalence of that wind from the West' – which are very closely similar to or almost identical with passages in the tale (pp. 150–1). But the differences in the narrative are profound.

Tuor's origin is left vague in the old story. There is a reference in the *Tale of Turambar* (p. 88) to 'those kindreds about the waters of Asgon whence after arose Tuor son of Peleg', but here it is said that Tuor did not dwell with his people (who 'wandered the forests and fells') but 'lived alone about that lake called Mithrim [< Asgon]', on which he journeyed in a small boat with a prow made like the neck of a swan. There is indeed scarcely any linking reference to other events, and of course no trace of the Grey-elves of Hithlum who in the later story fostered him, or of his outlawry and hunting by the Easterlings; but there are 'wandering Noldoli' in Dor Lómin (Hisilómë, Hithlum) – on whom see p. 65 – from whom Tuor learnt much, including their tongue, and it was they who guided him down the dark river-passage under the mountains. There is in this a premonition of Gelmir and Arminas, the Noldorin Elves who guided Tuor through the Gate of the Noldor (later *Tuor* pp. 21–2), and the story that the Noldoli 'made that hidden way at the prompting of Ulmo' survived in the much richer historical context of the later legend, where 'the Gate of the Noldor . . . was made by the skill of that people, long ago in the days of Turgon' (later *Tuor* p. 18).

The later *Tuor* becomes very close to the old story for a time when Tuor emerges out of the tunnel into the ravine (later called Cirith Ninniach, but still a name of Tuor's own devising); many features recur, such as the stars shining in the 'dark lane of sky above him', the echoes of his harping (in the tale of course without the literary echoes of Morgoth's cry and the voices of Fëanor's host that landed there), his doubt concerning the mournful calling of the gulls, the narrowing of the ravine where the incoming tide (fierce because of the west wind) met the water of the river, and Tuor's escape by climbing to the cliff-top (but in the tale the connection between Tuor's curiosity concerning the gulls and the saving of his life is not made: he climbed the cliff in response to the prompting of the Ainur). Notable is the retention of the idea that Tuor was the first of Men to reach the Sea, standing on the cliff-top with outspread arms, and of his 'sea-longing' (later *Tuor* p. 25). But the story of his dwelling in the cove of Falasquil and his adornment of it with carvings (and of course the floating of timber down the river to him by the Noldoli of Dor Lómin) was abandoned; in the later legend Tuor finds on the coast ruins of the ancient harbour-works of the Noldor from the days of Turgon's lordship in Nevrast, and of Turgon's former dwelling in these regions before he went to Gondolin there is in the old story no trace. Thus the entire Vinyamar episode is absent from it, and despite the frequent reminder that Ulmo was guiding Tuor as the instrument of his designs, the essential element in the later legend of the arms left for him by Turgon on Ulmo's instruction (*The Silmarillion* pp. 126, 238–9) is lacking.

The southward-flying swans (seven, not three, in the later *Tuor*) play essentially the same part in both narratives, drawing Tuor to continue his journey; but the emblem of the Swan was afterwards given a different origin, as 'the token of Annael and his foster-folk', the Grey-elves of Mithrim (later *Tuor* p. 25).

Both in the route taken (for the geography see p. 217) and in the seasons of the year my father afterwards departed largely from the original story of Tuor's journey to Gondolin. In the later *Tuor* it was the Fell Winter after the fall of Nargothrond, the winter of Túrin's return to Hithlum, when he and Voronwë journeyed in snow and bitter cold eastwards beneath the Mountains of Shadow. Here the journey takes far longer: he left Falasquil in 'the latest days of summer' (as still in the later *Tuor*) but he went down all the coast of Beleriand to the mouths of Sirion, and it was the summer of the following year when he lingered in the Land of Willows. (Doubtless the geography was less definite than it afterwards became, but its general resemblance to the later map seems assured by the description (p. 153) of the coast's trending after a time eastwards rather than southwards.)

Only in its place in the narrative structure is there resemblance between Ulmo's visitation of Tuor in the Land of Willows in a summer twilight and his tremendous epiphany out of the rising storm on the coast at Vinyamar. It is however most remarkable that the old vision of the Land of Willows and its drowsy beauty of river-flowers and butterflies was not lost, though afterwards it was Voronwë, not Tuor, who wandered there, devising names, and who stood enchanted 'knee-deep in the grass' (p. 155; later *Tuor* p. 35), until his fate, or Ulmo Lord of Waters, carried him down to the Sea. Possibly there is a faint reminiscence of the old story in Ulmo's words (later *Tuor* p. 28): 'Haste thou must learn, and *the pleasant road that I designed for thee* must be changed.'

In the tale, Ulmo's speech to Tuor (or at least that part of it that is reported) is far more simple and brief, and there is no suggestion there of Ulmo's 'opposing the will of his brethren, the Lords of the West'; but two essential elements of his later message are present, that Tuor will find the words to speak when he stands before Turgon, and the reference to Tuor's unborn son (in the later *Tuor* much less explicit: 'But it is not for thy valour only that I send thee, but to bring into the world a hope beyond thy sight, and a light that shall pierce the darkness').

(ii) *The journey of Tuor and Voronwë to Gondolin* (pp. 156–8)

Of Tuor's journey to Gondolin, apart from his sojourn in the Land of Willows, little is told in the tale, and Voronwë only appears late in its course as the one Noldo who was not too fearful to accompany him further; of Voronwë's history as afterwards related there is no word, and he is not an Elf of Gondolin.

It is notable that the Noldoli who guided Tuor northwards from the Land of Willows call themselves thralls of Melko. On this matter the *Tales* present a consistent picture. It is said in the *Tale of Tinúviel* (p. 9) that

> all the Eldar both those who remained in the dark or who had been lost upon the march from Palisor and those Noldoli too who fared back into the world after [Melko] seeking their stolen treasury fell beneath his power as thralls.

In *The Fall of Gondolin* it is said that the Noldoli did their service to Ulmo in secret, and 'out of fear of Melko wavered much' (p. 154), and Voronwë spoke to Tuor of 'the weariness of thraldom' (pp. 156–7); Melko sent out his army of spies 'to search out the dwelling of the Noldoli that had escaped his thraldom' (p. 166). These 'thrall-Noldoli' are represented as moving as it were freely about the lands, even to the mouths of Sirion, but they 'wandered as in a dream of fear, doing [Melko's] ill bidding, for the spell of bottomless dread was on them and they felt the eyes of Melko burn them from afar' (*Tale of Turambar*, p. 77). This expression is often used: Voronwë rejoiced in Gondolin that he no longer dreaded Melko with 'a binding terror' – 'and of a sooth that spell which Melko held over the Noldoli was one of bottomless dread, so that he seemed ever nigh them even were they far from the Hells of Iron, and their hearts quaked and they fled not even when they could' (p. 159). The spell of bottomless dread was laid too on Meglin (p. 169).

There is little in all this that cannot be brought more or less into harmony with the later narratives, and indeed one may hear an echo in the words of *The Silmarillion* (p. 156):

> But ever the Noldor feared most the treachery of those of their own kin, who had been thralls in Angband; for Morgoth used some of these for his evil purposes, and feigning to give them liberty sent them abroad, but their wills were chained to his, and they strayed only to come back to him again.

Nonetheless one gains the impression that at that time my father pictured the power of Melko when at its height as operating more diffusedly and intangibly, and perhaps also more universally, in the Great Lands. Whereas in *The Silmarillion* the Noldor who are not free are prisoners in Angband (whence a few may escape, and others with enslaved wills may be sent out), here all save the Gondothlim are 'thralls', controlled by Melko from afar, and Melko asserts that the Noldoli are all, by their very existence in the Great Lands, his slaves by right. It is a difference difficult to define, but that there is a difference may be seen in the improbability, for the later story, of Tuor being guided on his way to Gondolin by Noldor who were in any sense slaves of Morgoth.

The entrance to Gondolin has some general similarity to the far fuller and more precisely visualised account in the later *Tuor*: a deep river-gorge, tangled bushes, a cave-mouth – but the river is certainly Sirion (see the passage at the end of the tale, p. 195, where the exiles come back to the entrance), and the entrance to the secret way is in one of the steep river banks, quite unlike the description of the Dry River whose ancient bed was itself the secret way (later *Tuor* pp. 43–4). The long tunnel which Tuor and Voronwë traverse in the tale leads them at length not only to the Guard but also to sunlight, and they are 'at the foot of steep hills' and can see the city: in other words there is a simple conception of a plain, a ring-wall of mountains, and a tunnel through them leading to the outer world. In the later *Tuor* the approach to the city is much stranger: for the tunnel of the Guard leads to the ravine of Orfalch Echor, a great rift from top to bottom of the Encircling Mountains ('sheer as if axe-cloven', p. 46), up which the road climbed through the successive gates until it came to the Seventh Gate, barring the rift at the top. Only when this last gate was opened and Tuor passed through was he able to see Gondolin; and we must suppose (though the narrative does not reach this point) that the travellers had to descend again from the Seventh Gate in order to reach the plain.

It is notable that Tuor and Voronwë are received by the Guard without any of the suspicion and menace that greeted them in the later story (p. 45).

(iii)   *Tuor in Gondolin* (pp. 159–64)

With this section of the narrative compare *The Silmarillion*, p. 126:

Behind the circle of the mountains the people of Turgon grew and throve, and they put forth their skill in labour unceasing, so that Gondolin upon Amon Gwareth became fair indeed and fit to compare even with Elven Tirion beyond the sea. High and white were its walls, and smooth its stairs, and tall and strong was the Tower of the King. There shining fountains played, and in the courts of Turgon stood images of the Trees of old, which Turgon himself wrought with elven-craft; and the Tree which he made of gold was named Glingal, and the Tree whose flowers he made of silver was named Belthil.

The image of Gondolin was enduring, and it reappears in the glimpses given in notes for the continuation of the later *Tuor* (*Unfinished Tales* p. 56): 'the stairs up to its high platform, and its great gate . . . the Place of the Fountain, the King's tower on a pillared arcade, the King's house . . .' Indeed the only real difference that emerges from the original account concerns the Trees of Gondolin, which in the former were unfading, 'shoots of old from the glorious Trees of Valinor', but in *The Silmarillion* were images made of the precious metals. On the Trees of Gondolin see the entries *Bansil* and *Glingol* from the Name-list, given below pp. 214–16. The gift by the Gods of these 'shoots' (which 'blossomed eternally without abating') to Inwë and Nólemë at the time of the building of Kôr, each being given a shoot of either Tree, is mentioned in *The Coming of the Elves* (I.123), and in *The Hiding of Valinor* there is a reference to the uprooting of those given to Nólemë, which 'were gone no one knew whither, and more had there never been' (I.213).

But a deep underlying shift in the history of Gondolin separates the earlier and later accounts: for whereas in the *Lost Tales* (and later) Gondolin was only discovered *after* the Battle of Unnumbered Tears when the host of Turgon retreated southwards down Sirion, in *The Silmarillion* it had been found by Turgon of Nevrast more than four hundred years before (442 years before Tuor came to Gondolin in the Fell Winter after the fall of Nargothrond in the year 495 of the Sun). In the tale my father imagined a great age passing *between* the Battle of Unnumbered Tears and the destruction of the city ('unstaying labour *through ages of years* had not sufficed to its building and adornment whereat folk travailed yet', p. 163); afterwards, with radical changes in the chronology of the First Age after the rising of the Sun and Moon, this period was reduced to no more than (in the last extant version of 'The Tale of Years' of the First Age) thirty-eight years. But the old conception can still be felt in the passage on p. 240 of *The Silmarillion* describing the withdrawal of the people of Gondolin from all concern with the world outside after the Nirnaeth Arnoediad, with its air of long years passing.*

In *The Silmarillion* it is explicit that Turgon devised the city to be 'a memorial of Tirion upon Túna' (p. 125), and it became 'as beautiful as a memory of Elven Tirion' (p. 240). This is not said in the old story, and indeed in the *Lost Tales* Turgon himself had never known Kôr (he was born in the Great Lands after the return of the Noldoli from Valinor, I.167, 238, 240); one may feel nonetheless that the tower of the King, the fountains and stairs, the white marbles of Gondolin embody a recollection of Kôr as it is described in *The Coming of the Elves and the Making of Kôr* (I.122–3).

I have said above that 'despite the frequent reminder that Ulmo was guiding Tuor as the instrument of his designs, the essential element in the later legend of the arms left for him by Turgon on Ulmo's instruction is lacking'. Now however we seem to see the germ of this conception in Turgon's words to Tuor (p. 161): 'Thy coming was set in our books of wisdom, and it has been written that there would come to pass many great things in the homes of the Gondothlim whenso thou faredst hither.' Yet it is clear from Tuor's reply that as yet the establishment of Gondolin was no part of Ulmo's design, since 'there have come to the ears of Ulmo whispers of your dwelling and your hill of vigilance against the evil of Melko, and he is glad'.

* Of the story of Gondolin from Tuor's coming to its destruction my father wrote nothing after the version of 'The Silmarillion' made (very probably) in 1930; and in this the old conception of its history was still present. This was the basis for much of Chapter 23 in the published work.

In the tale, Ulmo foresaw that Turgon would be unwilling to take up arms against Melko, and he fell back, through the mouth of Tuor, on a second counsel: that Turgon send Elves from Gondolin down Sirion to the coasts, there to build ships to carry messages to Valinor. To this Turgon replied, decisively and unanswerably, that he had sent messengers down the great river with this very purpose 'for years untold', and since all had been unavailing he would now do so no more. Now this clearly relates to a passage in *The Silmarillion* (p. 159) where it is said that Turgon, after the Dagor Bragollach and the breaking of the Siege of Angband,

> sent companies of the Gondolindrim in secret to the mouths of Sirion and the Isle of Balar. There they built ships, and set sail into the uttermost West upon Turgon's errand, seeking for Valinor, to ask for pardon and aid of the Valar; and they besought the birds of the sea to guide them. But the seas were wild and wide, and shadow and enchantment lay upon them; and Valinor was hidden. Therefore none of the messengers of Turgon came into the West, and many were lost and few returned.

Turgon did indeed do so once more, after the Battle of Unnumbered Tears (*The Silmarillion* p. 196), and the only survivor of that last expedition into the West was Voronwë of Gondolin. Thus, despite profound changes in chronology and a great development in the narrative of the last centuries of the First Age, the idea of the desperate attempts of Turgon to get a message through to Valinor goes back to the beginning.

Another aboriginal feature is that Turgon had no son; but (curiously) no mention whatsoever is made in the tale of his wife, the mother of Idril. In *The Silmarillion* (p. 90) his wife Elenwë was lost in the crossing of the Helcaraxë, but obviously this story belongs to a later period, when Turgon was born in Valinor.

The tale of Tuor's sojourn in Gondolin survived into the brief words of *The Silmarillion* (p. 241):

> And Tuor remained in Gondolin, for its bliss and its beauty and the wisdom of its people held him enthralled; and he became mighty in stature and in mind, and learned deeply of the lore of the exiled Elves.

In the present tale he 'heard tell of Ilúvatar, the Lord for Always, who dwelleth beyond the world', and of the Music of the Ainur. Knowledge of the very existence of Ilúvatar was, it seems, a prerogative of the Elves; long afterwards in the garden of Mar Vanwa Tyaliéva (I. 49) Eriol asked Rúmil: 'Who was Ilúvatar? Was he of the Gods?' and Rúmil answered: 'Nay, that he was not; for he made them. Ilúvatar is the Lord for Always, who dwells beyond the world.'

(iv)   *The encirclement of Gondolin;*
the treachery of Meglin (pp. 164–71)

The king's daughter was from the first named 'Idril of the Silver Feet' (Irildë in the language of the 'Eldar', note 22); Meglin (later Maeglin) was his nephew, though the name of his mother (Turgon's sister) Isfin was later changed.

In this section of the narrative the story in *The Silmarillion* (pp. 241–2) preserved all the essentials of the original version, with one major exception. The wedding of Tuor and Idril took place with the consent and full favour of the king, and there was great joy in Gondolin among all save Maeglin (whose love of Idril is told earlier in *The Silmarillion*, p. 139, where the barrier of his being close kin to her, not mentioned in the tale, is emphasised). Idril's power of foreseeing and her foreboding of evil to come; the secret way of her devising (but in the tale this led south from the city, and the Eagles' Cleft was in the southern mountains); the loss of Meglin in the hills while seeking for ore; his capture by Orcs, his treacherous purchase of life, and his return to Gondolin to avert suspicion (with the detail of his changed mood thereafter and 'smiling face') – all this remained. Much is of course absent (whether rejected or merely passed over) in the succinct account devised for *The Silmarillion* – where there is no mention, for example, of Idril's dream concerning Meglin, the watch set on him when he went to the hills, the formation on Idril's advice of a guard bearing Tuor's emblem, the refusal of Turgon to doubt the invulnerability of the city and his trust in Meglin, Meglin's discovery of the secret way,* or the remarkable story that it was Meglin himself who conceived the idea of the monsters of fire and iron and communicated it to Melko – a valuable defector indeed!

The great difference between the versions lies of course in the nature of Melko/Morgoth's knowledge of Gondolin. In the tale, he had by means of a vast army of spies† already discovered it before ever Meglin was captured, and creatures of Melko had found the 'Way of Escape' and looked down on Gondolin from the surrounding heights. Meglin's treachery in the old story lay in his giving an exact account of the structure of the city and the preparations made for its defence – and in his advice to Melko concerning the monsters of flame. In *The Silmarillion*, on the other hand, there is the element, devised much later, of the unconscious betrayal by Húrin to Morgoth's spies of the general region in which Gondolin must be sought, in 'the mountainous land between

---

* This is in fact specifically denied in *The Silmarillion*: 'she contrived it that the work was known but to few, and no whisper of it came to Maeglin's ears.'

† It seems that the 'creatures of blood' (said to be disliked by the people of Gondolin, p. 166), snakes, wolves, weasels, owls, falcons, are here regarded as the natural servants and allies of Melko.

Anach and the upper waters of Sirion, whither [Morgoth's] servants had never passed' (p. 241); but 'still no spy or creature out of Angband could come there because of the vigilance of the eagles' – and of this rôle of the eagles of the Encircling Mountains (though hostile to Melko, p. 193) there is in the original story no suggestion.

Thus in *The Silmarillion* Morgoth remained in ignorance until Maeglin's capture of the precise location of Gondolin, and Maeglin's information was of correspondingly greater value to him, as it was also of greater damage to the city. The history of the last years of Gondolin has thus a somewhat different atmosphere in the tale, for the Gondothlim are informed of the fact that Melko has 'encompassed the vale of Tumladin around' (p. 167), and Turgon makes preparations for war and strengthens the watch on the hills. The withdrawal of all Melko's spies shortly before the attack on Gondolin did indeed bring about a renewal of optimism among the Gondothlim, and in Turgon not least, so that when the attack came the people were unprepared; but in the later story the shock of the sudden assault is much greater, for there has never been any reason to suppose that the city is in immediate danger, and Idril's foreboding is peculiar to herself and more mysterious.

(v)   *The array of the Gondothlim* (pp. 171–4)

Though the central image of this part of the story – the people of Gondolin looking out from their walls to hail the rising sun on the feast of the Gates of Summer, but seeing a red light rising in the north and not in the east – survived, of all the heraldry in this passage scarcely anything is found in later writings. Doubtless, if my father had continued the later *Tuor*, much would have re-emerged, however changed, if we judge by the rich 'heraldic' descriptions of the great gates and their guards in the Orfalch Echor (pp. 46–50). But in the concise account in *The Silmarillion* the only vestiges are the titles Ecthelion 'of the Fountain'* and Glorfindel 'chief of the House of the Golden Flower of Gondolin'. Ecthelion and Glorfindel are named also in *The Silmarillion* (p. 194) as Turgon's captains who guarded the flanks of the host of Gondolin in their retreat down Sirion from the Nirnaeth Arnoediad, but of other captains named in the tale there is no mention afterwards† – though it is significant that the eighteenth Ruling Steward of Gondor was named Egalmoth, as the

---

* In the later *Tuor* (p. 50) he is 'Lord of the Fountains', plural (the reading in the manuscript is certain).

† In the version of 'The Silmarillion' made in 1930 (see footnote on p. 208), the last account of the Fall of Gondolin to be written and the basis for that in chapter 23 of the published work, the text actually reads: '. . . much is told in *The Fall of Gondolin*: of the death of Rog without the walls, and of the battle of Ecthelion of the Fountain ', &c. I removed the reference to Rog (*The Silmarillion* p. 242) on the grounds that it was absolutely certain that my father would not have retained this name as that of a lord of Gondolin.

seventeenth and twenty-fifth were named Ecthelion (*The Lord of the Rings*, Appendix A (I,ii)).*

Glorfindel 'of the golden hair' (p. 192) remains 'yellow-haired Glorfindel' in *The Silmarillion*, and this was from the beginning the meaning of his name.

(vi)   *The battle of Gondolin* (pp. 174–88)

Virtually the entire history of the fighting in Gondolin is unique in the tale of *The Fall of Gondolin*; the whole story is summarised in *The Silmarillion* (p. 242) in a few lines:

> Of the deeds of desperate valour there done, by the chieftains of the noble houses and their warriors, and not least by Tuor, much is told in *The Fall of Gondolin*: of the battle of Ecthelion of the Fountain with Gothmog Lord of Balrogs in the very square of the King, where each slew the other, and of the defence of the tower of Turgon by the people of his household, until the tower was overthrown: and mighty was its fall and the fall of Turgon in its ruin.
>
> Tuor sought to rescue Idril from the sack of the city, but Maeglin had laid hands on her, and on Eärendil; and Tuor fought with Maeglin on the walls, and cast him far out, and his body as it fell smote the rocky slopes of Amon Gwareth thrice ere it pitched into the flames below. Then Tuor and Idril led such remnants of the people of Gondolin as they could gather in the confusion of the burning down the secret way which Idril had prepared.

(In this highly compressed account the detail that Maeglin's body struck the slopes of Amon Gwareth three times before it 'pitched' into the flames was retained.) It would seem from *The Silmarillion* account that Maeglin's attempt on Idril and Eärendil took place much later in the fighting, and indeed shortly before the escape of the fugitives down the tunnel; but I think that this is far more likely to be the result of compression than of a change in the narrative of the battle.

In the tale Gondolin is very clearly visualised as a city, with its markets and its great squares, of which there are only vestiges in later writing (see above, p. 207); and there is nothing vague in the description of the fighting. The early conception of the Balrogs makes them less terrible, and certainly more destructible, than they afterwards became: they

---

* In a very late note written on one of the texts that constitute chapter 16 of *The Silmarillion* ('Of Maeglin') my father was thinking of making the 'three lords of his household' whom Turgon appointed to ride with Aredhel from Gondolin (p. 131) Glorfindel, Ecthelion, and Egalmoth. He notes that Ecthelion and Egalmoth 'are derived from the primitive F[all of]G[ondolin]', but that they 'are well-sounding and have been in print' (with reference to the names of the Stewards of Gondor). Subsequently he decided against naming Aredhel's escort.

existed in 'hundreds' (p. 170),* and were slain by Tuor and the Gondothlim in large numbers: thus five fell before Tuor's great axe Dramborleg, three before Ecthelion's sword, and two score were slain by the warriors of the king's house. The Balrogs are 'demons of power' (p. 181); they are capable of pain and fear (p. 194); they are attired in iron armour (pp. 181, 194), and they have whips of flame (a character they never lost) and claws of steel (pp. 169, 179).

In *The Silmarillion* the dragons that came against Gondolin were 'of the brood of Glaurung', which 'were become now many and terrible'; whereas in the tale the language employed (p. 170) suggests that some at least of the 'Monsters' were inanimate 'devices', the construction of smiths in the forges of Angband. But even the 'things of iron' that 'opened about their middles' to disgorge bands of Orcs are called 'ruthless beasts', and Gothmog 'bade' them 'pile themselves' (p. 176); those made of bronze or copper 'were given hearts and spirits of blazing fire'; while the 'fire-drake' that Tuor hewed screamed and lashed with its tail (p. 181).

A small detail of the narrative is curious: what 'messengers' did Meglin send to Melko to warn him to guard the outer entrance of the Way of Escape (where he guessed that the secret tunnel must lead in the end)? Whom could Meglin trust sufficiently? And who would dare to go?

(vii)   *The escape of the fugitives and the battle in Cristhorn* (pp. 188–95)

The story as told in *The Silmarillion* (p. 243) is somewhat fuller in its account of the escape of the fugitives from the city and the ambush in the Eagles' Cleft (there called Cirith Thoronath) than in that of the assault and sack itself, but only in one point are the two narratives actually at variance – as already noticed, the Eagles' Cleft was afterwards moved from the southern parts of the Encircling Mountains to the northern, and Idril's tunnel led north from the city (the comment is made that it was not thought 'that any fugitives would take a path towards the north and the highest parts of the mountains and the nighest to Angband'). The tale provides a richness of detail and an immediacy that is lacking in the short version, where such things as the tripping over dead bodies in the hot and reeking underground passage have disappeared; and there is no mention of the Gondothlim who against the counsel of Idril and Tuor went to the Way of Escape and were there destroyed by the dragon lying in wait,† or of the fight to rescue Eärendel.

* The idea that Morgoth disposed of a 'host' of Balrogs endured long, but in a late note my father said that only very few ever existed – 'at most seven'.

† This element in the story was in fact still present in the 1930 'Silmarillion' (see footnote on p. 208), but I excluded it from the published work on account of evidence in a much later text that the old entrance to Gondolin had by this time been blocked up – a fact which was then written into the text in chapter 23 of *The Silmarillion*.

In the tale appears the keen-sighted Elf Legolas Greenleaf, first of the names of the Fellowship of the Ring to appear in my father's writings (see p. 217 on this earlier Legolas), followed by Gimli (an Elf) in the *Tale of Tinúviel*.

In one point the story of the ambush in Cristhorn seems difficult to follow: this is the statement on p. 193 that the moon 'lit not the path for the height of the walls'. The fugitives were moving southwards through the Encircling Mountains, and the sheer rockwall above the path in the Eagles' Cleft was 'of the right or westerly hand', while on the left there was 'a fall . . . dreadly steep'. Surely then the moon rising in the east would illuminate the path?

The name *Cristhorn* appears in my father's drawing of 'Gondolin and the Vale of Tumladin from Cristhorn', September 1928 (*Pictures by J. R. R. Tolkien*, 1979, no. 35).

(viii)   *The wanderings of the Exiles of Gondolin* (pp. 195–7)

In *The Silmarillion* (p. 243) it is said that 'led by Tuor son of Huor the remnant of Gondolin passed over the mountains, and came down into the Vale of Sirion'. One would suppose that they came down into Dimbar, and so 'fleeing southward by weary and dangerous marches they came at length to Nan-tathren, the Land of Willows'. It seems strange in the tale that the exiles were wandering in the wilderness for more than a year, and yet achieved only to the outer entrance of the Way of Escape; but the geography of this region may have been vaguer when *The Fall of Gondolin* was written.

In *The Silmarillion* when Tuor and Idril went down from Nan-tathren to the mouths of Sirion they 'joined their people to the company of Elwing, Dior's daughter, that had fled thither but a little while before'. Of this there is no mention here; but I postpone consideration of this part of the narrative.

§2   *Entries in the Name-list to The Fall of Gondolin*

On this list see p. 148, where the head-note to it is given. Specifically linguistic information from the list, including meanings, is incorporated in the Appendix on Names, but I collect here some statements of other kind (arranged in alphabetical order) that are contained in it.

Bablon 'was a city of Men, and more rightly *Babylon*, but such is the Gnomes' name as they now shape it, and they got it from Men aforetime.'

Bansil   'Now this name had the Gondothlim for that tree before their king's door which bore silver blossom and faded not – and its name had Elfriniel from his father Voronwë; and it meaneth "Fairgleam". Now that tree of which it was a shoot (brought in the deep ages out of Valinor by the Noldoli) had like properties, but greater, seeing that for half the twenty-four hours it lit all Valinor with silver light. This the Eldar still tell of as *Silpion* or "Cherry-moon", for its blossom was like that of a cherry in spring – but of that tree in Gondolin they know no name, and the Noldoli tell of it alone.'

Dor Lómin 'or the "Land of Shadows" was that region named of the Eldar Hisilómë (and this means Shadowy Twilights) where Melko shut Men, and it is so called by reason of the scanty sun which peeps little over the Iron Mountains to the east and south of it – there dwell now the Shadow Folk. Thence came Tuor to Gondolin.'

Eärendel 'was the son of Tuor and Idril and 'tis said the only being that is half of the kindred of the Eldalië and half of Men. He was the greatest and first of all mariners among Men, and saw regions that Men have not yet found nor gazed upon for all the multitude of their boats. He rideth now with Voronwë upon the winds of the firmament nor comes ever further back than Kôr, else would he die like other Men, so much of the mortal is in him.'

(For these last statements about Eärendel see pp. 264–5. The statement that Eärendel was 'the only being that is half of the kindred of the Eldalië and half of Men' is very notable. Presumably this was written when Beren was an Elf, not a Man (see p. 139); Dior son of Beren and Tinúviel appears in the *Tale of the Nauglafring*, but there Beren is an Elf, and Dior is not Half-elven. In the tale of *The Fall of Gondolin* itself it is said, but in a later replacement passage (p. 164 and note 22), that Tuor was the first but not the last to wed 'a daughter of Elfinesse'. On the extraordinary statement in the *Tale of Turambar* that Tamar Lamefoot was Half-elven see p. 130.)

Ecthelion 'was that lord of the house of the Fountain, who had the fairest voice and was most skilled in musics of all the Gondothlim. He won renown for ever by his slaying of Gothmog son of Melko, whereby Tuor was saved from death but Ecthelion was drowned with his foe in the king's fountain.'

Egalmoth was 'lord of the house of the Heavenly Arch, and got even out of the burning of Gondolin, and dwelt after at the mouth of Sirion, but was slain in a dire battle there when Melko seized Elwing'.
(See p. 258.)

Galdor 'was that valiant Gnome who led the men of the Tree in many a charge and yet won out of Gondolin and even the onslaught of Melko upon the dwellers at Sirion's mouth and went back to the ruins with Eärendel. He dwelleth yet in Tol Eressëa (said Elfriniel), and still do some of his folk name themselves *Nos Galdon*, for *Galdon* is a tree, and thereto Galdor's name akin.' The last phrase was emended to read: '*Nos nan Alwen*, for *Alwen* is a Tree.'

(For Galdor's return to the ruins of Gondolin with Eärendel see p. 258.)

Glingol 'meaneth "singing-gold" ('tis said), and this name was that which the Gondothlim had for that other of the two unfading trees in the king's square which bore golden bloom. It also was a shoot from the trees of Valinor (see rather where Elfrith has spoken of Bansil), but of Lindeloktë (which is "singing-cluster") or Laurelin [*emended from* Lindelaurë] (which is "singing-gold") which lit all Valinor with golden light for half the 24 hours.'

(For the name *Lindeloktë* see I. 22, 258 (entry *Lindelos*).)

Glorfindel 'led the Golden Flower and was the best beloved of the Gondothlim, save it be Ecthelion, but who shall choose. Yet he was hapless and fell slaying a Balrog in the great fight in Cristhorn. His name meaneth Goldtress for his hair was golden, and the name of his house in Noldorissa *Los'lóriol*' (emended from *Los Glóriol*).

Gondolin 'meaneth stone of song (whereby figuratively the Gnomes meant stone that was carven and wrought to great beauty), and this was the name most usual of the Seven Names they gave to their city of secret refuge from Melko in those days before the release.'

Gothmog 'was a son of Melko and the ogress Fluithuin and his name is Strife-and-hatred, and he was Captain of the Balrogs and lord of Melko's hosts ere fair Ecthelion slew him at the taking of Gondolin. The Eldar named him *Kosmoko* or *Kosomok(o)*, but 'tis a name that fitteth their tongue no way and has an ill sound even in our own rougher speech, said Elfrith [*emended from* Elfriniel].'

(In a list of names of the Valar associated with the tale of *The Coming of the Valar* (I. 93) it is said that Melko had a son 'by Ulbandi' called *Kosomot*; the early 'Qenya' dictionary gives *Kosomoko* = Gnomish *Gothmog*, I. 258. In the tale Gothmog is called the 'marshal' of the hosts of Melko (p. 184).

In the later development of the legends Gothmog was the slayer of Fëanor, and in the Battle of Unnumbered Tears it was he who slew Fingon and captured Húrin (*The Silmarillion* pp. 107, 193, 195). He is not of course called later 'son of Melkor'; the 'Children of the Valar' was a feature of the earlier mythology that my father discarded.

In the Third Age *Gothmog* was the name of the lieutenant of Minas Morgul (*The Return of the King* V.6).)

Hendor 'was a house-carle of Idril's and was aged, but bore Eärendel down the secret passage.'

Idril 'was that most fair daughter of the king of Gondolin whom Tuor loved when she was but a little maid, and who bare him Eärendel. Her the Elves name *Irildë*; and we speak of as *Idril Tal-Celeb* or Idril of the Silver Feet, but they *Irildë Taltelepta*.'

See the Appendix on Names, entry *Idril*.

Indor 'was the name of the father of Tuor's father, wherefore did the Gnomes name Eärendel *Gon Indor* and the Elves *Indorildo* or *Indorion*.'

Legolas 'or Green-leaf was a man of the Tree, who led the exiles over Tumladin in the dark, being night-sighted, and he liveth still in Tol Eressëa named by the Eldar there *Laiqalassë*; but the book of Rúmil saith further hereon.'
(See I. 267, entry *Tári-Laisi*.)

§3 *Miscellaneous Matters*

(i) *The geography of The Fall of Gondolin*

I have noticed above (p. 205) that in Tuor's journey all along the coast of what was afterwards Beleriand to the mouths of Sirion there is an unquestionable resemblance to the later map, in the trend of the coast from north-south to east-west. It is also said that after he left Falasquil 'the distant hills marched ever nearer to the margin of the sea', and that the spurs of the Iron Mountains 'run even to the sea' (pp. 152–3). These statements can likewise be readily enough related to the map, where the long western extension of the Mountains of Shadow (Ered Wethrin), forming the southern border of Nevrast, reached the sea at Vinyamar (for the equation of the Mountains of Iron and the Mountains of Shadow see I. 111–12).

Arlisgion, 'the place of reeds' (p. 153) above the mouths of Sirion, survived in Lisgardh 'the land of reeds at the Mouths of Sirion' in the later *Tuor* (p. 34); and the feature that the great river passed underground for a part of its course goes back to the earliest period, as does that of the Meres of Twilight, Aelin-uial ('the Pools of Twilight', p. 195). There is here however a substantial difference in the tale from *The Silmarillion* (p. 122), where Aelin-uial was the region of great pools and marshes where 'the flood of Sirion was stayed'; *south of the Meres* the river 'fell from the north in a mighty fall . . . and then he plunged suddenly underground into great tunnels that the weight of his falling waters delved'. Here on the other hand the Pools of Twilight are clearly *below* the 'cavern of the Tumultuous Winds' (never mentioned later) where Sirion dives underground. But the Land of Willows, below the region of Sirion's underground passage, is placed as it was to remain.

Thus the view I expressed (p. 141) of the geographical indications in the *Tale of Turambar* can be asserted also of those of *The Fall of Gondolin*.

(ii) *Ulmo and the other Valar in The Fall of Gondolin*

In the speech of Tuor inspired by Ulmo that he uttered at his first meeting with Turgon (p. 161) he said: 'the hearts of the Valar are angered . . . seeing the sorrow of the thraldom of the Noldoli and the wanderings of Men.' This is greatly at variance with what is told in *The Hiding of Valinor*, especially the following (I. 208–9):*

> The most of the Valar moreover were fain of their ancient ease and desired only peace, wishing neither rumour of Melko and his violence nor murmur of the restless Gnomes to come ever again among them to disturb their happiness; and for such reasons they also clamoured for the concealment of the land. Not the least among these were Vána and Nessa, albeit most even of the great Gods were of one mind. In vain did Ulmo of his foreknowing plead before them for pity and pardon on the Noldoli . . .

Subsequently Tuor said (p. 161): 'the Gods sit in Valinor, though their mirth is minished for sorrow and fear of Melko, and they hide their land and weave about it inaccessible magic that no evil come to its shores.' Turgon in his reply ironically echoed and altered the words: 'they that sit within [*i.e. in Valinor*] reck little of the dread of Melko or the sorrow of the world, but hide their land and weave about it inaccessible magic, that no tidings of evil come ever to their ears.'

How is this to be understood? Was this Ulmo's 'diplomacy'? Certainly Turgon's understanding of the motives of the Valar chimes better with what is said of them in *The Hiding of Valinor*.

But the Gnomes of Gondolin reverenced the Valar. There were 'pomps of the Ainur' (p. 165); a great square of the city and its highest point was Gar Ainion, the Place of the Gods, where weddings were celebrated (pp. 164, 186); and the people of the Hammer of Wrath 'reverenced Aulë the Smith more than all other Ainur' (p. 174).

Of particular interest is the passage (p. 165) in which a reason is given for Ulmo's choice of a Man as the agent of his designs: 'Now Melko was not much afraid of the race of Men in those days of his great power, and for this reason did Ulmo work through one of this kindred for the better deceiving of Melko, seeing that no Valar and scarce any of the Eldar or Noldoli might stir unmarked of his vigilance.' This is the only place where a reason is expressly offered, save for an isolated early note, where two reasons are given:

(1) 'the wrath of the Gods' (i.e. against the Gnomes);
(2) 'Melko did not fear Men — had he thought that any messengers were getting to Valinor he would have redoubled his vigilance and evil and hidden the Gnomes away utterly.'

---

* It also seems to be at variance with the story that all Men were shut in Hithlum by Melko's decree after the Battle of Unnumbered Tears; but 'wanderings' is a strange word in the context, since the next words are 'for Melko ringeth them in the Land of Shadows'.

But this is too oblique to be helpful.

The conception of 'the luck of the Gods' occurs again in this tale (pp. 188, 200 note 32), as it does in the *Tale of Turambar*: see p. 141. The Ainur 'put it into Tuor's heart' to climb the cliff out of the ravine of Golden Cleft for the saving of his life (p. 151).

Very strange is the passage concerning the birth of Eärendel (p. 165): 'In these days came to pass the fulfilment of the time of the desire of the Valar and the hope of the Eldalië, for in great love Idril bore to Tuor a son and he was called Eärendel.' Is it to be understood that the union of Elf and mortal Man, and the birth of their offspring, was 'the desire of the Valar' – that the Valar foresaw it, or hoped for it, as the fulfilment of a design of Ilúvatar from which great good should come? There is no hint or suggestion of such an idea elsewhere.

(iii) Orcs

There is a noteworthy remark in the tale (p. 159) concerning the origin of the Orcs (or *Orqui* as they were called in *Tuor A*, and in *Tuor B* as first written): 'all that race were bred of the subterranean heats and slime.' There is no trace yet of the later view that 'naught that had life of its own, nor the semblance of life, could ever Melkor make since his rebellion in the Ainulindalë before the Beginning', or that the Orcs were derived from enslaved Quendi after the Awakening (*The Silmarillion* p. 50). Conceivably there is a first hint of this idea of their origin in the words of the tale in the same passage: 'unless it be that certain of the Noldoli were twisted to the evil of Melko and mingled among these Orcs', although of course this is as it stands quite distinct from the idea that the Orcs were actually bred from Elves.

Here also occurs the name *Glamhoth* of the Orcs, a name that reappears in the later *Tuor* (pp. 39 and 54 note 18).

On Balrogs and Dragons in *The Fall of Gondolin* see pp. 212–13.

(iv) Noldorin in the Land of Willows

'Did not even after the days of Tuor Noldorin and his Eldar come there seeking for Dor Lómin and the hidden river and the caverns of the Gnomes' imprisonment; yet thus nigh to their quest's end were like to abandon it? Indeed sleeping and dancing here . . . they were whelmed by the goblins sped by Melko from the Hills of Iron and Noldorin made bare escape thence' (p. 154). This was the Battle of Tasarinan, mentioned in the *Tale of Turambar* (pp. 70, 140), at the time of the great expedition of the Elves from Kôr. Cf. Lindo's remark in *The Cottage of Lost Play* (I.16) that his father Valwë 'went with Noldorin to find the Gnomes'.

Noldorin (Salmar, companion of Ulmo) is also said in the tale to have fought beside Tulkas at the Pools of Twilight against Melko himself, though his name was struck out (p. 195 and note 38); this was after the Battle of Tasarinan. On these battles see pp. 278 ff.

(v)   The stature of Elves and Men

The passage concerning Tuor's stature on p. 159, before it was rewritten (see note 18), can only mean that while Tuor was not himself unusually tall for a Man he was nonetheless taller than the Elves of Gondolin, and thus agrees with statements made in the *Tale of Turambar* (see p. 142). As emended, however, the meaning is rather that Men and Elves were not greatly distinct in stature.

(vi)   *Isfin and Eöl*

The earliest version of this tale is found in the little *Lost Tales* notebook (see I. 171), as follows:

Isfin and Eöl

Isfin daughter of Fingolma loved from afar by Eöl (Arval) of the Mole-kin of the Gnomes. He is strong and in favour with Fingolma and with the Sons of Fëanor (to whom he is akin) because he is a leader of the Miners and searches after hidden jewels, but he is illfavoured and Isfin loathes him.

(Fingolma as a name for Finwë Nólemë appears in outlines for *Gilfanon's Tale*, I. 238–9.) We have here an illfavoured miner named Eöl 'of the Mole' who loves Isfin but is rejected by her with loathing; and this is obviously closely parallel to the illfavoured miner Meglin with the sign of the sable mole seeking the hand of Idril, who rejects him, in *The Fall of Gondolin*. It is difficult to know how to interpret this. The simplest explanation is that the story adumbrated in the little notebook is actually earlier than that in *The Fall of Gondolin*; that Meglin did not yet exist; and that subsequently the image of the 'ugly miner – unsuccessful suitor' became that of the son, the object of desire becoming Idril (niece of Isfin), while a new story was developed for the father, Eöl the dark Elf of the forest who ensnared Isfin. But it is by no means clear where Eöl the miner was when he 'loved from afar' Isfin daughter of Fingolma. There seems to be no reason to think that he was associated with Gondolin; more probably the idea of the miner bearing the sign of the Mole entered Gondolin with Meglin.

IV

THE NAUGLAFRING

We come now to the last of the original *Lost Tales* to be given consecutive narrative form. This is contained in a separate notebook, and it bears the title *The Nauglafring: The Necklace of the Dwarves*.

The beginning of this tale is somewhat puzzling. Before the telling of *The Fall of Gondolin* Lindo told Littleheart that 'it is the desire of all that you tell us the tales of Tuor and of Eärendel as soon as may be' (p. 144), and Littleheart replied: 'It is a mighty tale, and seven times shall folk fare to the Tale-fire ere it be rightly told; and so twined is it with those stories of the Nauglafring and of the Elf-march that I would fain have aid in that telling of Ailios here . . .' Thus Littleheart's surrender of the chair of the tale-teller to Ailios at the beginning of the present text, so that Ailios should tell of the Nauglafring, fits the general context well; but we should not expect the new tale to be introduced with the words 'But after a while silence fell', since *The Fall of Gondolin* ends 'And no one in all the Room of Logs spake or moved for a great while.' In any case, after the very long *Fall of Gondolin* the next tale would surely have waited till the following evening.

This tale is once again a manuscript in ink over a wholly erased original in pencil, but only so far as the words 'sate his greed' on page 230. From this point to the end there is only a primary manuscript in pencil in the first stage of composition, written in haste – in places hurled on to the page, with a good many words not certainly decipherable; and a part of this was extensively rewritten while the tale was still in progress (see note 13).

The Nauglafring
The Necklace of the Dwarves

But after a while silence fell, and folk murmured 'Eärendel', but others said 'Nay – what of the Nauglafring, the Necklace of the Dwarves.' Therefore said Ilfiniol, leaving the chair of the tale-teller: 'Yea, better would the tale be told if Ailios would relate the matters concerning that necklace,' and Ailios being nowise unwilling thus began, looking upon the company.

'Remember ye all how Úrin the Steadfast cast the gold of Glorund before the feet of Tinwelint, and after would not touch it

again, but went in sorrow back to Hisilómë, and there died?' And
all said that that tale was still fresh in their hearts.

'Behold then,' said Ailios, 'in great grief gazed the king upon
Úrin as he left the hall, and he was weary for the evil of Melko that
thus deceived all hearts; yet tells the tale that so potent were the
spells that Mîm the fatherless had woven about that hoard that,
even as it lay upon the floor of the king's halls shining strangely in
the light of the torches that burnt there, already were all who
looked upon it touched by its subtle evil.

Now therefore did those of Úrin's band murmur, and one said
to the king: "Lo, lord, our captain Úrin, an old man and mad, has
departed, but we have no mind to forego our gain."

Then said Tinwelint, for neither was he untouched by the
golden spell: "Nay then, know ye not that this gold belongs to the
kindred of the Elves in common, for the Rodothlim who won it
from the earth long time ago are no more, and no one has especial
claim[1] to so much as a handful save only Úrin by reason of his son
Túrin, who slew the Worm, the robber of the Elves; yet Túrin is
dead and Úrin will have none of it; and Túrin was my man."

At those words the outlaws fell into great wrath, until the king
said: "Get ye now gone, and seek not O foolish ones to quarrel
with the Elves of the forest, lest death or the dread enchantments
of Valinor find you in the woods. Neither revile ye the name of
Tinwelint their king, for I will reward you richly enough for your
travail and the bringing of the gold. Let each one now approach
and take what he may grasp with either hand, and then depart in
peace."

Now were the Elves of the wood in turn displeased, who long
had stood nigh gazing on the gold; but the wild folk did as they
were bid, and yet more, for some went into the hoard twice and
thrice, and angry cries were raised in that hall. Then would
the woodland Elves hinder them of their thieving, and a great
dissension arose, so that though the king would stay them none
heeded him. Then did those outlaws being fierce and fearless folk
draw swords and deal blows about them, so that soon there was a
great fight even upon the steps of the high-seat of the king.
Doughty were those outlaws and great wielders of sword and axe
from their warfare with Orcs,[2] so that many were slain ere the
king, seeing that peace and pardon might no longer be, summoned
a host of his warriors, and those outlaws being wildered with the
stronger magics of the king[3] and confused in the dark ways of
the halls of Tinwelint were all slain fighting bitterly; but the

king's hall ran with gore, and the gold that lay before his throne, scattered and spurned by trampling feet, was drenched with blood. Thus did the curse of Mîm the Dwarf begin its course; and yet another sorrow sown by the Noldoli of old in Valinor was come to fruit.[4]

Then were the bodies of the outlaws cast forth, but the woodland Elves that were slain Tinwelint let bury nigh to the knoll of Tinúviel, and 'tis said that the great mound stands there still in Artanor, and for long the fairies called it Cûm an-Idrisaith, the Mound of Avarice.

Now came Gwenniel to Tinwelint and said: "Touch not this gold, for my heart tells me it is trebly cursed. Cursed indeed by the dragon's breath, and cursed by thy lieges' blood that moistens it, and the death of those[5] they slew; but some more bitter and more binding ill methinks hangs over it that I may not see."

Then, remembering the wisdom of Gwenniel his wife, the king was minded to hearken to her, and he bade gather it up and cast it into the stream before the gates. Yet even so he might not shake off its spell, and he said to himself: "First will I gaze my last upon its loveliness ere I fling it from me for ever." Therefore he let wash it clean of its stains of blood in clear waters, and display it before him. Now such mighty heaps of gold have never since been gathered in one place; and some thereof was wrought to cups, to basons, and to dishes, and hilts there were for swords, and scabbards, and sheaths for daggers; but the most part was of red gold unwrought lying in masses and in bars. The value of that hoard no man could count, for amid the gold lay many gems, and these were very beautiful to look upon, for the fathers of the Rodothlim had brought them out of Valinor, a portion of that boundless treasury the Noldoli had there possessed.

Now as he gazed Tinwelint said: "How glorious is this treasure! And I have not a tithe thereof, and of the gems of Valinor none save that Silmaril that Beren won from Angamandi." But Gwenniel who stood by said: "And that were worth all that here lies, were it thrice as great."

Then arose one from among the company, and that was Ufedhin, a Gnome; but more had he wandered about the world than any of the king's folk, and long had he dwelt with the Nauglath and the Indrafangs their kin. The Nauglath are a strange race and none know surely whence they be; and they serve not Melko nor Manwë and reck not for Elf or Man, and some say that they have not heard of Ilúvatar, or hearing disbelieve.

Howbeit in crafts and sciences and in the knowledge of the virtues of all things that are in the earth[6] or under the water none excel them; yet they dwell beneath the ground in caves and tunnelled towns, and aforetime Nogrod was the mightiest of these. Old are they, and never comes a child among them, nor do they laugh. They are squat in stature, and yet are strong, and their beards reach even to their toes, but the beards of the Indrafangs are the longest of all, and are forked, and they bind them about their middles when they walk abroad. All these creatures have Men called 'Dwarves', and say that their crafts and cunning surpass that of the Gnomes in marvellous contrivance, but of a truth there is little beauty in their works of themselves, for in those things of loveliness that they have wrought in ages past such renegade Gnomes as was Ufedhin have ever had a hand. Now long had that Gnome forsaken his folk, becoming leagued with the Dwarves of Nogrod, and was at that time come to the realms of Tinwelint with certain other Noldoli of like mind bearing swords and coats of mail and other smithyings of exquisite skill in which the Nauglath in those days did great traffic with the free Noldoli, and, 'tis said, with the Orcs and soldiers of Melko also.

As he stood in that place the spell of the gold had pierced the heart of Ufedhin more deeply than the heart of any there, and he could not endure that it should all be cast away, and these were his words: "An evil deed is this that Tinwelint the king intends; or who hereafter shall say that the kindreds of the Eldalië love things of beauty if a king of the Eldar cast so great a store of loveliness into the dark woodland waters where none but the fishes may after behold it? Rather than this should be, I beg of thee, O King, to suffer the craftsmen of the Dwarves to try their skill upon this unwrought gold, that the name of the golden treasury of Tinwelint become heard in all lands and places. This will they do, I promise thee, for small guerdon, might they but save the hoard from ruin."

Then looked the king upon the gold and he looked upon Ufedhin, and that Gnome was clad very richly, having a tunic of golden web and a belt of gold set with tiny gems; and his sword was damasked in strange wise,[7] but a collar of gold and silver interlaced most intricate was round his neck, and Tinwelint's raiment could in no wise compare with that of the wayfarer in his halls. Again looked Tinwelint upon the gold, and it shone yet more alluring fair, nor ever had the sparkle of the gems seemed so brilliant, and Ufedhin said again: "Or in what manner, O King, dost thou guard that Silmaril of which all the world hath heard?"

Now Gwenniel warded it in a casket of wood bound with iron, and Ufedhin said it was shame so to set a jewel that should not touch aught less worthy than the purest gold. Then was Tinwelint abashed, and yielded, and this was the agreement that he made with Ufedhin. Half the gold should the king measure and give to the hands of Ufedhin and his company, and they should bear it away to Nogrod and the dwellings of the Dwarves. Now those were a very long journey southward beyond the wide forest on the borders of those great heaths nigh Umboth-muilin the Pools of Twilight, on the marches of Tasarinan. Yet after but seven full moons back would the Nauglath fare bearing the king's loan all wrought to works of greatest cunning, yet in no wise would the weight and purity of the gold be minished. Then would they speak to Tinwelint, and an he liked not the handiwork then would they return and say no more; yet if it seemed good to him then of that which remained would they fashion such marvellous things for his adornment and for Gwenniel the Queen as never had Gnome or Dwarf made yet.

"For," said Ufedhin, "the cunning of the Nauglath have I learnt, and the beauty of design that only can the Noldoli compass do I know – yet shall the wages of our labour be small indeed, and we will name it before thee when all is done."

Then by reason of the glamour of the gold the king repented his agreement with Ufedhin, and he liked not altogether his words, and he would not suffer so great a store of gold to be borne without surety out of his sight for seven moons to the distant dwellings of the Dwarves; yet was he minded nonetheless to profit by their skill. Therefore suddenly he let seize Ufedhin, and his folk, and he said unto them: "Here shall ye remain as hostages in my halls until I see again my treasury." Now Tinwelint thought in his heart that Ufedhin and his Gnomes were of the utmost service to the Dwarves, and no covetice would be strong enough to bring them to forsake him; but that Gnome was very wroth, saying: "The Nauglath are no thieves, O King, nor yet their friends"; but Tinwelint said: "Yet the light of overmuch gold has made many thieves, who were not so before," and Ufedhin perforce consented, yet he forgave not Tinwelint in his heart.

Therefore was the gold now borne to Nogrod by folk of the king guided by one only of Ufedhin's companions, and the agreement of Ufedhin and Tinwelint spoken to Naugladur, the king of those places.

Now during the time of waiting Ufedhin was kindly entreated

in the courts of Tinwelint, yet was he idle perforce, and he fretted
inwardly. In his leisure he pondered ever what manner of lovely
thing of gold and jewels he would after fashion for Tinwelint, but
this was only for the greater ensnaring of the king, for already he
began to weave dark plots most deep of avarice and revenge.

On the very day of the fullness of the seventh moon thereafter
the watchers on the king's bridge cried: "Lo! there comes a great
company through the wood, and all it seems are aged men, and
they bear very heavy burdens on their backs." But the king
hearing said: "It is the Nauglath, who keep their tryst: now mayst
thou go free, Ufedhin, and take my greeting to them, and lead
them straightway to my hall"; and Ufedhin sallied forth gladly,
but his heart forgot not its resentment. Therefore having speech
privily with the Nauglath he prevailed upon them to demand at
the end a very great reward, and one thereto that the king might
not grant unhumbled; and more of his designs also did he unfold,
whereby that gold might fare in the end to Nogrod for ever.

Now come the Dwarves nonetheless over the bridge and before
the chair of Tinwelint, and behold, the things of their workmanship they had conveyed thither in silken cloths, and boxes of rare
woods carven cunningly. In other wise had Úrin haled the treasure
thither, and half thereof lay yet in his rude sacks and clumsy chests;
yet when the gold was once more revealed, then did a cry of wonder
arise, for the things the Nauglath had made were more wondrous
far than the scanty vessels and the ornaments that the Rodothlim
wrought of old. Cups and goblets did the king behold, and some
had double bowls or curious handles interlaced, and horns there
were of strange shape, dishes and trenchers, flagons and ewers,
and all appurtenances of a kingly feast. Candlesticks there were
and sconces for the torches, and none might count the rings and
armlets, the bracelets and collars, and the coronets of gold;
and all these were so subtly made and so cunningly adorned that
Tinwelint was glad beyond the hope of Ufedhin.

But as yet the designs of Ufedhin came to nought, for in no wise
would Tinwelint suffer or him or those of the Nauglath to depart
to Nogrod with or without that portion of the unwrought gold that
yet remained, and he said: "How shall it be thought that after the
weariness of your burdened journeys hither I should let you so
soon be gone, to noise the lack of courtesy of Tinwelint abroad in
Nogrod? Stay now awhile and rest and feast, and afterward shall
ye have the gold that remains to work your pleasure on; nor shall
aught of help that I or my folk may afford be wanting in your

labour, and a reward rich and more than just awaits you at the end."

But they knew nonetheless that they were prisoners, and trying the exits privily found them strongly warded. Being therefore without counsel they bowed before the king, and the faces of the Dwarf-folk show seldom what they think. Now after a time of rest was that last smithying begun in a deep place of Tinwelint's abode which he caused to be set apart for their uses, and what their hearts lacked therein fear supplied, and in all that work Ufedhin had a mighty part.

A golden crown they made for Tinwelint, who yet had worn nought but a wreath of scarlet leaves, and a helm too most glorious they fashioned; and a sword of dwarven steel brought from afar was hilted with bright gold and damascened in gold and silver with strange figurings wherein was pictured clear the wolf-hunt of Karkaras Knife-fang, father of wolves. That was a more wonderful sword than any Tinwelint had seen before, and outshone the sword in Ufedhin's belt the king had coveted. These things were of Ufedhin's cunning, but the Dwarves made a coat of linked mail of steel and gold for Tinwelint, and a belt of gold. Then was the king's heart gladdened, but they said: "All is not finished," and Ufedhin made a silver crown for Gwenniel, and aided by the Dwarves contrived slippers of silver crusted with diamonds, and the silver thereof was fashioned in delicate scales, so that it yielded as soft leather to the foot, and a girdle he made too of silver blended with pale gold. Yet were those things but a tithe of their works, and no tale tells a full count of them.

Now when all was done and their smithcraft given to the king, then said Ufedhin: "O Tinwelint, richest of kings, dost thou think these things fair?" And he said: "Yea"; but Ufedhin said: "Know then that great store of thy best and purest gold remaineth still, for we have husbanded it, having a boon to ask of thee, and it is this: we would make thee a carcanet and to its making lay all the skill and cunning that we have, and we desire that this should be the most marvellous ornament that the Earth has seen, and the greatest of the works of Elves and Dwarves. Therefore we beg of thee to let us have that Silmaril that thou treasurest, that it may shine wondrously amid the Nauglafring, the Necklace of the Dwarves."

Then again did Tinwelint doubt Ufedhin's purpose, yet did he yield the boon, an they would suffer him to be present at that smithying.

None are that yet live,' quoth Ailios,[8] 'who have seen that most glorious thing, save only[9] Littleheart son of Bronweg, yet are many things told thereof. Not only was it wrought with the greatest skill and subtlety in the world but it had a magic power, and there was no throat so great or so slender whereon it sat not with grace and loveliness. Albeit a weight beyond belief of gold was used in the making, lightly it hung upon its wearer as a strand of flax; and all such as clasped it about their necks seemed, as it hung upon their breasts, to be of goodly countenance, and women seemed most fair. Gems uncounted were there in that carcanet of gold, yet only as a setting that did prepare for its great central glory, and led the eye thereto, for amidmost hung like a little lamp of limpid fire the Silmaril of Fëanor, jewel of the Gods. Yet alas, even had that gold of the Rodothlim held no evil spell still had that carcanet been a thing of little luck, for the Dwarves were full of bitterness, and all its links were twined with baleful thoughts. Now however did they bear it before the king in its new-gleaming splendour; and then was the joy of Tinwelint king of the woodland Elves come to its crowning, and he cast the Nauglafring about his throat, and straightway the curse of Mîm fell upon him. Then said Ufedhin: "Now, O Lord, that thou art pleased beyond thy hope, perchance thou wilt grant the craftsmen thy kingly reward, and suffer them to depart also in joy to their own lands."

But Tinwelint, bewildered by the golden spell and the curse of Mîm, liked not the memory of his tryst; yet dissembling he bid the craftsmen come before him, and he praised their handiwork with royal words. At length said he: "'Twas said to me by one Ufedhin that at the end such reward as ye wished ye would name before me, yet would it be small enough, seeing that the labour was of love and of Ufedhin's desire that the golden hoard be not cast away and lost. What then do ye wish that I may grant?"

Then said Ufedhin scornfully: "For myself, nothing, O Lord; indeed the guestkindliness of thy halls for seven moons and three is more than I desire." But the Dwarves said: "This do we ask. For our labours during seven moons each seven jewels of Valinor, and seven robes of magic that only Gwendelin[10] can weave, and each a sack of gold; but for our great labour during three moons in thy halls unwilling, we ask each three sacks of silver, and each a cup of gold wherein to pledge thy health, O King, and each a fair maiden of the woodland Elves to fare away with us to our homes."

Then was King Tinwelint wroth indeed, for what the Dwarves had asked was of itself a goodly treasury, seeing that their company was very great; and he had no mind thus to devour the dragon's hoard, but never could he deliver maidens of the Elves unto illshapen Dwarves without undying shame.

Now that demand they had made only by the design of Ufedhin, yet seeing the anger of the king's face they said: "Nay, but this is not all, for in payment of Ufedhin's captivity for seven moons seven stout Elves must come with us and abide seven times seven years among us as bondsmen and menials in our labour."

Thereat arose Tinwelint from his seat, and calling summoned his weaponed thanes and warriors, that these surrounded the Nauglath and those Gnomes. Then said he: "For your insolence each three stripes with stinging withes shall ye receive, and Ufedhin seven, and afterwards will we speak of recompense."

When this was done, and a flame of bitter vengeance lit in those deep hearts, he said: "Lo, for your labour of seven months six pieces of gold and one of silver each shall have, and for your labours in my halls each three pieces of gold and some small gem that I can spare. For your journey hither a great feast shall ye eat and depart with good store against your return, and ere ye go ye shall drink to Tinwelint in elfin wine; yet, mark ye, for the sustenance of Ufedhin seven idle months about my halls shall ye each pay a piece of gold, and of silver two, for he has not aught himself and shall not receive since he desires it not, yet methinks he is at the bottom of your arrogance."

Then were the Dwarves paid their reward like common smiths of bronze and iron, and constrained to yield once more therefrom payment for Ufedhin – "else," said the king, "never shall ye get him hence." Then sat they to a great feast and dissembled their mood; yet at the end the time of their going came, and they drank to Tinwelint in elfin wine, but they cursed him in their beards, and Ufedhin swallowed not and spat the wine from his mouth upon the threshold.

Now tells the tale that the Nauglath fared home again, and if their greed had been kindled when first the gold was brought to Nogrod now was it a fierce flame of desire, and moreover they burnt under the insults of the king. Indeed all that folk love gold and silver more dearly than aught else on Earth, while that treasury was haunted by a spell and by no means were they armed against it. Now one there had been, Fangluin* the aged, who had counselled them from the first never to return the king's loan, for

* In the margin of the manuscript is written: *Fangluin: Bluebeard*.

said he: "Ufedhin we may later seek by guile to release, if it seem good," but at that time this seemed not policy to Naugladur their lord, who desired not warfare with the Elves. Yet now did Fangluin jeer at them mightily on their return, saying they had flung away their labour for a botcher's wage and a draught of wine and gotten dishonour thereto, and he played upon their lust, and Ufedhin joined his bitter words thereto. Therefore did Naugladur hold a secret council of the Dwarves of Nogrod, and sought how he might both be avenged upon Tinwelint, and sate his greed.[11]

Yet after long pondering he saw not how he might achieve his purpose save by force, and there was little hope therein, both by reason of the great strength of numbers of the Elves of Artanor in those days, and of the woven magic of Gwenniel that guarded all those regions, so that men of hostile heart were lost and came not to those woods; nor indeed could any such come thither unaided by treachery from within.

Now even as those aged ones sat in their dark halls and gnawed their beards, behold a sound of horns, and messengers were come from Bodruith of the Indrafangs, a kindred of the Dwarves that dwelt in other realms. Now these brought tidings of the death of Mîm the fatherless at the hand of Úrin and the rape of Glorund's gold, which tale had but new come to Bodruith's ears. Now hitherto the Dwarves knew not the full tale concerning that hoard, nor more than Ufedhin might tell hearing the speech in Tinwelint's halls, and Úrin had not spoken the full count thereof ere he departed. Hearing therefore these tidings new wrath was added to their lust and a clamour arose among them, and Naugladur vowed to rest not ere Mîm was thrice avenged – "and more," said he, "meseems the gold belongs of right to the people of the Dwarves."

This then was the design; and by his deeds have the Dwarves been severed in feud for ever since those days with the Elves, and drawn more nigh in friendship to the kin of Melko. Secretly he let send to the Indrafangs that they prepare their host against a day that he would name, whenso the time should be ripe; and a hidden forging of bitter steel then was in Belegost the dwelling of the Indrafangs. Moreover he gathered about him a great host of the Orcs, and wandering goblins, promising them a good wage, and the pleasure of their Master moreover, and a rich booty at the end; and all these he armed with his own weapons. Now came unto Naugladur an Elf, and he was one of Tinwelint's folk, and he offered to lead that host through the magics of Gwendelin, for he was bitten by the gold-lust of Glorund's hoard, and so did the curse of Mîm come upon Tinwelint and treachery first arose among the Elves of Artanor. Then did Naugladur [?smile] bitterly, for he knew that the time was ripe and Tinwelint delivered to him. Now each year about the time of the great wolf-hunt of Beren Tinwelint was wont to keep the memory of that day by a hunt in the woods, and it was a very mighty chase and thronged with very many folk, and nights of merriment and feasting were there in the forest. Now Naugladur learnt of that Elf Narthseg, whose name is bitter to the Eldar yet, that the king would fare a-hunting at the next high moon but one, and straightway he sent the trysted sign, a bloodstained knife, to Bodruith at Belegost. Now all that host assembled on the confines of the woods, and no word came yet unto the king.

Now tells the tale that one came unto Tinwelint, and Tinwelint knew him not for the wild growth of his hair – and lo! it was Mablung, and he said: "Lo, even in the depths of the forest have we heard that this year you will celebrate the death of Karkaras with a high-tide greater than even before, O King – and behold I have returned to bear you company." And the king was full of mirth and fain to greet Mablung the brave; and at the words of Mablung that Huan captain of Dogs was come also into Artanor was he glad indeed.

Behold now Tinwelint the king rode forth a-hunting, and more glorious was his array than ever aforetime, and the helm of gold was above his flowing locks, and with gold were the trappings of his steed adorned; and the sunlight amid the trees fell upon his face, and it seemed to those that beheld it like to the glorious face of the sun at morning; for about his throat was clasped the Nauglafring, the Necklace of the Dwarves. Beside him rode Mablung the Heavyhand in the place of honour by reason of his deeds at that great hunt aforetime – but Huan of the Dogs was ahead of the hunters, and men thought that great dog bore him strangely, but mayhap there was something in the wind that day he liked not.

Now is the king far in the woods with all his company, and the horns grow faint in the deep forest, but Gwendelin sits in her bower and foreboding is in her heart and eyes. Then said an Elfmaid, Nielthi: "Wherefore, O Lady, art thou sorrowful at the hightide of the king?" And Gwendelin said: "Evil seeks our land, and my heart misgives me that my days in Artanor are speeding to their end, yet if I should lose Tinwelint then would I wish never to have wandered forth from Valinor." But Nielthi said: "Nay, O Lady Gwendelin, hast thou not woven great magic all about us, so that we fear not?" But the queen made answer: "Yet meseems there is a rat that gnaws the threads and all the web has come unwoven." Even at that word there was a cry about the doors, and suddenly it grew to a fierce noise . . . by the clash of steel. Then went Gwendelin unafraid forth from her bower, and behold, a sudden multitude of Orcs and Indrafangs held the bridge, and there was war within the cavernous gates; but that place ran with blood, and a great heap of slain lay there, for the onset had been secret and all unknown.

Then did Gwendelin know well that her foreboding was true, and that treachery had found her realm at last, yet did she hearten those few guards that remained to her and had fared not to the hunt, and valiantly they warded the palace of the king until the tide of numbers bore them back [and] fire and blood found all the halls and deep ways of that great fortress of the Elves.

Then did those Orcs and Dwarves ransack all the chambers seeking for treasure, and lo! one came and sate him in the high seat of the king laughing loud, and Gwendelin saw that it was Ufedhin, and mocking he bid her be seated in her ancient seat beside the king's. Then Gwendelin gazed upon him so that his glance fell, and she said: "Wherefore, O renegade, dost thou defile my lord's seat? Little had I thought to see any of the Elves sit there, a robber, stained with murder, a league-fellow of the truceless enemies of his kin. Or thinkest thou it is a glorious deed to assail an ill-armed house what time its lord is far away?" But Ufedhin said nought, shunning the bright eyes of Gwendelin, wherefore said she anew: "Get thee now gone with thy foul Orcs, lest Tinwelint coming repay thee bitterly."

Then at last did Ufedhin answer, and he laughed, but ill at ease, and he looked not at the queen, but he said listening to a sound without: "Nay, but already is he come." And behold, Naugladur entered now and a host of the Dwarves were about him, but he bore the head of Tinwelint crowned and helmed in gold; but the necklace of all wonder was clasped about the throat of Naugladur. Then did Gwendelin see in her heart all that had befallen, and how the curse of the gold had fallen on the realm of Artanor, and never has she danced or sung since that dark hour; but Naugladur bid gather all things of gold or silver or of precious stones and bear them to Nogrod — "and whatso remains of goods or folk may the

Orcs keep, or slay, as they desire. Yet the Lady Gwendelin Queen of Artanor shall fare with me."

Then said Gwendelin: "Thief and murderer, child of Melko, yet art thou a fool, for thou canst not see what hangs over thine own head." By reason of the anguish of her heart was her sight grown very clear, and she read by her fay-wisdon the curse of Mîm and much of what would yet betide.

Then did Naugladur in his triumph laugh till his beard shook, and bid seize her: but none might do so, for as they came towards her they groped as if in sudden dark, or stumbled and fell tripping each the other, and Gwendelin went forth from the places of her abode, and her bitter weeping filled the forest. Now did a great darkness fall upon her mind and her counsel and lore forsook her, that she wandered she knew not whither for a great while; and this was by reason of her love for Tinwelint the king, for whom she had chosen never to fare back to Valinor and the beauty of the Gods, dwelling always in the wild forests of the North; and now did there seem to her neither beauty nor joy be it in Valinor or in the Lands Without. Many of the scattered Elves in her wayward journeyings she met, and they took pity on her, but she heeded them not. Tales had they told her, but she hearkened not over much since Tinwelint was dead; nonetheless must ye know how even in the hour that Ufedhin's host brake the palace and despoiled it, and other companies as great and as terrible of the Orcs and Indrafangs fell with death and fire upon all the realm of Tinwelint, behold the brave hunt of the king were resting amid mirth and laughter, but Huan stalked apart. Then suddenly were the woods filled with noise and Huan bayed aloud; but the king and his company were all encircled with armed foes. Long they fought bitterly there among the trees, and the Nauglath – for such were their foes – had great scathe of them or ever they were slain. Yet in the end were they all fordone, and Mablung and the king fell side by side – but Naugladur it was who swept off the head of Tinwelint after he was dead, for living he dared not so near to his bright sword or the axe of Mablung.[12]

Now doth the tale know no more to tell of Huan, save that even while the swords still sang that great dog was speeding through the land, and his way led him as the [?wind] to the land of i·Guilwarthon, the living-dead, where reigned Beren and Tinúviel the daughter of Tinwelint. Not in any settled abode did those twain dwell, nor had their realm boundaries well-marked – and indeed no other messenger save Huan alone to whom all ways were known had ever found Beren and obtained his aid so soon.[13] Indeed the tale tells that even as that host of the Orcs were burning all the land of Tinwelint and the Nauglath and the Indrafangin were wending homeward burdened utterly with spoils of gold and precious things, came Huan to Beren's lodge, and it was dusk. Lo, Beren sat upon a tree root and Tinúviel danced on a green sward in the gloaming as he gazed upon her, when suddenly stood Huan before them, and Beren gave a cry of joy and wonder, for it was long since he and Huan had hunted together. But Tinúviel looking upon Huan saw that he bled, and there was a tale to read in his great eyes. And she said suddenly: "What evil then has fallen upon Artanor?" and Huan said: "Fire and death and the terror of Orcs; but Tinwelint is slain."

Then did both Beren and Tinúviel weep bitter tears; nor did the full tale of Huan dry their eyes. When then it was told to the end leapt Beren to his feet in white wrath, and seizing a horn that hung at his belt he blew a clear blast thereon that rang round all the neighbouring hills, and an elfin folk all clad in green and brown sprang as it were by magic towards him from every glade and coppice, stream and fell.

Now not even Beren knew the tale of those myriad folk that followed his horn in the woods of Hisilómë, and or ever the moon was high above the hills the host assembled in the glade of his abiding was very great, yet were they lightly armed and the most bore only knives and bows. "Yet," said Beren, "speed is that which now we need the most"; and certain Elves at his bidding fared like deer before him, seeking news of the march of the Dwarves and Indrafangs, but at dawn he followed at the head of the green Elves, and Tiñúviel abode in the glade and wept unto herself for the death of Tinwelint, and Gwendelin also she mourned as dead.

Now is to tell that the laden host of the Dwarves fared from the place of their ransacking, and Naugladur was at their head, and beside him Ufedhin and Bodruith; and ever as he rode Ufedhin sought to put the dread eyes of Gwendelin from his mind and could not, and all happiness was fled from his heart that shrivelled under the memory of that glance; nor was this the only disquiet that tortured him, for if ever he raised his eyes lo! they lighted on the Necklace of the Dwarves shining about the aged neck of Naugladur, and then all other thoughts save bottomless desire of its beauty were banished.

Thus did those three fare and with them all their host, but so great became the torment of Ufedhin's mind that in the end he might not endure it more, but at night when a halt was called he crept stealthily to the place where Naugladur slept, and coming upon that aged one wrapt in slumbers would slay that Dwarf and lay hands upon the wondrous Nauglafring. Now even as he sought to do so, behold one seized his throat suddenly from behind, and it was Bodruith, who filled with the same lust sought also to make that lovely thing his own; but coming upon Ufedhin would slay him by reason of his kinship to Naugladur. Then did Ufedhin stab suddenly backward at hazard in the dark with a keen knife long and slender that he had with him for the bane of Naugladur, and that knife pierced the vitals of Bodruith Lord of Belegost so that he fell dying upon Naugladur, and the throat of Naugladur and the magic carcanet were drenched anew with blood.

Thereat did Naugladur awake with a great cry, but Ufedhin fled gasping from that place, for the long fingers of the Indrafang had well-nigh choked him. Now when some bore torches swiftly to that place Naugladur thought that Bodruith alone had sought to rob him of the jewel, and marvelled how he had thus been timely slain, and he proclaimed a rich reward to the slayer of Bodruith if that man would come forward telling all that he had seen. Thus was it that none perceived the flight of Ufedhin for a while, and wrath awoke between the Dwarves of Nogrod and the Indrafangs, and many were slain ere the Indrafangs being in less number were scattered and got them as best they might to Belegost, bearing scant treasury with them. Of this came the agelong feud between those kindreds of the Dwarves that has spread to many lands and caused many a tale, whereof the Elves know little tidings and Men have seldom heard. Yet may it be seen how the curse of Mîm came early home to rest among his own kin, and would indeed it had gone no further and had visited the Eldar never more.

Lo, when the flight of Ufedhin came also to light then was Naugladur in wrath, and he let kill all the Gnomes that remained in the host. Then said he: "Now are we rid of Indrafangs and Gnomes and all traitors, and nought more do I fear at all."

But Ufedhin ranged the wild lands in great fear and anguish, for him seemed that he had become a traitor to his kin, blood-guilty to the Elves, and haunted with the [?burning] eyes of Gwendelin the queen, for nought but exile and misery, and no smallest part nor share had he in the gold of Glorund, for all his heart was afire with lust; yet few have pitied him.

Now tells the tale that he fell in with the rangers of Beren's folk, and these gaining from him sure knowledge of all the host and

array of Naugladur and the ways he purposed to follow, they sped
back like wind among the trees unto their lord; but Ufedhin
revealed not to them who he was, feigning to be an Elf of Artanor
escaped from bondage in their host. Now therefore they entreated
him well, and he was sent back to Beren that their captain might
. . . . his words, and albeit Beren marvelled at his
[?cowardly] . . . . . .[14] and downward glance it seemed to him that
he brought safe word, and he set a trap for Naugladur.

No longer did he march hotly on the trail of the Dwarves, but
knowing that they would essay the passage of the river Aros at a
certain time he turned aside, faring swiftly with his light-footed
Elves by straighter paths that he might reach Sarnathrod the
Stony Ford before them. Now the Aros is a fierce stream – and is it
not that very water that more near its spring runs swiftly past the
aged doors of the Rodothlim's caves and the dark lairs of Glorund[15]
– and in those lower regions by no means can be crossed by a great
host of laden men save at this ford, nor is it overeasy here. Never
would Naugladur have taken that way had he knowledge of Beren
– yet blinded by the spell and the dazzling gold he feared nought
either within or without his host, and he was in haste to reach
Nogrod and its dark caverns, for the Dwarves list not long to abide
in the bright light of day.

Now came all that host to the banks of Aros, and their array was
thus: first a number of unladen Dwarves most fully armed, and
amidmost the great company of those that bore the treasury of
Glorund, and many a fair thing beside that they had haled from
Tinwelint's halls; and behind these was Naugladur, and he bestrode
Tinwelint's horse, and a strange figure did he seem, for the legs of
the Dwarves are short and crooked, but two Dwarves led that
horse for it went not willingly and it was laden with spoil. But
behind these came again a mass of armed men but little laden; and
in this array they sought to cross Sarnathrod on their day of doom.

Morn was it when they reached the hither bank and high noon
saw them yet passing in long-strung lines and wading slowly the
shallow places of the swift-running stream. Here doth it widen out
and fare down narrow channels filled with boulders atween long
spits of shingle and stones less great. Now did Naugladur slip
from his burdened horse and prepare to get him over, for the
armed host of the vanguard had climbed already the further bank,
and it was great and sheer and thick with trees, and the bearers of
the gold were some already stepped thereon and some amidmost
of the stream, but the armed men of the rear were resting awhile.

Suddenly is all that place filled with the sound of elfin horns, and one . . . . .[16] with a clearer blast above the rest, and it is the horn of Beren, the huntsman of the woods. Then is the air thick with the slender arrows of the Eldar that err not neither doth the wind bear them aside, and lo, from every tree and boulder do the brown Elves and the green spring suddenly and loose unceasingly from full quivers. Then was there a panic and a noise in the host of Naugladur, and those that waded in the ford cast their golden burdens in the waters and sought affrighted to either bank, but many were stricken with those pitiless darts and fell with their gold into the currents of the Aros, staining its clear waters with their dark blood.

Now were the warriors on the far bank [?wrapped] in battle and rallying sought to come at their foes, but these fled nimbly before them, while [?others] poured still the hail of arrows upon them, and thus got the Eldar few hurts and the Dwarf-folk fell dead unceasingly. Now was that great fight of the Stony Ford . . . . . . nigh to Naugladur, for even though Naugladur and his captains led their bands stoutly never might they grip their foe, and death fell like rain upon their ranks until the most part broke and fled, and a noise of clear laughter echoed from the Elves thereat, and they forebore to shoot more, for the illshapen figures of the Dwarves as they fled, their white beards torn by the wind, filled them [with] mirth. But now stood Naugladur and few were about him, and he remembered the words of Gwendelin, for behold, Beren came towards him and he cast aside his bow, and drew a bright sword; and Beren was of great stature among the Eldar, albeit not of the girth and breadth of Naugladur of the Dwarves.

Then said Beren: "Ward thy life an thou canst, O crook-legged murderer, else will I take it," and Naugladur bid him even the Nauglafring, the necklace of wonder, that he be suffered to go unharmed; but Beren said: "Nay, that may I still take when thou art slain," and thereat he made alone upon Naugladur and his companions, and having slain the foremost of these the others fled away amid elfin laughter, and so Beren came upon Naugladur, slayer of Tinwelint. Then did that aged one defend himself doughtily, and 'twas a bitter fight, and many of the Elves that watched for love and fear of their captain fingered their bow-strings, but Beren called even as he fought that all should stay their hands.

Now little doth the tale tell of wounds and blows of that affray, save that Beren got many hurts therein, and many of his shrewdest blows did little harm to Naugladur by reason of the [?skill] and magic of his dwarfen mail; and it is said that three hours they fought and Beren's arms grew weary, but not those of Naugladur accustomed to wield his mighty hammer at the forge, and it is more than like that otherwise would the issue have been but for the curse of Mîm; for marking how Beren grew faint Naugladur pressed him ever more nearly, and the arrogance that was of that grievous spell came into his heart, and he thought: "I will slay this Elf, and his folk will flee in fear before me," and grasping his sword he dealt a mighty blow and cried: "Take here thy bane, O stripling of the woods," and in that moment his foot found a jagged stone and he stumbled forward, but Beren slipped aside from that blow and catching at his beard his hand found the carcanet of gold, and therewith he swung Naugladur suddenly off his feet upon his face: and Naugladur's sword was shaken from his grasp, but Beren seized it and slew him therewith, for he said: "I will not sully my bright blade with thy dark blood, since there is no need." But the body of Naugladur was cast into the Aros.

Then did he unloose the necklace, and he gazed in wonder at it – and beheld the Silmaril, even the jewel he won from Angband and gained undying glory by his deed; and he said: "Never have mine eyes beheld thee O Lamp of Faëry burn one half so fair as now thou dost, set in gold and gems and the magic of the Dwarves"; and that necklace he caused to be washed of its stains, and he cast it not away, knowing nought of its power, but bore it with him back into the woods of Hithlum.

But the waters of Aros flowed on for ever above the drowned hoard of Glorund, and so do still, for in after days Dwarves came from Nogrod and sought for it, and for the body of Naugladur; but a flood arose from the mountains and therein the seekers perished; and so great now is the gloom and dread of that Stony Ford that none seek the treasure that it guards nor dare ever to cross the magic stream at that enchanted place.

But in the vales of Hithlum was there gladness at the homecoming of the Elves, and great was the joy of Tinúviel to see her lord once more returning amidst his companies, but little did it ease her grief for the death of Tinwelint that Naugladur was slain and many Dwarves beside. Then did Beren seek to comfort her, and taking her in his arms he set the glorious Nauglafring about her neck, and all were blinded by the greatness of her beauty; and Beren said: "Behold the Lamp of Fëanor that thou

and I did win from Hell," and Tinúviel smiled, remembering the
first days of their love and those days of travail in the wild.

Now is it to be said that Beren sent for Ufedhin and well
rewarded him for his words of true guidance whereof the Dwarves
had been overcome, and he bid him dwell in . . . . among his folk,
and Ufedhin was little loth; yet on a time, no great space thereafter, did that thing betide which he least desired. For came there
a sound of very sorrowful singing in the woods, and behold, it was
Gwendelin wandering distraught, and her feet bore her to the
midmost of a glade where sat Beren and Tinúviel; and at that hour
it was new morning, but at the sound all nigh ceased their speaking
and were very still. Then did Beren gaze in awe upon Gwendelin,
but Tinúviel cried suddenly in sorrow mixed with joy: "O mother
Gwendelin, whither do thy feet bear thee, for methought thee
dead"; but the greeting of those twain upon the greensward was
very sweet. And Ufedhin fled from among the Elves, for he could
not endure to look upon the eyes of Gwendelin, and madness took
him, and none may say what was his unhappy weird thereafter;
and little but a tortured heart got he from the Gold of Glorund.

Now hearing the cries of Ufedhin Gwendelin looked in wonder
after him, and stayed her tender words; and memory came back
into her eyes so that she cried as in amaze beholding the Necklace
of the Dwarves that hung about the white throat of Tinúviel.
Then wrathfully she asked of Beren what it might portend, and
wherefore he suffered the accursed thing to touch Tinúviel; and
told Beren[17] all that tale such as Huan had told him, in deed or
guess, and of the pursuit and fighting at the ford he told also,
saying at the end: "Nor indeed do I see who, now that Lord
Tinwelint is fared to Valinor, should so fittingly wear that jewel of
the Gods as Tinúviel." But Gwendelin told of the dragon's ban
upon the gold and the [?staining] of blood in the king's halls, "and
yet another and more potent curse, whose arising I know not, is
woven therewith," said she, "nor methinks was the labour of the
Dwarves free from spells of the most enduring malice." But Beren
laughed, saying that the glory of the Silmaril and its holiness
might overcome all such evils, even as it burnt the [?foul] flesh of
Karkaras. "Nor," said he, "have I seen ever my Tinúviel so fair as
now she is, clasped in the loveliness of this thing of gold"; but
Gwendelin said: "Yet the Silmaril abode in the Crown of Melko,
and that is the work of baleful smiths indeed."

Then said Tinúviel that she desired not things of worth
or precious stones but the elfin gladness of the forest, and to

pleasure Gwendelin she cast it from her neck; but Beren was little pleased and he would not suffer it to be flung away, but warded it in his . . . .[18]

Thereafter did Gwendelin abide a while in the woods among them and was healed; and in the end she fared wistfully back to the land of Lórien and came never again into the tales of the dwellers of Earth; but upon Beren and Tinúviel fell swiftly that doom of mortality that Mandos had spoken when he sped them from his halls – and in this perhaps did the curse of Mîm have [?potency] in that it came more soon upon them; nor this time did those twain fare the road together, but when yet was the child of those twain, Dior[19] the Fair, a little one, did Tinúviel slowly fade, even as the Elves of later days have done throughout the world, and she vanished in the woods, and none have seen her dancing ever there again. But Beren searched all the lands of Hithlum and of Artanor ranging after her; and never has any of the Elves had more loneliness than his, or ever he too faded from life, and Dior his son was left ruler of the brown Elves and the green, and Lord of the Nauglafring.

Mayhap what all Elves say is true, that those twain hunt now in the forest of Oromë in Valinor, and Tinúviel dances on the green swards of Nessa and of Vána daughters of the Gods for ever more; yet great was the grief of the Elves when the Guilwarthon went from among them, and being leaderless and lessened of magic their numbers minished; and many fared away to Gondolin, the rumour of whose growing power and glory ran in secret whispers among all the Elves.

Still did Dior when come to manhood rule a numerous folk, and he loved the woods even as Beren had done; and songs name him mostly Ausir the Wealthy for his possession of that wondrous gem set in the Necklace of the Dwarves. Now the tales of Beren and Tinúviel grew dim in his heart, and he took to wearing it about his neck and to love its loveliness most dearly; and the fame of that jewel spread like fire through all the regions of the North, and the Elves said one to another: "A Silmaril of Fëanor burns in the woods of Hisilómë."

Now fare the long days of Elfinesse unto that time when Tuor dwelt in Gondolin; and children then had Dior the Elf,[20] Auredhir and Elwing, and Auredhir was most like to his forefather Beren, and all loved him, yet none so dearly as did Dior; but Elwing the fairy have all poesies named as beautiful as Tinúviel if that indeed may be, yet hard is it to say seeing the great loveliness of the elfin folk of yore. Now those were days of happiness in the vales of Hithlum, for there was peace with Melko and the Dwarves who had but one thought as they plotted against Gondolin, and Angband was full of labour; yet is it to tell that bitterness entered into the hearts of the seven sons of Fëanor, remembering their oath. Now Maidros, whom Melko maimed, was their leader; and he called to his brethren Maglor and Dinithel, and to Damrod, and to Celegorm, to Cranthor and to Curufin the Crafty, and he said to them how it was now known to him that a Silmaril of those their father Fëanor had made was now the pride and glory of Dior of the southern vales, "and Elwing his daughter bears it whitherso she goes – but do you not forget," said he, "that we swore to have no peace with Melko nor any of his folk, nor with any other of Earth-dwellers that held the Silmarils of Fëanor from us. For what," said Maidros, "do we suffer exile and wandering and rule over a scant and forgotten folk, if others gather to their hoard the heirlooms that are ours?"

Thus was it that they sent Curufin the Crafty to Dior, and told him of their oath, and bid him give that fair jewel back unto those whose right it was; but Dior gazing on the loveliness of Elwing would not do so, and he said that he could not endure that the Nauglafring, fairest of earthly craft, be so despoiled. "Then," said Curufin, "must the Nauglafring unbroken be given to the sons of Fëanor," and Dior waxed wroth, bidding him be gone, nor dare to claim what his sire Beren the Onehanded won with his hand from the [?jaws] of Melko – "other twain are there in the selfsame place," said he, "an your hearts be bold enow."

Then went Curufin unto his brethren, and because of their unbreakable oath and of their [?thirst] for that Silmaril (nor indeed was the spell of Mîm and of the dragon wanting) they planned war upon Dior – and the Eldar cry shame upon them for that deed, the first premeditated war of elfin folk upon elfin folk, whose name otherwise were glorious among the Eldalië for their sufferings. Little good came thereby to them; for they fell unawares upon Dior, and Dior and Auredhir were slain, yet behold, Evranin the nurse of Elwing, and Gereth a Gnome, took her unwilling in a flight swift and sudden from those lands, and they bore with them the Nauglafring, so that the sons of Fëanor saw it not; but a host of Dior's folk, coming with all speed yet late unto the fray, fell suddenly on their rear, and there was a great battle, and Maglor was slain with swords, and Mai . . . .[21] died of wounds in the wild, and Celegorm was pierced with a hundred arrows, and Cranthor beside him. Yet in the end were the sons of Fëanor masters of the field of slain, and the brown Elves and the green were scattered over all the lands unhappy, for they would not hearken to Maidros the maimed, nor to Curufin and Damrod who had slain their lord; and it is said that even on the day of that battle of the Elves Melko sought against Gondolin, and the fortunes of the Elves came to their uttermost waning.

Now was naught left of the seed of Beren Ermabwed son of Egnor save Elwing the Lovely, and she wandered in the woods, and of the brown Elves and the green a few gathered to her, and they departed for ever from the glades of Hithlum and got them to the south towards Sirion's deep waters, and the pleasant lands.

And thus did all the fates of the fairies weave then to one strand, and that strand is the great tale of Eärendel; and to that tale's true beginning are we now come.'

Then said Ailios: 'And methinks that is tale enow for this time of telling.'

NOTES

1   This sentence is a rewriting of the text, which had originally:

"Nay then, know ye not that this gold belongs to the kindred of the Elves, who won it from the earth long time ago, and no one among Men has claim . . ."

The remainder of this scene, ending with the slaughter of Úrin's band, was rewritten at many points, with the same object as in the passage just cited – to convert Úrin's band from Men to Elves, as was done also at the end of Eltas' tale (see p. 118 note 33). Thus original 'Elves' was changed to 'Elves of the wood, woodland Elves', and original 'Men' to 'folk, outlaws'; and see notes 2, 3, 5.

2   The original sentence here was:

Doughty were those Men and great wielders of sword and axe, and still in those unfaded days might mortal weapons wound the bodies of the elfin-folk.

See note 1.

3   The original sentence here was: 'and those Men being wildered with magics'. See note 1.

4   This sentence, from 'and yet another sorrow . . .', was added to the text later.

5   'those': the text has 'the Men', obviously left unchanged through oversight. See note 1.

6 'in the earth' is an emendation of the original reading 'on the earth'.

7 'damasked in strange wise', i.e. 'damascened', ornamentally inlaid
with designs in gold and silver. The word 'damascened' is used of
the sword of Tinwelint made by the Dwarves, on which were seen
images of the wolf-hunt (p. 227), and of Glorfindel's arms (p. 173).

8 The text has 'Eltas', but with 'Ailios' written above in pencil. Since
Ailios appears as the teller at the beginning of the tale, and not as the
result of emendation, 'Eltas' here was probably no more than a slip.

9 'save only' is a later emendation of the original 'not even'. See p. 256.

10 It is odd that *Gwendelin* appears here, not *Gwenniel* as hitherto in
this tale. Since the first part of the tale is in ink over an erased pencil
text, the obvious explanation is that the erased text had *Gwendelin*
and that my father changed this to *Gwenniel* as he went along,
overlooking it in this one instance. But the matter is probably more
complex – one of those small puzzles with which the texts of the *Lost
Tales* abound – for after the manuscript in ink ceases the form
Gwenniel occurs, though once only, and *Gwendelin* is then used
for all the rest of the tale. See *Changes made to Names*, p. 244.

11 Here the manuscript in ink ends; see p. 221.

12 Against this sentence my father wrote a direction that the story was
to be that the Nauglafring caught in the bushes and held the king.

13 A rejected passage in the manuscript here gives an earlier version of
the events, according to which it was Gwendelin, not Huan, who
brought the news to Beren:

> . . . and her bitter weeping filled the forest. Now there did
> Gwendeling [*sic*] gather to her many of the scattered woodland
> Elves and of them did she hear how matters had fared even as she
> had guessed: how the hunting party had been surrounded and
> o'erwhelmed by the Nauglath while the Indrafangs and Orcs fell
> suddenly with death and fire upon all the realm of Tinwelint, and
> not the least host was that of Ufedhin that slew the guardians of
> the bridge; and it was said that Naugladur had slain Tinwelint
> when he was borne down by numbers, and folk thought Narthseg
> a wild Elf had led the foemen hither, and he had been slain in the
> fighting.
>
> Then seeing no hope Gwendelin and her companions fared
> with the utmost speed out of that land of sorrow, even to the
> kingdom of i·Guilwarthon in Hisilómë, where reigned Beren and
> Tinúviel her daughter. Now Beren and Tinúviel lived not in any
> settled abode, nor had their realm boundaries well-marked, and
> no other messenger save Gwendelin daughter of the Vali had of a
> surety found those twain the living-dead so soon.

It is clear from the manuscript that the return of Mablung and Huan
to Artanor and their presence at the hunt (referred to in general
terms at the end of the *Tale of Tinúviel*, p. 41) was added to the

tale, and with this new element went the change in Gwendelin's movements immediately after the disaster. But though the textual history is here extremely hard to interpet, what with erasures and additions on loose pages, I think it is almost certain that this reshaping was done while the original composition of the tale was still in progress.

14 The first of these lacunae that I have left in the text contains two words, the first possibly 'believe' and the second probably 'best'. In the second lacuna the word might conceivably be 'pallor'.

15 This sentence, from 'and is it not that very water . . .', is struck through and bracketed, and in the margin my father scribbled: 'No [?that] is Narog.'

16 The illegible word might be 'brays': the word 'clearer' is an emendation from 'hoarser'.

17 'and told Beren': i.e., 'and Beren told'. The text as first written had 'Then told Beren . . .'

18 The illegible word might just possibly be 'treasury', but I do not think that it is.

19 *Dior* replaced the name *Ausir*, which however occurs below as another name for Dior.

20 'Dior the Elf' is an emendation from 'Dior then an aged Elf'.

21 The latter part of this name is quite unclear: it might be read as *Maithog*, or as *Mailweg*. See *Changes made to Names* under *Dinithel*.

Changes made to names in
The Tale of the Nauglafring

Ilfiniol (p. 221) here so written from the first: see p. 201.

Gwenniel is used throughout the revised section of the tale except at the last occurrence (p. 228), where the form is *Gwendelin*; in the pencilled part of the tale at the first occurrence of the queen's name it is again *Gwenniel* (p. 230), but thereafter always *Gwendelin* (see note 10).

The name of the queen in the *Lost Tales* is as variable as that of Littleheart. In *The Chaining of Melko* and *The Coming of the Elves* she is *Tindriel > Wendelin*. In the *Tale of Tinúviel* she is *Wendelin > Gwendeling* (see p. 50); in the type-script text of *Tinúviel Gwenethlin > Melian*; in the *Tale of Turambar Gwendeling > Gwedheling*; in the present tale *Gwendelin/Gwenniel* (the form *Gwendeling* occurs in the rejected passage given in note 13); and in the Gnomish dictionary *Gwendeling > Gwedhiling*.

Belegost At the first occurrence (p. 230) the manuscript has *Ost Belegost*, with *Ost* circled as if for rejection, and *Belegost* is the reading subsequently.

(*i*·)*Guilwarthon*   In the *Tale of Tinúviel*, p. 41, the form is *i·Cuilwarthon*. At the occurrence on p. 240 the ending of the name does not look like -*on*, but as I cannot say what it is I give *Guilwarthon* in the text.

Dinithel could also be read as *Durithel* (p. 241). This name was written in later in ink over an earlier name in pencil now scarcely legible, though clearly the same as that beginning *Mai* . . . . which appears for this son of Fëanor subsequently (see note 21).

Commentary on
The Tale of the Nauglafring

In this commentary I shall not compare in detail the *Tale of the Nauglafring* with the story told in *The Silmarillion* (Chapter 22, *Of the Ruin of Doriath*). The stories are profoundly different in essential features – above all, in the reduction of the treasure brought by Húrin from Nargothrond to a single object, the Necklace of the Dwarves, which had long been in existence (though not, of course, containing the Silmaril); while the whole history of the relation between Thingol and the Dwarves is changed. My father never again wrote any part of this story on a remotely comparable scale, and the formation of the published text was here of the utmost difficulty; I hope later to give an account of it.

While it is often difficult to differentiate what my father omitted in his more concise versions (in order to keep them concise) from what he rejected, it seems clear that a large part of the elaborate narrative of the *Tale of the Nauglafring* was early abandoned. In subsequent writing the story of the fighting between Úrin's band and Tinwelint's Elves disappeared, and there is no trace afterwards of Ufedhin or the other Gnomes that lived among the Dwarves, of the story that the Dwarves took half the unwrought gold ('the king's loan') away to Nogrod to make precious objects from it, of the keeping of Ufedhin hostage, of Tinwelint's refusal to let the Dwarves depart, of their outrageous demands, of their scourging and their insulting payment.

We meet here again the strong emphasis on Tinwelint's love of treasure and lack of it, in contrast to the later conception of his vast wealth (see my remarks, pp. 128–9). The Silmaril is kept in a wooden casket (p. 225), Tinwelint has no crown but a wreath of scarlet leaves (p. 227), and he is far less richly clad and accoutred than 'the wayfarer in his halls' (Ufedhin). This is very well in itself – the Woodland Elf corrupted by the lure of golden splendour, but it need not be remarked again how strangely at variance is this picture with that of Thingol Lord of Beleriand, who had a vast treasury in his marvellous underground realm of Menegroth, the Thousand Caves – itself largely contrived by the Dwarves of Belegost in the distant past (*The Silmarillion* pp. 92–3), and who most certainly did not need the aid of Dwarves at this time to make him a crown and a fine sword, or vessels to adorn his banquets. Thingol in the later conception is proud, and stern; he is also wise, and powerful, and greatly increased in stature and in knowledge through his union with a Maia. Could such a king have sunk to the level of miserly swindling that is portrayed in the *Tale of the Nauglafring*?

Great stress is indeed placed on the enormous size of the hoard – 'such mighty heaps of gold have never since been gathered in one place', p. 223 – which is made so vast that it becomes hard to believe that a band of wandering outlaws could have brought it to the halls of the woodland Elves, even granting that 'some was lost upon the way' (p. 114). There is perhaps some difference here from the account of the Rodothlim and their works in the *Tale of Turambar* (p. 81), where there is certainly no suggestion that the Rodothlim possessed treasures coming out of Valinor – though this idea remained through all the vicissitudes of this part of the story: it is said of the Lord of Nargothrond in *The Silmarillion* (p. 114) that 'Finrod had brought more treasures out of Tirion than any other of the princes of the Noldor'.

More important, the elements of 'spell' and 'curse' are dominant in this tale, to such a degree that they might almost be said to be the chief actors in it. The curse of Mîm on the gold is felt at every turn of the narrative. Vengeance for him is one motive in Naugladur's decision to attack the Elves of Artanor (p. 230). His curse is fulfilled in the 'agelong feud' between the kindreds of the Dwarves (p. 235) – of which all trace was afterwards effaced, with the loss of the entire story of Ufedhin's intent to steal the Necklace from Naugladur sleeping, the killing of Bodruith Lord of Belegost, and the fighting between the two clans of Dwarves. Naugladur was 'blinded by the spell' in taking so imprudent a course out of Artanor (p. 236); and the curse of Mîm is made the 'cause' of his stumbling on a stone in his fight with Beren (p. 238). It is even, and most surprisingly, suggested as a reason for the short second lives of Beren and Tinúviel (p. 240); and finally 'the spell of Mîm' is an element in the attack on Dior by the Fëanorians (p. 241). An important element also in the tale is the baleful nature of the Nauglafring, for the Dwarves made it with bitterness; and into the complex of curses and spells is introduced also 'the dragon's ban upon the gold' (p. 239) or 'the spell of the dragon' (p. 241). It is not said in the *Tale of Turambar* that Glorund had cursed the gold or enspelled it; but Mîm said to Úrin (p. 114): 'Has not Glorund lain long years upon it, and the evil of the drakes of Melko is on it, and no good can it bring to Man or Elf.' Most notably, Gwendelin implies, against Beren's assertion that 'its holiness might overcome all such evils', that the Silmaril itself is unhallowed, since it 'abode in the Crown of Melko' (p. 239). In the later of the two 'schemes' for the *Lost Tales* (see I. 107 note 3) it is said that the Nauglafring 'brought sickness to Tinúviel'.*

---

* It is said in the Gnomish dictionary that the curse of Mîm was 'appeased' when the Nauglafring was lost in the sea; see the Appendix on Names, entry *Nauglafring*.

But however much the chief actors in this tale are 'enspelled' or blindly carrying forward the mysterious dictates of a curse, there is no question but that the Dwarves in the original conception were altogether more ignoble than they afterwards became, more prone to evil to gain their ends, and more exclusively impelled by greed; that Doriath should be laid waste by mercenary Orcs under Dwarvish paymasters (p. 230) was to become incredible and impossible later. It is even said that by the deeds of Naugladur 'have the Dwarves been severed in feud for ever since those days with the Elves, and drawn more nigh in friendship to the kin of Melko' (p. 230); and in the outlines for *Gilfanon's Tale* the Nauglath are an evil people, associates of goblins (I.236–7). In a rejected outline for the *Tale of the Nauglafring* (p. 136) the Necklace was made 'by certain Úvanimor (Nautar or Nauglath)', Úvanimor being defined elsewhere as 'monsters, giants, and ogres'. With all this compare *The Lord of the Rings*, Appendix F (I): 'They [the Dwarves] are not evil by nature, and few ever served the Enemy of free will, whatever the tales of Men may have alleged.'

The account of the Dwarves in this tale is of exceptional interest in other respects. 'The beards of the Indrafangs' have been named in Tinúviel's 'lengthening spell' (pp. 19, 46); but this is the first description of the Dwarves in my father's writings – already with the spelling that he maintained against the unceasing opposition of proof-readers – and they are eminently recognisable in their dour and hidden natures, in their 'unloveliness' (*The Silmarillion* p. 113), and in their 'marvellous skill with metals' (*ibid.* p. 92). The strange statement that 'never comes a child among them' is perhaps to be related to 'the foolish opinion among Men' referred to in *The Lord of the Rings*, Appendix A (III), 'that there are no Dwarf-women, and that the Dwarves "grow out of stone".' In the same place it is said that 'it is because of the fewness of women among them that the kind of the Dwarves increases slowly'.

It is also said in the tale that it is thought by some that the Dwarves 'have not heard of Ilúvatar'; on knowledge of Ilúvatar among Men see p. 209.

According to the Gnomish dictionary *Indrafang* was 'a special name of the Longbeards or Dwarves', but in the tale it is made quite plain that the Longbeards were on the contrary the Dwarves of Belegost; the Dwarves of Nogrod were the Nauglath, with their king Naugladur. It must be admitted however that the use of the terms is sometimes confusing, or confused: thus the description of the Nauglath on pp. 223–4 seems to be a description of all Dwarves, and to include the Indrafangs, though this cannot have been intended. The reference to 'the march of the Dwarves and Indrafangs' (p. 234) must be taken as an ellipse, i.e. 'the Dwarves of Nogrod and the Indrafangs'. Naugladur of Nogrod and Bodruith of Belegost are said to have been akin (p. 235), though this perhaps only means that they were both Dwarves whereas Ufedhin was an Elf.

The Dwarf-city of Nogrod is said in the tale to lie 'a very long journey southward beyond the wide forest on the borders of those great heaths nigh Umboth-muilin the Pools of Twilight, on the marches of Tasarinan' (p. 225). This could be interpreted to mean that Nogrod was itself 'on the borders of those great heaths nigh Umboth-muilin'; but I think that this is out of the question. It would be a most improbable place for Dwarves, who 'dwell beneath the earth in caves and tunnelled towns, and aforetime Nogrod was the mightiest of these' (p. 224). Though mountains are not specifically mentioned here in connection with Dwarves, I think it extremely likely that my father at this time conceived their cities to be in the mountains, as they were afterwards. Further, there seems nothing to contradict the view that the configuration of the lands in the *Lost Tales* was essentially similar to that of the earliest and later 'Silmarillion' maps; and on them, 'a very long journey southward' is totally inappropriate to that between the Thousand Caves and the Pools of Twilight.

The meaning must therefore be, simply, 'a very long journey southward beyond the wide forest', and what follows places the wide forest, not Nogrod; the forest being, in fact, the Forest of Artanor.

The Pools of Twilight are described in *The Fall of Gondolin*, but the Elvish name does not there appear (see pp. 195–6, 217).

Whether Belegost was near to or far from Nogrod is not made plain; it is said in this passage that the gold should be borne away 'to Nogrod and the dwellings of the Dwarves', but later (p. 230) the Indrafangs are 'a kindred of the Dwarves that dwelt in other realms'.

In his association with the Dwarves Ufedhin is reminiscent of Eöl, Maeglin's father, of whom it is said in *The Silmarillion* (p. 133) that 'for the Dwarves he had more liking than any other of the Elvenfolk of old'; cf. *ibid.* p. 92: 'Few of the Eldar went ever to Nogrod or Belegost, save Eöl of Nan Elmoth and Maeglin his son.' In the early forms of the story of Eöl and Isfin (referred to in *The Fall of Gondolin*, p. 165) Eöl has no association with Dwarves. In the present tale there is mention (p. 224) of 'great traffic' carried on by the Dwarves 'with the free Noldoli' (with Melko's servants also) in those days: we may wonder who these free Noldoli were, since the Rodothlim had been destroyed, and Gondolin was hidden. Perhaps the sons of Fëanor are meant, or Egnor Beren's father (see p. 65).

The idea that it was the Dwarves of Nogrod who were primarily involved survived into the later narrative, but they became exclusively so, and those of Belegost specifically denied all aid to them (*The Silmarillion* p. 233).

Turning now to the Elves, Beren is here of course still an Elf (see p. 139), and in his second span of life he is the ruler, in Hithlum–Hisilómë, of an Elvish people so numerous that 'not even Beren knew the tale of those myriad folk' (p. 234); they are called 'the green Elves' and 'the brown Elves and the green', for they were 'clad in green and brown', and Dior ruled them in Hithlum after the final departure of Beren and Tinúviel. Who were they? It is far from clear how they are to be set into the conception of the Elves of the Great Lands as it appears in other Tales. We may compare the passage in *The Coming of the Elves* (I. 118–19):

> Long after the joy of Valinor had washed its memory faint [i.e., the memory of the journey through Hisilómë] the Elves sang still sadly of it, and told tales of many of their folk whom they said and say were lost in those old forests and ever wandered there in sorrow. Still were they there long after when Men were shut in Hisilómë by Melko, and still do they dance there when Men have wandered far over the lighter places of the Earth. Hisilómë did Men name Aryador, and the Lost Elves did they call the Shadow Folk, and feared them.

But in that tale the conception still was that Tinwelint ruled 'the scattered Elves of Hisilomë', and in the outlines for *Gilfanon's Tale* the 'Shadow Folk' of Hisilómë had ceased to be Elves (see p. 64). In any case, the expression 'green Elves', coupled with the fact that it was the Green-elves of Ossiriand whom Beren led to the ambush of the Dwarves at Sarn Athrad in the later story (*The Silmarillion* p. 235), shows which Elvish people they were to become, even though there is as yet no trace of Ossiriand beyond the river Gelion and the story of the origin of the Laiquendi (*ibid*. pp. 94, 96).

It was inevitable that 'the land of the dead that live' should cease to be in Hisilómë (which seems to have been in danger of having too many inhabitants), and a note on the manuscript of the *Tale of the Nauglafring* says: 'Beren must be in "Doriath beyond Sirion" on a . . . . . not in Hithlum.' Doriath beyond Sirion was the region called in *The Silmarillion* (p. 122) Nivrim, the West March, the woods on the west bank of the river between the confluence of Teiglin and Sirion and Aelin-uial, the Meres of Twilight. In the *Tale of Tinúviel* Beren and Tinúviel, called i·Cuilwarthon, 'became mighty fairies in the lands about the north of Sirion' (p. 41).

Gwendelin/Gwenniel appears a somewhat faint and ineffective figure by comparison with the Melian of *The Silmarillion*. Conceivably, an aspect of this is the far slighter protection afforded to the realm of Artanor by her magic than that of the impenetrable wall and deluding mazes of the Girdle of Melian (see p. 63). But the nature of the protection in the old conception is very unclear. In the *Tale of the Nauglafring* the coming of the Dwarves from Nogrod is only known when they approach the bridge before Tinwelint's caves (p. 226); on the other hand, it is said (p. 230) that the 'woven magic' of the queen was a defence against 'men of hostile heart', who could never make their way through the woods unless aided by treachery from within. Perhaps this provides an explanation of a sort of how the Dwarves bringing treasure from Nogrod were able to penetrate to the halls of Tinwelint without hindrance and apparently undetected (cf. also the coming of Úrin's band in the *Tale of Turambar*, p. 114). In the event, the protective magic was easily – too easily – overthrown by the simple device of a single treacherous Elf of Artanor who 'offered to lead the host through the magics of Gwendelin'. This was evidently unsatisfactory; but I shall not enter further into this question here. Extraordinary difficulties of narrative structure were caused by this element of the inviolability of Doriath, as I hope to describe at a future date.

It might be thought that the story of the drowning of the treasure at the Stony Ford (falling into the waters of the river with the Dwarves who bore it) was evolved from that in the rejected conclusion of the *Tale of Turambar* (p. 136) – Tinwelint 'hearing that curse [set on the treasure by Úrin] caused the gold to be cast into a deep pool of the river before his doors'. In the *Tale of the Nauglafring*, however, Tinwelint, influenced by the queen's foreboding words, still has the intention of doing this, but does not fulfil his intention (p. 223).

The account of the second departure of Beren and Tinúviel (p. 240) raises again the extremely difficult question of the peculiar fate that was decreed for them by the edict of Mandos, which I have discussed on pp. 59–60. There I have suggested that

the peculiar dispensation of Mandos in the case of Beren and Tinúviel as here conceived is therefore that their whole 'natural' destiny as Elves was changed: having died as Elves might die (from wounds or from grief) they were not reborn as new beings, but returned in their own persons – yet now 'mortal even as Men'.

Here however Tinúviel 'faded', and vanished in the woods; and Beren searched all Hithlum and Artanor for her, until he too 'faded from life'. Since this fading is here quite explicitly the mode in which 'that doom of mortality that Mandos had spoken' came upon them (p. 240), it is very notable that it is likened to, and even it seems identified with, the fading of 'the Elves of later days throughout the world' – as though in the original idea Elvish fading was a form of mortality. This is in fact made explicit in a later version.

The seven Sons of Fëanor, their oath (sworn not in Valinor but after the coming of the Noldoli to the Great Lands), and the maiming of Maidros appear in the outlines for *Gilfanon's Tale*; and in the latest of these outlines the Fëanorians are placed in Dor Lómin (= Hisilómë, Hithlum), see I.238, 240, 243. Here, in the *Tale of the Nauglafring*, appear for the first time the names of the Sons of Fëanor, five of them (Maidros, Maglor, Celegorm, Cranthor, Curufin) in the forms, or almost the forms, they were to retain, and Curufin already with his sobriquet 'the Crafty'. The names Amrod and Amras in *The Silmarillion* were a late change; for long these two sons of Fëanor were Damrod (as here) and Díriel (here Dinithel or Durithel, see *Changes made to Names*, p. 245).

Here also appear Dior the Fair, also called Ausir the Wealthy, and his daughter Elwing; his son Auredhir early disappeared in the development of the legends. But Dior ruled in 'the southern vales' (p. 241) of Hisilómë, not in Artanor, and there is no suggestion of any renewal of Tinwelint's kingdom after his death, in contrast to what was told later (*The Silmarillion* p. 236); moreover the Fëanorians, as noted above, dwelt also in Hisilómë – and how all this is to be related to what is said elsewhere of the inhabitants of that region I am unable to say: cf. the *Tale of Tinúviel*, p. 10: 'Hisilómë where dwelt Men, and thrall-Noldoli laboured, and few free-Eldar went.'

A very curious statement is made in this concluding part of the tale, that 'those were days of happiness in the vales of Hithlum, for there was peace with Melko and the Dwarves who had but one thought as they plotted against Gondolin' (p. 241). Presumably 'peace with Melko' means no more than that Melko had averted his attention from those lands; but nowhere else is there any reference to the Dwarves' plotting against Gondolin.

In the typescript version of the *Tale of Tinúviel* (p. 43) it is said that if Turgon King of Gondolin was the most glorious of the kings of the Elves who defied Melko, 'for a while the most mighty *and the longest free was* Thingol of the Woods'. The most natural interpretation of this expression is surely that Gondolin fell before Artanor; whereas in *The Silmarillion* (p. 240) 'Tidings were brought by Thorondor Lord of Eagles of the fall of Nargothrond, and after of the slaying of Thingol and of Dior his heir, and of the ruin of Doriath; but Turgon shut his ear to word of the woes without.' In the present tale we see the same chronology, in that many of the Elves who followed Beren went after his departure to Gondolin, 'the rumour of whose growing power and glory ran in secret whispers among all the Elves' (p. 240), though here the destruction of Gondolin is said to have taken place on the very day that Dior was attacked by the Sons of Fëanor (p. 242). To evade the discrepancy therefore we must interpret the passage in the *Tale of Tinúviel* to mean that Thingol remained free for a longer period of years than did Turgon, irrespective of the dates of their downfalls.

Lastly, the statements that Cûm an-Idrisaith, the Mound of Avarice, 'stands there still in Artanor' (p. 223), and that the waters of Aros still flow above the drowned hoard (p. 238), are noteworthy as indications that nothing analogous to the Drowning of Beleriand was present in the original conception.

V

THE TALE OF EÄRENDEL

The 'true beginning' of the *Tale of Eärendel* was to be the dwelling at Sirion's mouth of the Lothlim (the point at which *The Fall of Gondolin* ends: 'and fair among the Lothlim Eärendel grows in the house of his father', pp. 196–7) and the coming there of Elwing (the point at which the *Tale of the Nauglafring* ends: 'they departed for ever from the glades of Hithlum and got them to the south towards Sirion's deep waters, and the pleasant lands. And thus did all the fates of the fairies weave then to one strand, and that strand is the great tale of Eärendel; and to that tale's true beginning are we now come', p. 242). The matter is complicated, however, as will be seen in a moment, by my father's also making the *Nauglafring* the first part of the *Tale of Eärendel*.

But the great tale was never written; and for the story as he then conceived it we are wholly dependent on highly condensed and often contradictory outlines. There are also many isolated notes; and there are the very early Eärendel poems. While the poems can be precisely dated, the notes and outlines can not; and it does not seem possible to arrange them in order so as to provide a clear line of development.

One of the outlines for the *Tale of Eärendel* is the earlier of the two 'schemes' for the *Lost Tales* which are the chief materials for *Gilfanon's Tale*; and I will repeat here what I said of this in the first part (I.233):

There is no doubt that [the earlier of the two schemes] was composed when the *Lost Tales* had reached their furthest point of development, as represented by the latest texts and arrangements given in this book. Now when this outline comes to the matter of *Gilfanon's Tale* it becomes at once very much fuller, but then contracts again to cursory references for the tales of Tinúviel, Túrin, Tuor, and the Necklace of the Dwarves, and once more becomes fuller for the tale of Eärendel.

This scheme B (as I will continue to call it) provides a coherent if very rough narrative plan, and divides the story into seven parts, of which the first (marked 'Told') is 'The Nauglafring down to the flight of Elwing'. This sevenfold division is referred to by Littleheart at the beginning of *The Fall of Gondolin* (p. 144):

It is a mighty tale, and seven times shall folk fare to the Tale-fire ere it be rightly told; and so twined is it with those stories of the Nauglafring and of the Elf-march that I would fain have aid in that telling . . .

If the six parts following the *Tale of the Nauglafring* were each to be of comparable length, the whole *Tale of Eärendel* would have been somewhere near half the length of all the tales that were in fact written; but my father never afterwards returned to it on any ample scale.

I give now the concluding part of Scheme B.

Tale of Eärendel begins, with which is interwoven the Nauglafring and the March of the Elves. For further details see Notebook C.*

First part. The tale of the Nauglafring down to the flight of Elwing.

Second part. The dwelling at Sirion. Coming thither of Elwing, and the love of her and Eärendel as girl and boy. Ageing of Tuor – his secret sailing after the conches of Ulmo in Swanwing.

Eärendel sets sail to the North to find Tuor, and if needs be Mandos. Sails in Eärámë. Wrecked. Ulmo appears. Saves him, bidding him sail to Kôr – 'for for this hast thou been brought out of the Wrack of Gondolin'.

Third part. Second attempt of Eärendel to Mandos. Wreck of Falasquil and rescue by the Oarni.[1] He sights the Isle of Seabirds 'whither do all the birds of all waters come at whiles'. Goes back by land to Sirion.

Idril has vanished (she set sail at night). The conches of Ulmo call Eärendel. Last farewell of Elwing. Building of Wingilot.

Fourth part. Eärendel sails for Valinor. His many wanderings, occupying several years.

Fifth part. Coming of the birds of Gondolin to Kôr with tidings. Uproar of the Elves. Councils of the Gods. March of the Inwir (death of Inwë), Teleri, and Solosimpi.

Raid upon Sirion and captivity of Elwing.

Sorrow and wrath of Gods, and a veil dropped between Valmar and Kôr, for the Gods will not destroy it but cannot bear to look upon it.

Coming of the Eldar. Binding of Melko. Faring to Lonely Isle. Curse of the Nauglafring and death of Elwing.

Sixth part. Eärendel reaches Kôr and finds it empty. Fares home in sorrow (and sights Tol Eressëa and the fleet of the Elves, but a great wind and darkness carries him away, and he misses his way and has a voyage eastward).

Arriving at length at Sirion finds it empty. Goes to the ruins of Gondolin. Hears of tidings. Sails to Tol Eressëa. Sails to the Isle of Seabirds.

Seventh part. His voyage to the firmament.

* For 'Notebook C' see p. 254.

Written at the end of the text is: 'Rem[ainder] of Scheme in Notebook C'. These references in Scheme B to 'Notebook C' are to the little pocket-book which goes back to 1916–17 but was used for notes and suggestions throughout the period of the *Lost Tales* (see I.171). At the beginning of it there is an outline (here called 'C') headed 'Eärendel's Tale, Tuor's son', which is in fair harmony with Scheme B:

> Eärendel dwells with Tuor and Irildë[2] at Sirion's mouth by the sea (on the Isles of Sirion). Elwing of the Gnomes of Artanor[3] flees to them with the Nauglafring. Eärendel and Elwing love one another as boy and girl.
>
> Great love of Eärendel and Tuor. Tuor ages, and Ulmo's conches far out west over the sea call him louder and louder, till one evening he sets sail in his twilit boat with purple sails, Swanwing, Alqarámë.[4] Idril sees him too late. Her song on the beach of Sirion.
>
> When he does not return grief of Eärendel and Idril. Eärendel (urged also by Idril who is immortal) desires to set sail and search even to Mandos. [*Marginal addition*:] Curse of Nauglafring rests on his voyages. Ossë his enemy.
>
> Fiord of the Mermaid. Wreck. Ulmo appears at wreck and saves them, telling them he must go to Kôr and is saved for that.
>
> Elwing's grief when she learns Ulmo's bidding. 'For no man may tread the streets of Kôr or look upon the places of the Gods and dwell in the Outer Lands in peace again.'
>
> Eärendel departs all the same and is wrecked by the treachery of Ossë and saved only by the Oarni (who love him) with Voronwë and dragged to Falasquil.
>
> Eärendel makes his way back by land with Voronwë. Finds that Idril has vanished.[5] His grief. Prays to Ulmo and hears the conches. Ulmo bids him build a new and wonderful ship of the wood of Tuor from Falasquil. Building of Wingilot.

There are four items headed 'Additions' on this page of the notebook:

> Building of Eärámë (Eaglepinion).
> Noldoli add their pleading to Ulmo's bidding.
> Eärendel surveys the first dwelling of Tuor at Falasquil.
> The voyage to Mandos and the Icy Seas.

The outline continues:

> Voronwë and Eärendel set sail in Wingilot. Driven south. Dark regions. Fire mountains. Tree-men. Pygmies. Sarqindi or cannibal-ogres.
>
> Driven west. Ungweliantë. Magic Isles. Twilit Isle [*sic*]. Little-heart's gong awakes the Sleeper in the Tower of Pearl.[6]

Kôr is found. Empty. Eärendel reads tales and prophecies in the waters. Desolation of Kôr. Eärendel's shoes and self powdered with diamond dust so that they shine brightly.

Homeward adventures. Driven east – the deserts and red palaces where dwells the Sun.[7]

Arrives at Sirion, only to find it sacked and empty. Eärendel distraught wanders with Voronwë and comes to the ruins of Gondolin. Men are encamped there miserably. Also Gnomes searching still for lost gems (or some Gnomes gone back to Gondolin).

Of the binding of Melko.[8] The wars with Men and the departure to Tol Eressëa (the Eldar unable to endure the strife of the world). Eärendel sails to Tol Eressëa and learns of the sinking of Elwing and the Nauglafring. Elwing became a seabird. His grief is very great. His garments and body shine like diamonds and his face is in silver flame for the grief and . . . .

He sets sail with Voronwë and dwells on the Isle of Seabirds in the northern waters (not far from Falasquil) – and there hopes that Elwing will return among the seabirds, but she is seeking him wailing along all the shores and especially among wreckage.

After three times seven years he sails again for halls of Mandos with Voronwë – he gets there because [?only] those who still . . . . and had suffered may do so – Tuor is gone to Valinor and nought is known of Idril or of Elwing.

Reaches bar at margin of the world and sets sail on oceans of the firmament in order to gaze over the Earth. The Moon mariner chases him for his brightness and he dives through the Door of Night. How he cannot now return to the world or he will die.

He will find Elwing at the Faring Forth.

Tuor and Idril some say sail now in Swanwing and may be seen going swift down the wind at dawn and dusk.

The Co-events to Eärendel's Tale

Raid upon Sirion by Melko's Orcs and the captivity of Elwing.

Birds tell Elves of the Fall of Gondolin and the horrors of the fate of the Gnomes. Counsels of the Gods and uproar of the Elves. March of the Inwir and Teleri. The Solosimpi go forth also but fare along all the beaches of the world, for they are loth to fare far from the sound of the sea – and only consent to go with the Teleri under these conditions – for the Noldoli slew some of their kin at Kópas.

This outline then goes on to the events after the coming of the Elves of Valinor into the Great Lands, which will be considered in the next chapter.

Though very much fuller, there seems to be little in C that is certainly contradictory to what is said in B, and there are elements in the latter that are absent from the former. In discussing these outlines I follow the divisions of the tale made in B.

Second part. A little more is told in C of Tuor's departure from Sirion (in B there is no mention of Idril); and there appears the motive of Ossë's hostility to Eärendel and the curse of the Nauglafring as instrumental in his shipwrecks. The place of the first wreck is called the Fiord of the Mermaid. The word 'them' rather than 'him' in 'Ulmo saves them, telling them he must go to Kôr' is certain in the manuscript, which possibly suggests that Idril or Elwing (or both) were with Eärendel.

Third part. In B Eärendel's second voyage, like the first, is explicitly an attempt to reach Mandos (seeking his father), whereas in C it seems that the second is undertaken rather in order to fulfil Ulmo's bidding that he sail to Kôr (to Elwing's grief). In C Voronwë is named as Eärendel's companion on the second voyage which ended at Falasquil; but the Isle of Seabirds is not mentioned at this point. In C Wingilot is built 'of the wood of Tuor from Falasquil'; in *The Fall of Gondolin* Tuor's wood was hewed for him by the Noldoli in the forests of Dor Lómin and floated down the hidden river (p. 152).

Fourth part. Whereas B merely refers to Eärendel's 'many wanderings, occupying several years' in his quest for Valinor, C gives some glimpses of what they were to be, as Wingilot was driven to the south and then into the west. The encounter with Ungweliantë on the western voyage is curious; it is said in *The Tale of the Sun and Moon* that 'Melko held the North and Ungweliant the South' (see I. 182, 200).

In C we meet again the Sleeper in the Tower of Pearl (said to be Idril, though this was struck out, note 6) awakened by Littleheart's gong; cf. the account of Littleheart in *The Cottage of Lost Play* (I. 15):

> He sailed in Wingilot with Eärendel in that last voyage wherein they sought for Kôr. It was the ringing of this Gong on the Shadowy Seas that awoke the Sleeper in the Tower of Pearl that stands far out to west in the Twilit Isles.

In *The Coming of the Valar* it is said that the Twilit Isles 'float' on the Shadowy Seas 'and the Tower of Pearl rises pale upon their most western cape' (I. 68; cf. I. 125). But there is no other mention in C of Littleheart, Voronwë's son, as a companion of Eärendel, though he was named earlier in the outline, in a rejected phrase, as present at the Mouths of Sirion (see note 5), and in the *Tale of the Nauglafring* (p. 228) Ailios says that none still living have seen the Nauglafring 'save only Littleheart son of Bronweg' (where 'save only' is an emendation from 'not even').

Fifth and sixth parts. In C we meet the image of Eärendel's shoes

shining from the dust of diamonds in Kör, an image that was to survive
(*The Silmarillion* p. 248):

He walked in the deserted ways of Tirion, and the dust upon his
raiment and his shoes was a dust of diamonds, and he shone and
glistened as he climbed the long white stairs.

But in *The Silmarillion* Tirion was deserted because it was 'a time of
festival, and wellnigh all the Elvenfolk were gone to Valimar, or were
gathered in the halls of Manwë upon Taniquetil'; here on the other hand
it seems at least strongly implied, in both B and C, that Kôr was empty
because the Elves of Valinor had departed into the Great Lands, as a
result of the tidings brought by the birds of Gondolin. In these very early
narrative schemes there is no mention of Eärendel's speaking to the
Valar, as the ambassador of Elves and Men (*The Silmarillion* p. 249),
and we can only conclude, extraordinary as the conclusion is, that
Eärendel's great western voyage, though he attained his goal, was fruitless, that he was not the agent of the aid that did indeed come out of
Valinor to the Elves of the Great Lands, and (most curious of all) that
Ulmo's designs for Tuor had no issue. In fact, my father actually wrote in
the 1930 version of 'The Silmarillion':

Thus it was that the many emissaries of the Gnomes in after days came
never back to Valinor – save one: and he came too late.

The words 'and he came too late' were changed to 'the mightiest mariner
of song', and this is the phrase that is found in *The Silmarillion*, p. 102.
It is unfortunately never made clear in the earliest writings what was
Ulmo's purpose in bidding Eärendel sail to Kôr, for which he had been
saved from the ruin of Gondolin. What would he have achieved, had he
come to Kôr 'in time', more than in the event did take place after the
coming of tidings from Gondolin – the March of the Elves into the Great
Lands? In a curious note in C, not associated with the present outline,
my father asked: 'How did King Turgon's messengers get to Valinor or
gain the Gods' consent?' and answered: 'His messengers never got there.
Ulmo [*sic*] but the birds brought tidings to the Elves of the fate of
Gondolin (the doves and pigeons of Turgon) and they [?arm and march
away].'
   The coming of the message was followed by 'the councils (counsels C)
of the Gods and the uproar of the Elves', but in C nothing is said of 'the
sorrow and wrath of the Gods' or 'the veil dropped between Valmar and
Kôr' referred to in B: where the meaning can surely only be that the
March of the Elves from Valinor was undertaken in direct opposition to
the will of the Valar, that the Valar were bitterly opposed to the interven-
tion of the Elves of Valinor in the affairs of the Great Lands. There may
well be a connection here with Vairë's words (I. 19): 'When the fairies left

Kôr that lane [i.e. Olórë Mallë that led past the Cottage of Lost Play] *was blocked for ever with great impassable rocks'*. Elsewhere there is only one other reference to the effect of the message from across the sea, and that is in the words of Lindo to Eriol in *The Cottage of Lost Play* (I. 16):

> Inwë, whom the Gnomes call Inwithiel . . . . . was King of all the Eldar when they dwelt in Kôr. That was in the days before hearing the lament of the world [i.e. the Great Lands] Inwë led them forth to the lands of Men.

Later, Meril-i-Turinqi told Eriol (I. 129) that Inwë, her grandsire's sire, 'perished in that march into the world', but Ingil his son 'went long ago back to Valinor and is with Manwë'; and there is a reference to Inwë's death in B.

In C the Solosimpi only agreed to accompany the expedition on condition that they remain by the sea, and the reluctance of the Third Kindred, on account of the Kinslaying at Swanhaven, survived (*The Silmarillion* p. 251). But there is no suggestion that the Elves of Valinor were transported by ship, indeed the reverse, for the Solosimpi 'fare along all the beaches of the world', and the expedition is a 'March'; though there is no indication of how they came to the Great Lands.

Both outlines refer to Eärendel being driven eastwards on his homeward voyage from Kôr, and to his finding the dwellings at Sirion's mouth ravaged when he finally returned there; but B does not say who carried out the sack and captured Elwing. In C it was a raid by Orcs of Melko; cf. the entry in the Name-list to *The Fall of Gondolin* (p. 215): '*Egalmoth* . . . got even out of the burning of Gondolin, and dwelt after at the mouth of Sirion, but was slain in a dire battle there when Melko seized Elwing'.

Neither outline refers to Elwing's escape from captivity. Both mention Eärendel's going back to the ruins of Gondolin – in C he returns there with Voronwë and finds Men and Gnomes; another entry in the Name-list to *The Fall of Gondolin* (p. 215) bears on this: '*Galdor* . . . won out of Gondolin and even the onslaught of Melko upon the dwellers at Sirion's mouth and went back to the ruins with Eärendel.'

Both outlines mention the departure of the Elves from the Great Lands, after the binding of Melko, to Tol Eressëa, C adding a reference to 'wars with Men' and to the Eldar being 'unable to endure the strife of the world', and both refer to Eärendel's going there subsequently, but the order of events seems to be different: in B Eärendel on his way back from Kôr 'sights Tol Eressëa and the fleet of the Elves' (presumably the fleet returning from the Great Lands), whereas in C the departure of the Elves is not mentioned until after Eärendel's return to Sirion. But the nature of these outlines is not conveyed in print: they were written at great speed, catching fugitive thoughts, and cannot be pressed hard. However, with the fate of Elwing B and C seem clearly to part company:

in B there is a simple reference to her death, apparently associated with the curse of the Nauglafring, and from the order in which the events are set down it may be surmised that her death took place on the journey to Tol Eressëa; C specifically refers to the 'sinking' of Elwing and the Nauglafring – but says that Elwing became a seabird, an idea that survived (*The Silmarillion* p. 247). This perhaps gives more point to Eärendel's going to the Isle of Seabirds, mentioned in both B and C: in the latter he 'hopes that Elwing will return among the seabirds'.

Seventh part. In B the concluding part of the tale is merely sum-marised in the words 'His voyage to the firmament', with a reference to the other outline C, and in the latter we get some glimpses of a narrative. It seems to be suggested that the brightness of Eärendel (quite uncon-nected with the Silmaril) arose from the 'diamond dust' of Kôr, but also in some sense from the exaltation of his grief. An isolated jotting else-where in C asks: 'What became of the Silmarils after the capture of Melko?' My father at this time gave no answer to the question; but the question is itself a testimony to the relatively minor importance of the jewels of Fëanor, if also, perhaps, a sign of his awareness that they would not always remain so, that in them lay a central meaning of the mythology, yet to be discovered.

It seems too that Eärendel sailed into the sky in continuing search for Elwing ('he sets sail on the oceans of the firmament in order to gaze over the Earth'); and that his passing through the Door of Night (the entrance made by the Gods in the Wall of Things in the West, see I.215–16) did not come about through any devising, but because he was hunted by the Moon. With this last idea, cf. I.193, where Ilinsor, steersman of the Moon, is said to 'hunt the stars'.

The later of the two schemes for the *Lost Tales*, which gives a quite substantial outline for *Gilfanon's Tale*, where I have called it 'D' (see I.234), here fails us, for the concluding passage is very condensed, in part erased, and ends abruptly early in the *Tale of Eärendel*. I give it here, beginning at a slightly earlier point in the narrative:

Of the death of Tinwelint and the flight of Gwenethlin [see p. 51]. How Beren avenged Tinwelint and how the Necklace became his. How it brought sickness to Tinúviel [see p. 246], and how Beren and Tinúviel faded from the Earth. How their sons [*sic*] dwelt after them and how the sons of Fëanor came up against them with a host because of the Silmaril. How all were slain but Elwing daughter of Daimord [see p. 139] son of Beren fled with the Necklace.
Of Tuor's vessel with white sails.

How folk of the Lothlim dwelt at Sirion's Mouth. Eärendel grew fairest of all Men that were or are. How the mermaids (Oarni) loved him. How Elwing came to the Lothlim and of the love of Elwing and Eärendel. How Tuor fell into age, and how Ulmo beckoned to him at eve, and he set forth on the waters and was lost. How Idril swam after him.

(In the following passage my father seems at first to have written: 'Eärendel . . . . Oarni builded Wingilot and set forth in search of . . . . leaving Voronwë with Elwing', where the first lacuna perhaps said 'with the aid of', though nothing is now visible; but then he wrote 'Eärendel built Swanwing', and then partly erased the passage: it is impossible to see now what his intention was.)

Elwing's lament. How Ulmo forbade his quest but Eärendel would yet sail to find a passage to Mandos. How Wingilot was wrecked at Falasquil and how Eärendel found the carven house of Tuor there.

Here Scheme D ends. There is also a reference at an earlier point in it to 'the messengers sent from Gondolin. The doves of Gondolin fly to Valinor at the fall of that town.'

This outline seems to show a move to reduce the complexity of the narrative, with Wingilot being the ship in which Eärendel attempted to sail to Mandos and in which he was wrecked at Falasquil; but the outline is too brief and stops too soon to allow any certain conclusions to be drawn.

A fourth outline, which I will call 'E', is found on a detached sheet; in this Tuor is called Tûr (see p. 148).

Fall of Gondolin. The feast of Glorfindel. The dwelling by the waters of Sirion's mouth. The mermaids come to Eärendel.

Tûr groweth sea-hungry – his song to Eärendel. One evening he calls Eärendel and they go to the shore. There is a skiff. Tûr bids farewell to Eärendel and bids him thrust it off – the skiff fares away into the West. Eärendel hears a great song swelling from the sea as Tûr's skiff dips over the world's rim. His passion of tears upon the shore. The lament of Idril.

The building of Earum.[9] The coming of Elwing. Eärendel's reluctance. The whetting of Idril. The voyage and foundering of Earum in the North, and the vanishing of Idril. How the seamaids rescued Eärendel, and brought him to Tûr's bay. His coastwise journey.

The rape of Elwing. Eärendel discovers the ravaging of Sirion's mouth.

The building of Wingelot. He searches for Elwing and is blown far to the South. Wirilómë. He escapes eastward. He goes back westward; he descries the Bay of Faëry. The Tower of Pearl, the magic isles, the great shadows. He finds Kôr empty; he sails back, crusted with dust and his face afire. He learns of Elwing's foundering. He sitteth on the Isle of Seabirds. Elwing as a seamew comes to him. He sets sail over the margent of the world.

Apart from the fuller account of Tuor's departure from the mouths of Sirion, not much can be learned from this – it is too condensed. But even allowing for speed and compression, there seem to be essential differences from B and C. Thus in this outline (E) Elwing, as it appears, comes to Sirion at a later point in the story, after the departure of Tuor; but the raid and capture of Elwing seems to take place at an earlier point, while Eärendel is on his way back to Sirion from his shipwreck in the North (not, as in B and C, while he is on the great voyage in Wingilot that took him to Kôr). Here, it seems, there was to be only one northward journey, ending in the shipwreck of Earámë/Earum near Falasquil. Though it cannot be demonstrated, I incline to think that E was subsequent to B and C: partly because the reduction of two northward voyages ending in shipwreck to one seems more likely than the other way about, and partly because of the form Tûr, which, though it did not survive, replaced Tuor for a time (p. 148).

One or two other points may be noticed in this outline. The great spider, called Ungweliantë in C but here Wirilómë ('Gloomweaver', see I.152), is here encountered by Eärendel in the far South, not as in C on his westward voyage: see p. 256. Elwing in this version comes to Eärendel as a seabird (as she does in The Silmarillion, p. 247), which is not said in C and even seems to be denied.

Another isolated page (associated with the poem 'The Bidding of the Minstrel', see pp. 269–70 below) gives a very curious account of Eärendel's great voyage:

Eärendel's boat goes through North. Iceland. [Added in margin: back of North Wind.] Greenland, and the wild islands: a mighty wind and crest of great wave carry him to hotter climes, to back of West Wind. Land of strange men, land of magic. The home of Night. The Spider. He escapes from the meshes of Night with a few comrades, sees a great mountain island and a golden city [added in margin: Kôr] – wind blows him southward. Tree-men, Sun-dwellers, spices, fire-mountains, red sea: Mediterranean (loses his boat (travels afoot through wilds of Europe?)) or Atlantic.* Home. Waxes aged. Has a new boat builded. Bids adieu to his north land. Sails west again to the lip of the world, just as the Sun is diving into the sea. He sets sail upon the sky and returns no more to earth.

The golden city was Kôr and he had caught the music of the Solosimpë, and returns to find it, only to find that the fairies have departed from Eldamar. See little book. Dusted with diamond dust climbing the deserted streets of Kôr.

* The words in this passage ('Tree-men, Sun-dwellers . . .') are clear but the punctuation is not, and the arrangement here may not be that intended.

One would certainly suppose this account to be earlier than anything so far considered (both from the fact that Eärendel's history after his return from the great voyage seems to bear no relation to that in B and C, and from his voyage being set in the lands and oceans of the known world), were it not for the reference to the 'little book', which must mean 'Notebook C', from which the outline C above is taken (see p. 254). But I think it very probable (and the appearance of the MS rather supports this) that the last paragraph ('The golden city was Kôr . . .') was added later, and that the rest of the outline belongs with the earliest writing of the poem, in the winter of 1914.

It is notable that only here in the earliest writings is it made clear that the 'diamond dust' that coated Eärendel came from the streets of Kôr (cf. the passage from *The Silmarillion* cited on p. 257).

Another of the early Eärendel poems, 'The Shores of Faëry', has a short prose preface, which if not as old as the first composition of the poem itself (July 1915, see p. 271) is certainly not much later:

Eärendel the Wanderer who beat about the Oceans of the World in his white ship Wingelot sat long while in his old age upon the Isle of Seabirds in the Northern Waters ere he set forth upon a last voyage.

He passed Taniquetil and even Valinor, and drew his bark over the bar at the margin of the world, and launched it on the Oceans of the Firmament. Of his ventures there no man has told, save that hunted by the orbed Moon he fled back to Valinor, and mounting the towers of Kôr upon the rocks of Eglamar he gazed back upon the Oceans of the World. To Eglamar he comes ever at plenilune when the Moon sails a-harrying beyond Taniquetil and Valinor.*

Both here and in the outline associated with 'The Bidding of the Minstrel' Eärendel was conceived to be an old man when he journeyed into the firmament.

No other 'connected' account of the *Tale of Eärendel* exists from the earliest period. There are however a number of separate notes, mostly in the form of single sentences, some found in the little notebook C, others jotted down on slips. I collect these references here more or less in the sequence of the tale.

(i) 'Dwelling in the Isle of Sirion in a house of snow-white stone.' – In C (p. 254) it is said that Eärendel dwelt with Tuor and Idril at Sirion's mouth by the sea 'on the Isles of Sirion'.

---

* This preface is found in all the texts of the poem save the earliest, and the versions of it differ only in name-forms: *Wingelot/Vingelot* and *Eglamar/Eldamar* (varying in the same ways as in the accompanying versions of the poem, see textual notes p. 272), and *Kôr* > *Tûn* in the third text, *Tûn* in the fourth. For *Egla* = *Elda* see I.251 and II.338, and for *Tûn* see p. 292.

(ii) 'The Oarni give to Eärendel a wonderful shining silver coat that wets not. They love Eärendel, in Ossë's despite, and teach him the lore of boat-building and of swimming, as he plays with them about the shores of Sirion.' – In the outlines are found references to the love of the Oarni for Eärendel (D, p. 259), the coming of the mermaids to him (E, p. 260), and to Ossë's enmity (C, p. 254).

(iii) Eärendel was smaller than most men but nimble-footed and a swift swimmer (but Voronwë could not swim).

(iv) 'Idril and Eärendel see Tuor's boat dropping into the twilight and a sound of song.' – In B Tuor's sailing is 'secret' (p. 253), in C 'Idril sees him too late' (p. 254), and in E Eärendel is present at Tuor's departure and thrusts the boat out: 'he hears a great song swelling from the sea' (p. 260).

(v) 'Death of Idril? – follows secretly after Tuor.' – That Idril died is denied in C: 'Tuor and Idril some say sail now in Swanwing . . .' (p. 255); in D Idril swam after him (p. 260).

(vi) 'Tuor has sailed back to Falasquil and so back up Ilbranteloth to Asgon where he sits playing on his lonely harp on the islanded rock.' – This is marked with a query and an 'X' implying rejection of the idea. There are curious references to the 'islanded rock' in Asgon in the outlines for *Gilfanon's Tale* (see I. 238).

(vii) 'The fiord of the Mermaid: enchantment of his sailors. Mermaids are not Oarni (but are earthlings, or fays? – or both).' – In D (p. 259) Mermaids and Oarni are equated.

(viii) The ship Wingilot was built of wood from Falasquil with 'aid of the Oarni'. – This was probably said also in D: see p. 260.

(ix) Wingilot was 'shaped as a swan of pearls'.

(x) 'The doves and pigeons of Turgon's courtyard bring message to Valinor – only to Elves.' – Other references to the birds that flew from Gondolin also say that they came to the Elves, or to Kôr (pp. 253, 255, 257).

(xi) 'During his voyages Eärendel sights the white walls of Kôr gleaming afar off, but is carried away by Ossë's adverse winds and waves.' – The same is said in B (p. 253) of Eärendel's sighting of Tol Eressëa on his homeward voyage from Kôr.

(xii) 'The Sleeper in the Tower of Pearl awakened by Littleheart's gong: a messenger that was despatched years ago by Turgon and enmeshed in magics. Even now he cannot leave the Tower and warns them of the magic.' – In C there is a statement, rejected, that the Sleeper in the Tower of Pearl was Idril herself (see note 6).

(xiii) 'Ulmo's protection removed from Sirion in wrath at Eärendel's second attempt to Mandos, and hence Melko overwhelmed it.' – This note is struck through, with an 'X' written against it; but in D (p. 260) it is said that 'Ulmo forbade his quest but Eärendel would yet sail to find a passage to Mandos'. The meaning of this must be that it was contrary to Ulmo's purpose that Eärendel should seek to Mandos for his father, but must rather attempt to reach Kôr.

(xiv) 'Eärendel weds Elwing before he sets sail. When he hears of her loss he says that his children shall be "all such men hereafter as dare the great seas in ships".' – With this cf. *The Cottage of Lost Play* (I.13): 'even such a son of Eärendel as was this wayfarer', and (I.18): 'a man of great and excellent travel, a son meseems of Eärendel'. In an outline of Eriol's life (I.24) it is said that he was a son of Eärendel, born under his beam, and that if a beam from Eärendel fall on a child newborn he becomes 'a child of Eärendel' and a wanderer. In the early dictionary of Qenya there is an entry: *Eärendilyon* 'son of Eärendel (used of any mariner)' (I.251).

(xv) 'Eärendel goes even to the empty Halls of Iron seeking Elwing.' – Eärendel must have gone to Angamandi (empty after the defeat of Melko) at the same time as he went to the ruins of Gondolin (pp. 253, 255).

(xvi) The loss of the ship carrying Elwing and the Nauglafring took place on the voyage to Tol Eressëa with the exodus of the Elves from the Great Lands. – See my remarks, pp. 258–9. For the 'appeasing' of Mîm's curse by the drowning of the Nauglafring see the Appendix on Names, entry *Nauglafring*. The departure of the Elves to Tol Eressëa is discussed in the next chapter (p. 280).

(xvii) 'Eärendel and the northern tower on the Isle of Seabirds.' – In C (p. 255) Eärendel 'sets sail with Voronwë and dwells on the Isle of Seabirds in the northern waters (not far from Falasquil) – and there hopes that Elwing will return among the seabirds'; in B (p. 253) 'he sights the Isle of Seabirds "whither do all the birds of all waters come at whiles".' There is a memory of this in *The Silmarillion*, p. 250: 'Therefore there was built for [Elwing] a white tower northward upon the borders of the Sundering Seas; and thither at times all the seabirds of the earth repaired.'

(xviii) When Eärendel comes to Mandos he finds that Tuor is '*not* in Valinor, nor Erumáni, and neither Elves nor Ainu know where he is. (He is with Ulmo.)' – In C (p. 255) Eärendel, reaching the Halls of Mandos, learns that Tuor 'is gone to Valinor'. For the possibility that Tuor might be in Erumáni or Valinor see I.91 ff.

(xix) Eärendel 'returns from the firmament ever and anon with Voronwë to Kôr to see if the Magic Sun has been lit and the fairies have come back – but the Moon drives him back'. – On Eärendel's return from the firmament see (xxi) below; on the Rekindling of the Magic Sun see p. 286.

Two statements about Eärendel cited previously may be added here:

(xx) In the tale of *The Theft of Melko* (I.141) it is said that 'on the walls of Kôr were many dark tales written in pictured symbols, and runes of great beauty were drawn there too or carved upon stones, and Eärendel read many a wondrous tale there long ago'.

(xxi) The Name-list to *The Fall of Gondolin* has the following entry (cited on p. 215): '*Eärendel* was the son of Tuor and Idril and 'tis said the only being that is half of the kindred of the Eldalië and half of Men. He was the greatest and first of all mariners among Men, and saw regions that Men have not yet found nor gazed upon for all the multitude of their boats. He rideth now with Voronwë upon the winds of the firmament nor comes ever further back than Kôr, else would he die like other Men, so much of the mortal is in him.' – In the outline associated with the poem 'The Bidding of the Minstrel' Eärendel 'sets sail upon the sky and returns no more to earth' (p. 261); in the prose preface to 'The Shores of Faëry' 'to Eglamar he comes ever at plenilune when the Moon sails a-harrying beyond Taniquetil and Valinor' (p. 262); in outline C 'he cannot now return to the world or he will die' (p. 255); and in citation (xix) above he 'returns from the firmament ever and anon with Voronwë to Kôr'.

In *The Silmarillion* (p. 249) Manwë's judgement was that Eärendel and Elwing 'shall not walk ever again among Elves or Men in the Outer Lands'; but it is also said that Eärendel returned to Valinor from his 'voyages beyond the confines of the world' (*ibid.* p. 250), just as it is said in the Name-list to *The Fall of Gondolin* that he does not come ever further back than Kôr. The further statement in the Name-list, that if he did he would die like other Men, 'so much of the mortal is in him', was in some sense echoed long after in a letter of my father's written in 1967: '*Eärendil*, being in part descended from Men, was not allowed to set foot on Earth again, and became a star shining with the light of the Silmaril' (*The Letters of J. R. R. Tolkien* no. 297).

This brings to an end all the 'prose' materials that bear on the earliest form of the *Tale of Eärendel* (apart from a few other references to him that appear in the next chapter). With these outlines and notes we are at a very early stage of composition, when the conceptions were fluid and had not been given even preliminary narrative form: the myth was present in certain images that were to endure, but these images had not been articulated.

I have already noticed (p. 257) the remarkable fact that there is no hint of the idea that it was Eärendel who by his intercession brought aid out of the West; equally there is no suggestion that the Valar hallowed his ship and set him in the sky, nor that his light was that of the Silmaril. Nonetheless there were already present the coming of Eärendel to Kôr (Tirion) and finding it deserted, the dust of diamonds on his shoes, the changing of Elwing into a seabird, the passing of his ship through the Door of Night, and the sanction against his return to the lands east of the Sea. The raid on the Havens of Sirion appears in the early outlines, though that was an act of Melko's, not of the Fëanorians; and Tuor's departure also, but without Idril, whom he left behind. His ship was *Alqarámë*, Swanwing: afterwards it bore the name *Eärrámë*, with the meaning 'Sea-wing' (*The Silmarillion* p. 245), which retained, in form but not in meaning, the name of Eärendel's first ship *Eärámë* 'Eaglepinion' (pp. 253–4, and see note 9).

It is interesting to read my father's statement, made some half-century later (in the letter of 1967 referred to above), concerning the origins of Eärendil:

This name is in fact (as is obvious) derived from Anglo-Saxon *éarendel*. When first studying Anglo-Saxon professionally (1913–) – I had done so as a boyish hobby when supposed to be learning Greek and Latin – I was struck by the great beauty of this word (or name), entirely coherent with the normal style of Anglo-Saxon, but euphonic to a peculiar degree in that pleasing but not 'delectable' language. Also its form strongly suggests that it is in origin a proper name and not a common noun. This is borne out by the obviously related forms in other Germanic languages; from which amid the confusions and debasements of late traditions it at least seems certain that it belonged to astronomical-myth, and was the name of a star or star-group. To my mind the Anglo-Saxon uses seem plainly to indicate that it was a star presaging the dawn (at any rate in English tradition): that is what we now call *Venus*: the morning star as it may be seen shining brilliantly in the dawn, before the actual rising of the Sun. That is at any rate how I took it. Before 1914 I wrote a 'poem' upon Eärendel who launched his ship like a bright spark from the havens of the Sun. I adopted him into my mythology – in which he became a prime figure as a mariner, and eventually as a herald star, and a sign of hope to men. *Aiya Eärendil Elenion Ancalima* ([The Lord of the Rings] II.329) 'hail Eärendil brightest of Stars' is derived at long remove from *Éalá Éarendel engla beorhtast*.* But the name could not be adopted just like that: it had to be accommodated to the Elvish linguistic situation, at the same time as a place for this person was made in legend. From this, far back in the history of 'Elvish', which was beginning, after many tentative starts in boyhood, to take definite shape at the time of the name's adoption, arose eventually (a) the C[ommon]E[lvish] stem *AYAR 'sea', primarily applied to the Great Sea of the West, lying between Middle-earth and Aman the Blessed Realm of the Valar; and (b) the element, or verbal base (N)DIL, 'to love, be devoted to' – describing the attitude of one to a person, thing, cause, or occupation to which one is devoted for its own sake. Eärendil became a character in the earliest written (1916–17) of the major legends: *The Fall of Gondolin*, the greatest of the *Pereldar* 'Half-elven', son of *Tuor* of the most renowned House of the Edain, and *Idril* daughter of the King of Gondolin.

My father did not indeed here say that his *Eärendel* contained from the beginning elements that in combination give a meaning like 'Sea-lover'; but it is in any case clear that at the time of the earliest extant writings on

---

* From the Old English poem *Crist*: *éalá! éarendel engla beorhtast ofer mid-dangeard monnum sended*.

the subject the name was associated with an Elvish word *ea* 'eagle' – see p. 265 on the name of Eärendel's first ship *Eärámë* 'Eaglepinion'. In the Name-list to *The Fall of Gondolin* this is made explicit: '*Earendl* [*sic*] though belike it hath some kinship to the Elfin *ea* and *earen* "eagle" and "eyrie" (wherefore cometh to mind the passage of Cristhorn and the use of the sign of the Eagle by Idril [see p. 193]) is thought to be woven of that secret tongue of the Gondothlim [see p. 165].'

★

I give lastly four early poems of my father's in which Eärendel appears.

I

Éala Éarendel Engla Beorhtast

There can be little doubt that, as Humphrey Carpenter supposes (*Biography* p. 71), this was the first poem on the subject of Eärendel that my father composed, and that it was written at Phoenix Farm, Gedling, Nottinghamshire, in September 1914.[10] It was to this poem that he was referring in the letter of 1967 just cited – 'I wrote a "poem" upon Eärendel who launched his ship like a bright spark': cf. line 5 'He launched his bark like a silver spark . . .'

There are some five different versions, each one incorporating emendations made in the predecessor, though only the first verse was substantially rewritten. The title was originally 'The Voyage of Éarendel the Evening Star', together with (as customarily) an Old English version of this: *Scipfæreld Earendeles Æfensteorran*; this was changed in a later copy to *Éala Éarendel Engla Beorhtast* 'The Last Voyage of Eärendel', and in still later copies the modern English name was removed. I give it here in the last version, the date of which cannot be determined, though the handwriting shows it to be substantially later than the original composition; together with all the divergent readings of the earliest extant version in footnotes.

> Éarendel arose where the shadow flows
>   At Ocean's silent brim;
> Through the mouth of night as a ray of light
>   Where the shores are sheer and dim
> He launched his bark like a silver spark   4
>   From the last and lonely sand;
> Then on sunlit breath of day's fiery death
>   He sailed from Westerland.   8

He threaded his path o'er the aftermath
  Of the splendour of the Sun,
And wandered far past many a star
  In his gleaming galleon.   12
On the gathering tide of darkness ride
  The argosies of the sky,
And spangle the night with their sails of light
  As the streaming star goes by.   16

Unheeding he dips past these twinkling ships,
  By his wayward spirit whirled
On an endless quest through the darkling West
  O'er the margin of the world;   20
And he fares in haste o'er the jewelled waste
  And the dusk from whence he came
With his heart afire with bright desire
  And his face in silver flame.   24

The Ship of the Moon from the East comes soon
  From the Haven of the Sun,
Whose white gates gleam in the coming beam
  Of the mighty silver one.   28
Lo! with bellying clouds as his vessel's shrouds
  He weighs anchor down the dark,
And on shimmering oars leaves the blazing shores
  In his argent-timbered bark.   32

Readings of the earliest version:
1–8   Éarendel sprang up from the Ocean's cup
      In the gloom of the mid-world's rim;
    From the door of Night as a ray of light
      Leapt over the twilight brim,
    And launching his bark like a silver spark
      From the golden-fading sand
    Down the sunlit breath of Day's fiery Death
      He sped from Westerland.

10   splendour] glory
11   wandered] went wandering
16   streaming] Evening
17   Unheeding] But unheeding
18   wayward] wandering
19   endless] magic   darkling] darkening
20   O'er the margin] Toward the margent
22   And the dusk] To the dusk
25   The Ship] For the Ship
31   blazing] skiey
32   timbered] orbéd

Then Éarendel fled from that Shipman dread
  Beyond the dark earth's pale,
Back under the rim of the Ocean dim,
  And behind the world set sail;   36
And he heard the mirth of the folk of earth
  And the falling of their tears,
As the world dropped back in a cloudy wrack
  On its journey down the years.   40

Then he glimmering passed to the starless vast
  As an isléd lamp at sea,
And beyond the ken of mortal men
  Set his lonely errantry,   44
Tracking the Sun in his galleon
  Through the pathless firmament,
Till his light grew old in abysses cold
  And his eager flame was spent.   48

There seems every reason to think that this poem preceded all the
outlines and notes given in this chapter, and that verbal similarities to
the poem found in these are echoes (e.g. 'his face is in silver flame',
outline C, p. 255; 'the margent of the world', outline E, p. 260).

In the fourth verse of the poem the Ship of the Moon comes forth from
the Haven of the Sun; in the tale of *The Hiding of Valinor* (I. 215) Aulë
and Ulmo built two havens in the east, that of the Sun (which was 'wide
and golden') and that of the Moon (which was 'white, having gates of
silver and of pearl') – but they were both 'within the same harbourage'.
As in the poem, in the *Tale of the Sun and Moon* the Moon is urged on
by 'shimmering oars' (I. 195).

II

The Bidding of the Minstrel

This poem, according to a note that my father scribbled on one of the
copies, was written at St. John's Street, Oxford (see I. 27) in the winter
of 1914; there is no other evidence for its date. In this case the earliest
workings are extant, and on the back of one of the sheets is the outline

33   Then] And
38   And the falling of] And hearkened to

46–8   And voyaging the skies
       Till his splendour was shorn by the birth of Morn
       And he died with the Dawn in his eyes.

account of Eärendel's great voyage given on p. 261. The poem was then much longer than it became, but the workings are exceedingly rough; they have no title. To the earliest finished text a title was added hastily later: this apparently reads 'The Minstrel renounces the song'. The title then became 'The Lay of Eärendel', changed in the latest text to 'The Bidding of the Minstrel, from the Lay of Eärendel'.

There are four versions following the original rough draft, but the changes made in them were slight, and I give the poem here in the latest form, noting only that originally the minstrel seems to have responded to the 'bidding' much earlier – at line 5, which read 'Then harken – a tale of immortal sea-yearning'; and that 'Eldar' in line 6 and 'Elven' in line 23 are emendations, made on the latest text, of 'fairies', 'fairy'.

'Sing us yet more of Eärendel the wandering,
Chant us a lay of his white-oared ship,
More marvellous-cunning than mortal man's pondering,
Foamily musical out on the deep.
Sing us a tale of immortal sea-yearning   5
The Eldar once made ere the change of the light,
Weaving a winelike spell, and a burning
Wonder of spray and the odours of night;
Of murmurous gloamings out on far oceans;
Of his tossing at anchor off islets forlorn   10
To the unsleeping waves' never-ending sea-motions;
Of bellying sails when a wind was born,
And the gurgling bubble of tropical water
Tinkled from under the ringéd stem,
And thousands of miles was his ship from those wrought her   15
A petrel, a sea-bird, a white-wingéd gem,
Gallantly bent on measureless faring
Ere she came homing in sea-laden flight,
Circuitous, lingering, restlessly daring,
Coming to haven unlooked for, at night.'   20

'But the music is broken, the words half-forgotten,
The sunlight has faded, the moon is grown old,
The Elven ships foundered or weed-swathed and rotten,
The fire and the wonder of hearts is acold.
Who now can tell, and what harp can accompany   25
With melodies strange enough, rich enough tunes,
Pale with the magic of cavernous harmony,
Loud with shore-music of beaches and dunes,
How slender his boat; of what glimmering timber;
How her sails were all silvern and taper her mast,   30
And silver her throat with foam and her limber
Flanks as she swanlike floated past!

The song I can sing is but shreds one remembers
Of golden imaginings fashioned in sleep,
A whispered tale told by the withering embers   35
Of old things far off that but few hearts keep.'

III

The Shores of Faëry

This poem is given in its earliest form by Humphrey Carpenter, *Biography*, pp. 76–7.[11] It exists in four versions each as usual incorporating slight changes; my father wrote the date of its composition on three of the copies, viz. 'July 8–9, 1915'; 'Moseley and Edgbaston, Birmingham July 1915 (walking and on bus). Retouched often since – esp. 1924'; and 'First poem of my mythology, Valinor . . . . 1910'. This last cannot have been intended for the date of composition, and the illegible words preceding it may possibly be read as 'thought of about'. But it does not in any case appear to have been 'the first poem of the mythology': that, I believe, was *Éalá Éarendel Engla Beorhtast* – and my father's mention of this poem in his letter of 1967 (see p. 266) seems to suggest this also.

The Old English title was *Ielfalandes Strand* (The Shores of Elfland). It is preceded by a short prose preface which has been given above, p. 262. I give it here in the latest version (undateable), with all readings from the earliest in footnotes.

East of the Moon, west of the Sun
There stands a lonely hill;
Its feet are in the pale green sea,
Its towers are white and still,
Beyond Taniquetil   5
In Valinor.
Comes never there but one lone star
That fled before the moon;
And there the Two Trees naked are
That bore Night's silver bloom,   10
That bore the globéd fruit of Noon
In Valinor.
There are the shores of Faëry

Readings of the earliest version:

1   East . . . . . west] West . . . . . East
7   No stars come there but one alone
8   fled before] hunted with
9   For there the Two Trees naked grow
10 bore] bear   11   bore] bear

With their moonlit pebbled strand
Whose foam is silver music   15
On the opalescent floor
Beyond the great sea-shadows
On the marches of the sand
That stretches on for ever
To the dragonheaded door,   20
The gateway of the Moon,
Beyond Taniquetil
In Valinor.
West of the Sun, east of the Moon
Lies the haven of the star,   25
The white town of the Wanderer
And the rocks of Eglamar.
There Wingelot is harboured,
While Eärendel looks afar
O'er the darkness of the waters   30
Between here and Eglamar –
Out, out, beyond Taniquetil
In Valinor afar.

There are some interesting connections between this poem and the tale of *The Coming of the Elves and the Making of Kôr*. The 'lonely hill' of line 2 is the hill of Kôr (cf. the tale, I. 122: 'at the head of this long creek there stands a lonely hill which gazes at the loftier mountains'), while 'the golden feet of Kôr' (a line replaced in the later versions of the poem) and very probably 'the sand That stretches on for ever' are explained by the passage that follows in the tale:

Thither [i.e. to Kôr] did Aulë bring all the dust of magic metals that his great works had made and gathered, and he piled it about the foot of that hill, and most of this dust was of gold, and a sand of gold stretched away from the feet of Kôr out into the distance where the Two Trees blossomed.

18   marches] margent
20–21   To the dragonheaded door, The gateway of the Moon] From the golden feet of Kôr
24   West of the Sun, east of the Moon] O! West of the Moon, East of the Sun
27   rocks] rock
28   Wingelot] *Earliest text* Wingelot > Vingelot; *second text* Vingelot; *third text* Vingelot > Wingelot; *last text* Wingelot
30   O'er the darkness of the waters] On the magic and the wonder
31   Between] 'Tween

In the latest text *Elvenland* is lightly written over *Faëry* in line 13, and *Eldamar* against *Eglamar* in line 27 (only); *Eglamar* > *Eldamar* in the second text.

With the 'dragonheaded door' (line 20) cf. the description of the Door of·
Night in *The Hiding of Valinor* (I. 215–16):

Its pillars are of the mightiest basalt and its lintel likewise, but great
dragons of black stone are carved thereon, and shadowy smoke pours
slowly from their jaws.

In that description the Door of Night is not however 'the gateway of the
Moon', for it is the Sun that passes through it into the outer dark,
whereas 'the Moon dares not the utter loneliness of the outer dark by
reason of his lesser light and majesty, and he journeys still beneath the
world [i.e. through the waters of Vai]'.

IV

The Happy Mariners

I give lastly this poem whose subject is the Tower of Pearl in the Twilit
Isles. It was written in July 1915,[12] and there are six texts preceding the
version which was published (together with 'Why the Man in the Moon
came down too soon') at Leeds in 1923* and which is the first of the two
given here.

(1)

I know a window in a western tower
That opens on celestial seas,
And wind that has been blowing round the stars
Comes to nestle in its tossing draperies.
It is a white tower builded in the Twilight Isles, 5
Where Evening sits for ever in the shade;
It glimmers like a spike of lonely pearl
That mirrors beams forlorn and lights that fade;
And sea goes washing round the dark rock where it stands,
And fairy boats go by to gloaming lands 10
All piled and twinkling in the gloom
With hoarded sparks of orient fire

---

* *A Northern Venture:* see I.204, footnote. Mr Douglas A. Anderson has kindly
supplied me with a copy of the poem in this version, which had been very slightly altered
from that published in *The Stapeldon Magazine* (Exeter College, Oxford), June 1920
(Carpenter, p. 268). – *Twilight* in line 5 of the Leeds version is almost certainly an error,
for *Twilit*, the reading of all the original texts.

That divers won in waters of the unknown Sun –
And, maybe, 'tis a throbbing silver lyre,
Or voices of grey sailors echo up   15
Afloat among the shadows of the world
In oarless shallop and with canvas furled;
For often seems there ring of feet and song
Or twilit twinkle of a trembling gong.

O! happy mariners upon a journey long   20
To those great portals on the Western shores
Where far away constellate fountains leap,
And dashed against Night's dragon-headed doors,
In foam of stars fall sparkling in the deep.
While I alone look out behind the Moon   25
From in my white and windy tower,
Ye bide no moment and await no hour,
But chanting snatches of a mystic tune
Go through the shadows and the dangerous seas
Past sunless lands to fairy leas   30
Where stars upon the jacinth wall of space
Do tangle burst and interlace.
Ye follow Earendel through the West,
The shining mariner, to Islands blest;
While only from beyond that sombre rim   35
A wind returns to stir these crystal panes
And murmur magically of golden rains
That fall for ever in those spaces dim.

In *The Hiding of Valinor* (I. 215) it is told that when the Sun was first
made the Valar purposed to draw it beneath the Earth, but that

> it was too frail and lissom; and much precious radiance was spilled in
> their attempts about the deepest waters, and escaped to linger as secret
> sparks in many an unknown ocean cavern. These have many elfin
> divers, and divers of the fays, long time sought beyond the outmost
> East, even as is sung in the song of the Sleeper in the Tower of Pearl.

That 'The Happy Mariners' was in fact 'the song of the Sleeper in the
Tower of Pearl' seems assured by lines 10–13 of the poem.

For 'Night's dragon-headed doors' see p. 273. The meaning of *jacinth*
in 'the jacinth wall of space' (line 31) is 'blue'; cf. 'the deep-blue walls' in
The Hiding of Valinor (I. 215).

Many years later my father rewrote the poem, and I give this version
here. Still later he turned to it again and made a few further alterations
(here recorded in footnotes); at this time he noted that the revised
version dated from '1940?'.

(2)

I know a window in a Western tower
that opens on celestial seas,
and there from wells of dark behind the stars
blows ever cold a keen unearthly breeze.
It is a white tower builded on the Twilit Isles,   5
and springing from their everlasting shade
it glimmers like a house of lonely pearl,
where lights forlorn take harbour ere they fade.

Its feet are washed by waves that never rest.
There silent boats go by into the West   10
all piled and twinkling in the dark
with orient fire in many a hoarded spark
that divers won
in waters of the rumoured Sun.
There sometimes throbs below a silver harp,   15
touching the heart with sudden music sharp;
or far beneath the mountains high and sheer
the voices of grey sailors echo clear,
afloat among the shadows of the world
in oarless ships and with their canvas furled,   20
chanting a farewell and a solemn song:
for wide the sea is, and the journey long.

O happy mariners upon a journey far,
beyond the grey islands and past Gondobar,
to those great portals on the final shores   25
where far away constellate fountains leap,
and dashed against Night's dragon-headed doors
in foam of stars fall sparkling in the deep!
While I, alone, look out behind the moon
from in my white and windy tower,   30
ye bide no moment and await no hour,
but go with solemn song and harpers' tune
through the dark shadows and the shadowy seas
to the last land of the Two Trees,
whose fruit and flower are moon and sun,   35
where light of earth is ended and begun.

Last revisions:
3   and there *omitted*
4   blows ever cold] there ever blows
17   mountains] mountain
22   the journey] their journey
29   While I look out alone   30   imprisoned in the white and windy tower
31   ye] you   33–6   *struck through*

Ye follow Eärendel without rest,
the shining mariner, beyond the West,
who passed the mouth of night and launched his bark
upon the outer seas of everlasting dark.   40
Here only comes at whiles a wind to blow
returning darkly down the way ye go,
with perfume laden of unearthly trees.
Here only long afar through window-pane
I glimpse the flicker of the golden rain   45
that falls for ever on the outer seas.

I cannot explain the reference (in the revised version only, line 24) to
the journey of the mariners 'beyond the grey islands and past Gondobar'.
Gondobar ('City of Stone') was one of the seven names of Gondolin
(p. 158).

NOTES

1   Falasquil was the name of Tuor's dwelling on the coast (p. 152); the
     Oarni, with the Falmaríni and the Wingildi, are called 'the spirits of
     the foam and the surf of ocean' (I.66).
2   *Irildë*: the 'Elvish' name corresponding to Gnomish *Idril*. See the
     Appendix on Names, entry *Idril*.
3   'Elwing of the *Gnomes* of Artanor' is perhaps a mere slip.
4   For the Swan-wing as the emblem of Tuor see pp. 152, 164, 172,
     193.
5   The words 'Idril has vanished' replace an earlier reading: 'Sirion has
     been sacked and only Littleheart (Ilfrith) remained who tells the
     tale.' *Ilfrith* is yet another version of Littleheart's Elvish name (see
     pp. 201–2).
6   Struck out here: 'The Sleeper is Idril but he does not know.'
7   Cf. *Kortirion among the Trees* (I.36, lines 129–30): 'I need not
     know the desert or red palaces Where dwells the sun'; lines retained
     slightly changed in the second (1937) version (I. 39).
8   This passage, from 'Eärendel distraught...', replaced the following:
     '[*illegible name, possibly* Orlon] is [?biding] there and tells him of
     the sack of Sirion and the captivity of Elwing. The faring of the
     Koreldar and the binding of Melko.' Perhaps the words 'The faring
     of the Koreldar' were struck out by mistake (cf. Outline B).
9   *Earum* is emended (at the first occurrence only) from *Earam*; and
     following it stood the name *Earnhama*, but this was struck out.
     Earnhama is Old English, 'Eagle-coat', 'Eagle-dress'.

37   Ye] You   40   outer *omitted*
41–3   *struck through*   46   the] those
Line added at end: beyond the country of the shining Trees.

10 The two earliest extant texts date it thus, one of them with the
addition 'Ex[eter] Coll[ege] Essay Club Dec. 1914', and on a third is
written 'Gedling, Notts., Sept. 1913 [error for 1914] and later'. My
father referred to having read 'Eärendel' to the Essay Club in a letter
to my mother of 27 November 1914.

11 But *rocks* in line 27 (26) should read *rock*.

12 According to one note it was written at 'Barnt Green [see *Biography*
p. 36] July 1915 and Bedford and later', and another note dates it
'July 24 [1915], rewritten Sept. 9'. The original workings are on the
back of an unsent letter dated from Moseley (Birmingham) July 11,
1915; my father began military training at Bedford on July 19.

VI

THE HISTORY OF ERIOL OR ÆLFWINE AND THE END OF THE TALES

In this final chapter we come to the most difficult (though not, as I hope to show, altogether insoluble) part of the earliest form of the mythology: its end, with which is intertwined the story of Eriol/Ælfwine – and with that, the history and original significance of Tol Eressëa. For its eluci- dation we have some short pieces of connected narrative, but are largely dependent on the same materials as those that constitute *Gilfanon's Tale* and the story of Eärendel: scribbled plot-outlines, endlessly varying, written on separate slips of paper or in the pages of the little notebook 'C' (see p. 254). In this chapter there is much material to consider, and for convenience of reference within the chapter I number the various citations consecutively. But it must be said that no device of presentation can much diminish the inherent complexity and obscurity of the matter.

The fullest account (bald as it is) of the March of the Elves of Kôr and the events that followed is contained in notebook C, continuing on from the point where I left that outline on p. 255, after the coming of the birds from Gondolin, the 'counsels of the Gods and uproar of the Elves', and the 'March of the Inwir and Teleri', with the Solosimpi only agreeing to accompany the expedition on condition that they remain by the sea. The outline continues:

(1)   Coming of the Eldar. Encampment in the Land of Willows of first host. Overwhelming of Noldorin and Valwë. Wanderings of Noldorin with his harp.
        Tulkas overthrows Melko in the battle of the Silent Pools. Bound in Lumbi and guarded by Gorgumoth the hound of Mandos.
        Release of the Noldoli. War with Men as soon as Tulkas and Noldorin have fared back to Valinor.
        Noldoli led to Valinor by Egalmoth and Galdor.

There have been previous references in the *Lost Tales* to a battle in Tasarinan, the Land of Willows: in the *Tale of Turambar* (pp. 70, 140), and, most notably, in *The Fall of Gondolin* (p. 154), where when Tuor's sojourn in that land is described there is mention of events that would take place there in the future:

Did not even after the days of Tuor Noldorin and his Eldar come there seeking for Dor Lómin and the hidden river and the caverns of the Gnomes' imprisonment; yet thus nigh to their quest's end were like to abandon it? Indeed sleeping and dancing here . . . they were whelmed by the goblins sped by Melko from the Hills of Iron and Noldorin made bare escape thence.

Valwë has been mentioned once before, by Lindo, on Eriol's first evening in Mar Vanwa Tyaliéva (I.16): 'My father Valwë who went with Noldorin to find the Gnomes.' Of Noldorin we know also that he was the Vala Salmar, the twin-brother of Ómar-Amillo; that he entered the world with Ulmo, and that in Valinor he played the harp and lyre and loved the Noldoli (I.66, 75, 93, 126).

An isolated note states:

(2) Noldorin escapes from the defeat of the Land of Willows and takes his harp and goes seeking in the Iron Mountains for Valwë and the Gnomes until he finds their place of imprisonment. Tulkas follows. Melko comes to meet him.

The only one of the great Valar who is mentioned in these notes as taking part in the expedition to the Great Lands is Tulkas; but whatever story underlay his presence, despite the anger and sorrow of the Valar at the March of the Elves (see p. 257), is quite irrecoverable. (A very faint hint concerning it is found in two isolated notes: 'Tulkas gives – or the Elves take *limpë* with them', and '*Limpë* given by the Gods (Oromë? Tulkas?) when Elves left Valinor'; cf. *The Flight of the Noldoli* (I.166): 'no *limpë* had they [the Noldoli] as yet to bring away, for that was not given to the fairies until long after, when the March of Liberation was undertaken'.) According to (1) above Tulkas fought with and overthrew Melko 'in the battle of the Silent Pools'; and the Silent Pools are the Pools of Twilight, 'where Tulkas after fought with Melko's self' (*The Fall of Gondolin*, p. 195; the original reading here was 'Noldorin and Tulkas').

The name *Lumbi* is found elsewhere (in a list of names associated with the tale of *The Coming of the Valar*, I.93), where it is said to be Melko's third dwelling; and a jotting in notebook C, sufficiently mysterious, reads: 'Lumfad. Melko's dwelling after release. Castle of Lumbi.' But this story also is lost.

That the Noldoli were led back to Valinor by Egalmoth and Galdor, as stated in (1), is notable. This is contradicted in detail by a statement in the Name-list to *The Fall of Gondolin*, which says (p. 215) that Egalmoth was slain in the raid on the dwelling at the mouth of Sirion when Elwing was taken; and contradicted in general by the next citation to be given, which denies that the Elves were permitted to dwell in Valinor.

The only other statement concerning these events is found in the first of the four outlines that constitute *Gilfanon's Tale*, which I there called 'A' (I. 234). This reads:

(3)   March of the Elves out into the world.
The capture of Noldorin.
The camp in the Land of Willows.
Army of Tulkas at the Pools of Twilight . . . . . . and [?many]
Gnomes, but Men fall on them out of Hisilómë.
Defeat of Melko.
Breaking of Angamandi and release of captives.
Hostility of Men. The Gnomes collect some of the jewels.
Elwing and most of the Elves go back to dwell in Tol Eressëa. The
Gods will not let them dwell in Valinor.

This seems to differ from (1) in the capture of Noldorin and in the attack of Men from Hisilómë before the defeat of Melko; but the most notable statement is that concerning the refusal of the Gods to allow the Elves to dwell in Valinor. There is no reason to think that this ban rested only, or chiefly, on the Noldoli. The text, (3), does not refer specifically to the Gnomes in this connection; and the ban is surely to be related to 'the sorrow and wrath of the Gods' at the time of the March of the Elves (p. 253). Further, it is said in *The Cottage of Lost Play* (I. 16) that Ingil son of Inwë returned to Tol Eressëa with 'most of the fairest and the wisest, most of the merriest and the kindest, of all the Eldar', and that the town that he built there was named 'Koromas or "the Resting of the Exiles of Kôr".' This is quite clearly to be connected with the statement in (3) that 'Most of the Elves go back to dwell in Tol Eressëa', and with that given on p. 255: 'The wars with Men and the departure to Tol Eressëa (the Eldar unable to endure the strife of the world)'. These indications taken together leave no doubt, I think, that my father's original conception was of the Eldar of Valinor undertaking the expedition into the Great Lands against the will of the Valar; together with the rescued Noldoli they returned over the Ocean, but being refused re-entry into Valinor they settled in Tol Eressëa, as 'the Exiles of Kôr'. That some did return in the end to Valinor may be concluded from the words of Meril-i-Turinqi (I. 129) that Ingil, who built Kortirion, 'went long ago back to Valinor and is with Manwë'. But Tol Eressëa remained the land of the fairies in the early conception, the Exiles of Kôr, Eldar and Gnomes, speaking both *Eldarissa* and *Noldorissa*.

It seems that there is nothing else to be found or said concerning the original story of the coming of aid out of the West and the renewed assault on Melko.

★

The conclusion of the whole story as originally envisaged was to be rejected in its entirety. For it we are very largely dependent on the outline in notebook C, continuing on from citation (1) above; this is extremely rough and disjointed, and is given here in a very slightly edited form.

(4) After the departure of Eärendel and the coming of the Elves to Tol Eressëa (and most of this belongs to the history of Men) great ages elapse; Men spread and thrive, and the Elves of the Great Lands fade. As Men's stature grows theirs diminishes. Men and Elves were formerly of a size, though Men always larger.[1]

Melko again breaks away, by the aid of Tevildo (who in long ages gnaws his bonds); the Gods are in dissension about Men and Elves, some favouring the one and some the other. Melko goes to Tol Eressëa and tries to stir up dissension among the Elves (between Gnomes and Solosimpi), who are in consternation and send to Valinor. No help comes, but Tulkas sends privily Telimektar (Taimonto) his son.[2]

Telimektar of the silver sword and Ingil surprise Melko and wound him, and he flees and climbs up the great Pine of Tavrobel. Before the Inwir left Valinor Belaurin (Palúrien)[3] gave them a seed, and said that it must be guarded, for great tidings would one day come of its growth. But it was forgotten, and cast in the garden of Gilfanon, and a mighty pine arose that reached to Ilwë and the stars.[4]

Telimektar and Ingil pursue him, and they remain now in the sky to ward it, and Melko stalks high above the air seeking ever to do a hurt to the Sun and Moon and stars (eclipses, meteors). He is continually frustrated, but on his first attempt – saying that the Gods stole his fire for its making – he upset the Sun, so that Urwendi fell into the Sea, and the Ship fell near the ground, scorching regions of the Earth. The clarity of the Sun's radiance has not been so great since, and something of magic has gone from it. Hence it is, and long has been, that the fairies dance and sing more sweetly and can the better be seen by the light of the Moon – because of the death of Urwendi.

The 'Rekindling of the Magic Sun' refers in part to the Trees and in part to Urwendi.

Fionwë's rage and grief. In the end he will slay Melko.

'Orion' is only the image of Telimektar in the sky? [sic] Varda gave him stars, and he bears them aloft that the Gods may know he watches; he has diamonds on his sword-sheath, and this will go red when he draws his sword at the Great End.

But now Telimektar, and Gil[5] who follows him like a Blue Bee, ward off evil, and Varda immediately replaces any stars that Melko loosens and casts down.

Although grieved at the Gods' behest, the Pine is cut down; and

Melko is thus now out of the world – but one day he will find a way back, and the last great uproars will begin before the Great End.

The evils that still happen come about in this wise. The Gods can cause things to enter the hearts of Men, but not of Elves (hence their difficult dealings in the old days of the Exile of the Gnomes) – and though Melko sits without, gnawing his fingers and gazing in anger on the world, he can suggest evil to Men so inclined – but the lies he planted of old still grow and spread.

Hence Melko can now work hurt and damage and evil in the world only through Men, and he has more power and subtlety with Men than Manwë or any of the Gods, because of his long sojourn in the world and among Men.

In these early chartings we are in a primitive mythology, with Melko reduced to a grotesque figure chased up a great pine-tree, which is thereupon cut down to keep him out of the world, where he 'stalks high above the air' or 'sits without, gnawing his fingers', and upsets the Sun-ship so that Urwendi falls into the Sea – and, most strangely, meets her death.

That Ingil (Gil) who with Telimektar pursues Melko is to be identified with Ingil son of Inwë who built Kortirion is certain and appears from several notes; see the Appendix on Names to Vol. I, entries *Ingil*, *Telimektar*. This is the fullest statement of the Orion-myth, which is referred to in the *Tale of the Sun and Moon* (see I. 182, 200):

of Nielluin [Sirius] too, who is the Bee of Azure, Nielluin whom still may all men see in autumn or winter burning nigh the foót of Telimektar son of Tulkas whose tale is yet to tell.

In the Gnomish dictionary it is said (I. 256) that Gil rose into the heavens and 'in the likeness of a great bee bearing honey of flame' followed Telimektar. This presumably represents a distinct conception from that referred to above, where Ingil 'went long ago back to Valinor and is with Manwë' (I. 129).

With the reference to Fionwë's slaying of Melko 'in the end' cf. the end of *The Hiding of Valinor* (I. 219):

Fionwë Úrion, son of Manwë, of love for Urwendi shall in the end be Melko's bane, and shall destroy the world to destroy his foe, and so shall all things then be rolled away.

Cf. also the *Tale of Turambar*, p. 116, where it is said that Turambar 'shall stand beside Fionwë in the Great Wrack'.

For the prophecies and hopes of the Elves concerning the Rekindling of the Magic Sun see pp. 285–6.

The outline in C continues and concludes thus (again with some very slight and insignificant editing):

(5)   Longer ages elapse. Gilfanon is now the oldest and wisest Elf in Tol Eressëa, but is not of the Inwir – hence Meril-i-Turinqi is Lady of the Isle.

Eriol comes to Tol Eressëa. Sojourns at Kortirion. Goes to Tavrobel to see Gilfanon, and sojourns in the house of a hundred chimneys – for this is the last condition of his drinking *limpë*. Gilfanon bids him write down all he has heard before he drinks.

Eriol drinks *limpë*. Gilfanon tells him of things to be; that in his mind (although the fairies hope not) he believes that Tol Eressëa will become a dwelling of Men. Gilfanon also prophesies concerning the Great End, and of the Wrack of Things, and of Fionwë, Tulkas, and Melko and the last fight on the Plains of Valinor.

Eriol ends his life at Tavrobel but in his last days is consumed with longing for the black cliffs of his shores, even as Meril said.

The book lay untouched in the house of Gilfanon during many ages of Men.

The compiler of the Golden Book takes up the Tale: one of the children of the fathers of the fathers of Men. [*Against this is written*:] It may perhaps be much better to let Eriol himself see the last things and finish the book.

Rising of the Lost Elves against the Orcs and Nautar.[6] The time is not ready for the Faring Forth, but the fairies judge it to be necessary. They obtain through Ulmo the help of Uin,[7] and Tol Eressëa is uprooted and dragged near to the Great Lands, nigh to the promontory of Rôs. A magic bridge is cast across the intervening sound. Ossë is wroth at the breaking of the roots of the isle he set so long ago – and many of his rare sea-treasures grow about it – that he tries to wrench it back; and the western half breaks off, and is now the Isle of Íverin.

The Battle of Rôs: the Island-elves and the Lost Elves against Nautar, Gongs,[8] Orcs, and a few evil Men. Defeat of the Elves. The fading Elves retire to Tol Eressëa and hide in the woods.

Men come to Tol Eressëa and also Orcs, Dwarves, Gongs, Trolls, etc. After the Battle of Rôs the Elves faded with sorrow. They cannot live in air breathed by a number of Men equal to their own or greater; and ever as Men wax more powerful and numerous so the fairies fade and grow small and tenuous, filmy and transparent, but Men larger and more dense and gross. At last Men, or almost all, can no longer see the fairies.

The Gods now dwell in Valinor, and come scarcely ever to the world, being content with the restraining of the elements from utterly destroying Men. They grieve much at what they see; *but Ilúvatar is over all*.

On the page opposite the passage about the Battle of Rôs is written:

A great battle between Men at the Heath of the Sky-roof (now the Withered Heath), about a league from Tavrobel. The Elves and the Children flee over the Gruir and the Afros.
'Even now do they approach and our great tale comes to its ending.'
The book found in the ruins of the house of a hundred chimneys.

That Gilfanon was the oldest of the Elves of Tol Eressëa, though Meril held the title of Lady of the Isle, is said also in the *Tale of the Sun and Moon* (I.175): but what is most notable is that Gilfanon (not Ailios, teller of the *Tale of the Nauglafring*, whom Gilfanon replaced, see I.197 note 19 and 229ff.) appears in this outline, which must therefore be late in the period of the composition of the *Lost Tales*.

Also noteworthy are the references to Eriol's drinking *limpë* at Gilfanon's 'house of a hundred chimneys'. In *The Cottage of Lost Play* (I.17) Lindo told Eriol that he could not give him *limpë* to drink:

Turinqi only may give it to those not of the Eldar race, and those that drink must dwell always with the Eldar of the Island until such time as they fare forth to find the lost families of the kindred.

Meril-i-Turinqi herself, when Eriol besought her for a drink of *limpë*, was severe (I.98):

If you drink this drink . . . even at the Faring Forth, should Eldar and Men fall into war at the last, still must you stand by us against the children of your kith and kin, but until then never may you fare away home though longings gnaw you . . .

In the text described in I.229ff. Eriol bemoans to Lindo the refusal to grant him his desire, and Lindo, while warning him against 'thinking to overpass the bounds that Ilúvatar hath set', tells him that Meril has not irrevocably refused him. In a note to this text my father wrote: '. . . Eriol fares to Tavrobel – after Tavrobel he drinks of *limpë*.'

The statement in this passage of outline C that Eriol 'in his last days is consumed with longing for the black cliffs of his shores, even as Meril said' clearly refers to the passage in *The Chaining of Melko* from which I have cited above:

On a day of autumn will come the winds and a driven gull, maybe, will wail overhead, and lo! you will be filled with desire, remembering the black coasts of your home. (I.96).

Lindo's reference, in the passage from *The Cottage of Lost Play* cited above, to the faring forth of the Eldar of Tol Eressëa 'to find the lost families of the kindred' must likewise relate to the mentions in (5) of the Faring Forth (though the time was not ripe), of the rising of the Lost Elves against the Orcs and Nautar', and of 'the Island-elves and the Lost Elves' at the Battle of Rôs. Precisely who are to be understood by the 'Lost Elves' is not clear; but in *Gilfanon's Tale* (I. 231) all Elves of the Great Lands 'that never saw the light at Kôr' (Ilkorins), whether or not they left the Waters of Awakening, are called 'the lost fairies of the world', and this seems likely to be the meaning here. It must then be supposed that there dwelt on Tol Eressëa only the Eldar of Kôr (the 'Exiles') and the Noldoli released from thraldom under Melko; the Faring Forth was to be the great expedition from Tol Eressëa for the rescue of those who had never departed from the Great Lands.

In (5) we meet the conception of the dragging of Tol Eressëa back eastwards across the Ocean to the geographical position of England – it becomes England (see I. 26); that the part which was torn off by Ossë, the Isle of Íverin, is Ireland is explicitly stated in the Qenya dictionary. The promontory of Rôs is perhaps Brittany.

Here also there is a clear definition of the 'fading' of the Elves, their physical diminution and increasing tenuity and transparency, so that they become invisible (and finally incredible) to gross Mankind. This is a central concept of the early mythology: the 'fairies', as now conceived by Men (in so far as they are rightly conceived), have *become* so. They were not always so. And perhaps most remarkable in this remarkable passage, there is the final and virtually complete withdrawal of the Gods (to whom the Eldar are 'most like in nature', I. 57) from the concerns of 'the world', the Great Lands across the Sea. They watch, it seems, since they grieve, and are therefore not wholly indifferent to what passes in the lands of Men; but they are henceforward utterly remote, hidden in the West.

Other features of (5), the Golden Book of Tavrobel, and the Battle of the Heath of the Sky-roof, will be explained shortly. I give next a separate passage found in the notebook C under the heading 'Rekindling of the Magic Sun. Faring Forth.'

(6) The Elves' prophecy is that one day they will fare forth from Tol Eressëa and on arriving in the world will gather all their fading kindred who still live in the world and march towards Valinor – through the southern lands. This they will only do with the help of Men. If Men aid them, the fairies will take Men to Valinor – those that wish to go – fight a great battle with Melko in Erumáni and open Valinor.[9] Laurelin and Silpion will be rekindled, and the mountain wall being destroyed then soft radiance will spread over all the world, and the Sun and Moon will be recalled. If Men oppose them and aid Melko the Wrack of the Gods and the ending of the fairies will result – and maybe the Great End.

On the opposite page is written:

Were the Trees relit all the paths to Valinor would become clear to follow – and the Shadowy Seas open clear and free – Men as well as Elves would taste the blessedness of the Gods, and Mandos be emptied.

This prophecy is clearly behind Vairë's words to Eriol (I. 19–20): '. . . the Faring Forth, when if all goes well the roads through Arvalin to Valinor shall be thronged with the sons and daughters of Men.'

Since 'the Sun and Moon will be recalled' when the Two Trees give light again, it seems that here 'the Rekindling of the Magic Sun' (to which the toast was drunk in Mar Vanwa Tyaliéva, I. 17, 65) refers to the relighting of the Trees. But in citation (4) above it is said that 'the "Rekindling of the Magic Sun" refers in part to the Trees and in part to Urwendi', while in the *Tale of the Sun and Moon* (I. 179) Yavanna seems to distinguish the two ideas:

'Many things shall be done and come to pass, and the Gods grow old, and the Elves come nigh to fading, ere ye shall see the rekindling of these trees or the Magic Sun relit', and the Gods knew not what she meant, speaking of the Magic Sun, nor did for a long while after.

Citation (xix) on p. 264 does not make the reference clear: Eärendel 'returns from the firmament ever and anon with Voronwë to Kôr to see if the Magic Sun has been lit and the fairies have come back'; but in the following isolated note the Rekindling of the Magic Sun explicitly means the re-arising of Urwendi:

(7)   Urwendi imprisoned by Móru (upset out of the boat by Melko and only the Moon has been magic since). The Faring Forth and the Battle of Erumáni would release her and rekindle the Magic Sun.

This 'upsetting' of the Sun-ship by Melko and the loss of the Sun's 'magic' is referred to also in (4), where it is added that Urwendi fell into the sea and met her 'death'. In the tale of *The Theft of Melko* it is said (I. 151) that the cavern in which Melko met Ungweliant was the place where the Sun and Moon were imprisoned afterwards, for 'the primeval spirit Móru' was indeed Ungweliant (see I. 261). The Battle of Erumáni is referred to also in (6), and is possibly to be identified with 'the last fight on the plains of Valinor' prophesied by Gilfanon in (5). But the last part of (5) shows that the Faring Forth came to nothing, and the prophecies were not fulfilled.

There are no other references to the dragging of Tol Eressëa across the Ocean by Uin the great whale, to the Isle of Íverin, or to the Battle of Rôs; but a remarkable writing survives concerning the aftermath of the 'great battle between Men at the Heath of the Sky-roof (now the Withered Heath), about a league from Tavrobel' (end of citation (5)). This is a very hastily pencilled and exceedingly difficult text titled *Epilogue*. It begins with a short prefatory note:

(8) Eriol flees with the fading Elves from the Battle of the High Heath (Ladwen-na-Dhaideloth) and crosses the Gruir and the Afros.
     The last words of the book of Tales. Written by Eriol at Tavrobel before he sealed the book.

This represents the development mentioned as desirable in (5), that Eriol should 'himself see the last things and finish the book'; but an isolated note in C shows my father still uncertain about this even after the *Epilogue* was in being: 'Prologue by the writer of Tavrobel [*i.e., such a Prologue is needed*] telling how he found Eriol's writings and put them together. His epilogue after the battle of Ladwen Daideloth is written.'
     The rivers Gruir and Afros appear also in the passage about the battle at the end of (5). Since it is said there that the Heath was about a league from Tavrobel, the two rivers are clearly those referred to in the *Tale of the Sun and Moon*: 'the Tower of Tavrobel beside the rivers' (I.174, and see I.196 note 2). In scattered notes the battle is also called 'the Battle of the Heaven Roof' and 'the Battle of Dor-na-Dhaideloth'.[10]
     I give now the text of the *Epilogue*:

     And now is the end of the fair times come very nigh, and behold, all the beauty that yet was on earth – fragments of the unimagined loveliness of Valinor whence came the folk of the Elves long long ago – now goeth it all up in smoke. Here be a few tales, memories ill-told, of all that magic and that wonder twixt here and Eldamar of which I have become acquaint more than any mortal man since first my wandering footsteps came to this sad isle.
     Of that last battle of the upland heath whose roof is the wide sky – nor was there any other place beneath the blue folds of Manwë's robe so nigh the heavens or so broadly and so well encanopied – what grievous things I saw I have told.
     Already fade the Elves in sorrow and the Faring Forth has come to ruin, and Ilúvatar knoweth alone if ever now the Trees shall be relit while the world may last. Behold, I stole by evening from the ruined heath, and my way fled winding down the valley of the Brook of Glass, but the setting of the Sun was blackened with the reek of fires, and the waters of the stream were fouled with the war of men and grime of strife. Then was my heart bitter to see the bones of the good earth laid bare with winds where the destroying hands of men had torn the heather and the fern and burnt them to make sacrifice to Melko and to lust of ruin; and the thronging places of the bees that all day hummed among the whins and whortlebushes long ago bearing rich honey down

to Tavrobel – these were now become fosses and [?mounds] of stark
red earth, and nought sang there nor danced but unwholesome airs
and flies of pestilence.

Now the Sun died and behold, I came to that most magic wood
where once the ageless oaks stood firm amid the later growths of beech
and slender trees of birch, but all were fallen beneath the ruthless axes
of unthinking men. Ah me, here was the path beaten with spells,
trodden with musics and enchantment that wound therethrough, and
this way were the Elves wont to ride a-hunting. Many a time there have
I seen them and Gilfanon has been there, and they rode like kings unto
the chase, and the beauty of their faces in the sun was as the new
morning, and the wind in their golden hair like to the glory of bright
flowers shaken at dawn, and the strong music of their voices like the sea
and like trumpets and like the noise of very many viols and of golden
harps unnumbered. And yet again have I seen the people of Tavrobel
beneath the Moon, and they would ride or dance across the valley of
the two rivers where the grey bridge leaps the joining waters; and they
would fare swiftly as clad in dreams, spangled with gems like to the
grey dews amid the grass, and their white robes caught the long
radiance of the Moon . . . . and their spears shivered with
silver flames.

And now sorrow and . . . . . has come upon the Elves, empty is
Tavrobel and all are fled, [?fearing] the enemy that sitteth on
the ruined heath, who is not a league away; whose hands are red with
the blood of Elves and stained with the lives of his own kin, who has
made himself an ally to Melko and the Lord of Hate, who has fought
for the Orcs and Gongs and the unwholesome monsters of the world –
blind, and a fool, and destruction alone is his knowledge. The paths of
the fairies he has made to dusty roads where thirst [?lags wearily] and
no man greeteth another in the way, but passes by in sullenness.

So fade the Elves and it shall come to be that because of the
encompassing waters of this isle and yet more because of their
unquenchable love for it that few shall flee, but as men wax there and
grow fat and yet more blind ever shall they fade more and grow less;
and those of the after days shall scoff, saying Who are the fairies – lies
told to the children by women or foolish men – who are these fairies?
And some few shall answer: Memories faded dim, a wraith of vanishing
loveliness in the trees, a rustle of the grass, a glint of dew, some subtle
intonation of the wind; and others yet fewer shall say . . . . . 'Very small
and delicate are the fairies now, yet we have eyes to see and ears to
hear, and Tavrobel and Kortirion are filled yet with [?this] sweet folk.
Spring knows them and Summer too and in Winter still are they
among us, but in Autumn most of all do they come out, for Autumn is
their season, fallen as they are upon the Autumn of their days. What
shall the dreamers of the earth be like when their winter come.

Hark O my brothers, they shall say, the little trumpets blow; we hear a sound of instruments unimagined small. Like strands of wind, like mystic half-transparencies, Gilfanon Lord of Tavrobel rides out tonight amid his folk, and hunts the elfin deer beneath the paling sky. A music of forgotten feet, a gleam of leaves, a sudden bending of the grass,[11] and wistful voices murmuring on the bridge, and they are gone.

But behold, Tavrobel shall not know its name, and all the land be changed, and even these written words of mine belike will all be lost; and so I lay down the pen, and so of the fairies cease to tell.

Another text that bears on these matters is the prose preface to *Kortirion among the Trees* (1915), which has been given in Part I 25–6, but which I repeat here:

(9)   Now on a time the fairies dwelt in the Lonely Isle after the great wars with Melko and the ruin of Gondolin; and they builded a fair city amidmost of that island, and it was girt with trees. Now this city they called Kortirion, both in memory of their ancient dwelling of Kôr in Valinor, and because this city stood also upon a hill and had a great tower tall and grey that Ingil son of Inwë their lord let raise.

Very beautiful was Kortirion and the fairies loved it, and it became rich in song and poesy and the light of laughter; but on a time the great Faring Forth was made, and the fairies had rekindled once more the Magic Sun of Valinor but for the treason and faint hearts of Men. But so it is that the Magic Sun is dead and the Lonely Isle drawn back unto the confines of the Great Lands, and the fairies are scattered through all the wide unfriendly pathways of the world; and now Men dwell even on this faded isle, and care nought or know nought of its ancient days. Yet still there be some of the Eldar and the Noldoli of old who linger in the island, and their songs are heard about the shores of the land that once was the fairest dwelling of the immortal folk.

And it seems to the fairies and it seems to me who know that town and have often trodden its disfigured ways that autumn and the falling of the leaf is the season of the year when maybe here or there a heart among Men may be open, and an eye perceive how is the world's estate fallen from the laughter and the loveliness of old. Think on Kortirion and be sad – yet is there not hope?

★

At this point we may turn to the history of Eriol himself. My father's early conceptions of the mariner who came to Tol Eressëa are here again no more than allusive outlines in the pages of the little notebook C, and some of this material cannot be usefully reproduced. Perhaps the earliest is a collection of notes headed 'Story of Eriol's Life', which I gave in Vol.

I. 23–4 but with the omission of some features that were not there relevant. I repeat it here, with the addition of the statements previously omitted.

(10)   Eriol's original name was Ottor, but he called himself *Wǽfre* (Old English: 'restless, wandering') and lived a life on the waters. His father was named Eoh (Old English: 'horse'); and Eoh was slain by his brother Beorn, either 'in the siege' or 'in a great battle'. Ottor Wǽfre settled on the island of Heligoland in the North Sea, and wedded a woman named Cwén; they had two sons named Hengest and Horsa 'to avenge Eoh'.

Then sea-longing gripped Ottor Wǽfre (he was 'a son of Eärendel', born under his beam), and after the death of Cwén he left his young children. Hengest and Horsa avenged Eoh and became great chieftains; but Ottor Wǽfre set out to seek, and find, Tol Eressëa (*se uncúpa holm*, 'the unknown island').

In Tol Eressëa he wedded, being made young by *limpë* (here also called by the Old English word *líp*), Naimi (Éadgifu), niece of Vairë, and they had a son named Heorrenda.

It is then said, somewhat inconsequentially (though the matter is in itself of much interest, and recurs nowhere else), that Eriol told the fairies of *Wóden, Þunor, Tíw*, etc. (these being the Old English names of the Germanic gods who in Old Scandinavian form are *Óðinn, Þórr, Týr*), and they identified them with Manweg, Tulkas, and a third whose name is illegible but is not like that of any of the great Valar.

Eriol adopted the name of *Angol*.

Thus it is that through Eriol and his sons the *Engle* (i.e. the English) have the true tradition of the fairies, of whom the *Íras* and the *Wéalas* (the Irish and Welsh) tell garbled things.

Thus a specifically English fairy-lore is born, and one more true than anything to be found in Celtic lands.

The wedding of Eriol in Tol Eressëa is never referred to elsewhere; but his son Heorrenda is mentioned (though not called Eriol's son) in the initial link to *The Fall of Gondolin* (p. 145) as one who 'afterwards' turned a song of Meril's maidens into the language of his people. A little more light will be shed on Heorrenda in the course of this chapter.

Associated with these notes is a title-page and a prologue that breaks off after a few lines:

(11)   The Golden Book of Heorrenda
                        being the book of the
                        Tales of Tavrobel

                        ───────────

                    Heorrenda of Hægwudu

This book have I written using those writings that my father
Wǽfre (whom the Gnomes named after the regions of his home
Angol) did make in his sojourn in the holy isle in the days of the
Elves; and much else have I added of those things which his eyes
saw not afterward; yet are such things not yet to tell. For know

Here then the Golden Book was compiled from Eriol's writings by his
son Heorrenda – in contrast to (5), where it was compiled by someone
unnamed, and in contrast also to the *Epilogue* (8), where Eriol himself
concluded and 'sealed the book'.

As I have said earlier (I.24) *Angol* refers to the ancient homeland
of the 'English' before their migration across the North Sea (for the
etymology of *Angol/Eriol* 'ironcliffs' see I.24, 252).

(12)   There is also a genealogical table accompanying the outline (10)
and altogether agreeing with it. The table is written out in two forms that
are identical save in one point: for Beorn, brother of Eoh, in the one,
there stands in the other *Hasen of Isenóra* (Old English: 'iron shore').
But at the end of the table is introduced the cardinal fact of all these
earliest materials concerning Eriol and Tol Eressëa: Hengest and Horsa,
Eriol's sons by Cwén in Heligoland, and Heorrenda, his son by Naimi in
Tol Eressëa, are bracketed together, and beneath their names is written:

conquered Íeg
('seo unwemmede Íeg')
now called Englaland
and there dwell the Angolcynn or Engle.

Íeg is Old English, 'isle'; *seo unwemmede Íeg* 'the unstained isle'. I
have mentioned before (I.25, footnote) a poem of my father's written at
Étaples in June 1916 and called 'The Lonely Isle', addressed to England:
this poem bears the Old English title *seo Unwemmede Íeg*.

(13)   There follow in the notebook C some jottings that make precise
identifications of places in Tol Eressëa with places in England.

First the name *Kortirion* is explained. The element *Kôr* is derived
from an earlier *Qorǎ*, yet earlier *Guorǎ*; but from *Guorǎ* was also
derived (i.e. in Gnomish) the form *Gwâr*. (This formulation agrees with
that in the Gnomish dictionary, see I.257). Thus *Kôr = Gwâr*,
and *Kortirion = *Gwarmindon* (the asterisk implying a hypothetical,
unrecorded form). The name that was actually used in Gnomish had the
elements reversed, *Mindon-Gwar*. (*Mindon*, like *Tirion*, meant, and
continued always to mean, 'tower'. The meaning of *Kôr/Gwâr* is not
given here, but both in the tale of *The Coming of the Elves* (I.122) and
in the Gnomish dictionary (I.257) the name is explained as referring to
the *roundness* of the hill of Kôr.)

The note continues (using Old English forms): 'In Wíelisc *Caergwâr*, in Englisc *Warwíc*.' Thus the element *War-* in *Warwick* is derived from the same Elvish source as *Kor-* in *Kortirion* and *Gwar* in *Mindon-Gwar*.[12] Lastly, it is said that 'Hengest's capital was Warwick'.

Next, Horsa (Hengest's brother) is associated with *Oxenaford* (Old English: Oxford), which is given the equivalents Q[enya] *Taruktarna* and Gnomish **Taruithorn* (see the Appendix on Names, p. 347).

The third of Eriol's sons, Heorrenda, is said to have had his 'capital' at Great Haywood (the Staffordshire village where my parents lived in 1916–17, see I. 25); and this is given the Qenya equivalents *Tavaros*(*së*) and *Taurossë*, and the Gnomish *Tavrobel* and *Tavrost*; also 'Englisc [i.e. Old English] *Hægwudu se gréata*, *Gréata Hægwudu*'.[13]

These notes conclude with the statement that 'Heorrenda called Kôr or Gwâr "Tûn".' In the context of these conceptions, this is obviously the Old English word *tún*, an enclosed dwelling, from which has developed the modern word *town* and the place-name ending *-ton*. *Tûn* has appeared several times in the *Lost Tales* as a later correction, or alternative to *Kôr*, changes no doubt dating from or anticipating the later situation where the city was *Tûn* and the name *Kôr* was restricted to the hill on which it stood. Later still *Tûn* became *Túna*, and then when the city of the Elves was named *Tirion* the hill became *Túna*, as it is in *The Silmarillion*; by then it had ceased to have any connotation of 'dwelling-place' and had cut free from all connection with its actual origin, as we see it here, in Old English *tún*, Heorrenda's 'town'.

Can all these materials be brought together to form a coherent narrative? I believe that they can (granting that there are certain irreconcilable differences concerning Eriol's life), and would reconstruct it thus:

– The Eldar and the rescued Noldoli departed from the Great Lands and came to Tol Eressëa.

– In Tol Eressëa they built many towns and villages, and in Alalminórë, the central region of the island, Ingil son of Inwë built the town of Koromas, 'the Resting of the Exiles of Kôr' ('Exiles', because they could not return to Valinor); and the great tower of Ingil gave the town its name *Kortirion*. (See I. 16.)

– Ottor Wǽfre came from Heligoland to Tol Eressëa and dwelt in the Cottage of Lost Play in Kortirion; the Elves named him *Eriol* or *Angol* after the 'iron cliffs' of his home.

– After a time, and greatly instructed in the ancient history of Gods, Elves, and Men, Eriol went to visit Gilfanon in the village of Tavrobel, and there he wrote down what he had learnt; there also he at last drank *limpë*.

- In Tol Eressëa Eriol was wedded and had a son named Heorrenda (Half-elven!). (According to (5) Eriol died at Tavrobel, consumed with longing for 'the black cliffs of his shores'; but according to (8), certainly later, he lived to see the Battle of the Heath of the Sky-roof.)

- The Lost Elves of the Great Lands rose against the dominion of the servants of Melko; and the untimely Faring Forth took place, at which time Tol Eressëa was drawn east back across the Ocean and anchored off the coasts of the Great Lands. The western half broke off when Ossë tried to drag the island back, and it became the Isle of Íverin (= Ireland).

- Tol Eressëa was now in the geographical position of England.

- The great battle of Rôs ended in the defeat of the Elves, who retreated into hiding in Tol Eressëa.

- Evil men entered Tol Eressëa, accompanied by Orcs and other hostile beings.

- The Battle of the Heath of the Sky-roof took place not far from Tavrobel, and (according to (8)) was witnessed by Eriol, who completed the Golden Book.

- The Elves faded and became invisible to the eyes of almost all Men.

- The sons of Eriol, Hengest, Horsa, and Heorrenda, conquered the island and it became 'England'. They were not hostile to the Elves, and from them the English have 'the true tradition of the fairies'.

- Kortirion, ancient dwelling of the fairies, came to be known in the tongue of the English as Warwick; Hengest dwelt there, while Horsa dwelt at Taruithorn (Oxford) and Heorrenda at Tavrobel (Great Haywood). (According to (11) Heorrenda completed the Golden Book.)

This reconstruction may not be 'correct' in all its parts: indeed, it may be that any such attempt is artificial, treating all the notes and jottings as of equal weight and all the ideas as strictly contemporaneous and relatable to each other. Nonetheless I believe that it shows rightly in essentials how my father was thinking of ordering the narrative in which the *Lost Tales* were to be set; and I believe also that this was the conception that still underlay the *Tales* as they are extant and have been given in these books.

For convenience later I shall refer to this narrative as 'the *Eriol* story'. Its most remarkable features, in contrast to the later story, are the transformation of Tol Eressëa into England, and the early appearance of the mariner (in relation to the whole history) and his importance.

In fact, my father was exploring (before he decided on a radical transformation of the whole conception) ideas whereby his importance would be greatly increased.

(14)   From very rough jottings it can be made out that Eriol was to be so tormented with home longing that he set sail from Tol Eressëa with his son Heorrenda, against the command of Meril-i-Turinqi (see the passage cited on p. 284 from *The Chaining of Melko*); but his purpose in doing so was also 'to hasten the Faring Forth', which he 'preached' in the lands of the East. Tol Eressëa was drawn back to the confines of the Great Lands, but at once hostile peoples named the *Guiðlin* and the *Brithonin* (and in one of these notes also the *Rúmhoth*, Romans) invaded the island. Eriol died, but his sons Hengest and Horsa conquered the Guiðlin. But because of Eriol's disobedience to the command of Meril, in going back before the time for the Faring Forth was ripe, 'all was cursed'; and the Elves faded before the noise and evil of war. An isolated sentence refers to 'a strange prophecy that a man of good will, yet through longing after the things of Men, may bring the Faring Forth to nought'.

Thus the part of Eriol was to become cardinal in the history of the Elves; but there is no sign that these ideas ever got beyond this exploratory stage.

★

I have said that I think that the reconstruction given above ('the *Eriol* story') is in essentials the conception underlying the framework of the *Lost Tales*. This is both for positive and negative reasons: positive, because he is there still named *Eriol* (see p. 300), and also because Gilfanon, who enters (replacing Ailios) late in the development of the *Tales*, appears also in citation (5) above, which is one of the main contributors to this reconstruction; negative, because there is really nothing to contradict what is much the easiest assumption. There is no explicit statement anywhere in the *Lost Tales* that Eriol came from England. At the beginning (I.13) he is only 'a traveller from far countries'; and the fact that the story he told to Vëannë of his earlier life (pp. 4–7) agrees well with other accounts where his home is explicitly in England does no more than show that the story remained while the geography altered — just as the 'black coasts' of his home survived in later writing to become the western coasts of Britain, whereas the earliest reference to them is the etymology of *Angol* 'iron cliffs' (his own name, = *Eriol*, from the land 'between the seas', Angeln in the Danish peninsula, whence he came: see I.252). There is in fact a very early, rejected, sketch of Eriol's life in which essential features of the same story are outlined — the attack on his father's dwelling (in this case the destruction of Eoh's castle by his brother Beorn, see citation (10)), Eriol's captivity and escape — and in this note it is said that Eriol afterwards 'wandered over the wilds of the Central Lands to the Inland Sea, *Wendelsæ* [Old English, the Mediterranean], and hence to the shores of the Western Sea', whence his father had originally come. The mention in the typescript text of the *Link* to the *Tale of Tinúviel* (p. 6) of wild men out of the Mountains of the East, *which the duke could see from his tower*, seems likewise to imply that at this time Eriol's original home was placed in some 'continental' region.

The only suggestion, so far as I can see, that this view might not be correct is found in an early poem with a complex history, texts of which I give here.

The earliest rough drafts of this poem are extant; the original title was 'The Wanderer's Allegiance', and it is not clear that it was at first conceived as a poem in three parts. My father subsequently wrote in subtitles on these drafts, dividing the poem into three: *Prelude*, *The Inland City*, and *The Sorrowful City*, with (apparently) an overall title *The Sorrowful City*; and added a date, March 16–18, 1916. In the only later copy of the whole poem that is extant the overall title is *The Town of Dreams and the City of Present Sorrow*, with the three parts titled: *Prelude* (Old English *Foresang*), *The Town of Dreams* (Old English *Þæt Slæpende Tún*), and *The City of Present Sorrow* (Old English *Seo Wépende Burg*). This text gives the dates 'March 1916, Oxford and Warwick; rewritten Birmingham November 1916'. 'The Town of Dreams' is Warwick, on the River Avon, and 'The City of Present Sorrow' is Oxford, on the Thames, during the First War; there is no evident association of any kind with Eriol or the *Lost Tales*.

Prelude

In unknown days my fathers' sires
Came, and from son to son took root
Among the orchards and the river-meads
And the long grasses of the fragrant plain:
Many a summer saw they kindle yellow fires
Of iris in the bowing reeds,
And many a sea of blossom turn to golden fruit
In walléd gardens of the great champain.

★

There daffodils among the ordered trees
Did nod in spring, and men laughed deep and long
Singing as they laboured happy lays
And lighting even with a drinking-song.
There sleep came easy for the drone of bees
Thronging about cottage gardens heaped with flowers;
In love of sunlit goodliness of days
There richly flowed their lives in settled hours –
But that was long ago,

And now no more they sing, nor reap, nor sow,
And I perforce in many a town about this isle
Unsettled wanderer have dwelt awhile.

★

The Town of Dreams

Here many days once gently past me crept
In this dear town of old forgetfulness;
Here all entwined in dreams once long I slept
And heard no echo of the world's distress
Come through the rustle of the elms' rich leaves,
While Avon gurgling over shallows wove
Unending melody, and morns and eves
Slipped down her waters till the Autumn came,
(Like the gold leaves that drip and flutter then,
Till the dark river gleams with jets of flame
That slowly float far down beyond our ken.)

★

For here the castle and the mighty tower,
More lofty than the tiered elms,
More grey than long November rain,
Sleep, and nor sunlit moment nor triumphal hour,
Nor passing of the seasons or the Sun
Wakes their old lords too long in slumber lain.

★

No watchfulness disturbs their splendid dream,
Though laughing radiance dance down the stream;
And be they clad in snow or lashed by windy rains,
Or may March whirl the dust about the winding lanes,
The Elm robe and disrobe her of a million leaves
Like moments clustered in a crowded year,
Still their old heart unmoved nor weeps nor grieves,
Uncomprehending of this evil tide,
Today's great sadness, or Tomorrow's fear:
Faint echoes fade within their drowsy halls
Like ghosts; the daylight creeps across their walls.

★

The City of Present Sorrow

There is a city that far distant lies
And a vale outcarven in forgotten days –
There wider was the grass, and lofty elms more rare;
The river-sense was heavy in the lowland air.
There many willows changed the aspect of the earth and skies
Where feeding brooks wound in by sluggish ways,
And down the margin of the sailing Thames
Around his broad old bosom their old stems
Were bowed, and subtle shades lay on his streams
Where their grey leaves adroop o'er silver pools
Did knit a coverlet like shimmering jewels
Of blue and misty green and filtering gleams.

★

O agéd city of an all too brief sojourn,
I see thy clustered windows each one burn
With lamps and candles of departed men.
The misty stars thy crown, the night thy dress,
Most peerless-magical thou dost possess
My heart, and old days come to life again;
Old mornings dawn, or darkened evenings bring
The same old twilight noises from the town.
Thou hast the very core of longing and delight,
To thee my spirit dances oft in sleep
Along thy great grey streets, or down
A little lamplit alley-way at night –
Thinking no more of other cities it has known,
Forgetting for a while the tree-girt keep,
And town of dreams, where men no longer sing.
For thy heart knows, and thou shedst many tears
For all the sorrow of these evil years.
Thy thousand pinnacles and fretted spires
Are lit with echoes and the lambent fires
Of many companies of bells that ring
Rousing pale visions of majestic days
The windy years have strewn down distant ways;
And in thy halls still doth thy spirit sing
Songs of old memory amid thy present tears,
Or hope of days to come half-sad with many fears.
Lo! though along thy paths no laughter runs
While war untimely takes thy many sons,
No tide of evil can thy glory drown
Robed in sad majesty, the stars thy crown.

★

In addition, there are two texts in which a part of *The City of Present Sorrow* is treated as a separate entity. This begins with 'O aged city of an all too brief sojourn', and is briefer: after the line 'Thinking no more of other cities it has known' it ends:

> Forgetting for a while that all men weep
> It strays there happy and to thee it sings
> 'No tide of evil can thy glory drown,
> Robed in sad majesty, the stars thy crown!'

This was first called *The Sorrowful City*, but the title was then changed to *Wínsele wéste, windge reste réte berofene* (*Beowulf* lines 2456–7, very slightly adapted: 'the hall of feasting empty, the resting places swept by the wind, robbed of laughter').

There are also two manuscripts in which *The Town of Dreams* is treated as a separate poem, with a subtitle *An old town revisited*; in one of these the primary title was later changed to *The Town of Dead Days*.

Lastly, there is a poem in two parts called *The Song of Eriol*. This is found in three manuscripts, the later ones incorporating minor changes made to the predecessor (but the third has only the second part of the poem).

The Song of Eriol

Eriol made a song in the Room of the Tale-fire telling how his feet were set to wandering, so that in the end he found the Lonely Isle and that fairest town Kortirion.

I

> In unknown days my fathers' sires
> Came, and from son to son took root
> Among the orchards and the river-meads
> And the long grasses of the fragrant plain:
>
> Many a summer saw they kindle yellow fires
> Of flaglilies among the bowing reeds,
> And many a sea of blossom turn to golden fruit
> In walléd gardens of the great champain.
>
> There daffodils among the ordered trees
> Did nod in spring, and men laughed deep and long
> Singing as they laboured happy lays
> And lighting even with a drinking-song.

There sleep came easy for the drone of bees
Thronging about cottage gardens heaped with flowers;
In love of sunlit goodliness of days
There richly flowed their lives in settled hours –
    But that was long ago,
  And now no more they sing, nor reap, nor sow;
  And I perforce in many a town about this isle
  Unsettled wanderer have dwelt awhile.

2

Wars of great kings and clash of armouries,
Whose swords no man could tell, whose spears
Were numerous as a wheatfield's ears,
Rolled over all the Great Lands; and the Seas

Were loud with navies; their devouring fires
Behind the armies burned both fields and towns;
And sacked and crumbled or to flaming pyres
Were cities made, where treasuries and crowns,

Kings and their folk, their wives and tender maids
Were all consumed. Now silent are those courts,
Ruined the towers, whose old shape slowly fades,
And no feet pass beneath their broken ports.

★

There fell my father on a field of blood,
And in a hungry siege my mother died,
And I, a captive, heard the great seas' flood
Calling and calling, that my spirit cried

For the dark western shores whence long ago had come
Sires of my mother, and I broke my bonds,
Faring o'er wasted valleys and dead lands
Until my feet were moistened by the western sea,
Until my ears were deafened by the hum,
The splash, and roaring of the western sea –
    But that was long ago
  And now the dark bays and unknown waves I know,
  The twilight capes, the misty archipelago,
  And all the perilous sounds and salt wastes 'tween this isle
  Of magic and the coasts I knew awhile.

★

One of the manuscripts of *The Song of Eriol* bears a later note: 'Easington 1917–18' (Easington on the estuary of the Humber, see Humphrey Carpenter, *Biography*, p. 97). It may be that the second part of *The Song of Eriol* was written at Easington and added to the first part (formerly the *Prelude*) already in existence.

Little can be derived from this poem of a strictly narrative nature, save the lineaments of the same tale: Eriol's father fell 'on a field of blood', when 'wars of great kings . . . rolled over all the Great Lands', and his mother died 'in a hungry siege' (the same phrase is used in the *Link* to the *Tale of Tinúviel*, pp. 5–6); he himself was made a captive, but escaped, and came at last to the shores of the Western Sea (whence his mother's people had come).

The fact that the first part of *The Song of Eriol* is also found as the Prelude to a poem of which the subjects are Warwick and Oxford might make one suspect that the castle with a great tower overhanging a river in the story told by Eriol to Vëannë was once again Warwick. But I do not think that this is so. There remains in any case the objection that it would be difficult to accommodate the attack on it by men out of the Mountains of the East which the duke could see from his tower; but also I think it is plain that the original tripartite poem had been dissevered, and the *Prelude* given a new bearing: my father's 'fathers' sires' became Eriol's 'fathers' sires'. At the same time, certain powerful images were at once dominant and fluid, and the great tower of Eriol's home was indeed to become the tower of Kortirion or Warwick, when (as will be seen shortly) the structure of the story of the mariner was radically changed. And nothing could show more clearly than does the evolution of this poem the complex root from which the story rose.

Humphrey Carpenter, writing in his *Biography* of my father's life after he returned to Oxford in 1925, says (p. 169):

He made numerous revisions and recastings of the principal stories in the cycle, deciding to abandon the original sea-voyager 'Eriol' to whom the stories were told, and instead renaming him 'Ælfwine' or 'elf-friend'.

That *Eriol* was (for a time) displaced by *Ælfwine* is certain. But while it may well be that at the time of the texts now to be considered the name *Eriol* had actually been rejected, in the first version of 'The Silmarillion' proper, written in 1926, *Eriol* reappears, while in the earliest *Annals of Valinor*, written in the 1930s, it is said that they were translated in Tol Eressëa 'by Eriol of Leithien, that is Ælfwine of the Angelcynn'. On the other hand, at this earlier period it seems entirely justifiable on the evidence to treat the two names as indicative of different narrative projections – 'the *Eriol* story' and 'the *Ælfwine* story'.

'Ælfwine', then, is associated with a new conception, *subsequent to* the writing of the *Lost Tales*. The mariner is Ælfwine, not Eriol, in the second 'Scheme' for the *Tales*, which I have called 'an unrealised project for the revision of the whole work' (see I.234). The essential difference may be made clear now, before citing the difficult evidence: *Tol Eressëa is now in no way identified with England*, and the story of the drawing back of the Lonely Island across the sea has been abandoned. England is indeed still at the heart of this later conception, and is named *Luthany*.[14] The mariner, Ælfwine, is an Englishman sailing westward from the coast of Britain; and his role is diminished. For whereas in the writings studied thus far he comes to Tol Eressëa *before* the dénouement and disaster of the Faring Forth, and either he himself or his descendants witness the devastation of Tol Eressëa by the invasion of Men and their evil allies (in one line of development he was even to be responsible for it, p. 294), in the later narrative outlines he does not arrive until all the grievous history is done. His part is only to learn and to record.[15]

I turn now to a number of short and very oblique passages, written on separate slips, but found together and clearly dating from much the same time.

(15) Ælfwine of England dwelt in the South-west; he was of the kin of Ing, King of Luthany. His mother and father were slain by the sea-pirates and he was made captive.

He had always loved the fairies: his father had told him many things (of the tradition of Ing). He escapes. He beats about the northern and western waters. He meets the Ancient Mariner – and seeks for Tol Eressëa (*seo unwemmede íeg*), whither most of the unfaded Elves have retired from the noise, war, and clamour of Men.

The Elves greet him, and the more so when they learn of him who he is. They call him *Lúthien* the man of Luthany. He finds his own tongue, the ancient English tongue, is spoken in the isle.

The 'Ancient Mariner' has appeared in the story that Eriol told to Vëannë (pp. 5, 7), and much more will be told of him subsequently.

(16) Ælfwine of Englaland, [*added later*: driven by the Normans,] arrives in Tol Eressëa, whither most of the fading Elves have withdrawn from the world, and there fade now no more.

Description of the harbour of the southern shore. The fairies greet him well hearing he is from Englaland. He is surprised to hear them speak the speech of Ælfred of Wessex, though to one another they spoke a sweet and unknown tongue.

The Elves name him Lúthien for he is come from Luthany, as they call it ('friend' and 'friendship'). Eldaros or Ælfhâm. He is sped to Rôs their capital. There he finds the Cottage of Lost Play, and Lindo and Vairë.

He tells who he is and whence, and why he has long sought for the isle (by reason of traditions in the kin of Ing), and he begs the Elves to come back to Englaland.

Here begins (as an explanation of why they cannot) the series of stories called the Book of Lost Tales.

In this passage (16) Ælfwine becomes more firmly rooted in English history: he is apparently a man of eleventh-century Wessex – but as in (15) he is of 'the kin of Ing'. The capital of the Elves of Tol Eressëa is not Kortirion but Rôs, a name now used in a quite different application from that in citation (5), where it was a promontory of the Great Lands.

I have been unable to find any trace of the process whereby the name *Lúthien* came to be so differently applied afterwards (*Lúthien Tinúviel*). Another note of this period explains the name quite otherwise: 'Lúthien or Lúsion was son of Telumaith (Telumektar). Ælfwine loved the sign of Orion, and made the sign, hence the fairies called him Lúthien (Wanderer).' There is no other mention of Ælfwine's peculiar association with Orion nor of this interpretation of the name Lúthien; and this seems to be a development that my father did not pursue.

It is convenient to give here the opening passage from the second Scheme for the *Lost Tales*, referred to above; this plainly belongs to the same time as the rest of these 'Ælfwine' notes, when the *Tales* had been written so far as they ever went within their first framework.

(17)   Ælfwine awakens upon a sandy beach. He listens to the sea, which is far out. The tide is low and has left him.

Ælfwine meets the Elves of Rôs; finds they speak the speech of the English, beside their own sweet tongue. Why they do so – the dwelling of Elves in Luthany and their faring thence and back. They clothe him and feed him, and he sets forth to walk along the island's flowery ways.

The scheme goes on to say that on a summer evening Ælfwine came to Kortirion, and thus differs from (16), where he goes to 'Rôs their capital', in which he finds the Cottage of Lost Play. The name Rôs seems to be used here in yet another sense – possibly a name for Tol Eressëa.

(18)   He is sped to Ælfhâm (Elfhome) Eldos where Lindo and Vairë tell him many things: of the making and ancient fashion of the world: of the Gods: of the Elves of Valinor: of Lost Elves and Men: of the Travail of the Gnomes: of Eärendel: of the Faring Forth and the Loss of Valinor: of the disaster of the Faring Forth and the war with evil Men. The retreat to Luthany where Ingwë was king.

Of the home-thirst of the Elves and how the greater number sought back to Valinor. The loss of Elwing. How a new home was made by the Solosimpi and others in Tol Eressëa. How the Elves continually sadly leave the world and fare thither.

For the interpretation of this passage it is essential to realise (the key indeed to the understanding of this projected history) that 'the Faring Forth' does *not* here refer to the Faring Forth in the sense in which it has been used hitherto – that from Tol Eressëa for the Rekindling of the Magic Sun, which ended in ruin, but to the March of the Elves of Kôr and the 'Loss of Valinor' that the March incurred (see pp. 253, 257, 280). It is not indeed clear why it is here called a 'disaster': but this is evidently to be associated with 'the war with evil Men', and war between Elves and Men at the time of the March from Kôr is referred to in citations (1) and (3).

In 'the *Eriol* story' it is explicit that after the March from Kôr the Elves departed from the Great Lands to Tol Eressëa; here on the other hand 'the war with evil Men' is followed by 'the retreat to Luthany where Ingwë was king'. The (partial) departure to Tol Eressëa is from Luthany; the loss of Elwing seems to take place on one of these voyages. As will be seen, the 'Faring Forth' of 'the *Eriol* story' has disappeared as an event of Elvish history, and is only mentioned as a prophecy and a hope.

Schematically the essential divergence of the two narrative structures can be shown thus:

(*Eriol* story)	(*Ælfwine* story)
March of the Elves of Kôr to the Great Lands	March of the Elves of Kôr to the Great Lands (called 'the Faring Forth')
War with Men in the Great Lands	War with Men in the Great Lands
Retreat of the Elves to Tol Eressëa (loss of Elwing)	Retreat of the Elves to Luthany (> England) ruled by Ingwë
	Departure of many Elves to Tol Eressëa (loss of Elwing)
Eriol sails from the East (North Sea region) to Tol Eressëa	Ælfwine sails from England to Tol Eressëa
The Faring Forth, drawing of Tol Eressëa to the Great Lands; ultimately Tol Eressëa > England	

This is of course by no means a full statement of the *Ælfwine* story, and is merely set out to indicate the radical difference of structure. Lacking from it is the history of Luthany, which emerges from the passages that now follow.

(19)   *Luthany* means 'friendship', *Lúthien* 'friend'. Luthany the only land where Men and Elves once dwelt an age in peace and love.

How for a while after the coming of the sons of Ing the Elves throve again and ceased to fare away to Tol Eressëa.

How Old English became the sole mortal language which an Elf will speak to a mortal that knows no Elfin.

(20)   Ælfwine of England (whose father and mother were slain by the fierce Men of the Sea who knew not the Elves) was a great lover of the Elves, especially of the shoreland Elves that lingered in the land. He seeks for Tol Eressëa whither the fairies are said to have retired.

He reaches it. The fairies call him Lúthien. He learns of the making of the world, ... of Gods and Elves, of Elves and Men, down to the departure to Tol Eressëa.

How the Faring Forth came to nought, and the fairies took refuge in Albion or Luthany (the Isle of Friendship).

Seven invasions.

Of the coming of Men to Luthany, how each race quarrelled, and the fairies faded, until [?the most] set sail, after the coming of the Rúmhoth, for the West. Why the Men of the seventh invasion, the Ingwaiwar, are more friendly.

Ingwë and Eärendel who dwelt in Luthany before it was an isle and was [*sic*] driven east by Ossë to found the Ingwaiwar.

(21)   All the descendants of Ing were well disposed to Elves; hence the remaining Elves of Luthany spoke to [?them] in the ancient tongue of the English, and since some have fared . . . . . to Tol Eressëa that tongue is there understood, and all who wish to speak to the Elves, if they know not and have no means of learning Elfin speeches, must converse in the ancient tongue of the English.

In (20) the term 'Faring Forth' must again be used as it is in (18), of the March from Kôr. There it was called a 'disaster' (see p. 303), and here it is said that it 'came to nought': it must be admitted that it is hard to see how that can be said, if it led to the binding of Melko and the release of the enslaved Noldoli (see (1) and (3)).

Also in (20) is the first appearance of the idea of the Seven Invasions of Luthany. One of these was that of the Rúmhoth (mentioned also in (14)) or Romans; and the seventh was that of the Ingwaiwar, who were not hostile to the Elves.

Here something must be said of the name *Ing* (*Ingwë, Ingwaiar*) in these passages. As with the introduction of Hengest and Horsa, the association of the mythology with ancient English legend is manifest. But it would serve no purpose, I believe, to enter here into the obscure and speculative scholarship of English and Scandinavian origins: the

Roman writers' term *Inguaeones* for the Baltic maritime peoples from whom the English came; the name *Ingwine* (interpretable either as *Ing-wine* 'the friends of Ing' or as containing the same *Ingw-* seen in *Inguaeones*); or the mysterious personage *Ing* who appears in the Old English *Runic Poem*:

> Ing wæs ærest   mid East-Denum
> gesewen secgum   oþhe siþþan east
> ofer wæg gewat;   wæn æfter ran

– which may be translated: 'Ing was first seen by men among the East Danes, until he departed eastwards over the waves; his car sped after him.' It would serve no purpose, because although the connection of my father's *Ing*, *Ingwë* with the shadowy *Ing* (*Ingw-*) of northern historical legend is certain and indeed obvious he seems to have been intending no more than an *association* of his mythology with known traditions (though the words of the *Runic Poem* were clearly influential). The matter is made particularly obscure by the fact that in these notes the names *Ing* and *Ingwë* intertwine with each other, but are never expressly differentiated or identified.

Thus Ælfwine was 'of the kin of Ing, King of Luthany' (15, 16), but the Elves retreated 'to Luthany where Ingwë was king' (18). The Elves of Luthany throve again 'after the coming of the sons of Ing' (19), and the Ingwaiwar, seventh of the invaders of Luthany, were more friendly to the Elves (20), while Ingwë 'founded' the Ingwaiwar (20). This name is certainly to be equated with Inguaeones (see above), and the invasion of the Ingwaiwar (or 'sons of Ing') equally certainly represents the 'Anglo-Saxon' invasion of Britain. Can *Ing*, *Ingwë* be equated? So far as this present material is concerned, I hardly see how they can not be. Whether this ancestor-founder is to be equated with *Inwë* (whose son was *Ingil*) of the *Lost Tales* is another question. It is hard to believe that there is no connection (especially since *Inwë* in *The Cottage of Lost Play* is emended from *Ing*, I.22), yet it is equally difficult to see what that connection could be, since Inwë of the *Lost Tales* is an Elda of Kôr (Ingwë Lord of the Vanyar in *The Silmarillion*) while Ing(wë) of 'the *Ælfwine* story' is a Man, the King of Luthany and Ælfwine's ancestor. (In outlines for *Gilfanon's Tale* it is said that Ing King of Luthany was descended from Ermon, or from Ermon and Elmir (the first Men, I.236–7).)

The following outlines tell some more concerning Ing(wë) and the Ingwaiwar:

(22) How Ing sailed away at eld [i.e. in old age] into the twilight, and Men say he came to the Gods, but he dwells on Tol Eressëa, and will guide the fairies one day back to Luthany when the Faring Forth takes place.*

---

* The term 'Faring Forth' is used here in a prophetic sense, not as it is in (18) and (20).

How he prophesied that his kin should fare back again and possess Luthany until the days of the coming of the Elves.

How the land of Luthany was seven times invaded by Men, until at the seventh the children of the children of Ing came back to their own.

How at each new war and invasion the Elves faded, and each loved the Elves less, until the Rúmhoth came – and they did not even believe they existed, and the Elves all fled, so that save for a few the isle was empty of the Elves for three hundred years.

(23)   How Ingwë drank *limpë* at the hands of the Elves and reigned ages in Luthany.

How Eärendel came to Luthany to find the Elves gone.

How Ingwë aided him, but was not suffered to go with him. Eärendel blessed all his progeny as the mightiest sea-rovers of the world.[16]

How Ossë made war upon Ingwë because of Eärendel, and Ing longing for the Elves set sail, and all were wrecked after being driven far east.

How Ing the immortal came among the Dani OroDáni Urdainoth East Danes.

How he became the half-divine king of the Ingwaiwar, and taught them many things of Elves and Gods, so that some true knowledge of the Gods and Elves lingered in that folk alone.

Part of another outline that does not belong with the foregoing passages but covers the same part of the narrative as (23) may be given here:

(24)   Eärendel takes refuge with [Ingwë] from the wrath of Ossë, and gives him a draught of *limpë* (enough to assure immortality). He gives him news of the Elves and the dwelling on Tol Eressëa.

Ingwë and a host of his folk set sail to find Tol Eressëa, but Ossë blows them back east. They are utterly wrecked. Only Ingwë rescued on a raft. He becomes king of the Angali, Euti, Saksani, and Firisandi,* who adopt the title of Ingwaiwar. He teaches them much magic and first sets men's hearts to seafaring westward. . . . . .

After a great [?age of rule] Ingwë sets sail in a little boat and is heard of no more.

It is clear that the intrusion of Luthany, and Ing(wë), into the conception has caused a movement in the story of Eärendel: whereas in the older version he went to Tol Eressëa after the departure of the Eldar and Noldoli from the Great Lands (pp. 253, 255), now he goes to

* Angles, Saxons, Jutes, and Frisians.

Luthany; and the idea of Ossë's enmity towards Eärendel (pp. 254, 263) is retained but brought into association with the origin of the Ingwaiwar.

It is clear that the narrative structure is:

- Ing(wë) King of Luthany.
- Eärendel seeks refuge with him (after [many of] the Elves have departed to Tol Eressëa).
- Ing(wë) seeks Tol Eressëa but is driven into the East.
- Seven invasions of Luthany.
- The people of Ing(wë) are the Ingwaiwar, and they 'come back to their own' when they invade Luthany from across the North Sea.

(25)   Luthany was where the tribes first embarked in the Lonely Isle for Valinor, and whence they landed for the Faring Forth,* whence [also] many sailed with Elwing to find Tol Eressëa.

That Luthany was where the Elves, at the end of the great journey from Palisor, embarked on the Lonely Isle for the Ferrying to Valinor, is probably to be connected with the statement in (20) that 'Ingwë and Eärendel dwelt in Luthany before it was an isle'.

(26)   There are other references to the channel separating Luthany from the Great Lands: in rough jottings in notebook C there is mention of an isthmus being cut by the Elves, 'fearing Men now that Ingwë has gone', and 'to the white cliffs where the silver spades of the Teleri worked'; also in the next citation.

(27)   The Elves tell Ælfwine of the ancient manner of Luthany, of Kortirion or Gwarthyryn (Caer Gwâr),[17] of Tavrobel.
How the fairies dwelt there a hundred ages before Men had the skill to build boats to cross the channel – so that magic lingers yet mightily in its woods and hills.
How they renamed many a place in Tol Eressëa after their home in Luthany. Of the Second Faring Forth and the fairies' hope to reign in Luthany and replant there the magic trees – and it depends most on the temper of the Men of Luthany (since they first must come there) whether all goes well.

Notable here is the reference to 'the Second Faring Forth', which strongly supports my interpretation of the expression 'Faring Forth' in (18), (20), and (25); but the prophecy or hope of the Elves concerning

* In the sense of the March of the Elves from Kôr, as in (18) and (20).

the Faring Forth has been greatly changed from its nature in citation (6):
here, the Trees are to be replanted in Luthany.

(28)   How Ælfwine lands in Tol Eressëa and it seems to him like his own
       land made . . . . clad in the beauty of a happy dream. How the
       folk comprehended [his speech] and learn whence he is come by
       the favour of Ulmo. How he is sped to Kortirion.

With these two passages it is interesting to compare (9), the prose preface
to *Kortirion among the Trees*, according to which Kortirion was a city
built by the Elves in Tol Eressëa; and when Tol Eressëa was brought
across the sea, becoming England, Kortirion was renamed in the tongue
of the English *Warwick* (13). In the new story, Kortirion is likewise an
ancient dwelling of the Elves, but with the change in the fundamental
conception it is in Luthany; and the Kortirion to which Ælfwine comes
in Tol Eressëa is the second of the name (being called 'after their home in
Luthany'). There has thus been a very curious transference, which may
be rendered schematically thus:

(I)   Kortirion, Elvish dwelling in Tol Eressëa.
       Tol Eressëa ——→ England.
       Kortirion = Warwick.

(II)   Kortirion, Elvish dwelling in Luthany (> England).
       Elves ——→ Tol Eressëa.
       Kortirion (2) in Tol Eressëa named after Kortirion (1)
       in Luthany.

On the basis of the foregoing passages, (15) to (28), we may attempt to
construct a narrative taking account of all the essential features:

–   March of the Elves of Kôr (called 'the Faring Forth', or (by implica-
    tion in 27) 'the First Faring Forth') into the Great Lands, landing in
    Luthany (25), and the Loss of Valinor (18).
–   War with evil Men in the Great Lands (18).
–   The Elves retreated to Luthany (not yet an island) where Ing(wë)
    was king (18, 20).
–   Many [but by no means all] of the Elves of Luthany sought back west
    over the sea and settled in Tol Eressëa; but Elwing was lost (18, 25).
–   Places in Tol Eressëa were named after places in Luthany (27).
–   Eärendel came to Luthany, taking refuge with Ing(wë) from the
    hostility of Ossë (20, 23, 24).
–   Eärendel gave Ing(wë) *limpë* to drink (24), *or* Ing(wë) received
    limpë from the Elves before Eärendel came (23).

- Eärendel blessed the progeny of Ing(wë) before his departure (23).

- Ossë's hostility to Eärendel pursued Ing(wë) also (23, 24).

- Ing(wë) set sail (with many of his people, 24) to find Tol Eressëa (23, 24).

- Ing(wë)'s voyage, through the enmity of Ossë, ended in shipwreck, but Ing(wë) survived, and far to the East [i.e. after being driven across the North Sea] he became King of the Ingwaiwar the ancestors of the Anglo-Saxon invaders of Britain (23, 24).

- Ing(wë) instructed the Ingwaiwar in true knowledge of the Gods and Elves (23) and turned their hearts to seafaring westwards (24). He prophesied that his kin should one day return again to Luthany (22).

- Ing(wë) at length departed in a boat (22, 24), and was heard of no more (24), or came to Tol Eressëa (22).

- After Ing(wë)'s departure from Luthany a channel was made so that Luthany became an isle (26); but Men crossed the channel in boats (27).

- Seven successive invasions took place, including that of the Rúmhoth or Romans, and at each new war more of the remaining Elves of Luthany fled over the sea (20, 22).

- The seventh invasion, that of the Ingwaiwar, was however not hostile to the Elves (20, 21); and these invaders were 'coming back to their own' (22), since they were the people of Ing(wë).

- The Elves of Luthany (now England) throve again and ceased to leave Luthany for Tol Eressëa (19), and they spoke to the Ingwaiwar in their own language, Old English (21).

- Ælfwine was an Englishman of the Anglo-Saxon period, a descendant of Ing(wë), who had derived a knowledge of and love of the Elves from the tradition of his family (15, 16).

- Ælfwine came to Tol Eressëa, found that Old English was spoken there, and was called by the Elves Lúthien 'friend', the Man of Luthany (the Isle of Friendship) (15, 16, 19).

I claim no more for this than that it seems to me to be the only way in which these *disjecta membra* can be set together into a comprehensive narrative scheme. It must be admitted even so that it requires some forcing of the evidence to secure apparent agreement. For example, there seem to be different views of the relation of the Ingwaiwar to Ing(wë): they are 'the sons of Ing' (19), 'his kin' (22), 'the children of the children of Ing' (22), yet he seems to have become the king and teacher of North Sea peoples who had no connection with Luthany or the Elves (23, 24). (Over whom did he rule when the Elves first retreated to Luthany (18, 23)?) Again, it is very difficult to fit the 'hundred ages' during which the

Elves dwelt in Luthany before the invasions of Men began (27) to the rest of the scheme. Doubtless in these jottings my father was thinking with his pen, exploring independent narrative paths; one gets the impression of a ferment of ideas and possibilities rapidly displacing one another, from which no one stable narrative core can be extracted. A complete 'solution' is therefore in all probability an unreal aim, and this reconstruction no doubt as artificial as that attempted earlier for 'the *Eriol* story' (see p. 293). But here as there I believe that this outline shows as well as can be the direction of my father's thought at that time.

There is very little to indicate the further course of 'the *Ælfwine* story' after his sojourn in Tol Eressëa (as I have remarked, p. 301, the part of the mariner is only to learn and record tales out of the past); and virtually all that can be learned from these notes is found on a slip that reads:

(29)   How Ælfwine drank of *limpë* but thirsted for his home, and went back to Luthany; and thirsted then unquenchably for the Elves, and went back to Tavrobel the Old and dwelt in the House of the Hundred Chimneys (where grows still the child of the child of the Pine of Belawryn) and wrote the Golden Book.

Associated with this is a title-page:

(30)   The Book of Lost Tales
and the History of the Elves of Luthany
[?being]
The Golden Book of Tavrobel
the same that Ælfwine wrote and laid in the House of a Hundred
Chimneys at Tavrobel, where it lieth still to read for such as may.

These are very curious. Tavrobel the Old must be the original Tavrobel in Luthany (after which Tavrobel in Tol Eressëa was named, just as Kortirion in Tol Eressëa was named after Kortirion = Warwick in Luthany); and the House of the Hundred Chimneys (as also the Pine of Belawryn, on which see p. 281 and note 4) was to be displaced from Tol Eressëa to Luthany. Presumably my father intended to rewrite those passages in the 'framework' of the *Lost Tales* where the House of a Hundred Chimneys in Tavrobel is referred to; unless there was to be another House of a Hundred Chimneys in Tavrobel the New in Tol Eressëa.

Lastly, an interesting entry in the Qenya dictionary may be mentioned here: *Parma Kuluinen* 'the Golden Book – the collected book of legends, especially of Ing and Eärendel'.

★

In the event, of all these projections my father only developed the story of Ælfwine's youth and his voyage to Tol Eressëa to a full and polished form, and to this work I now turn; but first it is convenient to collect the passages previously considered that bear on it.

In the opening *Link* to the *Tale of Tinúviel* Eriol said that 'many years agone', when he was a child, his home was 'in an old town of Men girt with a wall now crumbled and broken, and a river ran thereby over which a castle with a great tower hung'.

My father came of a coastward folk, and the love of the sea that I had never seen was in my bones, and my father whetted my desire, for he told me tales that his father had told him before. Now my mother died in a cruel and hungry siege of that old town, and my father was slain in bitter fight about the walls, and in the end I Eriol escaped to the shoreland of the Western Sea.

Eriol told then of

his wanderings about the western havens, . . . of how he was wrecked upon far western islands until at last upon one lonely one he came upon an ancient sailor who gave him shelter, and over a fire within his lonely cabin told him strange tales of things beyond the Western Seas, of the Magic Isles and that most lonely one that lay beyond. . . .

'Ever after,' said Eriol, 'did I sail more curiously about the western isles seeking more stories of the kind, and thus it is indeed that after many great voyages I came myself by the blessing of the Gods to Tol Eressëa in the end . . .'

In the typescript version of this *Link* it is further told that in the town where Eriol's parents lived and died

there dwelt a mighty duke, and did he gaze from the topmost battlements never might he see the bounds of his wide domain, save where far to east the blue shapes of the great mountains lay – yet was that tower held the most lofty that stood in the lands of Men.

The siege and sack of the town were the work of 'the wild men from the Mountains of the East'.

At the end of the typescript version the boy Ausir assured Eriol that 'that ancient mariner beside the lonely sea was none other than Ulmo's self, who appeareth not seldom thus to those voyagers whom he loves'; but Eriol did not believe him.

I have given above (pp. 294–5) reasons for thinking that in 'the *Eriol* story' this tale of his youth was not set in England.

Turning to the passages concerned with the later, *Ælfwine* story, we learn from (15) that Ælfwine dwelt in the South-west of England and that his mother and father were slain by 'the sea-pirates', and from (20) that they were slain by 'the fierce Men of the Sea'; from (16) that he was 'driven by the Normans'. In (15) there is a mention of his meeting with 'the Ancient Mariner' during his voyages. In (16) he comes to 'the harbour of the southern shore' of Tol Eressëa; and in (17) he 'awakens upon a sandy beach' at low tide.

I come now to the narrative that finally emerged. It will be observed, perhaps with relief, that Ing, Ingwë, and the Ingwaiwar have totally disappeared.

ÆLFWINE OF ENGLAND

There are three versions of this short work. One is a plot-outline of less than 500 words, which for convenience of reference I shall call *Ælfwine* A; but the second is a much more substantial narrative bearing the title *Ælfwine of England*. This was written in 1920 or later: demonstrably not earlier, for my father used for it scraps of paper pinned together, and some of these are letters to him, all dated in February 1920.[18] The third text no doubt began as a fair copy in ink of the second, to which it is indeed very close at first, but became as it proceeded a complete rewriting at several points, with the introduction of much new matter, and it was further emended after it had been completed. It bears no title in the manuscript, but must obviously be called *Ælfwine of England* likewise.

For convenience I shall refer to the first fully-written version as *Ælfwine I* and to its rewriting as *Ælfwine II*. The relation of *Ælfwine A* to these is hard to determine, since it agrees in some respects with the one and in some with the other. It is obvious that my father had *Ælfwine I* in front of him when he wrote *Ælfwine II*, but it seems likely that he drew on *Ælfwine A* at the same time.

I give here the full text of *Ælfwine II* in its final form, with all noteworthy emendations and all important differences from the other texts in the notes (differences in names, and changes to names, are listed separately).

There was a land called England, and it was an island of the West, and before it was broken in the warfare of the Gods it was westernmost of all the Northern lands, and looked upon the Great Sea that Men of old called Garsecg;[19] but that part that was broken was called Ireland and many names besides, and its dwellers come not into these tales.

All that land the Elves named Lúthien[20] and do so yet. In Lúthien alone dwelt still the most part of the Fading Companies, the Holy Fairies that have not yet sailed away from the world, beyond the horizon of Men's knowledge, to the Lonely Island, or even to the Hill of Tûn[21] upon the Bay of Faëry that washes the western shores of the kingdom of the Gods. Therefore is Lúthien even yet a holy land, and a magic that is not otherwise lingers still in many places of that isle.

Now amidmost of that island is there still a town that is aged among Men, but its age among the Elves is greater far; and, for this is a book of the Lost Tales of Elfinesse, it shall be named in their tongue Kortirion, which the Gnomes call Mindon Gwar.[22] Upon the hill of Gwar dwelt in the days of the English a man and his name was Déor, and he came thither from afar, from the south of the island and from the forests and from the enchanted West, where albeit he was of the English folk he had long time wandered. Now the Prince of Gwar was in those days a lover of songs and no enemy of the Elves, and they lingered yet most of all the isle in those regions about Kortirion (which places they called Alalminórë, the Land of Elms), and thither came Déor the singer to seek the Prince of Gwar and to seek the companies of the Fading Elves, for he was an Elf-friend. Though Déor was of English blood, it is told that he wedded to wife a maiden from the West, from Lionesse as some have named it since, or Evadrien 'Coast of Iron' as the Elves still say. Déor found her in the lost land beyond Belerion whence the Elves at times set sail.

Mirth had Déor long time in Mindon Gwar, but the Men óf the North, whom the fairies of the island called Forodwaith, but whom Men called other names, came against Gwar in those days when they ravaged wellnigh all the land of Lúthien. Its walls availed not and its towers might not withstand them for ever, though the siege was long and bitter.

There Éadgifu (for so did Déor name the maiden of the West, though it was not her name aforetime)[23] died in those evil hungry days; but Déor fell before the walls even as he sang a song of ancient valour for the raising of men's hearts. That was a desperate sally, and the son of Déor was Ælfwine, and he was then but a boy left fatherless. The sack of that town thereafter was very cruel, and whispers of its ancient days alone remained, and the Elves that had grown to love the English of the isle fled or hid themselves for a long time, and none of Elves or Men were left in his old halls to lament the fall of Óswine Prince of Gwar.

Then Ælfwine, even he whom the unfaded Elves beyond the waters of Garsecg did after name Eldairon of Lúthien (which is

Ælfwine of England), was made a thrall to the fierce lords of the Forodwaith, and his boyhood knew evil days. But behold a wonder, for Ælfwine knew not and had never seen the sea, yet he heard its great voice speaking deeply in his heart, and its murmurous choirs sang ever in his secret ear between wake and sleep, that he was filled with longing. This was of the magic of Éadgifu, maiden of the West, his mother, and this longing unquenchable had been hers all the days that she dwelt in the quiet inland places among the elms of Mindon Gwar – and amidmost of her longing was Ælfwine her child born, and the Foamriders, the Elves of the Sea-marge, whom she had known of old in Lionesse, sent messengers to his birth. But now Éadgifu was gone beyond the Rim of Earth, and her fair form lay unhonoured in Mindon Gwar, and Déor's harp was silent, but Ælfwine laboured in thraldom until the threshold of manhood, dreaming dreams and filled with longing, and at rare times holding converse with the hidden Elves.

At last his longing for the sea bit him so sorely that he contrived to break his bonds, and daring great perils and suffering many grievous toils he escaped to lands where the Lords of the Forodwaith had not come, far from the places of Déor's abiding in Mindon Gwar. Ever he wandered southward and to the west, for that way his feet unbidden led him. Now Ælfwine had in a certain measure the gift of elfin-sight (which was not given to all Men in those days of the fading of the Elves and still less is it granted now), and the folk of Lúthien were less faded too in those days, so that many a host of their fair companies he saw upon his wandering road. Some there were dwelt yet and danced yet about that land as of old, but many more there were that wandered slowly and sadly westward; for behind them all the land was full of burnings and of war, and its dwellings ran with tears and with blood for the little love of Men for Men – nor was that the last of the takings of Lúthien by Men from Men, which have been seven, and others mayhap still shall be. Men of the East and of the West and of the South and of the North have coveted that land and dispossessed those who held it before them, because of its beauty and goodliness and of the glamour of the fading ages of the Elves that lingered still among its trees beyond its high white shores.[24]

Yet at each taking of that isle have many more of the most ancient of all dwellers therein, the folk of Lúthien, turned westward; and they have got them in ships at Belerion in the

West and sailed thence away for ever over the horizon of Men's knowledge, leaving the island the poorer for their going and its leaves less green; yet still it abides the richest among Men in the presence of the Elves. And it is said that, save only when the fierce fathers of Men, foes of the Elves, being new come under the yoke of Evil,[25] entered first that land, never else did so great a concourse of elfin ships and white-winged galleons sail to the setting sun as in those days when the ancient Men of the South set first their mighty feet upon the soil of Lúthien – the Men whose lords sat in the city of power that Elves and Men have called Rûm (but the Elves alone do know as Magbar).[26]

Now is it the dull hearts of later days rather than the red deeds of cruel hands that set the minds of the little folk to fare away; and ever and anon a little ship[27] weighs anchor from Belerion at eve and its sweet sad song is lost for ever on the waves. Yet even in the days of Ælfwine there was many a laden ship under elfin sails that left those shores for ever, and many a comrade he had, seen or half-unseen, upon his westward road. And so he came at last to Belerion, and there he laved his weary feet in the grey waters of the Western Sea, whose great roaring drowned his ears. There the dim shapes of Elvish[28] boats sailed by him in the gloaming, and many aboard called to him farewell. But he might not embark on those frail craft, and they refused his prayer – for they were not willing that even one beloved among Men should pass with them beyond the edge of the West, or learn what lies far out on Garsecg the great and measureless sea. Now the men who dwelt thinly about those places nigh Belerion were fishermen, and Ælfwine abode long time amongst them, and being of nature shaped inly thereto he learned all that a man may of the craft of ships and of the sea. He recked little of his life, and he set his ocean-paths wider than most of those men, good mariners though they were; and there were few in the end who dared to go with him, save Ælfheah the fatherless who was with him in all ventures until his last voyage.[29]

Now on a time journeying far out into the open sea, being first becalmed in a thick mist, and after driven helpless by a mighty wind from the East, he espied some islands lying in the dawn, but he won not ever thereto for the winds changing swept him again far away, and only his strong fate saved him to see the black coasts of his abiding once again. Little content was he with his good fortune, and purposed in his heart to sail some time again yet further into the West, thinking unwitting it was

the Magic Isles of the songs of Men that he had seen from afar.
Few companions could he get for this adventure. Not all men
love to sail a quest for the red sun or to tempt the dangerous seas
in thirst for undiscovered things. Seven such found he in the
end, the greatest mariners that were then in England, and Ulmo
Lord of the Sea afterward took them to himself and their names
are now forgotten, save Ælfheah only.[30] A great storm fell upon
their ship even as they had sighted the isles of Ælfwine's desire,
and a great sea swept over her; but Ælfwine was lost in the
waves, and coming to himself saw no sign of ship or comrades,
and he lay upon a bed of sand in a deep-walled cove. Dark and
very empty was the isle, and he knew then that these were not
those Magic Isles of which he had heard often tell.[31]

There wandering long, 'tis said, he came upon many hulls of
wrecks rotting on the long gloomy beaches, and some were
wrecks of many mighty ships of old, and some were treasure-
laden. A lonely cabin looking westward he found at last upon
the further shore, and it was made of the upturned hull of a
small ship. An ancient man dwelt there, and Ælfwine feared
him, for the eyes of the man were as deep as the unfathomable
sea, and his long beard was blue and grey; great was his stature,
and his shoes were of stone,[32] but he was all clad in tangled rags,
sitting beside a small fire of drifted wood.

In that strange hut beside an empty sea did Ælfwine long
abide for lack of other shelter or of other counsel, thinking his
ship lost and his comrades drowned. But the ancient man grew
kindly toward him, and questioned Ælfwine concerning his
coming and his goings and whither he had desired to sail before
the storm took him. And many things before unheard did
Ælfwine hear tell of him beside that smoky fire at eve, and
strange tales of wind-harried ships and harbourless tempests in
the forbidden waters. Thus heard Ælfwine how the Magic Isles
were yet a great voyage before him keeping a dark and secret
ward upon the edge of Earth, beyond whom the waters of
Garsecg grow less troublous and there lies the twilight of the
latter days of Fairyland. Beyond and on the confines of the
Shadows lies the Lonely Island looking East to the Magic
Archipelago and to the lands of Men beyond it, and West into
the Shadows beyond which afar off is glimpsed the Outer Land,
the kingdom of the Gods – even the aged Bay of Faëry whose
glory has grown dim. Thence slopes the world steeply beyond
the Rim of Things to Valinor, that is God-home, and to the

Wall and to the edge of Nothingness whereon are sown the stars. But the Lonely Isle is neither of the Great Lands or of the Outer Land, and no isle lies near it.

In his tales that aged man named himself the Man of the Sea, and he spoke of his last voyage ere he was cast in wreck upon this outer isle, telling how ere the West wind took him he had glimpsed afar off bosomed in the deep the twinkling lanterns of the Lonely Isle. Then did Ælfwine's heart leap within him, but he said to that aged one that he might not hope to get him a brave ship or comrades more. But that Man of the Sea said: 'Lo, this is one of the ring of Harbourless Isles that draw all ships towards their hidden rocks and quaking sands, lest Men fare over far upon Garsecg and see things that are not for them to see. And these isles were set here at the Hiding of Valinor, and little wood for ship or raft does there grow on them, as may be thought;[33] but I may aid thee yet in thy desire to depart from these greedy shores.'

Thereafter on a day Ælfwine fared along the eastward strands gazing at the many unhappy wrecks there lying. He sought, as often he had done before, if he might see perchance any sign or relic of his good ship from Belerion. There had been that night a storm of great violence and dread, and lo! the number of wrecks was increased by one, and Ælfwine saw it had been a large and well-built ship of cunning lines such as the Forodwaith then loved. Cast far up on the treacherous sands it stood, and its great beak carven as a dragon's head still glared unbroken at the land. Then went the Man of the Sea out when the tide began to creep in slow and shallow over the long flats. He bore as a staff a timber great as a young tree, and he fared as if he had no need to fear tide or quicksand until he came far out where his shoulders were scarce above the yellow waters of the incoming flood to that carven prow, that now alone was seen above the water. Then Ælfwine marvelled watching from afar, to see him heave by his single strength the whole great ship up from the clutches of the sucking sand that gripped its sunken stern; and when it floated he thrust it before him, swimming now with mighty strokes in the deepening water. At that sight Ælfwine's fear of the aged one was renewed, and he wondered what manner of being he might be; but now the ship was thrust far up on the firmer sands, and the swimmer strode ashore, and his mighty beard was full of strands of sea-weed, and sea-weed was in his hair.

When that tide again forsook the Hungry Sands the Man of the Sea bade Ælfwine go look at that new-come wreck, and going he saw it was not hurt; but there were within nine dead men who had not long ago been yet alive. They lay abottom gazing at the sky, and behold, one whose garb and mien still proclaimed a chieftain of Men lay there, but though his locks were white with age and his face was pale in death, still a proud man and a fierce he looked. 'Men of the North, Forodwaith, are they,' said the Man of the Sea, 'but hunger and thirst was their death, and their ship was flung by last night's storm where she stuck in the Hungry Sands, slowly to be engulfed, had not fate thought otherwise.'

'Truly do you say of them, O Man of the Sea; and him I know well with those white locks, for he slew my father; and long was I his thrall, and Orm men called him, and little did I love him.'

'And his ship shall it be that bears you from this Harbourless Isle,' said he; 'and a gallant ship it was of a brave man, for few folk have now so great a heart for the adventures of the sea as have these Forodwaith, who press ever into the mists of the West, though few live to take back tale of all they see.'

Thus it was that Ælfwine escaped beyond hope from that island, but the Man of the Sea was his pilot and steersman, and so they came after few days to a land but little known.[34] And the folk that dwell there are a strange folk, and none know how they came thither in the West, yet are they accounted among the kindreds of Men, albeit their land is on the outer borders of the regions of Mankind, lying yet further toward the Setting Sun beyond the Harbourless Isles and further to the North than is that isle whereon Ælfwine was cast away. Marvellously skilled are these people in the building of ships and boats of every kind and in the sailing of them; yet do they fare seldom or never to the lands of other folk, and little do they busy themselves with commerce or with war. Their ships they build for love of that labour and for the joy they have only to ride the waves in them. And a great part of that people are ever aboard their ships, and all the water about the island of their home is ever white with their sails in calm or storm. Their delight is to vie in rivalry with one another with their boats of surpassing swiftness, driven by the winds or by the ranks of their long-shafted oars. Other rivalries have they with ships of great seaworthiness, for with these will they contest who will weather the fiercest storms (and these are fierce indeed about that isle, and it is iron-coasted save for one cool harbour in the North). Thereby is the craft of their shipwrights proven; and these people are called by Men the Ythlings,[35] the Children of the Waves, but the Elves call the island Eneadur, and its folk the Shipmen of the West.[36]

Well did these receive Ælfwine and his pilot at the thronging quays of their harbour in the North, and it seemed to Ælfwine that the Man of the Sea was not unknown to them, and that they held him in the greatest awe and reverence, hearkening to his requests as though they were a king's commands. Yet greater was his amaze when he met amid the throngs of that place two of his comrades that he had thought lost in the sea; and learnt that those seven mariners of England were alive in that land, but the ship had been broken utterly on the black shores to the south, not long after the night when the great sea had taken Ælfwine overboard.

Now at the bidding of the Man of the Sea do those islanders with great speed fashion a new ship for Ælfwine and his fellows, since he would fare no further in Orm's ship; and its timbers were cut, as the ancient sailor had asked, from a grove of magic oaks far inland that grew about a high place of the Gods, sacred to Ulmo Lord of the Sea, and seldom were any of them felled. 'A ship that is wrought of this wood,' said the Man of the Sea, 'may be lost, but those that sail in it shall not in that voyage lose their lives; yet may they perhaps be cast where they little think to come.'

But when that ship was made ready that ancient sailor bid them climb aboard, and this they did, but with them went also Bior of the Ythlings, a man of mighty sea-craft for their aid, and one who above any of that strange folk was minded to sail at times far from the land of Eneadur to West or North or South. There stood many men of the Ythlings upon the shore beside that vessel; for they had builded her in a cove of the steep shore that looked to the West, and a bar of rock with but a narrow opening made here a sheltered pool and mooring place, and few like it were to be found in that island of sheer cliffs. Then the ancient one laid his hand upon her prow and spoke words of magic, giving her power to cleave uncloven waters and enter unentered harbours, and ride untrodden beaches. Twin rudder-paddles, one on either side, had she after the fashion of the Ythlings, and each of these he blessed, giving them skill to steer when the hands that held them failed, and to find lost courses, and to follow stars that were hid. Then he strode away,

and the press of men parted before him, until climbing he came
to a high pinnacle of the cliffs. Then leapt he far out and down
and vanished with a mighty flurry of foam where the great
breakers gathered to assault the towering shores.

Ælfwine saw him no more, and he said in grief and amaze:
'Why was he thus weary of life? My heart grieves that he is
dead,' but the Ythlings smiled, so that he questioned some that
stood nigh, saying: 'Who was that mighty man, for meseems ye
know him well,' and they answered him nothing. Then thrust
they forth that vessel valiant-timbered[37] out into the sea, for no
longer would Ælfwine abide, though the sun was sinking to the
Mountains of Valinor beyond the Western Walls. Soon was her
white sail seen far away filled with a wind from off the land, and
red-stained in the light of the half-sunken sun; and those aboard
her sang old songs of the English folk that faded on the sailless
waves of the Western Seas, and now no longer came any sound
of them to the watchers on the shore. Then night shut down and
none on Eneadur saw that strong ship ever more.[38]

So began those mariners that long and strange and perilous
voyage whose full tale has never yet been told. Nought of their
adventures in the archipelagoes of the West, and the wonders
and the dangers that they found in the Magic Isles and in seas
and sound unknown, are here to tell, but of the ending of their
voyage, how after a time of years sea-weary and sick of heart
they found a grey and cheerless day. Little wind was there, and
the clouds hung low overhead; while a grey rain fell, and nought
could any of them descry before their vessel's beak that moved
now slow and uncertain over the long dead waves. That day had
they trysted to be the last ere they turned their vessel homeward
(if they might), save only if some wonder should betide or any
sign of hope. For their heart was gone. Behind them lay the
Magic Isles where three of their number slept upon dim strands
in deadly sleep, and their heads were pillowed on white sand
and they were clad in foam, wrapped about in the agelong spells
of Eglavain. Fruitless had been all their journeys since, for ever
the winds had cast them back without sight of the shores of the
Island of the Elves.[39] Then said Ælfheah[40] who held the helm:
'Now, O Ælfwine, is the trysted time! Let us do as the Gods and
their winds have long desired — cease from our heart-weary
quest for nothingness, a fable in the void, and get us back if the
Gods will it seeking the hearths of our home.' And Ælfwine

yielded. Then fell the wind and no breath came from East or West, and night came slowly over the sea.

Behold, at length a gentle breeze sprang up, and it came softly from the West; and even as they would fill their sails therewith for home, one of those shipmen on a sudden said: 'Nay, but this is a strange air, and full of scented memories,' and standing still they all breathed deep. The mists gave before that gentle wind, and a thin moon they might see riding in its tattered shreds, until behind it soon a thousand cool stars peered forth in the dark. 'The night-flowers are opening in Faëry,' said Ælfwine; 'and behold,' said Bior,[41] 'the Elves are kindling candles in their silver dusk,' and all looked whither his long hand pointed over their dark stern. Then none spoke for wonder and amaze, seeing deep in the gloaming of the West a blue shadow, and in the blue shadow many glittering lights, and ever more and more of them came twinkling out, until ten thousand points of flickering radiance were splintered far away as if a dust of the jewels self-luminous that Fëanor made were scattered on the lap of the Ocean.

'Then is that the Harbour of the Lights of Many Hues,' said Ælfheah, 'that many a little-heeded tale has told of in our homes.' Then saying no more they shot out their oars and swung about their ship in haste, and pulled towards the never-dying shore. Near had they come to abandoning it when hardly won. Little did they make of that long pull, as they thrust the water strongly by them, and the long night of Faërie held on, and the horned moon of Elfinesse rode over them.

Then came there music very gently over the waters and it was laden with unimagined longing, that Ælfwine and his comrades leant upon their oars and wept softly each for his heart's half-remembered hurts, and memory of fair things long lost, and each for the thirst that is in every child of Men for the flawless loveliness they seek and do not find. And one said: 'It is the harps that are thrumming, and the songs they are singing of fair things; and the windows that look upon the sea are full of light.' And another said: 'Their stringéd violins complain the ancient woes of the immortal folk of Earth, but there is a joy therein.' 'Ah me,' said Ælfwine, 'I hear the horns of the Fairies shimmering in magic woods – such music as I once dimly guessed long years ago beneath the elms of Mindon Gwar.'

And lo! as they spoke thus musing the moon hid himself, and the stars were clouded, and the mists of time veiled the shore, and nothing could they see and nought more hear, save the sound of the surf of the seas in the far-off pebbles of the Lonely Isle; and soon the wind blew even that faint rustle far away. But Ælfwine stood forward with wide-open eyes unspeaking, and suddenly with a great cry he sprang forward into the dark sea, and the waters that filled him were warm, and a kindly death it seemed enveloped him. Then it seemed to the others that they awakened at his voice as from a dream; but the wind now suddenly grown fierce filled all their sails, and they saw him never again, but were driven back with hearts all broken with regret and longing. Pale elfin boats awhile they would see beating home, maybe, to the Haven of Many Hues, and they hailed them; but only faint echoes afar off were borne to their ears, and none led them ever to the land of their desire; who after a great time wound back all the mazy clue of their long tangled ways, until they cast anchor at last in the haven of Belerion, aged and wayworn men. And the things they had seen and heard seemed after to them a mirage, and a phantasy, born of hunger and sea-spells, save only to Bior of Eneadur of the Ship-folk of the West.

Yet among the seed of these men has there been many a restless and wistful spirit thereafter, since they were dead and passed beyond the Rim of Earth without need of boat or sail. But never while life lasted did they leave their sea-faring, and their bodies are all covered by the sea.[42]

★

The narrative ends here. There is no trace of any further continuation, though it seems likely that *Ælfwine of England* was to be the beginning of a complete rewriting of the *Lost Tales*. It would be interesting to know for certain when *Ælfwine II* was written. The handwriting of the manuscript is certainly changed from that of the rest of the *Lost Tales*; yet I am inclined to think that it followed *Ælfwine I* at no great interval, and the first version is unlikely to be much later than 1920 (see p. 312).

At the end of *Ælfwine II* my father jotted down two suggestions: (1) that Ælfwine should be made 'an early pagan Englishman who fled to the West'; and (2) that 'the Isle of the Old Man' should be cut out and all should be shipwrecked on Eneadur, the Isle of the Ythlings. The latter would (astonishingly) have entailed the abandonment of the foundered ship, with the Man of the Sea thrusting it to shore on the incoming tide, and the dead Vikings 'lying abottom gazing at the sky'.

In this narrative – in which the 'magic' of the early Elves is most intensely conveyed, in the seamen's vision of the Lonely Isle beneath 'the horned moon of Elfinesse' – Ælfwine is still placed in the context of the figures of ancient English legend: his father is Déor the Minstrel. In the great Anglo-Saxon manuscript known as the Exeter Book there is a little poem of 42 lines to which the title of *Déor* is now given. It is an utterance of the minstrel Déor, who, as he tells, has lost his place and been supplanted in his lord's favour by another bard, named Heorrenda; in the body of the poem Déor draws examples from among the great misfortunes recounted in the heroic legends, and is comforted by them, concluding each allusion with the fixed refrain *þæs ofereode; þisses swa mæg*, which has been variously translated; my father held that it meant 'Time has passed since then, this too can pass'.[43]

From this poem came both Déor and Heorrenda. In 'the *Eriol* story' Heorrenda was Eriol's son born in Tol Eressëa of his wife Naimi (p. 290), and was associated with Hengest and Horsa in the conquest of the Lonely Isle (p. 291); his dwelling in England was at Tavrobel (p. 292). I do not think that my father's Déor the Minstrel of Kortirion and Heorrenda of Tavrobel can be linked more closely to the Anglo-Saxon poem than in the names alone – though he did not take the names at random. He was moved by the glimpsed tale (even if, in the words of one of the poem's editors, 'the autobiographical element is purely fictitious, serving only as a pretext for the enumeration of the heroic stories'); and when lecturing on *Beowulf* at Oxford he sometimes gave the unknown poet a name, calling him *Heorrenda*.

Nor, as I believe, can any more be made of the other Old English names in the narrative: Óswine prince of Gwar, Éadgifu, Ælfheah (though the names are doubtless in themselves 'significant': thus *Óswine* contains *ós* 'god' and *wine* 'friend', and *Éadgifu éad* 'blessedness' and *gifu* 'gift'). The Forodwaith are of course Viking invaders from Norway or Denmark; the name Orm of the dead ship's captain is well-known in Norse. But all this is a mise-en-scène that is historical only in its bearings, not in its structure.

The idea of the seven invasions of Lúthien (Luthany) remained (p. 314), and that of the fading and westward flight of the Elves (which indeed was never finally lost),[44] but whereas in the outlines the invasion of the Ingwaiwar (i.e. the Anglo-Saxons) was the seventh (see citations (20) and (22)), here the Viking invasions are portrayed as coming upon the English – 'nor was that the last of the takings of Lúthien by Men from Men' (p. 314), obviously a reference to the Normans.

There is much of interest in the 'geographical' references in the story. At the very beginning there is a curious statement about the breaking off of Ireland 'in the warfare of the Gods'. Seeing that 'the *Ælfwine* story' does not include the idea of the drawing back of Tol Eressëa eastwards across the sea, this must refer to something quite other than the story in (5), p. 283, where the Isle of Íverin was broken off when Ossë tried to wrench back Tol Eressëa. What this was I do not know; but it seems conceivable that this is the first trace or hint of the great cataclysm at the end of the Elder Days, when Beleriand was drowned. (I have found no trace of any connection between the harbour of *Belerion* and the region of *Beleriand*.)

Kortirion (Mindon Gwar) is in this tale of course 'Kortirion the Old', the original Elvish dwelling in Lúthien, after which Kortirion in Tol Eressëa was named (see pp. 308, 310); in the same way we must suppose that the name Alalminórë (p. 313) for the region about it ('Warwickshire') was given anew to the midmost region of Tol Eressëa.

Turning to the question of the islands and archipelagoes in the Great Sea, what is said in *Ælfwine of England* may first be compared with the passages of geographical description in *The Coming of the Valar* (I. 68) and *The Coming of the Elves* (I. 125), which are closely similar the one to the other. From these passages we learn that there are many lands and islands in the Great Sea before the Magic Isles are reached; beyond the Magic Isles is Tol Eressëa; and beyond Tol Eressëa are the Shadowy Seas, 'whereon there float the Twilit Isles', the first of the Outer Lands. Tol Eressëa itself 'is held neither of the Outer Lands or of the Great Lands' (I. 125); it is far out in mid-ocean, and 'no land may be seen for many leagues' sail from its cliffs' (I. 121). With this account *Ælfwine of England* agrees closely; but to it is added now the archipelago of the Harbourless Isles.

As I have noted before (I. 137), this progression from East to West of Harbourless Isles, Magic Isles, the Lonely Isle, and then the Shadowy Seas in which were the Twilit Isles, was afterwards changed, and it is said in *The Silmarillion* (p. 102) that at the time of the Hiding of Valinor

the Enchanted Isles were set, and all the seas about them were filled with shadows and bewilderment. And these isles were strung as a net in the Shadowy Seas from the north to the south, before Tol Eressëa, the Lonely Isle, is reached by one sailing west. Hardly might any vessel pass between them, for in the dangerous sounds the waves sighed for ever upon dark rocks shrouded in mist. And in the twilight a great weariness came upon mariners and a loathing of the sea; but all that ever set foot upon the islands were there entrapped, and slept until the Change of the World.

As a conception, the Enchanted Isles are derived primarily from the old Magic Isles, set at the time of the Hiding of Valinor and described in that Tale (I. 211): 'Ossë set them in a great ring about the western limits of the mighty sea, so that they guarded the Bay of Faëry', and

all such as stepped thereon came never thence again, but being woven in the nets of Oinen's hair the Lady of the Sea, and whelmed in agelong slumber that Lórien set there, lay upon the margin of the waves, as those do who being drowned are cast up once more by the movements of the sea; yet rather did these hapless ones sleep unfathomably and the dark waters laved their limbs . . .

Here three of Ælfwine's companions

slept upon dim strands in deadly sleep, and their heads were pillowed on white sand and they were clad in foam, wrapped about in the agelong spells of Eglavain (p. 320).

(I do not know the meaning of the name *Eglavain*, but since it clearly contains *Egla* (Gnomish, = *Elda*, see I.251) it perhaps meant 'Elfinesse'.) But the Enchanted Isles derive also perhaps from the Twilit Isles, since the Enchanted Isles were likewise in twilight and were set in the Shadowy Seas (cf. I.224); and from the Harbourless Isles as well, which, as Ælfwine was told by the Man of the Sea (p. 317), were set at the time of the Hiding of Valinor – and indeed served the same purpose as did the Magic Isles, though lying far further to the East.

Eneadur, the isle of the Ythlings (Old English *ýð* 'wave'), whose life is so fully described in *Ælfwine of England*, seems never to have been mentioned again. Is there in Eneadur and the Shipmen of the West perhaps some faint foreshadowing of the early Númenóreans in their cliff-girt isle?

The following passage (pp. 316–17) is not easy to interpret:

Thence [i.e. from the Bay of Faëry] slopes the world steeply beyond the Rim of Things to Valinor, that is God-home, and to the Wall and to the edge of Nothingness whereon are sown the stars.

In the *Ambarkanta* or 'Shape of the World' of the 1930s a map of the world shows the surface of the Outer Land sloping steeply westwards from the Mountains of Valinor. Conceivably it is to this slope that my father was referring here, and the Rim of Things is the great mountain-wall; but this seems very improbable. There are also references in *Ælfwine of England* to 'the Rim of Earth', beyond which the dead pass (pp. 314, 322); and in an outline for the *Tale of Eärendel* (p. 260) Tuor's boat 'dips over the world's rim'. More likely, I think, the expression refers to the rim of the horizon ('the horizon of Men's knowledge', p. 313).

The expression 'the sun was sinking to the Mountains of Valinor beyond the Western Walls' (p. 320) I am at a loss to explain according to what has been told in the *Lost Tales*. A possible, though scarcely convincing, interpretation is that the sun was sinking towards Valinor, *whence it would pass* 'beyond the Western Walls' (i.e. through the Door of Night, see I.215–16).

Lastly, the suggestion (p. 313) is notable that the Elves sailing west from Lúthien might go beyond the Lonely Isle and reach even back to Valinor; on this matter see p. 280.

★

Before ending, there remains to discuss briefly a matter of a general nature that has many times been mentioned in the texts, and especially in these last chapters: that of the 'diminutiveness' of the Elves.

It is said several times in the *Lost Tales* that the Elves of the ancient days were of greater bodily stature than they afterwards became. Thus in *The Fall of Gondolin* (p. 159): 'The fathers of the fathers of Men were of less stature than Men now are, and the children of Elfinesse of greater growth'; in an outline for the abandoned tale of Gilfanon (I.235) very similarly: 'Men were almost of a stature at first with Elves, the fairies being far greater and Men smaller than now'; and in citation (4) in the present chapter: 'Men and Elves were formerly of a size, though Men always larger.' Other passages suggest that the ancient Elves were of their nature of at any rate somewhat slighter build (see pp. 142, 220).

The diminishing in the stature of the Elves of later times is very explicitly related to the coming of Men. Thus in (4) above: 'Men spread and thrive, and the Elves of the Great Lands fade. As Men's stature grows theirs diminishes'; and in (5): 'ever as Men wax more powerful and numerous so the fairies fade and grow small and tenuous, filmy and transparent, but Men larger and more dense and gross. At last Men, or almost all, can no longer see the fairies.' The clearest picture that survives of the Elves when they have 'faded' altogether is given in the *Epilogue* (p. 289):

> Like strands of wind, like mystic half-transparencies, Gilfanon Lord of Tavrobel rides out tonight amid his folk, and hunts the elfin deer beneath the paling sky. A music of forgotten feet, a gleam of leaves, a sudden bending of the grass, and wistful voices murmuring on the bridge, and they are gone.

But according to the passages bearing on the later '*Ælfwine*' version, the Elves of Tol Eressëa who had left Luthany were unfaded, or had ceased to fade. Thus in (15): 'Tol Eressëa, whither most of the unfaded Elves have retired from the noise, war, and clamour of Men'; and (16): 'Tol Eressëa, whither most of the fading Elves have withdrawn from the world, and there fade now no more'; also in *Ælfwine of England* (p. 313): 'the unfaded Elves beyond the waters of Garsecg'.

On the other hand, when Eriol came to the Cottage of Lost Play the doorward said to him (I.14):

> Small is the dwelling, but smaller still are they that dwell here – for all who enter must be very small indeed, or of their own good wish become as very little folk even as they stand upon the threshold.

I have commented earlier (I.32) on the oddity of the idea that the Cottage and its inhabitants were peculiarly small, in an island entirely inhabited by Elves. But my father, if he had ever rewritten *The Cottage of Lost Play*, would doubtless have abandoned this; and it may well be that he was in any case turning away already at the time of *Ælfwine II* from the idea that the 'faded' Elves were diminutive, as is suggested by his rejection of the word 'little' in 'little folk', 'little ships' (see note 27).

Ultimately, of course, the Elves shed all associations and qualities that would be now commonly considered 'fairylike', and those who remained in the Great Lands in Ages of the world at this time unconceived were to grow greatly in stature and in power: there was nothing filmy or transparent about the heroic or majestic Eldar of the Third Age of Middle-earth. Long afterwards my father would write, in a wrathful comment on a 'pretty' or 'ladylike' pictorial rendering of Legolas:

> He was tall as a young tree, lithe, immensely strong, able swiftly to draw a great war-bow and shoot down a Nazgûl, endowed with the tremendous vitality of Elvish bodies, so hard and resistant to hurt that he went only in light shoes over rock or through snow, the most tireless of all the Fellowship.

★

This brings to an end my rendering and analysis of the early writings bearing on the story of the mariner who came to the Lonely Isle and learned there the true history of the Elves. I have shown, convincingly as I hope, the curious and complex way in which my father's vision of the significance of Tol Eressëa changed. When he jotted down the synopsis (10), the idea of the mariner's voyage to the Island of the Elves was of course already present; but he journeyed out of the East and the Lonely Isle of his seeking was – England (though not yet the land of the English and not yet lying in the seas where England lies). When later the entire concept was shifted, England, as 'Luthany' or 'Lúthien', remained pre-eminently the Elvish land; and Tol Eressëa, with its meads and coppices, its rooks' nests in the elm-trees of Alalminórë, seemed to the English mariner to be remade in the likeness of his own land, which the Elves had lost at the coming of Men: for it was indeed a re-embodiment of Elvish Luthany far over the sea.

All this was to fall away afterwards from the developing mythology; but Ælfwine left many marks on its pages before he too finally disappeared.

Much in this chapter is necessarily inconclusive and uncertain; but I believe that these very early notes and projections are rightly disinterred. Although, as 'plots', abandoned and doubtless forgotten, they bear witness to truths of my father's heart and mind that he never abandoned. But these notes were scribbled down in his youth, when for him Elvish magic 'lingered yet mightily in the woods and hills of Luthany'; in his old age all was gone West-over-sea, and an end was indeed come for the Eldar of story and of song.

NOTES

1   On this statement about the stature of Elves and Men see pp. 326–7.

2   For the form *Taimonto* (*Taimondo*) see I.268, entry *Telimektar*.

3   *Belaurin* is the Gnomish equivalent of *Palúrien* (see I.264).

4   A side-note here suggests that perhaps the Pine should not be in Tol Eressëa. – For *Ilwë*, the middle air, that is 'blue and clear and flows among the stars', see I.65, 73.

5   *Gil* = *Ingil*. At the first occurrence of *Ingil* in this passage the name was written *Ingil* (*Gil*), but (*Gil*) was struck out.

6   The word *Nautar* occurs in a rejected outline for the *Tale of the Nauglafring* (p. 136), where it is equated with *Nauglath* (Dwarves).

7   *Uin*: 'the mightiest and most ancient of whales', chief among those whales and fishes that drew the 'island-car' (afterwards Tol Eressëa) on which Ulmo ferried the Elves to Valinor (I.118–20).

8   *Gongs*: these are evil beings obscurely related to Orcs: see I.245 note 10, and the rejected outlines for the *Tale of the Nauglafring* given on pp. 136–7.

9   A large query is written against this passage.

10 The likeness of this name to *Dor Daedeloth* is striking, but that is the name of the realm of Morgoth in *The Silmarillion*, and is interpreted 'Land of the Shadow of Horror'; the old name (whose elements are *dai* 'sky' and *teloth* 'roof') has nothing in common with the later except its form.

11 Cf. *Kortirion among the Trees* (I.34, 37, 41): *A wave of bowing grass*.

12 The origin of *Warwick* according to conventional etymology is uncertain. The element *wic*, extremely common in English place-names, meant essentially a dwelling or group of dwellings. The earliest recorded form of the name is *Wæring wic*, and *Wæring* has been thought to be an Old English word meaning a dam, a derivative from *wer*, Modern English *weir*: thus 'dwellings by the weir'.

13 Cf. the title-page given in citation (11): *Heorrenda of Hægwudu*. – No forms of the name of this Staffordshire village are actually recorded from before the Norman Conquest, but the Old English form was undoubtedly *hæg-wudu* 'enclosed wood' (cf. the *High Hay*, the great hedge that protected Buckland from the Old Forest in *The Lord of the Rings*).

14 The name Luthany, of a country, occurs five times in Francis

Thompson's poem *The Mistress of Vision*. As noted previously (I. 29) my father acquired the Collected Poems of Francis Thompson in 1913–14; and in that copy he made a marginal note against one of the verses that contains the name *Luthany* – though the note is not concerned with the name. But whence Thompson derived *Luthany* I have no idea. He himself described the poem as 'a fantasy' (Everard Meynell, *The Life of Francis Thompson*, 1913, p. 237).

This provides no more than the origin of the name as a series of sounds, as with *Kôr* from Rider Haggard's *She*,* or *Rohan* and *Moria* mentioned in my father's letter of 1967 on this subject (*The Letters of J. R. R. Tolkien*, pp. 383–4), in which he said:

> This leads to the matter of 'external history': the actual way in which I came to light on or choose certain sequences of sound to use as names, *before* they were given a place inside the story. I think, as I said, this is unimportant: the labour involved in my setting out what I know and remember of the process, or in the guess-work of others, would be far greater than the worth of the results. The spoken forms would simply be mere audible forms, and when transferred to the prepared linguistic situation in my story would receive meaning and significance according to that situation, and to the nature of the story told. It would be entirely delusory to refer to the sources of the sound-combination to discover any meanings overt or hidden.

15   The position is complicated by the existence of some narrative outlines of extreme roughness and near-illegibility in which the mariner is named Ælfwine and yet essential elements of 'the *Eriol* story' are present. These I take to represent an intermediate stage. They are very obscure, and would require a great deal of space to present and discuss; therefore I pass them by.

16   Cf. p. 264 (xiv).

17   *Caer Gwâr*: see p. 292.

18   It may be mentioned here that when my father read *The Fall of Gondolin* to the Exeter College Essay Club in the spring of 1920 the mariner was still *Eriol*, as appears from the notes for his preliminary remarks on that occasion (see *Unfinished Tales* p. 5). He said here, very strangely, that 'Eriol lights by accident on the Lonely Island'.

19   *Garsecg* (pronounced *Garsedge*, and so written in *Ælfwine* A) was one of the many Old English names of the sea.

20   In *Ælfwine I* the land is likewise named *Lúthien*, not *Luthany*. In *Ælfwine* A, on the other hand, the same distinction is made as in the outlines: 'Ælfwine of England (whom the fairies after named

---

* There is no external evidence for this, but it can hardly be doubted. In this case it might be thought that since the African Kôr was a city built on the top of a great mountain standing in isolation the relationship was more than purely 'phonetic'.

Lúthien (friend) of Luthany (friendship)).' – At this first occurrence (only) of *Lúthien* in *Ælfwine II* the form *Leithian* is
pencilled above, but *Lúthien* is not struck out. *The Lay of Leithian*
was afterwards the title of the long poem of Beren and Lúthien
Tinúviel.

21 The *Hill of Tûn*, i.e. the hill on which the city of Tûn was built: see
p. 292.

22 *Mindon Gwar*: see p. 291.

23 *Éadgifu*: in 'the *Eriol* story' this Old English name (see p. 323) was
given as an equivalent to Naimi, Eriol's wife whom he wedded in
Tol Eressëa (p. 290).

24 In *Ælfwine I* the text here reads: 'by reason of her beauty and
goodliness, even as that king of the Franks that was upon a time
most mighty among men hath said . . .' [*sic*]. In *Ælfwine II* the
manuscript in ink stops at 'high white shores', but after these words
my father pencilled in: 'even as that king of the Franks that was
in those days the mightiest of earthly kings hath said . . .' [*sic*]. The
only clue in *Ælfwine of England* to the period of Ælfwine's life is
the invasion of the Forodwaith (Vikings); the mighty king of the
Franks may therefore be Charlemagne, but I have been unable
to trace any such reference.

25 *Evil* is emended from *Melko*. *Ælfwine I* does not have the phrase.

26 *Ælfwine I* has: 'when the ancient Men of the South from
Micelgeard the Heartless Town set their mighty feet upon the soil
of Lúthien.' This text does not have the reference to Rûm and
Magbar. The name *Micelgeard* is struck through, but *Mickleyard*
is written at the head of the page. *Micelgeard* is Old English (and
Mickleyard a modernisation of this in spelling), though it does
not occur in extant Old English writings and is modelled on Old
Norse *Mikligarðr* (Constantinople). – The peculiar hostility of
the Romans to the Elves of Luthany is mentioned by implication in
citation (20), and their disbelief in their existence in (22).

27 The application, frequent in *Ælwine I*, of 'little' to the fairies
(Elves) of Lúthien and their ships was retained in *Ælfwine II* as
first written, but afterwards struck out. Here the word is twice
retained, perhaps unintentionally.

28 *Elvish* is a later emendation of *fairy*.

29 This sentence, from 'save Ælfheah . . .', was added later in
Ælfwine II; it is not in *Ælfwine I*. – The whole text to this point
in *Ælfwine I* and *II* is compressed into the following in *Ælfwine A*:

> Ælfwine of England (whom the fairies after named Lúthien
> (friend) of Luthany (friendship)) born of Déor and Éadgifu.
> Their city burned and Déor slain and Éadgifu dies. Ælfwine a
> thrall of the Winged Helms. He escapes to the Western Sea
> and takes ship from Belerion and makes great voyages. He is

seeking for the islands of the West of which Éadgifu had told him in his childhood.

30   *Ælfwine I* has here: 'But three men could he find as his companions; and Ossë took them unto him.' *Ossë* was emended to *Neorth*; and then the sentence was struck through and rewritten: 'Such found he only three; and those three Neorth after took unto him and their names are not known.' Neorth = Ulmo; see note 39.

31   *Ælfwine A* reads: 'He espies some islands lying in the dawn but is swept thence by great winds. He returns hardly to Belerion. He gathers the seven greatest mariners of England; they sail in spring. They are wrecked upon the isles of Ælfwine's desire and find them desert and lonely and filled with gloomy whispering trees.' This is at variance with *Ælfwine I* and *II* where Ælfwine is cast on to the island alone; but agrees with *II* in giving Ælfwine seven companions, not three.

32   A clue that this was Ulmo: cf. *The Fall of Gondolin* (p. 155): 'he was shod with mighty shoes of stone.'

33   In *Ælfwine A* they were 'filled with gloomy whispering trees' (note 31).

34   From the point where the Man of the Sea said: 'Lo, this is one of the ring of Harbourless Isles . . .' (p. 317) to here (i.e. the whole episode of the foundered Viking ship and its captain Orm, slayer of Ælfwine's father) there is nothing corresponding in *Ælfwine I*, which has only: 'but that Man of the Sea aided him in building a little craft, and together, guided by the solitary mariner, they fared away and came to a land but little known.' For the narrative in *Ælfwine A* see note 39.

35   At one occurrence of the name *Ythlings* (Old English *ȳð* 'wave') in Ælfwine I it is written *Ythlingas*, with the Old English plural ending.

36   *The Shipmen of the West*: emendation from *Eneathrim*.

37   Cf. in the passage of alliterative verse in my father's *On Translating Beowulf* (*The Monsters and the Critics and Other Essays*, 1983, p. 63): *then away thrust her to voyage gladly valiant-timbered.*

38   The whole section of the narrative concerning the island of the Ythlings is more briefly told in *Ælfwine I* (though, so far as it goes, in very much the same words) with several features of the later story absent (notably the cutting of timber in the grove sacred to Ulmo, and the blessing of the ship by the Man of the Sea). The only actual difference of structure, however, is that whereas in *Ælfwine II* Ælfwine finds again his seven companions in the land of the Ythlings, and sails west with them, together with Bior of the Ythlings, in *Ælfwine I* they were indeed drowned, and he got seven companions from among the Ythlings (among whom Bior is not named).

39   The plot-outline *Ælfwine A* tells the story from the point where
Ælfwine and his seven companions were cast on the Isle of the Man
of the Sea (thus differing from *Ælfwine I* and *II*, where he came
there alone) thus:

> They wander about the island upon which they have been cast
> and come upon many decaying wrecks – often of mighty ships,
> some treasure-laden. They find a solitary cabin beside a lonely
> sea, built of old ship-wood, where dwells a solitary and strange
> old mariner of dread aspect. He tells them these are the Harbour-
> less Isles whose enchanted rocks draw all ships thither, lest men
> fare over far upon Garsedge [*see note 19*] – and they were
> devised at the Hiding of Valinor. Here, he says, the trees are
> magical. They learn many strange things about the western world
> of him and their desire is whetted for adventure. He aids them to
> cut holy trees in the island groves and to build a wonderful
> vessel, and shows them how to provision it against a long voyage
> (that water that drieth not save when heart fails, &c.). This he
> blesses with a spell of adventure and discovery, and then dives
> from a cliff-top. They suspect it was Neorth Lord of Waters.
>
> They journey many years among strange western islands hear-
> ing often many strange reports – of the belt of Magic Isles which
> few have passed; of the trackless sea beyond where the wind
> bloweth almost always from the West; of the edge of the twilight
> and the far-glimpsed isle there standing, and its glimmering
> haven. They reach the magic island [*read* islands?] and three
> are enchanted and fall asleep on the shore.
>
> The others beat about the waters beyond and are in despair –
> for as often as they make headway west the wind changes and
> bears them back. At last they tryst to return on the morrow if
> nought other happens. The day breaks chill and dull, and they
> lie becalmed looking in vain through the pouring rain.

This narrative differs from both *Ælfwine I* and *II* in that here
there is no mention of the Ythlings; and Ælfwine and his seven
companions depart on their long western voyage from the Harbourless Isle of the ancient mariner. It agrees with *Ælfwine I* in the
name Neorth; but it foreshadows *II* in the cutting of sacred trees
to build a ship.

40   In *Ælfwine I* Ælfheah does not appear, and his two speeches in
this passage are there given to one *Gelimer*. Gelimer (Geilamir) was
the name of a king of the Vandals in the sixth century.

41   In *Ælfwine I* Bior's speech is given to Gelimer (see note 40).

42   *Ælfwine I* ends in almost the same words as *Ælfwine II*, but with a
most extraordinary difference; Ælfwine does not leap overboard,
but returns with his companions to Belerion, and so never comes to

Tol Eressëa! 'Very empty thereafter were the places of Men for Ælfwine and his mariners, and of their seed have been many restless and wistful folk since they were dead . . .' Moreover my father seems clearly to have been going to say the same in *Ælfwine II*, but stopped, struck out what he had written, and introduced the sentence in which Ælfwine leapt into the sea. I cannot see any way to explain this.

Ælfwine A ends in much the same way as *Ælfwine II*:

As night comes on a little breath springs up and the clouds lift. They hoist sail to return – when suddenly low down in the dusk they see the many lights of the Haven of Many Hues twinkle forth. They row thither, and hear sweet music. Then the mist wraps all away and the others rousing themselves say it is a mirage born of hunger, and with heavy hearts prepare to go back, but Ælfwine plunges overboard and swims into the dark until he is overcome in the waters, and him seems death envelops him. The others sail away home and are out of the tale.

43   Literally, as he maintained: 'From that (grief) one moved on; from this in the same way one can move on.'

44   There are long roots beneath the words of *The Fellowship of the Ring* (I. 2): 'Elves . . . could now be seen passing westward through the woods in the evening, passing and not returning; but they were leaving Middle-earth and were no longer concerned with its troubles.' '"That isn't anything new, if you believe the old tales,"' said Ted Sandyman, when Sam Gamgee spoke of the matter.

I append here a synopsis of the structural differences between the three versions of *Ælfwine of England*.

A	I	II
Æ. sails from Belerion and sees 'islands in the dawn'.	As in A	As in A, but his companion Ælfheah is named.
Æ. sails again with 7 mariners of England. They are shipwrecked on the isle of the Man of the Sea but all survive.	Æ. has only 3 companions, and he alone survives the shipwreck.	Æ. has 7 companions, and is alone on the isle of the Man of the Sea, believing them drowned.
The Man of the Sea helps them to build a ship but does not go with them.	The Man of the Sea helps Æ. to build a boat and goes with him.	Æ. and the Man of the Sea find a stranded Viking ship and sail away in it together.

A	I	II
The Man of the Sea dives into the sea from a cliff-top of his isle.	They come to the Isle of the Ythlings. The Man of the Sea dives from a cliff-top. Æ. gets 7 companions from the Ythlings.	As in I, but Æ. finds his 7 companions from England, who were not drowned; to them is added Bior of the Ythlings.
On their voyages 3 of Æ.'s companions are enchanted in the Magic Isles.	As in A, but in this case they are Ythlings.	As in A
They are blown away from Tol Eressëa after sighting it; Æ. leaps overboard, and the others return home.	They are blown away from Tol Eressëa, and all, including Æ., return home.	As in A

Changes made to names, and differences in names,
in the texts of *Ælfwine of England*

Lúthien   The name of the land in I and II; in A *Luthany* (see note 20).
Déor   At the first occurrence only in I *Déor* < *Heorrenda*, subsequently *Déor*; A *Déor*.
Evadrien   In I < *Erenol*. *Erenol* = 'Iron Cliff'; see I.252, entry *Eriol*.
Forodwaith   II has *Forodwaith* < *Forwaith* < *Gwasgonin*; I has *Gwâsgonin or the Winged Helms*; A has *the Winged Helms*.
Outer Land   < *Outer Lands* at both occurrences in II (pp. 316–17).
Ælfheah   I has *Gelimer* (at the first occurrence only < *Helgor*).
Shipmen of the West   In II < *Eneathrim*.

APPENDIX
NAMES IN THE *LOST TALES* – PART II

This appendix is designed only as an adjunct and extension to that in Part One. Names that have already been studied in Part One are not given entries in the following notes, if there are entries under that name in Part One, e.g. *Melko, Valinor*; but if, as is often the case, the etymological information in Part One is contained in an entry under some other name, this is shown, e.g. '*Gilim*   See I.260 (*Melko*)'.

Linguistic information from the Name-list to *The Fall of Gondolin* (see p. 148) incorporated in these notes is referred to 'NFG'. 'GL' and 'QL' refer to the Gnomish and Qenya dictionaries (see I.246ff.). *Qenya* is the term used in both these books and is strictly the name of the language spoken in Tol Eressëa; it does not appear elsewhere in the early writings, where the distinction is between 'Gnomish' on the one hand and 'Elfin', 'Eldar', or 'Eldarissa' on the other.

★

Alqarámë   For the first element Qenya *alqa* 'swan' see I.249 (*Alqaluntë*). Under root RAHA QL gives *râ* 'arm', *rakta* 'stretch out, reach', *ráma* 'wing', *rámavoitë* 'having wings'; GL has *ram* 'wing, pinion', and it is noted that Qenya *ráma* is a confusion of this and a word *róma* 'shoulder'.

Amon Gwareth   Under root AM(U) 'up(wards)' QL gives *amu* 'up(wards)', *amu-* 'raise', *amuntë* 'sunrise', *amun(d)* 'hill'; GL has *am* 'up(wards)', *amon* 'hill, mount', adverb 'uphill'.

GL gives the name as *Amon 'Wareth* 'Hill of Ward', also *gwareth* 'watch, guard, ward', from the stem *gwar-* 'watch' seen also in the name of *Tinfang Warble* (*Gwarbilin* 'Birdward', I.268). See *Glamhoth, Gwarestrin*.

Angorodin   See I.249 (*Angamandi*) and I.256 (*Kalormë*).

Arlisgion   GL gives *Garlisgion* (see I.265 (*Sirion*)), as also does NFG, which has entries '*Garlisgion* was our name, saith Elfrith, for the Place of Reeds which is its interpretation', and '*lisg* is a reed (*liskë*)'. GL has *lisg, lisc* 'reed, sedge', and QL *liskë* with the same meaning. For *gar* see I.251 (*Dor Faidwen*).

Artanor   GL has *athra* 'across, athwart', *athron* adverb 'further, beyond', *athrod* 'crossing, ford' (changed later to *adr(a), adron, adros*). With *athra, adr(a)* is compared Qenya *arta*. Cf. also the name *Dor Athro* (p. 41). It is clear that both *Artanor* and *Dor Athro* meant 'the Land Beyond'. Cf. *Sarnathrod*.

Asgon   An entry in NFG says: '*Asgon* A lake in the "Land of Shadows" Dor Lómin, by the Elves named *Aksan*.'

Ausir   GL gives *avos* 'fortune, wealth, prosperity,' *avosir, Ausir* 'the same (personified)'; also *ausin* 'rich', *aus(s)aith* or *avosaith* 'avarice'. Under root AWA in QL are *autë* 'prosperity, wealth; rich', *ausië* 'wealth'.

Bablon   See p. 214.

Bad Uthwen   Gnomish *uthwen* 'way out, exit, escape', see I.251 (*Dor Faidwen*). The entry in NFG says: '*Bad Uthwen* [emended from *Uswen*] meaneth but "way of escape" and is in Eldarissa *Uswevandë*.' For *vandë* see I.264 (*Qalvanda*).

Balcmeg   In NFG it is said that Balcmeg 'was a great fighter among the *Orclim* (*Orqui* say the Elves) who fell to the axe of Tuor – 'tis in meaning "heart of evil".' (For *-lim* in *Orclim* see *Gondothlim*.) The entry for *Balrog* in NFG says: '*Bal* meaneth evilness, and *Balc* evil, and *Balrog* meaneth evil demon.' GL has *balc* 'cruel': see I.250 (*Balrog*).

Bansil   For the entry in NFG, where this name is translated 'Fair-gleam', see p. 214; and for the elements of the name see I.272 (*Vána*) and I.265 (*Sil*).

Belaurin   See I.264 (*Palúrien*).

Belcha   See I.260 (*Melko*). NFG has an entry: '*Belca* Though here [i.e. in the Tale] of overwhelming custom did Bronweg use the elfin names, this was the name aforetime of that evil Ainu.'

Beleg   See I.254 (*Haloisi Velikë*).

Belegost   For the first element see *Beleg*. GL gives *ost* 'enclosure, yard – town', also *oss* 'outer wall, town wall', *osta-* 'surround with walls, fortify', *ostor* 'enclosure, circuit of walls'. QL under root OSO has *os(t)* 'house, cottage', *osta* 'homestead', *ostar* 'township', *ossa* 'wall and moat'.

bo-   A late entry in GL: '*bo (bon)* (cf. Qenya *vô, vondo* "son") as patronymic prefix, *bo- bon-* "son of"'; as an example is given *Tuor bo-Beleg*. There is also a word *bôr* 'descendant'. See *go-*, *Indorion*.

Bodruith   In association with *bod-* 'back, again' GL has the words *bodruith* 'revenge', *bodruithol* 'vengeful (by nature)', *bodruithog* 'thirsting for vengeance', but these were struck out. There is also *gruith* 'deed of horror, violent act, vengeance'. – It may be that Bodruith Lord of Belegost was supposed to have received his name from the events of the *Tale of the Nauglafring*.

Cópas Alqalunten   See I.257 (*Kópas*) and I.249 (*Alqaluntë*).

Cris Ilbranteloth   GL gives the group *crisc* 'sharp', *criss* 'cleft, gash, gully', *crist* 'knife', *crista-* 'slash, cut, slice'; NFG: '*Cris* meaneth much as doth *falc*, a cleft, ravine, or narrow way of waters with high walls'. QL under root KIRI 'cut, split' has *kiris* 'cleft, crack' and other words.

For *ilbrant* 'rainbow' see I.256 (*Ilweran*). The final element is *teloth* 'roofing, canopy': see I.267–8 (*Teleri*).

Cristhorn For *Cris* see *Cris Ilbranteloth*, and for *thorn* see I.266 (*Sorontur*). In NFG is the entry: '*Cris Thorn* is Eagles' Cleft or *Sornekiris*.'

Cuilwarthon For *cuil* see I.257 (*Koivië-néni*); the second element is not explained.

Cûm an-Idrisaith For cûm 'mound' see I.250 (*Cûm a Gumlaith*). *Idrisaith* is thus defined in GL: 'cf. *avosaith*, but that means avarice, money-greed, but *idrisaith* = excessive love of gold and gems and beautiful and costly things' (for *avosaith* see *Ausir*). Related words are *idra* 'dear, precious', *idra* 'to value, prize', *idri* (*îd*) 'a treasure, a jewel', *idril* 'sweetheart' (see *Idril*).

Curufin presumably contains *curu* 'magic'; see I.269 (*Tolli Kuruvar*).

Dairon GL includes this name but without etymological explanation: '*Dairon* the fluter (Qenya *Sairon*).' See *Mar Vanwa Tyaliéva* below.

Danigwiel In GL the Gnomish form is *Danigwethil*; see I.266 (*Taniquetil*). NFG has an entry: '*Danigwethil* do the Gnomes call *Taniquetil*; but seek for tales concerning that mountain rather in the elfin name.'

(bo-)Dhrauthodavros '(Son of) the weary forest'. Gnomish *drauth* 'weary, toilworn', *drauthos* 'toil, weariness', *drautha-* 'to be weary'; for the second element *tavros* see I.267 (*Tavari*).

Dor Athro See *Artanor, Sarnathrod*.

Dor-na-Dhaideloth For Gnomish *dai* 'sky' see I.268 (*Telimektar*), and for *teloth* 'roofing, canopy' see *ibid.* (*Teleri*); cf. *Cris Ilbranteloth*.

Dramborleg NFG has the following entry: '*Dramborleg* (or as it may be named *Drambor*) meaneth in its full form Thudder-sharp, and was the axe of Tuor that smote both a heavy dint as of a club and cleft as a sword; and the Eldar say *Tarambor* or *Tarambolaika*.' QL gives *Tarambor, Tarambolaike* 'Tuor's axe' under root TARA, TARAMA 'batter, thud, beat', with *taran, tarambo* 'buffet', and *taru* 'horn' (included here with a query: see *Taruithorn*). No Gnomish equivalents are cited in GL.

The second element is Gnomish *leg, lêg* 'keen, piercing', Qenya *laika*; cf. *Legolast* 'keen-sight', I.267 (*Tári-Laisi*).

Duilin NFG has the following entry: '*Duilin* whose name meaneth Swallow was the lord of that house of the Gondothlim whose sign was the swallow and was surest of the archers of the Eldalië, but fell in the fall of Gondolin. Now the names of those champions appear but in Noldorissa, seeing that Gnomes they were, but his name would be in Eldarissa *Tuilindo*, and that of his house (which the Gnomes called *Nos Duilin*) *Nossë Tuilinda.'* *Tuilindo* '(spring-singer), swallow' is given in QL, see I.269 (*Tuilérë*); GL has *duilin(g)* 'swallow', with *duil, duilir* 'Spring', but these last were struck through and in another part of the book appear *tuil, tuilir* 'Spring' (see I.269).

For *nossë* 'kin, people' see I.272 (*Valinor*); GL does not give *nos* in this sense, but has *nosta-* 'be born', *nost* 'birth; blood, high birth; birthday', and *noss* (changed to *nôs*) 'birthday'. Cf. *Nost-na-Lothion* 'the Birth of Flowers', *Nos Galdon, Nos nan Alwen*.

Eärámë For *ea* 'eagle' see I.251 (*Eärendel*), and for *rámë* see *Alqarámë*. GL has an entry *Iorothram, -um* '= Qenya *Eärámë* or Eaglepinion, a name of one of Eärendel's boats'. For Gnomish *ior, ioroth* 'eagle' see I.251 (*Eärendel*), and cf. the forms *Earam, Earum* as the name of the ship (pp. 260, 276).

Eärendel See pp. 266–7 and I.251.

Eärendilyon See I.251 (*Eärendel*), and *Indorion*.

Ecthelion Both GL and NFG derive this name from *ecthel* 'fountain', to which corresponds Qenya *ektelë*. (This latter survived: cf. the entry *kel-* in the Appendix to *The Silmarillion*: 'from *et-kelē* "issue of water, spring" was derived, with transposition of the consonants, Quenya *ehtelë*, Sindarin *eithel*'. A later entry in GL gives *aithil* (< *ektl*) 'a spring'.) – A form *kektelē* is also found in Qenya from root KELE, KELU: see I.257 (*Kelusindi*).

Egalmoth NFG has the following entry: '*Egalmoth* is a great name, yet none know clearly its meaning – some have said its bearer was so named in that he was worth a thousand Elves (but Rúmil says nay) and others that it signifies the mighty shoulders of that Gnome, and so saith Rúmil, but perchance it was woven of a secret tongue of the Gondothlim' (for the remainder of this entry see p. 215). For Gnomish *moth* '1000' see I.270 (*Uin*).

GL interprets the name as Rúmil did, deriving it from *alm* (< *alðam-*) 'the broad of the back from shoulder to shoulder, back, shoulders', hence *Egalmoth* = 'Broadshoulder'; the name in Qenya is said to be *Aikaldamor*, and an entry in QL of the same date gives *aika* 'broad, vast', comparing Gnomish *eg, egrin*. These in turn GL glosses as 'far away, wide, distant' and 'wide, vast, broad; far' (as in *Egla*; see I.251 (*Eldar*)).

Eglamar See I.251 (*Eldamar*). NFG has the following entry: '*Egla* said the son of Bronweg was the Gnome name of the Eldar (now but seldom used) who dwelt in Kôr, and they were called *Eglothrim* [emended from *Eglothlim*] (that is *Eldalië*), and their tongue *Lam Eglathon* or *Egladrin*. Rúmil said these names *Egla* and *Elda* were akin, but Elfrith cared not overmuch for such lore and they seem not over alike.' With this cf. I. 251 (*Eldar*). GL gives *lam* 'tongue', and *lambë* is found in QL: a word that survived into later Quenya. In QL it is given as a derivative of root LAVA 'lick', and defined 'tongue (of body, but also of land, or even = "speech")'.

Eldarissa appears in QL ('the language of the Eldar') but without explanation of the final element. Possibly it was derived from the root ISI: *ista* 'know', *issë* 'knowledge, lore', *iswa, isqa* 'wise', etc.

Elfrith See pp. 201–2, and I. 255 (*Ilverin*).

Elmavoitë 'One-handed' (Beren). See *Ermabwed*.

Elwing GL has the following entry: '*Ailwing* older spelling of *Elwing* = "lake foam". As a noun = "white water-lily". The name of the maiden loved by Ioringli' (*Ioringli* = *Eärendel*, see I. 251). The first element appears in the words *ail* 'lake, pool', *ailion* 'lake', Qenya *ailo, ailin* – cf. later *Aelin-uial*. The second element is *gwing* 'foam': see I. 273 (*Wingilot*).

Erenol See I. 252 (*Eriol*).

Ermabwed 'One-handed' (Beren). GL gives *mab* 'hand', *amabwed, mabwed* 'having hands', *mabwedri* 'dexterity', *mabol* 'skilful', *mablios* 'cunning', *mablad, mablod* 'palm of hand', *mabrin(d)* 'wrist'. A related word in Qenya was said in GL to be *mapa* (root MAPA) 'seize', but this statement was struck out. QL has also a root MAHA with many derivatives, notably *mā* (= *maha*) 'hand', *mavoitë* 'having hands' (cf. *Elmavoitë*).

Faiglindra 'Long-tressed' (Airin). Gnomish *faigli* 'hair, long tresses (especially used of women)'; *faiglion* 'having long hair', and *faiglim* of the same meaning, 'especially as a proper name', *Faiglim, Aurfaiglim* 'the Sun at noon'. With this is bracketed the word *faiglin(d)ra*.

Failivrin Together with *fail* 'pale, pallid', *failthi* 'pallor', and *Failin* a name of the Moon, GL gives *Failivrin*: '(1) a maid beloved by Silmo; (2) a name among the Gnomes of many maidens of great beauty, especially Failivrin of the Rothwarin in the Tale of Turumart.' (In the Tale *Rothwarin* was replaced by *Rodothlim*.)

The second element is *brin*, Qenya *vírin*, 'a magic glassy substance of great lucency used in fashioning the Moon. Used of things of great and pure transparency.' For *vírin* see I. 192–3.

Falasquil Three entries in NFG refer to this name (for *falas* see also I. 253 (*Falman*)):

'*Falas* meaneth (even as *falas* or *falassë* in Eldar) a beach.'

'*Falas-a-Gwilb* the "beach of peace" was *Falasquil* in Elfin where Tuor at first dwelt in a sheltered cove by the Great Sea.' *-a-Gwilb* is struck through and above is written, apparently, '*Wilb or Wilma*.

'*Gwilb* meaneth "full of peace", which is *gwilm*.'

GL gives *gwîl, gwilm, gwilthi* 'peace', and *gwilb* 'quiet, peaceful'.

Fangluin 'Bluebeard'. See *Indrafang*. For *luin* 'blue' see I. 262 (*Nielluin*).

Foalókë Under a root FOHO 'hide, hoard, store up' QL gives *foa* 'hoard, treasure', *foina* 'hidden', *fólë* 'secrecy, a secret', *fólima* 'secretive', and *foalókë* 'name of a serpent that guarded a treasure'. *lókë* 'snake' is derived from a root LOKO 'twine, twist, curl'.

GL originally had entries *fû, fûl, fûn* 'hoard', *fûlug* 'a dragon (who guards treasure)', and *ulug* 'wolf'. By later changes this construction was altered to *fuis* 'hoard', *fuithlug, -og* (the form that appears in the text, p. 70), *ulug* 'dragon' (cf. Qenya *lókë*). An entry in NFG reads: '*Lûg* is *lókë* of the Eldar, and meaneth "drake".'

Fôs'Almir (Earlier name of *Faskala-númen*; translated in the text (p. 115) 'the bath of flame'.) For *fôs* 'bath' see I. 253 (*Faskala-númen*). GL gives three names: '*Fôs Aura, Fôs'Almir,* and *Fôs na Ngalmir,* i.e. Sun's bath = the Western Sea.' For *Galmir, Aur,* names of the Sun, see I. 254 and I. 271 (*Ûr*).

Fuithlug See *Foalókë*.

Galdor For the entry in NFG concerning Galdor see p. 215; as first written *galdon* was there said to mean 'tree', and Galdor's people to be named *Nos Galdon*. *Galdon* is not in GL. Subsequently *galdon* > *alwen*, and *alwen* does appear in GL, as a word of poetic vocabulary: *alwen* '= *orn*'. – Cf. Qenya *alda* 'tree' (see I. 249 (*Aldaron*)), and the later relationship Quenya *alda*, Sindarin *galadh*.

Gar Thurion NFG has the earlier form *Gar Furion* (p. 202), and GL has *furn, furion* 'secret, concealed', also *fûr* 'a lie' (Qenya *furu*) and *fur-* 'to conceal; to lie'. QL has *furin* and *hurin* 'hidden, concealed' (root FURU or HURU). With *Thurion* cf. *Thuringwethil* 'Woman of Secret Shadow', and *Thurin* 'the Secret', Finduilas' name for Túrin (*Unfinished Tales* pp. 157, 159).

Gil See I. 256 (*Ingil*).

Gilim See I. 260 (*Melko*).

Gimli GL has *gimli* '(sense of) hearing', with *gim-* 'hear', *gimriol* 'attentive' (changed to 'audible'), *gimri* 'hearkening, attention'. The hearing of Gimli, the captive Gnome in the dungeons of Tevildo, 'was the keenest that has been in the world' (p. 29).

Glamhoth GL defines this as 'name given by the Goldothrim to the Orcin: People of Dreadful Hate' (cf. 'folk of dreadful hate', p. 160). For *Goldothrim* see I. 262 (*Noldoli*). The first element is *glâm* 'hatred, loathing'; other words are *glamri* 'bitter feud', *glamog* 'loathsome'. An entry in NFG says: '*Glam* meaneth "fierce hate" and even as *Gwar* has no kindred words in Eldar.'

For *hoth* 'folk' see I. 264 (*orchoth* in entry *Orc*), and cf. *Goldothrim, Gondothlim, Rúmhoth, Thornhoth*. Under root HOSO QL gives *hos* 'folk', *hossë* 'army, band, troop', *hostar* 'tribe', *horma* 'horde, host'; also *Sankossi* 'the Goblins', equivalent of Gnomish *Glamhoth*, and evidently compounded of *sankë* 'hateful' (root sṇkṇ 'rend, tear') and *hossë*.

Glend Perhaps connected with Gnomish *glenn* 'thin, fine', *glendrin* 'slender', *glendrinios* 'slenderness', *glent, glentweth* 'thinness'; Qenya root LENE 'long', which developed its meaning in different directions: 'slow, tedious, trailing', and 'stretch, thin': *lenka* 'slow', *lenwa* 'long and thin, straight, narrow', *lenu-* 'stretch', etc.

Glingol For the entry in NFG, where the name is translated 'singing-gold', see p. 216; and see I.258 (*Lindelos*). The second element is *culu* 'gold', for which see I.255 (*Ilsaluntë*); another entry in NFG reads: '*Culu* or *Culon* is a name we have in poesy for *Glor* (and Rúmil saith that it is the Elfin *Kulu*, and *-gol* in our *Glingol*).'

Glorfalc For *glor* see I.258 (*Laurelin*). NFG has an entry: '*Glor* is gold and is that word that cometh in verse of the Kôr-Eldar *laurë* (so saith Rúmil).'

Falc is glossed in GL '(1) cleft, gash; (2) cleft, ravine, cliffs' (also given is *falcon* 'a great two-handed sword, twibill', which was changed to *falchon*, and so close to English *falchion* 'broad-sword'). NFG has: '*Falc* is cleft and is much as *Cris*; being Elfin *Falqa*'; and under root FḶKḶ in QL are *falqa* 'cleft, mountain pass, ravine' and *falqan* 'large sword'. GL has a further entry: *Glorfalc* 'a great ravine leading out of Garioth'. *Garioth* is here used of Hisilómë; see I.252 (*Eruman*). Cf. later *Orfalch Echor*.

Glorfindel For the entry in NFG, where the name is rendered 'Gold-tress', see p. 216. For *glor* see I.258 (*Laurelin*), and *Glorfalc*. GL had an entry *findel* 'lock of hair', together with *fith* (*fidhin*) 'a single hair', *fidhra* 'hairy', but *findel* was struck out; later entries are *finn* 'lock of hair' (see *fin-* in the Appendix to *The Silmarillion*) and *fingl* or *finnil* 'tress'. NFG: '*Findel* is "tress", and is the Elfin *Findil*.' Under root FIRI QL gives *findl* 'lock of hair' and *firin* 'ray of the sun'.

In another place in GL the name *Glorfindel* was given, and translated 'Goldlocks', but it was changed later to *Glorfinn*, with a variant *Glorfingl*.

Glorund For *glor* see I.258 (*Laurelin*), and *Glorfalc*. GL gives *Glorunn* 'the great drake slain by Turumart'. Neither of the Qenya forms *Laurundo, Undolaurë* (p. 84) appear in QL, which gives an earlier name for 'the great worm', *Fentor*, together with *fent* 'serpent', *fenumë* 'dragon'. As this entry was first written it read 'the great worm slain by Ingilmo'; to this was added 'or Turambar'.

Golosbrindi (Earlier name of Hirilorn, rendered in the text (p. 51) 'Queen of the Forest'.) A word *goloth* 'forest' is given in GL, derived from **gwōloth*, which is itself composed of *aloth* (*alos*), a verse word meaning 'forest' (= *taur*), and the prefix **ngua* > *gwa*, unaccented *go*, 'together, in one', 'often used merely intensively'.

The corresponding word in Qenya is said to be *málos*, which does not appear in QL.

Gondobar   See *Gondolin*, and for *-bar* see I. 251 (*Eldamar*). In GL the form *Gondobar* was later changed to *Gonthobar*.

Gondolin   To the entries cited in I. 254 may be added that in NFG: '*Gond* meaneth a stone, or stone, as doth Elfin *on* and *ondo*.' For the statement about Gondolin (where the name is rendered 'stone of song') in NFG see p. 216; and for the latest formulation of the etymology of *Gondolin* see the Appendix to *The Silmarillion*, entry *gond*.

Gondothlim   GL has the following entry concerning the word *lim* 'many', Qenya *limbë* (not in QL): 'It is frequently suffixed and so becomes a second plural inflexion. In the singular it = English "many a", as *golda-lim*. It is however most often suffixed to the plural in those nouns making their plural in *-th*. It then changes to *-rim* after *-l*. Hence great confusion with *grim* "host" and *thlim* "race", as in *Goldothrim* ("the people of the Gnomes").' NFG has an entry: '*Gondothlim* meaneth "folk of stone" and (saith Rúmil) is *Gond* "stone", whereto be added *Hoth* "folk" and that *-lim* we Gnomes add after to signify "the many".' Cf. *Lothlim*, *Rodothlim*, and *Orclim* in entry *Balcmeg*; for *hoth* see *Glamhoth*.

Gondothlimbar   See *Gondolin*, *Gondothlim*, and for *-bar* see I. 251 (*Eldamar*). In GL the form *Gondothlimbar* was later changed to '*Gonthoflimar* or *Gonnothlimar*'.

go-   An original entry in GL, later struck out, was: *gon- go-* 'son of, patronymic prefix (cf. suffix *ios/ion/io* and Qenya *yô*, *yondo*)'. The replacement for this is given above under *bo-*. See *Indorion*.

Gon Indor   See *go-*, *Indorion*.

Gothmog   See pp. 67, 216, and I. 258 (*Kosomot*). GL has *mog-* 'detest, hate', *mogri* 'detestation', *mogrin* 'hateful'; Qenya root MOKO 'hate'. In addition to *goth* 'war, strife' (Qenya root KOSO 'strive') may be noted *gothwen* 'battle', *gothweg* 'warrior', *gothwin* 'Amazon', *gothriol* 'warlike', *gothfeng* 'war-arrow', *gothwilm* 'armistice'.

Gurtholfin   GL: *Gurtholfin* 'Urdolwen, a sword of Turambar's, Wand of Death'. Also given is *gurthu* 'death' (Qenya *urdu*; not in QL). The second element of the name is *olfin(g)* (also *olf*) 'branch, wand, stick' (Qenya *olwen(n)*).

It may be noted that in QL Turambar's sword is given as *Sangahyando* 'cleaver of throngs', from roots SANGA 'pack tight, press' (*sanga* 'throng') and HYARA 'plough through' (*hyar* 'plough', *hyanda* 'blade, share'). *Sangahyando* 'Throng-cleaver' survived to become the name of a man in Gondor (see the Appendix to *The Silmarillion*, entry *thang*).

Gwar   See I. 257 (*Kôr*, *korin*).

Gwarestrin   Rendered in the Tale (p. 158) as 'Tower of Guard', and so also in NFG; GL glosses it 'watchtower (especially as a name of Gondolin)'. A late entry in GL gives *estirin, estirion, estrin* 'pinnacle', beside *esc* 'sharp point, sharp edge'. The second element of this word is *tiri(o)n*; see I.258 (*Kortirion*). For *gwar* see *Amon Gwareth*.

Gwedheling   See I.273 (*Wendelin*).

Heborodin   'The Encircling Hills.' Gnomish preposition *heb* 'round about, around'; *hebrim* 'boundary', *hebwirol* 'circumspect'. For *orod* see I.256 (*Kalormë*).

Hirilorn   GL gives *hiril* 'queen (a poetic use), princess; feminine of *bridhon*'. For *bridhon* see *Tevildo*. The second element is *orn* 'tree'. (It may be mentioned here that the word *neldor* 'beech' is found in QL; see the Appendix to *The Silmarillion*, entry *neldor*).

Idril   For Gnomish *idril* 'sweetheart' see *Cûm an-Idrisaith*. There is another entry in GL as follows: *Idhril* 'a girl's name often confused with *Idril*. *Idril* = "beloved" but *Idhril* = "mortal maiden". Both appear to have been the names of the daughter of Turgon – or apparently *Idril* was the older and the Kor-eldar called her *Irildë* (= *Idhril*) because she married Tuor.' Elsewhere in GL appear *idhrin* 'men, earth-dwellers; especially used as a folk-name contrasted with *Eglath* etc.; cf. Qenya *indi*', and *Idhru, Idhrubar* 'the world, all the regions inhabited by Men; cf. Qenya *irmin*'. In QL these words *indi* and *irmin* are given under root IRI 'dwell?', with *irin* 'town', *indo* 'house', *indor* 'master of house' (see *Indor*), etc.; but *Irildë* does not appear. Similar words are found in Gnomish: *ind, indos* 'house, hall', *indor* 'master (of house), lord'.

   After the entry in NFG on *Idril* which has been cited (p. 216) a further note was added: 'and her name meaneth "Beloved", but often do Elves say *Idhril* which more rightly compares with *Irildë* and that meaneth "mortal maiden", and perchance signifies her wedding with Tuor son of Men.' An isolated note (written in fact on a page of the *Tale of the Nauglafring*) says: 'Alter name of *Idril* to *Idhril*. The two were confused: *Idril* = "beloved", *Idhril* = "maiden of mortals". The Elves thought this her name and called her *Irildë* (because she married Tuor Pelechthon).'

Ilbranteloth   See *Cris Ilbranteloth*.

Ilfiniol, Ilfrith   See I.255 (*Ilverin*).

Ilúvatar   An entry in NFG may be noticed here: '*En* do the mystic sayings of the Noldoli also name *Ilathon* [emended from *Âd Ilon*], who is Ilúvatar – and this is like the Eldar *Enu*.' QL gives *Enu*, the Almighty Creator who dwells without the world. For *Ilathon* see I.255–6 (*Ilwë*).

Indor   (Father of Tuor's father Peleg). This is perhaps the word *indor* 'master (of house), lord' (see *Idril*) used as a proper name.

Indorion   See *go-*. QL gives *yô, yond-* as poetic words for 'son', adding: 'but very common as *-ion* in patronymics (and hence practically = "descendant")'; also *yondo* 'male descendant, usually (great) grandson' (cf. Eärendel's name *Gon Indor*). Cf. *Eärendilyon*.

Indrafang   GL has *indra* 'long (also used of time)', *indraluin* 'long ago'; also *indravang* 'a special name of the *nauglath* or dwarves', on which see p. 247. These forms were changed later to *in(d)ra*, *in(d)rafang, in(d)raluin/idhraluin*.

An original entry in GL was *bang* 'beard' = Qenya *vanga*, but this was struck out; and another word with the same meaning as *Indravang* was originally entered as *Bangasur* but changed to *Fangasur*. The second element of this is *sûr* 'long, trailing', Qenya *sóra*, and a later addition here is *Surfang* 'a long-beard, a *naugla* or *inrafang*'. Cf. *Fangluin*, and later *Fangorn* 'Treebeard'.

Irildë   See *Idril*.

Isfin   NFG has this entry: '*Isfin* was the sister of Turgon Lord of Gondolin, whom Eöl at length wedded; and it meaneth either "snow-locks" or "exceeding-cunning".' Long afterwards my father, noting that *Isfin* was 'derived from the earliest (1916) form of *The Fall of Gondolin*', said that the name was 'meaningless'; but with the second element cf. *finn* 'lock of hair' (see *Glorfindel*) or *fim* 'clever', *finthi* 'idea, notion', etc. (see I. 253 (*Finwë*)).

Ivárë   GL gives *Ior* 'the famous "piper of the sea", Qenya *Ivárë*.'

Íverin   A late entry in GL gives *Aivrin or Aivrien* 'an island off the west coast of Tol Eressëa, Qenya *Iwerin* or *Iverindor*.' QL has *Íverind-* 'Ireland'.

Karkaras   In GL this is mentioned as the Qenya form; the Gnomish name of 'the great wolf-warden of Belca's door' was *Carcaloth* or *Carcamoth*, changed to *Carchaloth, Carchamoth*. The first element is *carc* 'jag, point, fang'; QL under root KṚKṚ has *karka* 'fang, tooth, tusk', *karkassë, karkaras* 'row of spikes or teeth'.

Kosmoko   See *Gothmog*.

Kurûki   See I. 269 (*Tolli Kuruvar*).

Ladwen-na-Dhaideloth   'Heath of the Sky-roof'. See *Dor-na-Dhaideloth*. GL gives *ladwen* '(1) levelness, flatness; (2) a plain, heath; (3) a plane; (4) surface.' Other words are *ladin* 'level, smooth; fair, equable' (cf. *Tumladin*), *lad* 'a level' (cf. *mablad* 'palm of hand' mentioned under *Ermabwed*), *lada-* 'to smooth out, stroke, soothe, beguile', and *ladwinios* 'equity'. There are also words *bladwen* 'a plain' (see I. 264 (*Palúrien*)), and *fladwen* 'meadow' (with *flad* 'sward' and *Fladweth Amrod (Amrog)* 'Nomad's Green', 'a place in *Tol Erethrin* where Eriol sojourned a while; nigh to Tavrobel.' *Amrog, amrod* = 'wanderer', 'wandering', from *amra-* 'go up and down, live in the mountains, wander'; see *Amon Gwareth*).

Laiqalassë See I. 267 (*Tári-laisi*), I. 254 (*Gar Lossion*).

Laurundo See *Glorund*.

Legolas See *Laiqalassë*.

Lindeloktë See I. 258 (*Lindelos*).

Linwë Tinto See I. 269 (*Tinwë Linto*).

Lókë See *Foalókë*.

Lôs See I. 254 (*Gar Lossion*). The later form *loth* does not appear in GL (which has however *lothwing* 'foamflower'). NFG has '*Lôs* is a flower and in Eldarissa *lossë* which is a rose' (all after the word 'flower' struck out).

Lósengriol As with *lôs*, the later form *lothengriol* does not appear in GL. *Losengriol* is translated 'lily of the valley' in GL, which gives the Gnomish words *eng* 'smooth, level', *enga* 'plain, vale', *engri* 'a level', *engriol* 'vale-like; of the vale'. NFG says '*Eng* is a plain or vale and *Engriol* that which liveth or dwelleth therein', and translates *Lósengriol* 'flower of the vale or lily of the valley'.

Los 'lóriol (changed from *Los Glóriol*; the Golden Flower of Gondolin). See I. 254 (*Gar Lossion*), and for *glóriol* 'golden' see I. 258 (*Laurelin*).

Loth, Lothengriol See *Lôs, Lósengriol*.

Lothlim See *Lôs* and *Gondothlim*. The entry in NFG reads: '*Lothlim* being for *Loslim* meaneth folk of the flower, and is that name taken by the Exiles of Gondolin (which city they had called *Lôs* aforetime).'

Mablung For *mab* 'hand' see *Ermabwed*. The second element is *lung* 'heavy; grave, serious'; related words are *lungra-* 'weigh, hang heavy', *luntha* 'balance, weigh', *lunthang* 'scales'.

Malkarauki See I. 250 (*Balrog*).

Mar Vanwa Tyaliéva See I. 260 and add: a late entry in GL gives the Gnomish name, *Bara Dhair Haithin*, the Cottage of Lost Play; also *daira-* 'play' (with *dairwen* 'mirth', etc.), and *haim or haithin* 'gone, departed, lost' (with *haitha-* 'go, walk', etc.). Cf. *Dairon*.

Mathusdor (Aryador, Hisilómë). In GL are given *math* 'dusk', *mathrin* 'dusky', *mathusgi* 'twilight', *mathwen* 'evening'. See *Umboth-muilin*.

Mavwin A noun *mavwin* 'wish' in GL was struck out, but related words allowed to stand: *mav-* 'like', *mavra* 'eager after', *mavri* 'appetite', *mavrin* 'delightful, desirable', *mavros* 'desire', *maus* 'pleasure; pleasant'. Mavwin's name in Qenya, *Mavoinë*, is not in QL, unless it is to be equated with *maivoinë* 'great longing'.

Meleth A noun *meleth* 'love' is found in GL; see I. 262 (*Nessa*).

Melian, Melinon, Melinir None of these names occur in the

glossaries, but probably all are derivatives of the stem *mel-* 'love';
see I. 262 (*Nessa*). The later etymology of *Melian* derived the name
from *mel-* 'love' (*Melyanna* 'dear gift').

Meoita, Miaugion, Miaulë   See *Tevildo*.

Mindon-Gwar   For *mindon* 'tower' see I. 260 (*Minethlos*); and for
Gwar see p. 291 and I. 257 (*Kôr, korin*).

Morgoth   See p. 67 and *Gothmog*. For the element *mor-* see I. 261
(*Mornië*).

Mormagli, Mormakil   See I. 261 (*Mornië*) and I. 259 (*Makar*).

Nan Dumgorthin   See p. 62. For *nan* see I. 261 (*Nandini*).

Nantathrin   This name does not occur in the *Lost Tales*, where the
Land of Willows is called *Tasarinan*, but GL gives it (see I. 265
(*Sirion*)) and NFG has an entry: '*Dor-tathrin* was that Land of
Willows of which this and many a tale tells.' GL has *tathrin*
'willow', and QL *tasarin* of the same meaning.

Nauglafring   GL has the following entry: '*Nauglafring* = *Fring na
Nauglithon*, the Necklace of the Dwarves. Made for Ellu by the
Dwarves from the gold of Glorund that Mîm the fatherless cursed
and that brought ruin on Beren Ermabwed and Damrod his son and
was not appeased till it sank with Elwing beloved of Eärendel
to the bottom of the sea.' For Damrod (Daimord) son of Beren see
pp. 139, 259, and for the loss of Elwing and the Nauglafring
see pp. 255, 264. This is the only reference to the 'appeasing' of
Mîm's curse. – Gnomish *fring* means 'carcanet, necklace' (Qenya
firinga).

Níniel   Cf. Gnomish *nîn* 'tear', *ninios* 'lamentation', *ninna-* ,'weep';
see I. 262 (*Nienna*).

Nínin-Udathriol   ('Unnumbered Tears'). See *Níniel*. GL gives *tathn*
'number', *tathra-* 'number, count', *udathnarol, udathriol*
'innumerable'. *Û-* is a 'negative prefix with any part of speech'. (QL
casts no light on *Nieriltasinwa*, p. 84, apart from the initial element
nie 'tear', see I. 262 (*Nienna*).)

Noldorissa   See *Eldarissa*.

Nos Galdon, Nos nan Alwen   See *Duilin, Galdor*.

Nost-na-Lothion   See *Duilin*.

Parma Kuluinen   The Golden Book, see p. 310. This entry is given
in QL under root PARA: *parma* 'skin, bark; parchment; book,
writings'. This word survived in later Quenya (*The Lord of the
Rings* III. 401). For *Kuluinen* see *Glingol*.

Peleg   (Father of Tuor). GL has a common noun *peleg* 'axe', verb
pelectha- 'hew' (QL *pelekko* 'axe', *pelekta-* 'hew'). Cf. Tuor's
name *Pelecthon* in the note cited under *Idril*.

Ramandur   See I. 259 (*Makar*).

Rog   GL gives an adjective *rôg, rog* 'doughty, strong'. But with the Orcs' name for Egnor Beren's father, Rog the Fleet, cf. *arog* 'swift, rushing', and *raug* of the same meaning; Qenya *arauka*.

Rôs   GL gives yet another meaning of this name: 'the Sea' (Qenya *Rása*).

Rodothlim   See *Rothwarin* (earlier form replaced by *Rodothlim*).

Rothwarin   GL has this name in the forms *Rothbarin, Rosbarin*: '(literally "cavern-dwellers") name of a folk of secret Gnomes and also of the regions about their cavernous homes on the banks of the river.' Gnomish words derived from the root ROTO 'hollow' are *rod* 'tube, stem', *ross* 'pipe', *roth* 'cave, grot', *rothrin* 'hollow', *rodos* 'cavern'; QL gives *rotsë* 'pipe', *róta* 'tube', *ronta, rotwa* 'hollow', *rotelë* 'cave'.

Rúmhoth   See *Glamhoth*.

Rúsitaurion   GL gives a noun *rûs (rôs)* 'endurance, longsuffering, patience', together with adjective *rô* 'enduring, longsuffering; quiet, gentle', and verb *rô-* 'remain, stay; endure'. For *taurion* see I. 267 (*Tavari*).

Sarnathrod   Gnomish *sarn* 'a stone'; for *athrod* 'ford' see *Artanor*.

Sarqindi   ('Cannibal-ogres'). This must derive from the root SṚKṚ given in QL, with derivatives *sarko* 'flesh', *sarqa* 'fleshy', *sarkuva* 'corporeal, bodily'.

Silpion   An entry in NFG (p. 215) translates the name as 'Cherry-moon'. In QL is a word *pio* 'plum, cherry' (with *piukka* 'blackberry', *piosenna* 'holly', etc.), and also *Valpio* 'the holy cherry of Valinor'. GL gives *Piosil* and *Silpios*, without translation, as names of the Silver Tree, and also a word *piog* 'berry'.

Taimonto   See I. 268 (*Telimektar*).

Talceleb, Taltelepta   (Name of *Idril/Irildë*, 'of the Silver Feet'.) The first element is Gnomish *tâl* 'foot (of people and animals)'; related words are *taltha* 'foot (of things), base, pedestal, pediment', *talrind, taldrin* 'ankle', *taleg, taloth* 'path' – another name for the Way of Escape into Gondolin was *Taleg Uthwen* (see *Bad Uthwen*). QL under root TALA 'support' gives *tala* 'foot', *talwi* (dual) 'the feet', *talas* 'sole', etc. For the second element see I. 268 (*Telimpë*). QL gives the form *telepta* but without translation.

Tarnin Austa   For *tarn* 'gate' see I. 261 (*Moritarnon*). GL gives *aust* 'summer'; cf. *Aur* 'the Sun', I. 271 (*Ûr*).

Taruithorn, Taruktarna   (Oxford). GL gives *târ* 'horn' and *tarog* 'ox' (Qenya *taruku-*), *Taruithron* older *Taruitharn* 'Oxford'. Immediately following these words are *tarn* 'gate' and *taru* '(1) cross (2) crossing'. QL has *taru* 'horn' (see *Dramborleg*), *tarukka* 'horned', *tarukko, tarunko* 'bull', *Taruktarna* 'Oxford', and under root TARA *tara-* 'cross, go athwart', *tarna* 'crossing, passage'.

Tasarinan   See *Nantathrin*.

Taurfuin   See I. 267 (*Tavari*) and I. 253 (*Fui*).

Teld Quing Ilon   NFG has an entry: '*Cris a Teld Quing Ilon* signifieth Gully of the Rainbow Roof, and is in the Eldar speech *Kiris Iluqingatelda*'; a *Teld Quing Ilon* was struck out and replaced by *Ilbranteloth*. Another entry reads: '*Ilon* is the sky'; in GL *Ilon* (= Qenya *Ilu*) is the name of *Ilúvatar* (see I. 255 (*Ilwë*)). *Teld* does not appear in GL, but related words as *telm* 'roof' are given (see I. 267–8 (*Teleri*)); and *cwing* = 'a bow'. QL has *iluqinga* 'rainbow' (see I. 256 (*Ilweran*)) and *telda* 'having a roof' (see I. 268 (*Telimektar*)). For *Cris, Kiris* see *Cris Ilbranteloth*.

Tevildo, Tifil   For the etymology see I. 268, to which can be added that the earlier Gnomish form *Tifil* (later *Tiberth*) is associated in GL with a noun *tîf* 'resentment, ill-feeling, bitterness'.

    Vardo Meoita 'Prince of Cats': for *Vardo* see I. 273 (*Varda*). QL gives *meoi* 'cat'.

    Bridhon Miaugion 'Prince of Cats': *bridhon* 'king, prince', cf. *Bridhil*, Gnomish name of Varda (I. 273). Nouns *miaug, miog* 'tomcat' and *miauli* 'she-cat' (changed to *miaulin*) are given in GL, where the Prince of Cats is called *Tifil Miothon* or *Miaugion*. *Miaulë* was the name of Tevildo's cook (p. 28).

Thorndor   See I. 266 (*Sorontur*).

Thornhoth   See *Glamhoth*.

Thorn Sir   See I. 265 (*Sirion*).

Tifanto   This name is clearly to be associated with the Gnomish words (*tif-, tifin*) given in I. 268 (*Tinfang*).

Tifil   See *Tevildo*.

Tirin   See I. 258 (*Kortirion*).

Tôn a Gwedrin   *Tôn* is a Gnomish word meaning 'fire (on a hearth)', related to *tan* and other words given under *Tanyasalpë* (I. 266–7); *Tôn a Gwedrin* 'the Tale-fire' in *Mar Vanwa Tyaliéva*. Cf. *Tôn Sovriel* 'the fire lake of Valinor' (*sovriel* 'purification', *sovri* 'cleansing'; *sôn* 'pure, clean', *soth* 'bath', *sô-* 'wash, clean, bathe').

    Gwedrin belongs with *cwed-* (preterite *cwenthi*) 'say, tell', *cweth* 'word', *cwent* 'tale, saying', *cwess* 'saying, proverb', *cwedri* 'telling (of tales)', *ugwedriol* 'unspeakable, ineffable'. In QL under root QETE are *qet-* (*qentë*) 'speak, talk', *quent* 'word', *qentelë* 'sentence', *Eldaqet = Eldarissa*, etc. Cf. the Appendix to *The Silmarillion*, entry *quen-* (*quet-*).

Tumladin   For the first element, Gnomish *tûm* 'valley', see I. 269 (*Tombo*), and for the second, *ladin* 'level, smooth' see *Ladwen na Dhaideloth*.

Turambar   For the first element see I. 260 (*Meril-i-Turinqi*). QL gives *amarto, ambar* 'Fate', and also (root MṚTṚ) *mart* 'a piece of luck', *marto* 'fortune, fate, lot', *mart-* 'it happens' (impersonal). GL has *mart* 'fate', *martion* 'fated, doomed, fey'; also *umrod* and *umbart* 'fate'.

Turumart   See *Turambar*.

Ufedhin   Possible connections of this name are Gnomish *uf* 'out of, forth from', or *fedhin* 'bound by agreement, ally, friend'.

Ulbandi   See I. 260 (*Melko*).

Ulmonan   The Gnomish name was *Ingulma(n)* (*Gulma* = *Ulmo*), with the prefix *in-* (*ind-, im-*) 'house of' (*ind* 'house', see *Idril*). Other examples of this formation are *Imbelca, Imbelcon* 'Hell (house of Melko)', *inthorn* 'eyrie', *Intavros* 'forest' (properly 'the forest palace of Tavros').

Umboth-muilin   Gnomish *umboth, umbath* 'nightfall'; *Umbathor* is a name of Garioth (see I. 252 (*Eruman*)). This word is derived from **mbaþ-*, related to **maþ-* seen in *math* 'dusk': see *Mathusdor*. The second element is *muil* 'tarn', Qenya *moilë*.

Undolaurë   See *Glorund*.

Valar   NFG has the following entry: '*Banin* [emended from *Banion*] or *Bandrim* [emended from *Banlim*]. Now these dwell, say the Noldoli, in *Gwalien* [emended from *Banien*] but they are spoken of ever by Elfrith and the others in their Elfin names as the *Valar* (or *Vali*), and that glorious region of their abode is *Valinor*.' See I. 272 (*Valar*).

SHORT GLOSSARY OF OBSOLETE, ARCHAIC, AND RARE WORDS

Words that have been given in the similar glossary to Part I (such as *an* 'if', *fain*, *lief*, *meed*, *rede*, *ruth*) are not as a rule repeated here. Some words of current English used in obsolete senses are included.

acquaint   old past participle, superseded by *acquainted*, 287
ardour   burning heat, 38, 170 (modern sense 194)
bested   beset, 193
bravely   splendidly, showily, 75
broidure   embroidery, 163. Not recorded, but *broid-* varied with *broud-* etc. in Middle English, and *broudure* 'embroidery' is found.
burg   walled and fortified town, 175
byrnie   body-armour, corslet, coat-of-mail, 163
carcanet   ornamental collar or necklace, 227–8, 235, 238
carle   (probably) serving-man, 85; **house-carle** 190
chain   linear measure (a chain's length), sixty-six feet, 192
champain   level, open country, 295, 298
clue   thread, 322
cot   small cottage, 95, 141
damasked   224, **damascened** 173, 227, ornamentally inlaid with designs in gold and silver.
diapered   covered with a small pattern, 173
dight   arrayed, fitted out, 173
drake   dragon, 41, 46, 85–7, etc. (*Drake* is the original English word, Old English *draca*, derived from Latin; *dragon* was from French).
drolleries   comic plays or entertainments, 190
enow   enough, 241–2
enthralled   enslaved, 97, 163, 196, 198
entreat   treat, 26, 77, 87, 236 (modern sense 38)
errant   wandering, 42
estate   situation, 97
ewer   pitcher for water, 226
eyot   small island, 7
fathom   linear measure (six feet), formerly not used only of water, 78
fell in dread   fell into dread, 106
force   waterfall, 105 (Northern English, from Scandinavian).
fordone   overcome, 233
fosses   pits, 288
fretted   adorned with elaborate carving, 297

glamour   enchantment, spell, 314
greaves   armour for the lower leg, 163
guestkindliness   hospitality, 228. Apparently not recorded; used in I.175.
haply   perhaps, 13, 94, 99
hie   hasten; **hie thee**, hasten, 75
high-tide   festival, 231
house-carle   190, see **carle**.
inly   inwardly, 315
jacinth   blue, 274
kempt   combed, 75; **unkempt**, uncombed, 159
kirtle   long coat or tunic, 154
knave   male child, boy, 96 (the original sense of the word, long since lost).
lair   in **the dragon's lair**, 105, the place where the dragon was lying (i.e. happened at that time to be lying).
lambent   (of flame) playing lightly on a surface without burning, 297
league   about three miles, 171, 189, 201
lealty   loyalty, 185
let   desisted, 166; allowed, 181; **had let fashion**, had had fashioned, 174, **let seize**, had (him) seized, 225, **let kill**, had (them) killed, 235
like   please, 41; **good liking**, good will, friendly disposition, 169
list   wish, 85, 101; like, 236
or ever   before ever, 5–6, 38, 80, 110, 233–4, 240
or . . . or   either . . . or, 226
pale   boundary, 269
ports   gateways, 299
prate   chatter, speak to no purpose, 75
puissance   power, 168
repair   make one's way, go, 162
runagate   deserter, 15, 44 (the same word in origin as **renegade**, 15, 44, 224, 232)
scathe   hurt, harm, 99, 233
scatterlings   wanderers, stragglers, 182
sconces   brackets fastened on a wall, to carry candle or torch, 226
scullion   menial kitchen-servant, drudge, 17, 45
shallop   274. See I.275; but here the boat is defined as oarless.
silvern   silver, 270 (the original Old English adjective).
slot   track of an animal, 38, 96 (=**spoor** 38).
stead   farm, 89
stricken   in **the Stricken Anvil**, struck, beaten, 174, 179
swinge   stroke, blow, 194
thews   strength, bodily power, 33
tilth   cultivated (tilled) land, 4, 88, 101
tithe   tenth part, 188, 223, 227

travail   hardship, suffering, 77, 82, 239; toil, 168; **travailed**, toiled, 163; **travailing**, enduring hardship, 75

trencher   large dish or platter, 226

uncouth   85 perhaps has the old meaning 'strange', but elsewhere (13, 75, 115) has the modern sense.

vambrace   armour for the fore-arm, 163

weird   fate, 85–6, 111, 155, 239

whin   gorse, 287

whortle   whortleberry, bilberry; **whortlebush** 287

withe   withy, flexible branch of willow, 229

worm   serpent, dragon, 85–8, etc.

wrack   downfall, ruin, 116, 253, 283, 285

INDEX

This index is made on the same basis as that to Part I, but selected references are given in rather more cases, and the individual *Lost Tales* are not included. In view of the large number of names that appear in Part II fairly full cross-references are provided to associated names (earlier and later forms, equivalents in different languages, etc.). As in the index to Part I, the more important names occurring in *The Silmarillion* are not given explanatory definitions; and references sometimes include passages where the person or place is not actually named.

especially 61, and see *Doriath*, *Land(s) Beyond*. References to the protection of Artanor by the magic of the Queen: 9, 35–6, 43, 47–8, 63, 76, 122, 132, 137, 230–2, 249–50

Arval   An early name of Eöl. 220

Arvalin   286

Aryador   'Land of Shadow', name of Hisilómë among Men. 15, 42, 44, 50–1, 61, 70, 202, 249. See *Dor Lómin*, *Hisilómë*, *Hithlum*, *Land of Shadow(s)*, *Mathusdor*.

Asgon   Earlier name of (Lake) Mithrim. 70, 88, 202, 204, 263. See *Mithrim*.

Atlantic Ocean   261

Aulë   19, 46, 174, 218, 269, 272

Auredhir   Son of Dior. 240–1, 251

Ausir   (1) 'The Wealthy', name of Dior. 240, 244, 251. (2) A boy of Mar Vanwa Tyaliéva. 5, 7–8, 40–2, 50, 59, 311

Avari   64

Avon, River   295–6

Bablon   Gnomish form of *Babylon*. 196, 203, 214; *Babylon* 203, 214

Bad Uthwen   The Way of Escape into the plain of Gondolin. 189, 203; earlier *Bad Uswen*, *Bad Usbran* 203. See *Way of Escape*.

Balar, Isle of   209

Balcmeg   Orc slain by Tuor in Gondolin. 181

Balrog(s)   15, 34, 44, 67, 85, 156, 169–70, 174–6, 178–84, 186, 189, 193–4, 212–13, 216. Numbers of, 170, 179, 184, 213; described, 169, 181, 194, 212–13. See *Malkarauki*.

Bansil   'Fair-gleam', the Tree of Gondolin with silver blossom. 160, 184, 186, 203, 207, 214, 216; later form *Banthil* 203. See *Belthil*.

Barad-dûr   67

Baragund   Father of Morwen. 139

Barahir   Father of Beren. 43, 51. (Replaced *Egnor*.)

Battle of Unnumbered Tears   Called also *the Battle of Tears*, *of Uncounted Tears*, *of Lamentation*, and *the great battle*. 9–10, 17, 43–5, 65–6, 70, 73, 77, 83–4, 88, 91, 101, 120–1, 140, 142, 157, 198, 200, 208–9, 216, 218. See *Nieriltasinwa*, *Nínin-Udathriol*.

Bay of Faëry   See *Faëry*.

Bee of Azure   Sirius. 282; *Blue Bee* 281. See *Nielluin*.

Belaurin   Gnomish form of *Palúrien*. 281, 328; *Belawryn* 310

Belcha   Gnomish name of Melko. *Belcha Morgoth* 44, 67

Beleg   21, 47, 59, 62, 73, 76–83, 102, 118, 121–4, 141–2. Called 'wood-ranger', 'hunter', 'huntsman' 73, 76–7, 81, 123; a Noldo 78, 122–3; later surname *Cúthalion* 'Strongbow' 59, 62, 124

Belegost   City of the Indrafang Dwarves. 230–1, 235, 244–8; *Ost Belegost* 244

Beleriand   64, 128, 205, 217, 245, 324; Drowning of Beleriand 251, 324

Belerion   Harbour in the west of Britain. 313–15, 317, 322, 324, 330–3

Belthil   The Tree of Gondolin with silver flowers, made by Turgon. 207. See *Bansil*.

Belthronding   The bow of Beleg. 123

Beorn   Uncle of Ottor Wǽfre (Eriol). 290–1, 294. See *Hasen of Isenóra*.

Beowulf   298, 323; J. R. R. Tolkien, *On Translating Beowulf*, 331

Beren   11–19, 21–31, 33–41, 43–5, 48–9, 52–63, 65–8, 71–3, 116, 123–4, 137, 139–40, 144–5, 215, 223, 231, 233–43, 246, 248–51, 259, 330. Called *the One-handed, of the One Hand* (see *Ermabwed, Elmavoitë*); *Beren of the Hills* 49; *huntsman of the Noldoli, of the woods* 13, 237. For Beren as Man or Elf see 52, 116, 139, 215, 248

Bethos   Chief of the Woodmen. 101–2, 106, 111, 130, 142; Bethos' wife (a Noldo) 101, 130

Bidding of the Minstrel, The   (poem) 269–71; associated outline 261–2, 265

Bior   Man of the Ythlings who accompanied Ælfwine. 319, 321–2, 331–2, 334

Bitter Hills   See *Iron Mountains*.

Blacksword   Name of Túrin among the Rodothlim (later Nargo-thrond). 84, 128. See *Mormagli, Mormakil, Mormegil*.

Blessed Realm(s)   34, 82, 266

Blue Bee   See *Bee of Azure*.

bo-Dhuilin, bo-Dhrauthodavros, bo-Rimion   'son of' Duilin, etc.; see the names. (*bo-* replaced *go-*)

Bodruith   Lord of Belegost. 230–1, 234–5, 246–7

Brandir   130–4. (Replaced *Tamar*.)

Brethil, Forest of   125, 130, 132, 135, 141

Britain   294, 301, 305, 309

Brithonin   Invaders of Tol Eressëa. 294

Brittany   285

Brodda   Lord of men in Hisilómë. 89–90, 93, 126–8

Bronweg   Gnomish form of *Voronwë*. 144–5, 148–9, 156–7, 160, 197–8, 228, 256. See *Voronwë*.

Brook of Glass   Near Tavrobel. 287

Brown Elves   See *Green Elves*.

Buckland   328

Cabed-en-Aras   'The Deer's Leap', ravine in the Teiglin. 134–5

Caergwâr, Caer Gwâr   Name of Kortirion in Welsh. 292, 307

Carcaras   See *Karkaras*.

Carcharoth   58–9, 68; 'the Red Maw' 68

Carpenter, Humphrey   69; *J. R. R. Tolkien, A Biography*, 146, 267, 271, 273, 277, 300

Gilim   A Giant ('Winter'?) 19, 46, 67–8

Gimli   A Gnome, captive in the castle of Tevildo. 29, 55, 214

Glamhoth   'Folk of dreadful hate', Gnomish name for Orcs. 160, 219

Glaurung   68, 125–6, 129, 131–2, 134–5, 143, 213. See *Glorund*.

Glend   The sword of the giant Nan. 67

Glingol   'Singing-gold', the Tree of Gondolin with golden blossom.
160, 184–6, 207, 216. Later form *Glingal* (Tree of Gondolin made
of gold by Turgon) 207

Gloomweaver   The Great Spider. 160. See *Wirilómë*, *Ungwe-
liant(ë)*.

Glorfalc   'Golden Cleft', by which Tuor came to the Sea. 150, 202.
See *Cris Ilbranteloth*, *Golden Cleft*, *Teld Quing Ilon*.

Glorfindel   Lord of the people of the Golden Flower in Gondolin;
called *Glorfindel of the golden hair*, *golden Glorfindel*, *Gold-
tress* (216). 173, 175, 182–3, 186, 192–4, 196, 211–12, 216, 243,
260

Glorund   The Dragon, precursor of Glaurung. References include
passages where he is called *the drake*, etc; see also *Foalókë*. 19,
41, 46, 68, 84–8, 94–8, 103–16, 118, 123, 125–6, 128–37, 140–4,
221–3, 229–31, 235–6, 238–9, 241, 246; *Glorunt* 84. See *Laurundo*,
Undolaurë.

Gnomes   Selected references (including *Noldoli*). Slaves of Melko
9–11, 31, 42–3, 65, 77–8, 154, 156–7, 159, 161, 163, 166, 170,
205–6, 219, 279; free Noldoli 44, 65, 77, 82, 248; in Artanor 9, 43,
65, 122, 254, 276; in Dor Lómin 15, 43, 52, 65, 149, 204; among the
Dwarves 224, 245; confusion with Orcs 159; tongue of 148–9, 158,
198, 216–17; art of 224; lanterns of 78, 80–1, 123, 153; steel,
chainmail of 83, 85, 164; miners 168; release of, and return into the
West 161–2, 278, 280, 285

Goblins   Frequently used as alternative term to Orcs (cf. *Melko's
goblins, the Orcs of the hills* 157, but sometimes apparently
distingished, 31, 230). 14, 31, 35, 67, 76–80, 154, 156–7, 159,
176–7, 179–82, 219, 230, 247, 279. See *Orcs*.

go-Dhuilin, *go-Dhrauthodauros*, *go-Rimion* 'son of' Duilin, etc.;
see the names. (*go-* replaced by *bo-*)

Gods   See *Valar*.

Golden Book, The   283, 285, 287, 291, 293, 310. See *Parma Kuluinen*.

Golden Cleft   150, 153, 219. See *Glorfalc*.

Golden Flower, The   Name of one of the kindreds of the Gondothlim,
ruled by Glorfindel. 173, 182, 186, 195, 211, 216. See *Los'lóriol*.

Golosbrindi   Earlier name of Hirilorn. 51

Gondobar   'City of Stone', one of the Seven Names of Gondolin. 158,
172; in another application 275–6. See *City of Stone*.

Gondolin   'Stone of Song'. 43–4, 65, 70, 77, 119–20, 130, 158–64,
166, 168–72, 175, 178, 184–6, 188–91, 193, 195–9, 201, 203–16,
218, 220, 240–2, 248, 251, 253, 255, 257–8, 260, 266, 276, 289; the

Littleheart Son of Bronweg (Voronwë), called 'the Gong-warden' (of Mar Vanwa Tyaliéva). 197, 201, 221, 228, 244, 252, 254, 256, 263, 276. For his Elvish names see 201–2, 276.

Lókë Name in Eldarissa for the dragons of Melko. 85. See *Foalókë*, *Fuithlug*.

Lonely Isle, Lonely Island 4–5, 7, 34, 148, 253, 289, 298, 301, 307, 311, 313, 316–17, 322–4, 326–7, 329; *the Isle* 42, 144, 283–4; *the holy isle* 291; *Island of the Elves* 320, 327; Old English *se uncúpa holm* 290, *seo unwemmede Íeg* 291, 301; speech of 34, 148; poem *The Lonely Isle* 291. See *Tol Eressëa*.

Longbeards See *Indrafangs*.

Lord of the Rings, The 211, 247, 266, 328; *The Fellowship of the Ring* 333; *The Two Towers* 140; *The Return of the King* 67, 216

Lord of Wolves Thû (the Necromancer). 54

Lords of the West The Valar. 205

Lórien 8–9, 33, 42–3, 240, 324

Lôs Earlier form of the name *Loth* of Gondolin. 202

Lósengriol Earlier form of the name *Lothengriol* of Gondolin. 202

Los'lóriol Name in Noldorissa of the Golden Flower (kindred of the Gondothlim); earlier *Los Glóriol*. 216

Lost Elves Elves of the Great Lands. 9 (of Artanor), 40, 42, 283, 285, 293, 302; tongue of 22, 47. *Lost Elves of Hisilómë* 63–4, 249

Loth 'The Flower', one of the Seven Names of Gondolin. 158, 202. (Replaced *Lôs*.)

Lothengriol 'Flower of the Plain', one of the Seven Names of Gondolin. 158, 202. See I.172 and *Flower of the Plain*.

Lothlim 'People of the Flower', name taken by the survivors of Gondolin at the mouth of Sirion. 196, 201, 252, 259–60

Lug Orc slain by Tuor in Gondolin. 181

Lumbi A place where Melko dwelt after his defeat. 278–9

Lúsion = *Lúthien* (2). 302

Luthany England. 301–10, 323, 326–30, 334. See *Lúthien* (1) and (3), *Leithian*.

Lúthien (1) 'Man of Luthany', name given to Ælfwine by the Elves of Tol Eressëa. 301, 304, 309; explained as meaning 'Wanderer', 302. (2) Son of Telumektar 302. (3) = *Luthany* (England). 312–15, 323–4, 326–7, 329–30, 334. (4) Tinúviel. 52–8, 66, 302, 330

Mablung 'The Heavy-hand(ed)', chief of the thanes of Tinwelint. 38–41, 49–50, 56, 59, 121, 128–30, 134, 231, 233, 243

Maeglin Later form for Meglin. 210–12, 248

Magbar Elvish name of Rome. 315, 330. See *Rûm*.

Magic Isles 5, 7, 254, 260, 311, 316, 320, 324–5, 332, 334; *Magic Archipelago* 316

Magic Sun 264, 281–2, 285–6, 289, 303; see especially 285–6

Oarni   Spirits of the Sea (identified with 'mermaids' 259, identity denied 263). 253−4, 259−60, 263, 276. See *Mermaids.*

Oikeroi   A cat, thane of Tevildo, slain by Huan. 27−8, 30−2, 55−8

Oinen   See *Uinen.*

Old English   (including citations, words, titles of poems) 197, 200, 266−7, 271, 276, 290−2, 294−5, 298, 301, 304−5, 309, 323, 325, 328−31. Old English spoken by the Elves of Tol Eressëa 301−2, 304, 309

Old Forest   328

Olórë Mallë   'The Path of Dreams'. 48, 70, 119, 258. See *Way of Dreams.*

Olwë   Lord of the Solosimpi in Thingol's place. 50. See *Ellu* (2).

Ómar   Youngest of the great Valar, called also *Amillo.* 279

Ónen   Earlier name of Uinen. 51

Orcobal   Champion of the Orcs, slain by Ecthelion in Gondolin. 181

Orcs   Selected references: origin of 14, 159, 219; *children of Melko* 193; described 99, 159−60; sight and hearing of 78−9, 165−6; wolfriders 44, 67, 84, 190, 195; Orcs' blood in Meglin 165; *sons of the Orcs* 165; mercenaries of the Dwarves 230, 247. Singular *Ork* 202, plural *Orqui* 136, 202, 219. See *Goblins.*

Orfalch Echor   The great rift in the Encircling Mountains by which Gondolin was approached. 207, 211

Orgof   Elf of Artanor, slain by Túrin. 74−6, 122, 142

Orion   281−2, 302. See *Telimektar.*

Orlin   Man of Hisilómë, slain in Brodda's hall by Turambar. 90

Orm   Sea-captain of the Forodwaith, slayer of Déor Ælfwine's father. 318−19, 323, 331

Orodreth   Lord of the Rodothlim. 82−4, 98, 117, 123−4

Oromë   8, 42, 240, 279

Orqui   Earlier plural of *Orc* (*Ork*). See *Orcs.*

Ossë   150, 197, 254, 256, 263, 283, 285, 293, 304, 306−9, 323−4, 331

Ossiriand   249

Ost Belegost   See *Belegost.*

Oswine   Prince of Gwar (Kortirion). 313, 323

Óðinn   290. See *Wóden.*

Othrod   A lord of the Orcs, slain by Tuor in Gondolin. 181

Ottor Wæfre   Eriol. 290, 292; *Wæfre* 291

Outer Dark   273, 276

Outer Land(s)   (1) The Great Lands (Middle-earth). 254, 265. See *Lands Without.* (2) The lands West of the Great Sea. 316−17, 324−5, 334

Outer Oceans, Outer Sea(s)   154, 160, 276. See *Vai.*

Oxford   146, 269, 292−3, 295, 300, 323; (Old English) *Oxenaford* 292; poem *The City of Present Sorrow* 295−8. See *Taruithorn, Taruktarna.*

Oxford English Dictionary   69, 147

Tolkien, J.R.

The book of lost tales, Part II

105800

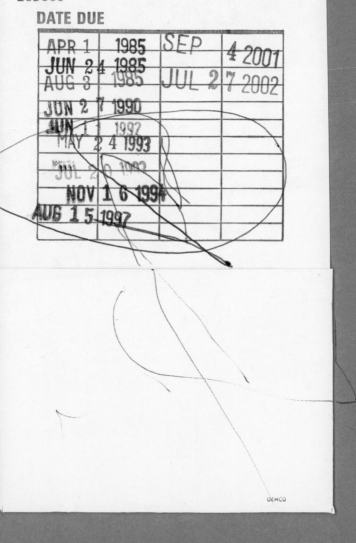